I0829661

Pregnant Pages

Maternity of Words

Pregnant Pages
Maternity of Words

by
Heinz G. Ross

2024

Copyright Notice

Copyright © 2024
All rights reserved
Heinz G. Ross
Gold Coast, Australia

The author appreciates the support and respect of readers, fellow authors, and the broader creative community in upholding the principles of copyright protection. Your adherence to these rights helps to foster creativity, encourage innovation, and promote the continued production of meaningful literary works.

Thank you for your understanding and compliance with this copyright notice.

ISBN: 978-0-6459281-2-9 (Hardcover)
ISBN: 978-0-6459281-3-6 (e-book)

BISAC codes:

FIC002000 (FICTION / Action & Adventure)
FIC010000 (FICTION /Fairy, Folk Tales, Legends & Mythology)
FIC067000 (FICTION / Animals)
FIC029000 (FICTION / Short Stories (single author)
LCO000000 (LITERARY COLLECTIONS / General)
FIC009020 (FICTION / Fantasy / Epic)
FIC009080 (FICTION / Fantasy / Humorous)
FIC037000 (FICTION / Political)
FIC027260 (FICTION / Romance / Action & Adventure)
FIC052000 (FICTION / Satire)
CGN033000 (COMICS & GRAPHIC NOVELS / Satire)
FAM002000 (FAMILY & RELATIONSHIPS / Activities)
MUS050000 (MUSIC / Individual Composer & Musician)
FAM014000 (FAMILY&RELATIONSHIPS/ Death, Grief, Bereavement)

Disclaimer

In the context of this literary work, 'Pregnant Pages: Maternity of Words' metaphorically explores the birthing and nurturing of creative ideas. It is unrelated to the conventional sense of child bearing or maternity.

The contents of this book, titled 'Pregnant Pages,' are intended for entertainment, creative exploration, and intellectual stimulation. The author would like to provide the following disclaimer to ensure clarity and understanding for readers:

Fictitious Nature: The stories, characters, events, and scenarios portrayed in this book are primarily products of the author's imagination. Any resemblance to actual persons, living or dead, or to real events is purely coincidental. The author has taken creative liberties to construct fictional narratives for the purpose of storytelling.

Literary License: The author has employed literary license throughout the book. Certain words, phrases, or expressions may be used metaphorically, symbolically, or in a manner that deviates from their literal or conventional meanings. Readers are encouraged to approach the text with an open mind, recognising the author's intention to evoke emotions, provoke thought, and create a unique literary experience.

Satirical and Tongue-in-Cheek Content: Some sections of the book may include satirical elements, humour, or a 'tongue-in-cheek' approach to certain subjects. Readers should interpret such content with an understanding of the author's intention to entertain and engage in social commentary.

'Pregnant Pages' includes AI-generated images, as well as illustrations and photographs to enhance the visual aspect of the text (approx. 294).

Individual Interpretation: The themes, ideas, and messages conveyed in 'Pregnant Pages' are subject to individual interpretation. Readers are encouraged to engage with the text critically and form their own perspectives based on their personal experiences and beliefs.

The author appreciates readers' engagement with the book and encourages an open dialogue about its contents. However, the author cannot be held responsible for any personal reactions, opinions, or actions arising from the reading or interpretation of 'Pregnant Pages.'

Table_of_Contents

Links

Website: http://www.heinzross.com
Email: mailto:info@hrexposure.com
All Videos: Youtube Video link
Music Videos playlist: Music Videos
Music & Video: reverbnation
Music (Audio only): https://heinzross.bandcamp.com/
Music (Audio only): https://soundcloud.com/heinz-ross

14

Preface (Pregnant Pages)

Welcome to 'Pregnant Pages,' a captivating collection that chronicles years of my creative journey, presenting a diverse array of self-contained short stories, articles, and thought-provoking musings.

Embark on a captivating exploration of imagination and introspection within these pages. While the characters and events may bear resemblance to real-life, they are primarily products of my imagination. Any resemblance is coincidental; these fictitious narratives exist for storytelling and artistic expression.

This book features several self-contained stories, each with their own preface. These works offer unique lenses for exploring diverse topics, inviting you on mini literary adventures within the larger tapestry.

'Pregnant Pages' also houses published articles touching on real-world topics, adopting light-hearted or satirical approaches. Some articles are metaphorical, symbolic, satirical, or outright absurd. Approach them with a figurative lens, embracing the interplay of wit, humour, and social commentary.

'Pregnant Pages' weaves personal introspection and lived experiences into its fabric. These reflections provide glimpses into my life and inspirations, enriching the collection.

Given its extensive content, 'Pregnant Pages' is not designed for a single sitting. Each self-contained story within this collection is a complete narrative in itself and holds no connection to the next. Feel free to savour its richness over time, knowing that you can put the book down after any story and return whenever you're ready. This allows diverse voices and perspectives to unfold gradually, offering a unique and fulfilling reading experience.

Encounter a variety of words used under literary license, serving to evoke emotion, ignite imagination, and breathe life into stories and ideas. May they transport you to new realms, challenging perceptions and illuminating the human experience.

'Pregnant Pages' is enhanced with approximately 294 images, many of which are AI-generated, to complement and enrich the reading experience. These visuals add a vibrant dimension to the stories, creating a visually immersive journey that harmonizes with the diverse tales within these pages. Additionally, where deemed necessary, trigger warnings or parental guidance are included to alert readers to sensitive content, ensuring a thoughtful and considerate engagement with the narratives.

Thank you for joining this literary odyssey. May the pages of 'Pregnant Pages' ignite your imagination, provoke contemplation, and offer moments of wonder as you navigate its intricate tapestry.

In forthcoming works, I'll unequivocally employ the name Heinz G. Ross, adorned with my unique HR logo, differentiating myself from others sharing the name 'Heinz Ross,' while emphasizing my location in Gold Coast, Australia.

Heinz G. Ross

Short Stories...

Preface (What's an 'anything?')

"What's an anything?" is a thought-provoking journey into the realm of dreams, desires, and the power of belief. In this captivating tale, we follow the introspective conversations between Aphra and her wise companion, Tomoko, as they unravel the significance of a dream that left Aphra with a beautiful feeling upon awakening.

Aphra's dream introduces the concept of the "anything," an enigmatic object that possesses the remarkable ability to transform into whatever one desires. As Aphra navigates the possibilities offered by these mysterious "anythings," she discovers the delicate balance between fulfilling personal desires and using this power to make a positive impact on the world.

Through their engaging dialogue, Aphra and Tomoko explore the intricacies of dreams, language, and the human psyche. They delve into the nuances of intention, emphasising the importance of choosing our words carefully, as dreams often take them literally. They also touch upon the fear of greed and the responsibility that comes with possessing the ability to have anything one wishes for.

As Aphra contemplates the boundless potential of the "anything," she ponders noble causes and envisions a world free from strife and suffering. Her journey of self-discovery leads her to consider the impact her choices could have on others and how she might utilise this extraordinary power for the greater good.

"What's an anything?" invites readers to reflect on their own dreams, aspirations, and the hidden power that lies within each of us. It encourages us to question the boundaries of what we believe is possible and to explore the transformative nature of our desires. Ultimately, this book serves as a reminder that our words and beliefs shape our reality and that we hold the key to unlocking the infinite potential of the human spirit.

Join Aphra and Tomoko on their enchanting quest as they unravel the mysteries of dreams, uncover the essence of true desire, and embark on a profound exploration of the boundless possibilities that lie within the realm of the mind.

Prepare to be captivated, inspired, and awakened to the wonders that await when we dare to dream and believe that anything is possible.

Heinz G. Ross

What's an 'anything?'

"Last night I had this dream and when I woke up I had this beautiful feeling."

"Did you now?" answered Tomoko. "What did you dream about, Aphra?"

"It was about anything."
"It would have been better if it was about something," Tomoko replied.

"No, no, anything was more than just something. You see, in this dream I was in a house and it felt like my house," I said. "I was sitting on the bed in the bedroom and around the whole room was a narrow shelf, about a foot wide. It would have been just above my head. It was all around the room."

"On the shelf was a blue object of no particular shape. I wondered what it was. The voice in my dream said that the blue thing was an 'anything'. First I didn't understand it, but the voice explained if I ever needed anything at all, then I could just use the 'anything' and it becomes whatever I need. The voice said I got to be careful what I wish for."
"Oh, that's good," said Tomoko, "what happened then?"

"We'll, I got four more of them, this time in red. Four more of those 'anythings' I mean."
"That was clever," answered Tomoko, but I could see she thought I must have gone a bit nuts.
"What happened then, Aphra?" she asked.
"As I was sitting on the bed, I could see water coming into the room. I guess the bathtub must have been overflowing. The water was maybe 2 or 3 inches deep."
"Oh my goodness," said Tomoko.
"The funny thing is that it didn't worry me in the slightest. I was high and dry sitting on the bed and actually had to grin. I thought it would be a good idea to try out the 'anything.' So, I

threw the blue one on the floor, in the water, and it became a stepping stone. When I stepped on it my feet were dry."

"And then?" asked Tomoko.
"Well, I had four more, but I thought if I use them all up then I haven't got anything left. It felt like a waste to use a good 'anything' for something so simple."

"Aphra, tell me, what happened then?" asked Tomoko, eager to hear the outcome. That's when I woke up Tomoko. I felt so happy. It was like an answer for any problem one might has to face," said I.

"Wouldn't it be good, if we had an endless supply of 'anythings'?"
"Ah yes, and then I went shopping. The big sign said 'Anything for sale,' but they didn't have anything I wanted."
"What did you want?" asked Tomoko.

"I wanted something."
"Then you mustn't look for anything if you want something. You should have looked for something," said Tomoko in a very wise manner. "You're right Tomoko," I said.

"That's why you didn't find anything," reiterated Tomoko, "and you didn't want to use one of your special 'anythings' to turn them into a something." She grinned when she said that. "No, no. I couldn't do that Tomoko. I want to use them for something special."

Then Tomoko's face lit up and she said, "I've got an idea."
I asked, "What?"
"These 'anythings' could become something, right?"

"Yes." I replied.
"And that something could be anything, right?" Tomoko said.
"Yes. Well, I think so," I replied.

"So all you got to do is get one of those anythings and turn it into a dozen somethings, but don't specify what they are. And then you have twelve anythings you can use," said Tomoko.
"Good idea," I said and Tomoko answered, "If you do it right, you'll have an endless supply of anything at all. Then you can do something."

Her face was shining like a light bulb.
"I could," said I and wondered if I was becoming greedy if I did.

Then Tomoko said, "Let's say you look into your fridge and you had run out of eggs."
"Yes."
"You wouldn't just ask for 1 egg, would you?" she said.

"No, perhaps not," said I.
"You'd ask for a dozen," Tomoko suggested.
"Yes, most likely I would."

Tomoko's face became more thoughtful when she said, "But you got to be careful with dreams."
"Why is that Tomoko?"
"They take you word for word," Tomoko answered, "not by what you mean, but exactly by the word and by what the word means. Not what you mean when you say it."

I must have looked a bit puzzled when she explained.
"Let's say you are angry with your cat, and you say 'bloody cat', what you mean by that is not that the cat is covered in blood, do you?"
"No."
"But your dream takes your word exactly as you say it and then it becomes a cat in blood, to the dream," said Tomoko.

"I see," said I, but Tomoko was quick to correct me, "No, what you meant is: 'I understand'."
"You are so lucky, Aphra," said Tomoko, "no wonder you were happy when you woke up."

"But it was just a dream," said I.

"What? Don't you know anything? A dream is a message," said Tomoko. "It is telling you that you can have anything you want. You better believe it," she added, and she was very convinced about it.

"The 'anything' in your dream is everything. Don't you get it?" she said and looked really seriously at me. "But I'm afraid," I said. "Of what, Aphra?"
"What if it doesn't work, I'm back to an ordinary life. And what if it does work? What if I ask for the wrong things and when I get it I may want to change my mind and then I've wasted it?"

"If I do nothing, at least I can believe that it may be true," I said, "but if I try it and it fails to work I may lose my belief." Tomoko just laughed.
"I am afraid of becoming greedy if it does work," said I.

Tomoko continued to laugh. After a while, she asked, "Let's go back to the dream. You threw the blue 'anything' into the water on the floor. That's what you said."
"I did."
"And what happened, Aphra? It turned into a stepping stone, right?"
"It did."
"What colour was the stepping stone? Was it blue?" she asked.

"No. It was the colour of stone and flat at the top."
"And you stepped on it and it was still a stone?" she asked.
"Yes. It felt solid, just like a real stone."
"And then you woke up," said Tomoko.

"A little later I woke up. I figured to get to the bathroom would have been about eight steps. I knew the four other 'anythings' would not have been enough to cover the distance. I stood on the stepping-stone and tried to figure out a way to get to the bathroom without wasting all my 'anythings.'

"I thought I could get by using just one more. Each step I could have bent backwards and pick up the last stone to move that one in front of me and so on."
"Did you?" she asked.
"No. I thought the stone would be heavy to lift and I may slip and fall into the water. Then I thought what a waste to use the special 'anythings' just to keep my feet dry."

"I thought of asking for more 'anythings,' but I didn't ask, for fear of becoming greedy."
"And then?" asked Tomoko.
"That's when I woke up. And I had this happy feeling when I woke up."

She pondered for a moment and then said, "The dream told you all you needed to know. Just go for it. Turn anything into whatever you desire."
She smiled like one of those blessed people with an inner calm.

"But Tomoko, I left my 'anythings' in the dream," I said.

"Silly you, don't you get it? Anything will do!" she said.
"Let's try it with something that is red. Use a red bottle top or a red capsicum. It doesn't matter what it is. Have you got any tomatoes?" she asked.
"No. I ran out of them yesterday," I said.
"Aphra! You did not run out of your tomatoes yesterday," she said. "You better watch your language, and I mean every word you say, otherwise you could do more harm than good."
"How can tomatoes be anything?" I asked.

"You see my car over there, in the carport?"

"Yes." I answered.
"If there is anything in the carport, what is it?" Tomoko asked.
"Yes, your car."
"Therefore a car is anything, the same with tomatoes. Anything is just a metaphor for any one thing, whatever that thing is doesn't matter."
"How can tomatoes turn into something else?" I asked.

"That's not your problem, Aphra. The dream said it could be done. Let the dream worry about how that is done." said Tomoko, and I think she meant it.

"Aphra, let me tell you this," Tomoko said, "dreams are stupid. They don't know what you mean. They only know what you say."

Then she added, "It's actually the other way around. We are the stupid ones, because we always say what we don't mean. And even while I'm saying this, I realise that this is wrong too, because sometimes we can say what we mean. But not all too often."

Then I thought for a while and said, "Tomoko, if I could have anything I want...", but Tomoko interrupted me.

"Wrong," she said.

"What's wrong?" I asked.

"What you just said," she replied.

"What have I said?"

"You said 'could'. You should have said 'I can have anything I want, etc, etc, etc,'" said Tomoko. "Why were you happy this morning when you woke up?"

"Because I had this lovely dream," I said.

"Wrong," said Tomoko. "You were happy because you believed in the dream. You were happy because you were wishing 'what if' that was real. You were happy because it felt as if it is real."

"I guess so."

"You must never forget that feeling. You must keep the same belief in every word you say," said Tomoko. "If you say 'could' you start to throw doubt on your own belief and bye, bye, it's all over."

"OK." I said, "If I can have anything I want..."

"Aphra, no 'if's' if you please," she interjected.

"...anything I want, wouldn't it make me feel rather special?" I continued my line of thought.

"Aren't you?" she questioned.

"But if I would get every wish granted, would I not get bored? What else is there to look forward to?" I said.

"Aren't there lots of other people who would deserve it more, others who have a real need for such a special gift?" I wondered.

"Listen to me, Aphra," said Tomoko with a voice like my teacher in Grade 7. "The dream was just a reminder to you, so that you are aware of the gifts that are within you. Other people have them too."

"But...," and Tomoko cut me short.

"Aphra, you ask too many questions," she said, "be glad that you've been given an answer and don't question it."

"Tomoko, what I wanted to say before you interrupted me, was trying to find something that is worthwhile wishing for," I said, "just in case the endless supply of 'anythings' doesn't work."

"I need to find a good and noble cause, so that the wish does the most good."

This time Tomoko did not interrupt me and waited for more.

"If I wished for all the hospital to shut down, because no one was going to need them, no one was going to be sick," I said, "but imagine, how much one of those 'anythings' could be worth?"

"What if I wished for peace on earth? That's a good thing to wish for," said I. "Can you just grasp how much that is worth? There is not enough money in the whole world to buy health or peace on earth. How can the little 'anything' I have be worth that much?"

Tomoko didn't say a word and within a few seconds I had a whole list of good wishes that would be ideal to sacrifice an 'anything' for.

"Peace on earth, enough food for all, no more fighting and arguments, a healthier environment, climate change, endangered species, enough money in everyone's pockets, happiness for everybody. Oh, there are a million things I could do," and I started to feel that I could.

Tomoko held her chin while I was rattling on.

"Just think a cure for any illness, an answer for any question, a solution to any problem. It would be great, fantastic."

Tomoko sat in silence. Her elbow was on the table and with her hand she held her chin and she listened to me with a smile.

"I could wish for no accidents ever, no more crime, no violence, nothing that could hurt another person in any which shape or form," I said, and I could feel I was on a roll.

"Tomoko, just think, no plane could ever fall out of the sky, no ship could sink, no train or car could crash, and nothing could go wrong. Wouldn't it be wonderful?" I said.

Tomoko took a sip of her coffee and had happiness in her face. "I could make more 'anythings' and just give them away by the hundreds, thousands, by the millions," said I, "and everyone could wish for their own dream."

Tomoko had finished her coffee and said, "Can I have another cuppa?"

"Sorry, I'm out of coffee. That was the last I had," I said.
"And what about yourself, Aphra? Isn't there anything you wish for yourself?" she asked.
"No. I don't want anything."
"I've got all I need."
"I don't wish for anything," I said.
Then I looked at Tomoko. She swallowed and then shut her eyes and a tear ran down her cheek.

End

Preface (In the Shadow of the Sun)

The language of 'In the Shadow of the Sun' is poetic and metaphorical, creating a lyrical and expressive style. In the realm of human emotions, few are as captivating and elusive as love. It weaves its intricate tapestry in the hearts and minds of those who dare to venture into its depths, casting shadows and illuminating paths unknown. It is within this ethereal realm that 'In the Shadow of the Sun' unfolds, revealing a tender exploration of love's complexities, its yearnings, and the profound impact it holds on our lives.

From the tender age of five, when petals plucked from a flower held the power to reveal love's truth, we embark on a journey alongside the narrator. The simple act of counting petals becomes a metaphor for the uncertainties and hopes that reside within every heart. Through evocative prose, we witness the narrator's youthful innocence and the unwavering belief in the power of love's affirmation.

As the years pass, the narrator's understanding of love evolves, guided by encounters with the sun, mirrors, echoes, and the vastness of the ocean. These encounters become catalysts for self-reflection and introspection, awakening a newfound awareness of the complexities of love's presence. The interplay between light and shadow mirrors the ebb and flow of their connection with a loved one, as they navigate the intricacies of distance, longing, and the yearning for unity.

Through heartfelt dialogue and profound introspection, the narrative delves into the nature of love itself. It explores the intangible essence of love, its boundless nature that transcends borders and defies conventional constraints. The narrator grapples with the challenges of distance, longing to bridge the physical and emotional gaps that separate one from the other.

As the passage of time unfolds, the narrative weaves a web of emotions, capturing the deep ache and profound yearning that arises from a love unfulfilled. Their connection, though constrained by circumstance, remains a beacon of hope, reminding us of the power of love's enduring presence even in the face of adversity.

Throughout the pages of 'In the Shadow of the Sun,' we are invited to contemplate the significance of each breath we take and the profound longing that resides within our hearts. The narrative challenges us to question our fears, to confront the uncertainties that hold us back from embracing love's transformative power. It reminds us that love, in all its forms and colours, has the ability to shape and define our existence, transcending the boundaries of time and space.

As you embark on this poignant exploration of love's intricacies, may the words on these pages resonate within your own heart. May they serve as a reminder of the power of love to illuminate even the darkest shadows, to inspire us to take the leap, and to embrace the transformative nature of love's embrace.

Heinz G. Ross

In the shadow of the sun

Three petals I picked when I was five.
"He loves me; he loves me not; he loves me."

I was so glad to be alive when I was five.

Four petals I picked when I was six.
"He loves me; he loves me not. He loves me; he loves me not."
Oh, what a fix when I was six!

At seven, I had worked out that if I picked five petals, he would love me. If I picked 7, 9, or 11, he would love me too. With six, eight, and twelve petals, I ripped one off before I started counting. I could make sure he always loved me.

The sun shone down, and I looked up and said, "Hey sun, you do see everything. You shine in all directions."
"That is not so," the sun replied. "I cannot see behind you."
"That is correct, and neither can I," this said I.

"But you shine everywhere at once," I said, "That is sheer magic."
"That is not so," the sun replied. "I cannot shine upon myself."
"Oh dear, I am so sorry," so said I, and began to ponder and wonder.

Then I stood, turned, and looked in all directions, and I could see everything except one thing. I could not see myself. I saw the bits of me, the arms, the legs, but never all of me at once. And then I saw the magic of a mirror that could see everything except itself. I brought it face-to-face with another, and then it saw itself for the first time.
It said, "This is not how you see me. My left is left, my right is right; it should be the other way around. This is not me, I see."

Then I stood on the edge of a gorge and called out loud. The echo returned, repeating my words, my proof that I had spoken.

Then I picked a flower with so many petals. I did not count them before I started. I was hopeful that he loved me. It would have worked out, but the last three petals had become four when I discovered another hidden between them.

Then I cried my heart out on a wall. Every sop I made came echoed from the wall until I realised it had no ears, nor had it words of soothing.

I went to the ocean, and the fin of a shark taught me: "Move forwards or you will drown; don't stop; don't give up hope; or you will perish. I would if I stopped."
So I did, advancing forwards, wherever that was. Mostly, I moved ahead, towards, or away from now.

Forwards I walked into the future, but it had a fence across my path. "You cannot enter," said the future, "walk in the present. There's your place."

He loves me; he loves me not; he loves me. "That's nice to know," I heard me say, "but if he does, where is he?"
"I'm here," I heard his thoughts, "and I do love you," his thoughts conveyed.

And then we met. His eyes were blue, and mine are green and blue eyes I had never seen. In the shine of the sun, I saw them sparkle, and he saw mine shine.

One summer we played, and another. We laughed, and loved, and bothered. Somehow, the sun had moved and cast a shadow. Two silhouettes stood in the shade on the grass, and we couldn't tell each other apart. So similar in many ways that the sun rose up for another day.

One day the sun rose, and late in the afternoon it started to lower, and then it would no longer move. It stopped setting and stayed fixed to throw a long shadow. From that low, it could not reflect from their eyes.

"I love you," he did say.
"And I do you," my heart responded. "Why are we apart?"
"Love is free," he said to me. "Love has no bounds, no borders."
"Love is...," and then he said what love is: "Love."
"So if you love me, why don't you?" I said, but his thoughts cut me short. "The 'if' is in the way," he said.
"But the flower said you love me," I said.
"I do," said he to me.
"Why don't you come then?" this I said.
"I am with you, but mostly in my thoughts," said he.
"How can you love me from afar?" said I.
"I do," said he, "your arrow pierced me."

"Each morning I awake with you by my side in thoughts."
"And so do I," said I.
"Throughout the day, I am with you," I knew.
"So what's the answer?" I did say
"Love is an answer in itself," said he.
"What does that mean?" asked I.
"Love is," he said to me.

Another month went by. Another month went past. Each month had four weeks, and sometimes it had more. Each week had seven days; sometimes they seemed longer. Each day had 24 hours, some of which they slept. And each day of every week of every month, he thought of her. And so did she of him.

"This is a sin," he said to me.
"But if you love me, could you not..."
"Love is," he said again

Do you not miss me?" this I asked.
"I do more than you know," said he.
"And I miss you," said I.
He cried.

Another month and more went by, each aching for the other and filling time with bother.
"But if you love me, could you not..."
"I do," said he. "You know I do."

"How many breaths of air have you inhaled?" he asked.
"How would I know? I never counted," said I.
"How many breaths will you have left?" he asked.
"I do not know the answer," said I.
"How many breaths are due to you?" he said.
"What sort of question is this? Is there a measure?" I replied.
He did not answer but asked again, "Do you not take the air to fill your lungs? Do you not fill its hunger?"
"I do," said I.
"Is there not a longing in your heart for love?" he asked.
"There is," I said.
"Why don't you let it in?" he said.
"I would, but..." he did not let me answer.
"And there is your answer," said he.
"Which of the breaths you took have you ever refused? Which breaths did you take by choice? Which breaths did you ever question before inhaling?" said he in asking.
"Possibly none, and all, and none, to answer all three," I said to him. "My lung could not live without it," said I as a reply.
"And your heart can?" said he, his answer as a question.

Another month with many days and many hours went from now to the past.
"What do we do?" he asked.
"Perhaps we shall get over it," I try. Time shall pass by.
"Love is life. Life unlived is unthinkable. Love unloved is incomprehensible," he said to me.

"Oh, I do love you from afar," I said.
"And so do I," said he.

And months went by, and each one cried, and none knew how to solve it. So close they lived yet as far apart as day and night. By chance, they would most likely never meet.
"And it is I; I cry," said I.
"Me too, for you," he said to me.
"How can it be that you have not found another?" they both asked of each other. No need to answer; they both knew because of 'love'.

Another minute grew to an hour, to become a day that grew to a week, which swelled to another month, which was surpassed by another with a different name.

"Is it not such a waste?" said I.
"It is reason to cry," he said to me.
"I did," said I.
"And so did I," said he to me.

"He loves me, he loves me not, he loves me, he loves me not, he loves me, he loves me not, he loves me."
"How many petals will you pick before you can accept their answer?" he said to me.
"As many as I need to know, to be certain," said she.
"I will breathe you; I will breathe you not; I will breathe you," said he, and laughed at me.
"I'll love you when I'm certain," I said.
"You love me," he said.
"I do," said I. "I do love you."
"So why don't you do what love needs you doing," he said to me.
"I am afraid," said I.
"Of me or of love?" he questioned.
"Both, I think," said I.

"I am afraid to see you," said I, "afraid you will draw me close."
"I will, and that you know," said he.
"I know, and I would come to you," said I.
"Are you afraid that if you do, you shall deny you to the one that colours your dream?" he said to me.
"How did you know?" I asked.
He cried.

"Are you not looking? You're free to do it," said I.
"I know. Love won't allow me," this he said.
"I want my love in the colour green," said I.
"Love is in every colour," said he.
"I don't want every colour. I want green," said I.
"Does it matter which colour love is?" he said to me.
I said, "It does to me."
"If that's a must, then wear coloured lenses so that it shows to you in green," he said to me as an answer.

"That would be an illusion. It is not green; for that, I know if I remove the coloured lens," said I in my reply.
"Love is a gift, given as it is, with all its beauty," he said to me.
She said, "I want it in a certain way. I want it to be green."
"It is beyond my comprehension that you can criticise the gift that is yours for the taking," said he.
"I had a vision in my mind that it was green," said I.
"What do you drink to quench your thirst?" he asked of me.
"What's that got to do with it? It's water I drink, clear, pure water," I said in reply.
"Would you drink mud?" he asked.
"I? Me? My? Mud? No, never," I responded.

"Would you say mud insults you if it were offered?" he said.

"I would," I said.
"Four weeks in a desert and your water had run out long ago, your insides screaming for any type of moisture, and there you find a pit of mud. Would it not be the greatest gift you

could hope to find? Would you not smile in gratefulness to quench your thirst with mud?" said he.

"That is not fair. It is a matter of survival; perhaps I have a taste because I must, to quench my thirst," I said in reply.

"This mud would be a gift of life. That's all the desert could manage to offer. The desert gave you all it had to give," he said to me.

"If I refused the mud, I'd die. But with love, it's not the same," I said.

"Do you not starve your heart of love because it is not green?" he said to me.

I said to him, "I'll manage."

"Perhaps you hope to find the green in someone else," he said to me.

"I cannot answer this out of fear of hurting you," I said, and cried, "turn green for me".

"Let's say I could. Let's say I am. My love for you is green," he said to answer me.

"Yes. Now I can be with you," I said.

And together, they walked to the ocean. They stood near the edge of the water. The sun reflected the ocean's blue onto the green of his love.

"Your green has a tinge of blue," I said.

"The water changes my colour. Let us walk inside a park," he said suggesting.

And together, they walked inside the park. They stood near bushes with flowers in bloom. Yellow and orange they shone. Again, the reflection coloured it green.

"Your green has a tinge of orange and yellow," I said.

"The flowers reflect it on the green," he said, "It's not my doing. My love is green. That I do know. I made it green for you."

"But I see it tinged. It is not pure green," I replied.

"But the love has not changed; I coloured it for you," he said to me. "Love is, no matter how you see it."

"I want it green, I want it strong, and I never want it changing," I did say.

"That is a demand. Love cannot oblige. Love is," he said to me. "Air cannot change. Water cannot change. Love cannot change. Love is."

"Water and air can change; why can't love make me happy?" I replied.

"Water and air only appear to change; they are constantly reborn and will return to their pure state of being, and so is love," he said to me, yet I could not understand it.

"The sun brings warmth and light. Those who know how to use it will prosper. Those that don't will be harmed," this he did say to me.

"What do you mean?"

"Is love like the rays of the sun?" I asked him to explain.

"Does it not bring life?" he answered short.

"But I can live without love if I have to," I said.

"Is not your heart aching for love?" he said to me.

"It is," said I, "I long to see love green and never changing."

"Can plants demand the type of rays the sun is giving? Can soil demand the type of raindrops it prefers? Either the sun burns or is too far away. Either the soil is dry or flooded, the two extremes. Is it not mostly in between that life unfolds in all its glory?" It's this, he said.

"If love is like a cold drop of water, it cannot remain cold when it falls into a boiling pot. If love is like a warm drop and heat is added, it will change and rise. No longer will it be a drop."

"If you ask me to change, you risk changing me. And if I change, so will the love I have to give," he did say.

"Perhaps it's this I'm asking," this said I.

"Then I will not know who I am," he said.

"But I'll find what I'm wanting in you." I did answer.

"I will no longer be if I don't know who I've become. I shall be lost not knowing who I am," he did answer.

"But I'll be happy," I said. He cried instead.

So close, so far, they grow each day older, each on their own. None could cry on the other's shoulder.

"I miss your voice. I miss your face. I miss your touch and closeness. I miss the kisses that we shared. I miss the laughter and your happiness," he said to me. "I miss your love."
"Turn green," I answered.
"Each sunrise and each sunset, each cloud would change my coat of green. Green is not me," was his reply.
"Then I shall never see you," she said and cried.

And so did he. And the clouds opened up and joined them both. It rained for a long time. It rained for twenty days and more. The waters rose. The fields were covered with tears from heaven. They walked knee-deep in water and went about their daily chores. The clouds called for more and more, and they came, and the rain poured for another 20 days and more. They did their chores as best they could as the water reached their shoulders. The clouds called for more, and more did come. The rain did fall and cover all the plants and trees. There was no green that could be seen anywhere. And then the rain stopped.

They each found a mountain above the water. There they sat, apart.

"Did you do that?" I asked him.
"No, I did not," he said to me.
"Is there any green you see?" he asked me.
I said, "No."
"I do," he said.
"Where?" I asked.
"The green is in your eyes," he said. "Don't turn your head."
"Why not?" I said.
"You will not like the green I see behind your head," he said.
I turned, and there I saw the green that brought me fear.
"Can you love me as I am?" he said to me.
"You know what I want," I said instead.

The clouds gathered. Among them was a dark green cloud that reached higher than all of the others combined.
"I miss your love," he said to me.

"How can you think of love in times like these?" I answered.
"How can you think of me at all? I have not seen you for a year, nor have your eyes seen me. The voice you hear is not from me, but from the memory of me," said I.
"But every day you're with me," he did say, "each night you're in my arms."
"That is not I," I said. He cried.
"I set you free. Go find another; there are others that need love," I said.

"You cannot set me free," said he. "You see, it's me."
"What are you saying?" I did say.
"Once I give love, I cannot take it back and give it to another," he said.
"I see," I said.
"Then you shall love what you won't see. Perhaps I have another," I did say.
"Perhaps you have. I would not know it if you did," said he.
"Is he green?"

"No, do not answer. I don't know how to cope if that was so," he did say.
"If you love me, would you not want to see me happy?" I did ask.
"I know that 'yes' should be the answer," he did said.
"So what is it?" I did want to know.
He could not answer me. He would not say. He could not speak to me.

"How can it be that you love me, and yet your love is not for me? I cannot see," he said to me. He could not understand it.

"You are not green," I said. I heard him sigh.
Then he said, "Why?"
What could I say? 'Because?'

Then the clouds moved in and the rain came down to raise the water's level. The green cloud poured its contents out and raised the level ten times higher. He stood on his toes on the mountain he found. The water had risen in all directions. He had to raise his head and form his lips to the shape of a kiss. This was the only way for the water to avoid flooding the inside of his mouth. There he stood, like reaching for a kiss from heaven, balancing on his toes.

The rain stopped. All it takes is one more drop, and the water tension will break, and his lips will not be able to stop the water from filling him.
"If you cry, you die," I said.
He knew.
What could he do?
What could I do?

57

"Why did you leave the last page blank?"
"I couldn't think of anything," he said, "except I tried to find another word that rhymes with others that I'd found."
"What do you mean?" I said.
"A, b, c, d," said he to me, "Ai, bye, cry, d..."
"I need to find another word instead," he said.
"'Ai' is not a word," said I.
"I know. I made it up," said he, "but that's not the one I'm after."
"I know one with 'd' that has two meanings," I said.
"It's not the one I can use. My head will be inclined to use the meaning of the one I do not wish to use," he said.
"Then use the opposite of 'wet'," I said instead.
"Dry. Good try," he said, sighing.

And there he stood. His lips shaped like a funnel, pointing up to keep the water out. Close by his eye, an ant was looking to find land that was dry. It climbed up on his lips and tickled with every step it took.
"For miles around there is no land except the lips on which I stand," said she, the ant, to the lips, the land.
"I live in trees. My home was a leaf. I had to leave as the seas kept rising," the ant did say.

"There is no tree for me to see," she said to me. "From where did all the water come?"
"If I tell you, you will cry. And if you do, we both shall... "
"I cannot say the word," he said.

"Then I shall try not to cry, but I need to know the answer to why I lost my home," the ant did say, "and if you don't then I shall bite you."

"It's about the love that I offered to the one that filled my heart. All went well until she stood and said she didn't want it anymore," said he.

"So what's the problem?" said the ant.

"In the first week that went by, I looked her in the eye and said, 'I'll never leave you'," he said.

"What did you say to her?" the ant replied.

"No. I made this promise to myself," he said.

"Then that's your problem," said the ant.

"I know," he said.

"The heavens cry for love must never d..," he said.

"I cannot say the word," he added.

The ant stood on its hind legs. It looked everywhere and then said what it had found: "I cannot see her anywhere. There is no living thing I see; there is no tree at all. And all I see is just the sea, and in it are just you and me."

"Where is she then?" the ant did ask.

"She's in my head; she's in my heart," he said.

"Then love your heart and love your head if she's in there instead," she said.

"I cannot fill myself with the love I have inside," he said.

"To me, love is a tree," said she, the ant, "and if there's only you and me, then give your love to me."

"Describe yourself. I cannot see. My eyes are underwater," he said.

"My legs are tinged a reddish brown. Sometimes I frown. My body is the colour of my home, the leaf."

"You mean it's green?" he said.

"Yes, green. I am a green ant," she said.

He laughed and said, "Oh my. You are the colour of her eye."

"How can I love you? You are a different species," he did said.

"A tree will do for me," she said.

"Is not a tree for me another species?" she added.

"The tree was my home. It was everything to me," she said.
"You are not of my kind," he said.
"This I don't mind," said she.
"I cannot love a tree," he said. "I do love trees, but in another way. Another kind of love," he said to me.
"How could I love an ant? You can bite," he said.
"Anything can bite, you see," said she.

It was then that the ant had enough. She let out a puff. She stood up again, looked around, and saw something that made her frown.
"All I see of you is just a ridge of lips stretching through the water. I know nothing else about you. I see no tree for me. I see no sign of her, the 'she' that's in your head. You have a choice to love your head or me instead," she said.
"Love has one demand, she said, "it needs to be loved."
"I'll tell you what I see instead," she said.

"Far in the distance is lightning. The heavens are rumbling. The sky is thundering. You can dream of the sun, but it's not going to come unless you love me," said she, the ant on the land of lips in the sea.
Said he, "Oh my, oh my..."
Then he started to...

End

Preface (Only for now)

'Only for now' is a journey through the fascinating perspective of an eye, the silent witness to a world filled with beauty, tragedy, and everything in between. In this introspective exploration, we delve into the complexities of perception, memory, and the lasting impressions etched upon the soul.

The eye, a gateway to the inner core, has no choice but to absorb the visuals of the world it beholds. It is a relentless observer, capturing every colour, shape, and motion in its unyielding gaze. Yet, behind its unwavering sight lies a profound longing to understand and make sense of the seen.

Through the eye, we encounter moments both joyous and heart-wrenching. We witness the flares of joy ignited by the presence of loved ones and the profound ache when they are lost. We confront the haunting images of tragedy, the shattered innocence of a child, the pain etched on trusted faces, and the cold stare of lifeless eyes.

But amidst the beauty and the anguish, questions arise. Can the seen be trusted? Is it reality or merely a dream? The eye, a silent witness to events, becomes plagued with doubt. It yearns for clarity, for a glimpse of truth within the vast expanse of the seen.

As we probe deeper into the mysteries of the eye, we uncover its intricacies and capabilities. We marvel at its co-ordination, the perfect harmony of muscles that allow it to track objects and perceive depth. We explore its ability to see the past, to focus billions of years into a single point, forever imprinted in memory.

Yet, even with its remarkable faculties, the eye is not infallible. It shows everything it sees, overwhelming the mind with a deluge of sights and leaving it to grapple with the weight of perception. It is a double-edged sword, offering clarity and insight while burdening the soul with indelible imprints.

Throughout this journey, we come to realise that the eye is not separate from the self, it is an integral part of our being. It carries the essence of who we are, reflecting the diverse hues that make us human. Whether blue, violet, hazel, or a mixture of all, the eye remains an enigmatic gateway to our perception of the world.

Once invites us to explore the untrodden paths of the seen, to seek the traces of our past, and to embrace the lasting impact of the sights we encounter. It challenges us to confront the bittersweet nature of memory and the unyielding presence of the seen in our lives.

With each turn of the page, we embark on a poignant journey of self-discovery, where the eye is both observer and protagonist. It is an invitation to ponder the true nature of reality, to question the boundaries between dream and waking life, and to unravel the profound connection between what is seen and who we are.

So join us as we embark on this introspective odyssey, where the eye reigns supreme, and the seen unfolds in all its bewildering splendour. Once you begin, you will find it impossible to look away, for the eye, in all its complexity, has a story to tell, a story that resonates within us all.

Through cryptic prose and introspective questions, this enigmatic narrative urges us to seek the traces of our past, tracing back to when we were but innocent children, our eyes captivated by the lines drawn by a host's hand. Those pencil lines, forming letters and words of warning, now beckon us to embark on a profound journey of self-discovery.

As we navigate deeper into the text, we encounter the enigmatic symbols of X and Y, which stand not merely for mathematical variables, but for something far more profound, the interconnectedness of ourselves and others. The story unfolds, revealing that within the shadows of our existence lies a war, not one fought between nations or ideologies, but a war within ourselves. It is a conflict between the outer and the inner, a yearning for peace amidst the chaos.

The author prompts us to examine the curtains that shroud our vision, obscuring our ability to perceive the world in its true essence. Through tears shed and a cleansing of the soul, the curtains can be changed, gradually aligning our inner peace with the outer reality. This quest for balance between the seen and the unseen, between what is and what could be, becomes our guiding light.

Within the narrative's labyrinthine passages, memories are revisited, fragments of time and place that have shaped our understanding of the world. Yet, we are cautioned against carrying the burdens of the past unnecessarily, for the key lies in focusing on the present and what lies ahead.

The eye, a marvel of evolution spanning millions of years, is both a witness and a victim of deception. Its inherent limitations become apparent, revealing a truth obscured by assumptions, fears, and distorted perspectives. And yet, amid these limitations, there is hope, moments of clarity, of pure sight unburdened by curtains, when the true nature of the seen is unveiled.

Ultimately, "Only for now" challenges us to re-evaluate our relationship with the seen and to question our desire for repetition, for the illusory pursuit of an ultimate satisfaction. Life, as the narrative reminds us, is dynamic and ever-changing, and true understanding lies not in the fixation on a single moment, but in embracing the constant ebb and flow of existence.

As we embark on this introspective voyage, let us heed the voice that whispers between the lines and discover the hidden truths that lie within our own perception. For in the exploration of the seen and the unseen, we may find the wisdom to unlock the mysteries of our existence and embrace the fullness of our being.

At its core, "Only for now" explores the multifaceted nature of vision and the limitations of the eye. The text invites us to un-breathe a breath, un-trace a trace, and un-live life, urging us to contemplate the very essence of our existence and the interconnectedness of all things. Through enigmatic conversations with a mirror-like figure, we are encouraged to look beyond the surface of what we see and look into the profound depths of our being.

The narrative reminds us that the eye, despite its remarkable abilities to gather light and construct visual images, is merely a conduit for information. It is through the collaboration of our senses, the integration of our experiences, and the interpretation by our consciousness that the true understanding of the world emerges. The text challenges us to transcend the limitations of sight and embrace a holistic perception that encompasses the full spectrum of our senses.

As we embark on this journey of self-discovery, we are invited to explore the interconnectedness of all things. The reflection in the mirror serves as a metaphor for the unseen forces that shape our existence, both within and outside ourselves. It calls us to Recognise the inherent unity that binds us to the world, to nature, and to one another.

The narrative also presents the idea that true vision goes beyond the physical act of seeing. It encourages us to immerse ourselves in the present moment, to engage all our senses, and to embrace the fullness of our experience. By doing so, we can transcend the confines of perception and tap into a deeper understanding of the world around us.

Through its poetic and enigmatic prose, "Only for now" challenges us to question our preconceptions, to shed our assumptions, and to open ourselves to new possibilities. It invites us to examine the nature of reality, the role of perception, and the intricacies of our own existence. It is a call to expand our vision, both within and beyond the confines of the eye, and to embrace the profound mysteries that lie within the seen and the unseen.

As we navigate the pages of this text, let us be open to its profound insights and thought-provoking questions. May it inspire us to see beyond the surface, to embrace the interconnectedness of all things, and to embark on a journey of self-discovery that transcends the limitations of sight and touches the very essence of our being.

Heinz G. Ross

Only for now

Once

Once vision like blurred haze, I did not know then who I was, or what I was to do or be. The vision cleared and I learned, I was about becoming. In becoming, I became.
I became eye.
Eye is I.
Eye I am.
I have no choice in what I see. It is always there, in front of me.
Eye is I.
The eye I am.
The eye absorbs the visuals of the world that appears to be in front. Unique the world this eye can see. The iris cannot shut it out. Retina will not blur it. Only the eyelids keep the vision out, the vision of the world around.
I deal with colour, shape and motion, in the attached brain with emotion. I am not one, but two, though one has never seen the other, neither had it seen me. It and I, both as one, we deal with depth, perception in space and shades of

brightness, which is how it seems. The brain turns some into bleak darkness. There, right in front, blackness is coloured, rarely ever without light.

Once, both shone. They glittered in the sun. What had I seen that was pleasing? So many things that sparked the flares of joy, mostly it was you, whenever it I saw. The harmony of you is more than just the visual view of you. Each picture's worth remembering, worthy of recalling without fear. Eyes, that soaked you in, were absorbing all of you. But now it aches, seeking the eyes it knew, the sight that never failed to soothe. Your eyes, which I will never find again.

What do I do, with the light I let in, which left its traces that will not fade? The views of muddy boots that stepped into the pass filled sores. One face changed to agony, while the face of the other roared to laughter.

What do I do, with the sight of oozing brain escaping from a fractured skull? The 'oh so cute' slammed by a brute. What do I do, with the seen that saw eyes staring lifeless into space? The cold dead stare of frozen eyes.

The eye is I, always absorbing, taking everything in.

The only things I give are tears. I cry. Tears fail to wash it clean, from the visions that the eye had seen.

I've seen the five-year-old child that tried to run across the road. The bumper bar of an approaching car hit him. The kid bounced like a soccer ball for sixty yards, and then he lay there, on the boiling bitumen. At least fourteen eyes saw it happening.

I was a witness.

Each saw it from another angle, another point of view. We all joined the silence, in shock. There was not a mark on him, not on the outside. He never made a sound. Eyes could not hear it either way, but his mouth did not move. He did not try to scream. The first hit knocked him out.

What do I do, with the visions of a trusted face, once that trust took flight? The brain, attached to the signal carriers, stunned. It is unable to fathom the change.

This eye had seen a trusted face and welcomed it, opening the iris, taking in more. Perception changed in time. No rewind is ever possible.

I have failed the host. I have been deceived. Can I ever rely on the seen? If this face can turn, so can anything. Is seen reality or is it dream?

The eye is a one-way street.

So much traffic is coming down, busy as a highway. On the other end, it is trying to make sense of all that is coming in. Retina retention, projection screen within, as funnel to the brain.

Who goes to sort it out?

Did he once, she never, he ever, she once, perhaps a million times. Therefore, what I see is real, is false, is just not happening, is incomprehensible and is absurd, falsehood to the extreme.

Even if I shut down, will still create the phantom visions, the ghostly apparitions, the never-ending views of things that appear to have no point.

A point there always is with eyes.

Even the night does not bring blackness, the grey tinged and the white is never pure.

For what I seek, I am powerless to find. I am not head. I cannot turn direction, cannot select the visions that I crave.

The eye is I, the silent witness of events.

Eyes have no guards have no protection. Eyes have no filters. Eyes are gates to the inner core. Gates that will only shut once, and when they do life will have drained.

Eyes that move and can track any object it aims in their sights. Six muscles provide perfect co-ordination; each eyeball rotates around its centre. Massive calculations of space and distance, motion of subject and movement of self. All is automatic co-ordination with little lag in time. Eyes can flutter rapidly as the host is sleeping.

Eyes that converge and diverge, to absorb whatever size the object be it sees, up to a point, down to a point.

Eyes can see the past. Focus billions of years to a finite point. That point being the purpose. That point contains the total of the seen. Billions of points, billions of instances of the now, the never stopping moments, each leaving impacts, compounding, each seeking some sort of comprehension, each wanting to become a point that be understood.

The yesterday to now is gettable. Yet not a single image can ever become 'unseen'. Rewind the seen, impossible, not even one seen instant clears to become blank. Unseeing is unobtainable, unless?

This then is eye, admiring, adoring, longing, gazing, dreaming and deceiving, evil, envious, loving and hating, staring and caring. This we are, three inch away from me and I.

Try as you may to seek the past, all is there, yet so much hidden. Fear remembers and fear disguises seen.

How does it work?

How does it work, the eye?

Eyes shooting out rays toward the sight, bounced back by the object in its path. Is the object of the seen radiating its vision into the eye, or is it neither?

This special eye, sharp and observing, almost accurate rendition of the seen is too good for its own good.

Therein it fails in its perfection. Instead of finding, it shows everything. Instead of singling out, it unloads its pregnant weight of sight. Eye failed by the system that bulks in dissecting the streams of its surrounds.

Eye is I. Blue, violet and why am I grey? I am eye, amber, green, hazel, but not yellow, hey? Eye I am, brown and black or some mixture of all. Whichever colour I am, the colours I see cannot be counted.

I can be red and glazed, hazed and dazed, laced with poison darts that spit from its core.

I have no scream, no voice at all. I cannot hear the screams I see. Rarely ever do I feel pain, but I can see the pain in you. I cannot feel it. That is not my job. I do not have the facilities. I gather the outside to a single point that is all I do. That is all I can do. My host deals with the rest. I can see you longing, I can trace your steps, I can freeze your vision and can never forget.

I can see one thing whilst seeing another. Yet if I see two or many, I can only see one. Sometimes I see and am unable to register the seen. Despite, the seen is seen.

I can see the bush you once planted. The once two-inch stick has grown to seven feet. I can see the dress you once wore, the shoes that no other foot has touched since. I see the words on your shopping list, which you once wrote, so many years ago. So much of you I see, and then through tear-blurred vision, I see you. Too far to touch, too faint to clearly see, too vague to accept as real, but there you are, the memory of gratefulness. All this, while staring at a lake.

Whichever path I trace, I leave no trace behind. The path traced within the eye is the one that carves deep gauges. It leaves its marks. Shades and shapes that will not vanish. You, path, have been absorbed. You have marked me. I let you. I looked at you, that is how I let you into me. You, tree, however tall you will grow, this instance of you I shall carry.

Seek your past

Eye in the mirror seek your past. Seek the trace of a Tuesday. Step through the years. Further. A Tuesday, it was in May. Not May, the woman, May, the month. The calendar showed the number 12. Follow the rhythm of your time and you will find the year. You will work it out. The season was spring.
Look closer.
The apple trees covered in white. Not snow, not in May. Blossoms, you see apple blossoms. The trees you had seen a million times looked oh so different on this Tuesday. As if you had never seen them before. This day, you, mirrored eye, had seen them in their magic. From this day on, you had learned to see a tree.
You are I.

Eye I am.

The oaks that I saw, once I had seen the apple blossoms, had a remarkable presence that I was never aware of.

Oaks, which I had seen as trees, became tables, chairs and the polished sides of a coffin. Beautiful oak died for the dead. They had died for the dead, when the dead were still breathing. When the dead were alive, the live tree was cut from its roots. Dead eyes do not see polished grain. Polished grain is not going to take root, no matter how deeply planted. No sawn-off lumber is ever going to grow into anything. Polished grain, prepared for tear-filled eyes of mourners that are unable to take in its essence.

I saw the blood of walnuts. The blood of chestnut, white birch, pear and cherry, I saw the blood of so many trees. Their blood is red. Their blood seeps like tears. It streams down their trunks. A bleeding tree is a sad sight. It is enough to make you cry. Yet trees do not sigh. They bleed in silence. Often trees bleed from four spots or more. The pulped remains of its kind, processed into paper and posters, nailed to a trunk, proclaiming a 30% discount on wooden floors, or whatever. The irony of being a tree, cut down for posterity. Used as a sign for all to see, your strength to sway will be how long?

Eye in the mirror, return to the Tuesday. Count thirty-two days back from that day. What did you see then, midday?

That's right, white.

It was a different white, the white of nothing, the empty white. It blurred. I could not tell the source of light, no depth and no dimension. I adjusted my focus, as if I discovered a tool that had never been used before. At close focus, I saw wriggly things, seemingly swimming right in front. Further away, the blur of white, beyond the blur the hazy face of a flat white wall. Flat ceiling, flat right wall, flat left wall, shapeless walls, avoid of any features.

What else was white?

It took a while to learn the game of focus. Don't know how long the while was, but it was fascinating, absorbing, even amusing. Almost everything was white. The sheets were white, bed sheets, bright lights and white linen bed sheets. White ceiling lights, lights glaring into me. A white bedpan placed under the body I was in. Then I lost the control of the focus. Still, I kept trying. Little else I could do.

Seeking identity

Who were you?
I can't remember.
Who were you then?
I can't recall.
Were you the eye of a female or male, young or old, animal, ghost, what?
I do not know to whom I belonged.
I had no sense of being. Had no sensations, had no memory to compare.
What was the name of your host?
I have no idea. I didn't know I lived in a host.
What body were you in?
I was not aware that I was in a body. Everything was white. I could barely move, I seemed paralysed. White bandages were everywhere. Was I dead?
Count back six hours from that moment.
There was a very strong white, a brilliant electric white, and there were figures in white coats and face-masks, ghostly figures.
What did they do?
There were so many, racing around, looking in. First only one, then another, and again more came and stuck their heads in front. As if I was something they had discovered. Something they had never seen. What was there to look at? What did they want? Who were they? Each one poked their head into view, so many. I wanted to hide behind my lids, but they would not allow me.
All I saw was the bright dazzling light, and all those masked heads so close to me. One blocked out the light a little. For

ten seconds I could rest from the bright shining light. His lips moved and he showed fingers that he had. He showed his thumb, his index and middle finger. Have no idea what was so special about his fingers. His lips moved all the time, and then he turned away and let the light burn my insides. I had focus then. The wires burned emitting the light.

The light slowly dimmed darker, and I was glad to find relief from its hurting glare. The eyelid lowered like a shutting gate.

I was so defenceless. Fading into darkness brought a welcome escape. The white, not as bright as the light that burned the retina inside, was what I saw. Recall was none. Being a being became the only awareness.

The unknown of self, so very strange, foreign, as if being grown before the shape reached its final form. The sense of forming, shaping, becoming, yet I was. I did not need becoming. I already was. Just did not know what I was. Meaning had no meaning, as everything was a blank.

The beginning

A clean slate of history is of little use. Awareness without concept, with no sense of life, death, or spirit, that is where I had to begin. Void of knowledge, vacant identity. I had no sense of loss, as I had no consciousness of ever been. That was the beginning.

I seemed to be known to those that came. To them I seemed familiar. I must have been before. That is an assumption without proof. Unless they are all actors playing a stupid game on me. The white had dimension, had depth. I deduct, the eye three inch away from me is all right.

Who are all these people that claim to know us?

So many lips form words that have no visual counterpart. How do I behave? What are the expectations? Am I a fraud if I play along? If I have no knowing, and they seem to have so much, should I accept what they say I am? At least I get an identity, a sense of self, a chance of becoming. Whatever it is that they say I am, was, or perhaps were at one stage. One needs to know the language when trying to read lips.

Tell me about trees?

What is a tree? Then, just some letters that were without meaning. Is it something that I should have known?

Show me the ceiling and call it a tree, I would have to believe you, then. What other choice did I have? They all seemed convinced about it. I could not detect any contradictions. To be honest, most likely I would not even have an awareness of what contradiction is, not then. I did adopt what they said I was, I became. They seemed to mean well. In any case, I was trapped.

My host must have gone through hell. I cannot see my host. There is a leg hoisted to a pole. A pin goes right through the heel protruding on both sides. Connected to this is a wire that lifts the leg two feet at the foot end. Hard plaster covered the leg from the foot to the place it grew from. I didn't know that in the beginning. That's what I discovered as I learned to get the focus back. The post fixed to a bed. I didn't know what a bed was, let alone a tree.

They were kind and concerned. They came every day. They stayed, went, and came again. So, I did allow a quasi adoption, since the white room offered little stimulation. One day they carried the host. In doing that, I was moved.

For the first time in life, I saw a colour named 'blue'. It seemed like the first time, but perhaps it was not. How would I know? I had lost my measure.

Driven through streets, the outside world whizzed by in constant motion, until it stopped. It was there that I saw the apple tree. Even then, I did not know this was a tree. It stood in silence. The sunlight made it glow. I was fixed by this vision. I was in awe. I soaked it in, every detail, colour, shading, shape and light, reflection, contours and motion.

Above the tree, the world was blue, beneath it green, I'd never seen. White and blue and green, the colours I had seen that day together.

Never did a tree look grander than that apple tree in bloom. It was a Tuesday in the month of May. It stood proud in rounded shape. I could grab it into the cone of vision. Could take it all at once into my core. Once within, condensed to a point, that point defined the apple tree. That point defined a tree.

Apple blossoms, like upside-down short skirts, each that little bit different. Soft pink coloration edges the white petals, five open to the sun surrounding the yellow stems. More petals beneath the five, like a layered skirt. Bees were dancing amongst the countless blooms. Combined, each played its part, to glow in harmony of form and beauty. So intricate the detail, I feasted in wondrous admiration.

The trunk stood strong with a slight lean towards lee. Branches reaching for the light, each uniquely shaped. Twigs twisting, stretching, each one seeking the best spot in the sun, that is the duty to the host. The host that feeds them all provides. Then I learned its name is tree, belonging to a family, named apple.

Behind, beside, around, so many more trees, each one vying for light. Saw I did, nine in all. Each pleasing, each easing and each showing me what can be, if you're a tree.

What did it teach you, this tree of grandeur?

Stay there, go back a little, the first one, go to that moment when you saw it for the very first time.

I see it. Yes?

You had no identity and there you see this tree. This tree, he, it or she, showed you what you could be. In that, it left its trace for you to carry.

I have an affinity with trees. A knowing that I can't describe. A comprehension that links me to their spirit. But I am eye, not tree or leaf or fruit or seed.

The oak, the walnut, peach and cherry, each left their trace for you to carry.

Perhaps they did. No matter which tree I see, there is a kinship. The strength, the power, the beauty, the softness, the complex arrangement, shed old and renew, reach out, produce, provide and shelter, yes all these combined I cherish.

Bees, bugs and insects, birds, butterflies, grubs, worms and children, strings for swings and hugs from lovers, as they frolic in the harbour of the cooling shade those trees will render for them all.

Perhaps it was a phylogenetic relationship of sorts between you and tree.

Eye is I, is my answer.

Did this tree leave more than a trace?

No, its trace was like any other. The tree is not at fault. You allowed hypnotisation by its august glory. You placed a mark. That mark will throw a shadow over many years and it will cause pain. Do not fear. It will also guide you; give you strength beyond your needs. The mark defines your being.

How do you know all this?

That is easy. You can see the past to now, as you watch your own reflection. I always see the other side, as I see towards the other direction. I look towards the 'from', you would say. A reversed vision that is unknown to you. The direction is to towards from, from your point of view.

Void filled

Eye is I, I am not tree. How can it be inside, and shape into my being?

You were void. The tree, the first thing that you have seen, which pleased you, did entrance you with its beauty.

You needed more and you did find it in the tree.

You saw the strength, the solid trunk, rooted firmly in the ground. The tree stands fast, not easily swayed. That filled part of your void. You saw the tree branch in all directions, each kissed by the sun. That is a part of you as well. You will wither next to a hi-rise building or if caged by walls of any kind. Trees cannot find the bees. Bees will find trees. They will find you, and this I know, is so in you. The fruits you bear fill many bellies and tease taste buds. The seeds contained within, each are copies with the same potential. Duplicates they are not. Each is unique. And there, you eye, have all this on the inside.

Go beyond that Tuesday. Count back the number of the year of now, in days. You are half the age than on that Tuesday.

2007.

Yes. Come closer.

Look at the white around the colours.

The white I see.

Seek the vessels that feed you with life.

I see them.

The white once was black, 2007 days away from that Tuesday.

I don't believe you.

Trust, I know the truth.

The white was black?

Yes.

How could that happen?

The white was many colours. Once white was red, turning to black. You were ill. The tiny vessels seeping blood, they burst from straining. The pressure was high and so was the temperature, so very high inside this eye. The blood turned the white to red. The colour of this eye not affected. The pupil did not suffer damage. You reached the edge of burning out. The eye was steaming tears.

How come, that I don't know all this?

You knew it once, you knew it then, but you had lost all sense of knowing.

How is it that you know more than I do about myself?

Each cell remembers everything, wherever, whenever, whatever, however it comes to be.

The red blood reached every part of the white, and then it died. As it died, it changed colour, turning black. This eye carried life and death within, all at once. In time, life rebuilds the eye. The black shed. The black transformed to yellow. It was not a pretty sight. There were smudges of imperfections.

It was a transitional phase. You came back from the edge when the black turned yellow, and then it changed to white.
Look at it now. Did it not do an excellent job?
If that is the truth, then it did.
It is the truth. What reason would I have to lie to the eye that is I?
Thank you.
The shadow cast for many years, the one that causes pain, the remnants of the tree that once I saw, when will that be?
You are in this shadow now. Did you not know?
Is this shadow the one that makes the tears flow, the tears that will not cease to stream?
It is.
Why is this happening?
You are not free.
I am not free from what?
You are not free from the tree. The tree has served you well.
It has.
Is the first tree that once I saw, now the cause of tears to flow?
In a way it is.
The tree is not at fault. The chainsaw is not the answer. Seek the line that casts its shadows, from the mountains to the meadows, from the hi-rise to the ghettos and then turn.
What does that mean?

Become

Be free of the tree. The tree is within. You are not tree. Realise this and become.
Become what?
I am eye.
Eye I am.
No, you are not.
I have been eye all my life. This much I know, if little else.
Yes, eye, but you are with the spirit of tree. Become free of the tree and learn to see.

Have I been wrong all my life?
No.
Why now? Why do I need becoming when I am?
The seasons have changed. Your wells are running low. The tree within is desiccating your reservoir. It claims more than its share. There is no reason to fear.
But I have seen so much. The seen is still living. The projector never shuts down.
I have the knowing. We are at the mercy of our host. It carries us, it feeds us, it steps through the world. We have no say in it. We bring the world in. We are also in the world, the same world we seem to absorb.
Am I trapped in a room with collared drapes?
Come closer. Come closer still.
Come much closer. Focus in the black and you will see a cat. That cat walked much of the shadow for you.
The black cat I see, the wildcat?
Yes.
The drapes were of other patterns, all seem so different and are so much alike. That cat's vision was nine times sharper than yours is now. It saw even more than its own eyes could handle.
How can I comprehend this? How can I try to understand?
You know about light.
Yes.
What does it do?
It touches every surface.
Does light have a choice in the surfaces it meets?
No.
The light that shines on lovers, on guns, on blood and plovers, on trees, on steel, on sheets, on seeds, on anyone it greets and anything around it meets, does it carry all these things?
No.
Why do you?
Are you not bleeding, weeding, seeding, pleading, feeding, all you have seen before, whilst weeping?
I am.

I am eye, the eye I am. I am, I do.
Be.
I am trying.
What are you looking at?
A mirror.
What do you see in this mirror?
I see an eye. The eye is I.
No, it is not.
It is.
Close one and look with the other.
Which one is closed, which one is open? Does not the mirror
lie?
The right is closed, the mirror shows it looking.
Turn left.
I do. I did.
What do you see?
The frame of a door I see. Behind is a bush in bloom. Beyond
is a field.
You are now looking at a mirror of a different kind. What else
is there to see?
Trees.
They had to be. Forgive that I am laughing.
What do they do, the trees?
They are reaching.
What are they reaching for?
They reach for the light.
Why do you not do that too?
I try, but often I cry.
Are you feeding the tree inside with tears from your eye?
I do not know. Why do I cry?
To be cleansed. Each eye must cry or else will dry and die.
Those I'm not meaning.
Answer brings knowing.
How much closer can the answer bring its knowing? So close,
that nothing can be closer than a tear inside your eye. And
you look through the answer. You are seeing everything else,

but the answer. You bear questions, seek knowing and fail to see the showing.

When do you cry?

I wish I knew. It happens whenever, out of the blue, unexpectedly.

Why does it hurt to see a knife staked through the eye?

Why does it pain to see someone bleeding?

Why does it not ever let go?

The bleeding tree, the pleading weed, the fleeting seed, the hungry need, the selfish greed, the sailing fleet, the tired feet, all cause the tears to flow.

Then look again and you shall find 'them', 'those' and 'these', all mirrors of the self and us.

Mirrors of the self?

Yes. You, I, them, those, these, all us?

Yes.

I see.

You do.

Welcome to self and all of you.

What is a tear?

Oil, salt, water, food and medicine, tear is a blend of all. Tear is a sphere of liquid clarity, if it were to float in space. Its surface reflects in every direction, light enters from outside to in. Light exits from inside to out. Tear is the coating that covers the eye. It allows breathing and stops it becoming dry. An even film of tear spread across the eye. It breaks the angle of incoming light, and breaks it again on leaving.

There is more to a tear than that.

Yes, such as tears of compassion and tenderness and empathy for what is breathing.

What is a tear, 'the answer tear', the one I fail to fathom?

Did I not tell you already? The vision is your mirror.

You do not see 'it'.

'It' is you.

'It' is I.

It is.

The knife that staked through the eye, the once seen, is not in the eye of the one you saw. It is in you. You are the seen.
You are the seen as well as the seeing. Both are the same. Is it any wonder that your tears flow? Are not the blood and tears so very similar, so much alike?
Is not the light at night the same as throughout the day? Does not the moon reflect the sun, even at night?

What is a tear, you ask. Tear is born from the rising crystal. Tear is from the source of life. Tears you bear carry within the source of life. It is from, and it becomes. The tear you shed, shed infinite times before, in the circle around.
A tear drops into the ocean; could you ever reclaim just the drop? Has it not become part of the ocean? Has it not become part of life? Has it not always been part of life?

Peace in war, war in peace

Seek the trace that once you followed, as the host's hand drew the lines. So very long ago, you were a child's eye. Pencil lines they were, forming letters, words of warning.

Seek the end of a sentence, drawn in lead, the words were these: ... find X and Y.

X and Y stood for something else.

You and I?

No.

I can't retrace the seen, so many lines of lead I drew.

Here is a hint, one you love, one you hate?

Peace and war?

Yes.

You did not like it when the lead traced the page. It was so long ago. You wished the order of words reversed, but that your host could not do.

The host's hands faster than thought had no knowledge of the power of words.

The shadow is your war. You feel it; you know these are different times. It is not as you expected. No war ever is. This is not a war in the conventional sense of the word, not a war between countries or beliefs'. It is uniquely yours. You have found it. You are facing your fears. You are aching to get out of it.

Recall another host, the one with white wings, the host that carried you so close to the jewels where sharp edged rocks shredded the bird to bits. It carried you near to the gates of doom. A few more turns in the spiral and you would have seen the sign.

What did it say, the sign?

'Welcome to your dream come true', but you never got that far. Recall the time. There was one moment in the funnel where you could detach from fear. Three seconds you allowed for this rare moment of sight, insight. That was a war too.

I do not like being in war or at war.

Few do, if any.

You are in conflict. The outside differs from the inside. It is as a war within, a war in a partial peace. Perhaps you have also seen peace in a partial war. You are eye. Your host carries you. You cry because you seek peace in peace.
Change the curtains. They are the barrier to your vision. How can you not see war with these curtains? You see with tainted vision. The seen renders contamination. As the seen is within so you turn and become infected.
How can I change the curtains?
You are already changing them. You are crying, are you not? In that, you are cleaning more than the eye. You clean the blood that feeds you. You clean your host. Even through the curtains of war, you become aware of the seen. When you become sick and tired of it, your curtains will have changed. Each tear you cry, becomes part of the circle of life. Each drop returning home. Bring the outer into balance with the inner. Peace is within. Within you find the likeness of the outer, the inner of another eye.
Are not the wells low and almost depleted?
Yes.
They will replenish. You know what to do.
I need to be free of the tree. Will I then be able to see and be free?
What else is in the shadow?
Tell me the answer.
Why do you not answer?
Will you be able to see, you ask. Sight is many things. Will you choose to see through curtains? Will you choose to see the seen that has been? Will you choose to view the seen as from a window of a house with many rooms?
Are there different ways to see?
You know it.
Recall the cold and snow, trees were bare, no green seen anywhere. You spotted a coin in the ice. All that you saw then turned out to be false. It seemed so real. Whichever room you were in at the time, coloured all the seen with falsehood.

There was another time you could not see green. Your eyes trapped underwater. Other eyes described the view.

Once water brought you fear. The spout of a tap filled the bathtub. You looked from the water towards the tap. It seemed like a waterfall. You had never seen so much water at once.

Recall the first time when you saw the ocean, there were large mountains of shells. Almost as high as a house, they were the remains of once living shells. Did not everything seem so different, so tinged by the stamp of time and place? Was it not like seeing from another room with other curtains, while your host stood on top of dead shells? Your vision from that window lasted six weeks. Never before had you seen such carnage. Never again did you go to that room, nor the place.

Why not?

The answer is not in the past. Why carry more than you need to carry.

I want to know.

You want to be able to see and be free, and take on the burden of the past as well?

I need to know what happened there.

I will not tell you, with good reason. I will tell you this: In all you have seen until now, millions of instances, countless moments, years of seen, you have only ever seen a couple of minutes at the most, without any curtains at all. These couple of minutes accumulated as fractions of seconds at a time. All the rest of your time spent seeing in blinding sight. You, the eye, fooled oh so many times into believing what you saw is real.

Illusions they were, seemingly real. The eye absorbing distorted views, each stained. How many windows are at your choosing? You, eye and I, the victims of deception. Did not desire, anger, vanity, hatred, hope and despair cloud your sight?

How much have you seen through fearful eyes? Flames in the house, rooms filled with smoke, one could not tell which way to get out. The fear of entrapment and the fear of boiling eyes were overwhelming.

The same fear, when the host fell, then rolling down a hill, at the edge of the rocks was the cliff, beneath that, the depth of no return. The river below laced with whirlpools, the fear of becoming sucked down to the bottom of the river. The eye filled with fear never let go. Fear had curtains like woven steel wires. You fed fear, you feared fear, and it fed you.

Once you did actually take in the seen. It was a September morning with rising fog, a Monday. Thick grey fog laden with droplets obscured the surrounds. There was little to focus on but the tiny droplets of suspended moisture. Your host walked you into the spheres. The pupils fully opened as you were carried through the countless numbers of floating spheres. It all seemed like space travel, each a planet without a sun. The eyelids prevented collisions with most. Some became part of the spread tear that covers your lens. That moment you saw with awareness. You had no curtains at all.

Two minutes later a car stopped beside you. You could barely see anything through the wires of fear. You have lost the memory of that.

You and I, eye. Eye has a history of 540 million years of evolution. Yet in all this time, you cannot tell what is coming or going, you have no depth of sight, often you assume without facts and have little visual sharpness. You can never rest. As soon as you stop moving, your vision fails.

Is it black, is it white, you cannot tell the difference. Is it there, is it not, you do not know. A fixed view has motion within, which it does not have at all. You are so easily taken for a ride. Most of your seen are assumptions. Eye started with colour some 35 million years ago, and to this day, you have never seen it.

You can take in one third of the circle, but all you really see is the centre, a tiny spot in focus, the rest a gradual decrease in sharpness. Whatever holds your attention appears sharp in your sight. The little cone of view magnifies its importance. Do not assume for a moment that all your vision is that good, it has failed you more times than not. You can detect faint glimpses of light, down to a photon, but not in your focus. Despite, it is enough. If you knew how to see, the seen could reveal much more.

What would you know? You're just a reflection and a poor one at that. You are not I. I am eye. The eye I am. You are a distorted image of me. You seem like a copy but you are not. There is no blood feeding your hollow sphere. You are not even a sphere. You are flat. You have no insides. If I move out of view, you are gone. You'll follow me to the edge of the glass and then you are no more. You will vanish from view and then drop off the edge. Yet I, the eye I am, will still be there. Not there, but here where I am now.

How wrong and right you are. More than you realise.

Yet you want to re-see the seen, whatever for?

The pink curtains that colour everything rosy, do you want to see through them again. You know that seen is false, yet it appears so very pleasing. It is a dreaming, deceiving; longing will recall it with pain.

Watch your host. What is it that appeals the sense of taste?

It could be chocolate. I've seen it many times.

Is there ever THE piece of chocolate that could quench the desire?

It appears not.

Which is the BEST that you have ever seen? The seen that would fill your craving, would set your eye at rest, so that the need of seeing any more is no longer.

The thought is absurd. If I were to see it, I would want to see more of it. I would want repetition of the same.

Life is dynamic. Each moment is unique. No moment can ever happen twice. Each apparent repetition is a new event.

Eye is I.

The eye I am.

I need to know where I've been, so that I know who I am.

Awareness

Does the 'where' define who you are? You are. There is your definition. Are not the moments with full awareness the ones that turn to treasures? Treasures you treasure balanced by pain.

Let me show you when you were aware. It was 10.5 million minutes before the moment of now. Your host is travelling on a long journey. It was night-time, the journey being 1380 miles long. Your host was tired and you were fatigued. The time was 2:14 am. The bright glare of spotlights cut through your daze and woke you up. In this fraction of a second, you could analyse the situation and give your host all the information needed to make the only decision that prevented disaster. That was one of your most brilliant moments.

Did not your whole world appear so different in that instant?

Another time you got it all wrong. You judged the speed correctly, you calculated it down to the smallest fraction, and your anticipated evasive action by your host could have worked out perfectly. You allowed for minimal but adequate safety margin. You did everything right, in an instant, except one thing. Repetition stopped and you anticipated repetition. In that it showed you, how unique each moment is. Having just gone through all these calculations, adjustments, focus and refocus, aimed to prevent any damage, you had to restart instantly. This time accepting that there will be damage, you exceeded your host's expectations keeping damage to a bearable minimum.

Analysis of incoming moments, kinetic depth perception, time to crash distance calculations and frantic search to find another inch that may reduce the impact to lessen the price.

In these moments, you worked like a high performance machine, two, perhaps three seconds at the most. It was 15 minutes later, when you became aware of that point in time, a kind of time-lapse to recover before you could count your blessings.

Once more, much further in the past, your host was swimming in a lake. The weather turned quickly and a violent thunderstorm came out of nowhere. Your host stayed in the water. A massive downpour whipped up the water. Each drop broke through the surface of the water, lifting it up, multiplying the droplets. This display of magic you had never seen with the eyes at the surface of the lake. Your moment of awareness began when the storm started. It lasted until it unleashed all its fury. You had a good six minutes of seeing with all your capacity of sight.

Does all this tell you who you are?

Another recall, you are near a shopping centre. You saw a finger on the trigger of a rifle. As in slow motion, the trigger moved all the way. You saw the blur of a bullet leaving the barrel. The bullet entered a head, right between the eyes.

No blood came out. All you could see was the small hole it had left in the skull. He fell backwards with a surprised frozen stare, a look of disbelieve, unthinkable, that this could happen to him. Like the inevitable realisation, that from this moment forward he will be dead forever. He will be dead for the rest of his life. The rest of his life is no longer. He is dead. His eyes have become mere hollow balls without purpose.

He had just filled up the tank of his motorbike with fuel that he would never use in riding. The moment already surpassed by another. From this moment on, the world lost a life and gained a murderer. And that moment gone as well, as a newborn cries from a nearby room, just two seconds old, now three and four and more. A six-second-old newborn crying this instant, with a yet unlived life that is beginning its journey now.

The last moments of life in the eyes of the now dead, saw the bullet leave the barrel as a slow ticking freeze-frame event. The fascinating sight of an approaching bullet mesmerising as it advanced toward the eye. His eyes were incapable of moving out of the way, unable to respond to the danger, too busy absorbing, yet aware of what is nearing. The bullet spared the eyes. It knocked out all vision of the host, while the eyes were still feeding the funnel to his brain.

Do you know who you are now?

Does this, the seen define you?

There are twelve more instances, different settings, other conditions, but twelve more times you had seen the light of death. Four times, you were witness to the candle of life beginning.

I have recall of some.

Each time you could see. In the time that followed, you lost the seen. Mostly you applied a kind of double vision, the eyes capturing the aftermath, while at the same time adding the moment that had already transpired, a sort of reliving.

So many more moments brought you full vision. Once you had a kind of vision even with your eyes closed. August 17th at 11:24pm, a straight stretch of highway, your host rode a 275kg motorcycle. Speed was 102 miles per hour. You shut your eyes for a count of ten. The first time you stole a peek through the eyelashes, but not the second and third time.

Does facing death awaken your sight?

I have no wish to die.

When you could only see the white, and when your white turned black, and in the spiral with the cutting jewels, was it not death that stood nearby?

When you could not see green, the fall near the cliff, the suction of the whirlpools, was it not there the same?

You narrowly missed several accidents; each could have been your last moment, the swimming in the lake in a vicious thunderstorm, was it not the thrill of surviving the lightning? Was it not being close to death that helped you see? Did you not dare the lightning bolt to strike close?

The bullet, the barrel, did it not occur that it could have been you?

Closed eyes at 102 miles per hour, were you not tempting death once more? There are many more examples, each time near death made you see light in a different way. Also the other is true, the starting of life, light with a different magic.

I'm unable to recall all the seen.

The ones you cannot recall happened before you saw the tree.

Your roots are still firmly in the ground. You are still not free of the tree. What do you see when you look away from this mirror, at 7 degrees to your left?

A bush is in bloom.

What else is near the bush?

There are bees and butterflies.

Pick any of them and become one. It can lift your roots out of the ground.

What do I hold on to?

Does the butterfly hold onto anything? The bee, does it fly with a stick?

They are at the mercy of the wind.

Despite, somehow they manage.

Can it control where it wants to be?

The eye is, wherever it is. Where would it want to be? It is a part of the host. The host decides where it is going to be. The host is its carrier.

Eye is I.

Yes. You reinforced that so many times. Eye pronounced I. The letter 'I' is reaching up and reaching down. Eye is two times an 'e' and the letter 'y'.

In a small classroom, the letter 'e' was on an ego trip and wanted to change the Alphabet into the Elphabet. No one played along. E went on strike and when it refused its sound, it took everything down. E was not happy.

Take two 'e's' out of 'eye' and you are left with a 'y'. Three arms stretching in each direction. Like three rays converging to a point at its centre. Three primary colours you see, all other colours a blend of either or neither. All primaries in the same measure are white; none shows to you as black. It takes precious little to throw everything out of balance.

I am eye. The eye I am. I have seen more than that.

See what I mean? Are you not on an ego trip? You have seen more than that. Yes, you have. You have even seen two worlds at once and vision made no sense at all.

Have I?

A tumour behind one eye moved it out of place. Each eye showed the world, but each from a different viewpoint. Double vision is of little use to your host, caused by a small growth that threw a lot out of balance. It moved you.

What do you mean with ego trip?

The seen, the been, the rays that got in, all so important, clouding the vision you are seeing.

What do you see?

I have good vision.

What do you see?

A mirror, right in front of me.

What does it reflect?

Whatever is in front.

What did it reflect yesterday?

The same.

No, it did not. The earth travelled a different path yesterday. That put the sun in a different position. This was visible in yesterday's reflection. The bush lost 29 leaves. The grass was a little shorter. There were different particles in the air; the humidity was not the same. Oh, so many things have changed since yesterday.

Have you not tried a million times and more, to hold the yesterdays? To trap them, capture them in some way. Did you not sacrifice so many moments when you looked through the viewfinder? No picture is alive. No 'then' will ever turn to 'now'. Was it not all a futile effort to be eternal? Did you not try to live on through time?

There is only one way to see forever, and that way is not to be.

What do you mean?

Have every cell within you join its parent. Re-awaken every cell that died. Slow the wind, then hold its path, freeze the rays of the sun, freeze the waves of the oceans, hold the flow of the currents and stop the planet's rotation. Stop light in its travel, un-see the seen; reverse the flow of a tear. When you can do all that, each living thing must do the same, perhaps then you can see forever.

But not before a bark is unbarked, a song is unsung, a kill is unkilled, or a knowing is unknown. Un-breathe a breath, un-trace a trace, stop a ball in flight, stop motion, un-grow growth, un-beat the beat of a heart, and un-live life; capture a photon.

Can you do all that?

That's stupid.

Even if you could stop a photon, if nothing moves you will be blind.

Who are you?

To you, I am just a mirror, as you said, a flat no-body.

What are you?

A reflection is I.

Are you the one the cat found in the snow?

I am.

How can that be? That was so far away, so long ago.

My time is now. However long ago to you, it was now to me. I am reflection. I am in many things. I am even in you.

In me?

I am in your tear; I am on a shiny leaf, in the eyes of every eye you see, well most. A polished apple, a rain covered stool, a wet wooden floor.

Look at the surface of a still lake. What will you see?

The reflection of the sky I'd see.

If you were to look closer, what would you see then?

I'd see myself.

Yes, but you mean vision, I mean substance. Are you not seeing the self? I do not mean the reflection of eye that is a hollow ball, but the being in the seen. Do you not see that you are within? Can you not find the answer right here. The sought found. Can you not see this? Can you not see that I am within you and on you? That I reflect from you and reflect into you? Can you not see that we are both of the same?

I am eye. The eye I am. Eye is I.

Where does this lake come from?

A spring.

Who feeds the spring?

The clouds, the rain, the run-off water from the land around it.

This lake contains the breath of your ancestors, contains the blood of your kind, harbours remnants of your forebears. You and this lake are relatives. This lake and so many others have links to you. Every cloud contains a part of your history. Each played a part, however long ago, that in time allowed you this view. Your heritage is in front of you.

I can see, but I cannot see what you describe.

Then know this, you cannot see.

I can, I always have.

You cannot see.

You are a hollow ball with a hole that has a lens. You gather light and focus it to a point. You collect light in the various intensities of the primary colours and the countless shades of brightness. All this gathered in cones, yet none of this enables you to see. You are in effect unable to see, even when you can see. All the seen become signals. Your host dissects these and builds a picture of the outside world. That picture combined with the signals from all eyes forms your host's vision. Thus the world outside becomes a world within, but not within the eye. This, you have never seen before.

That is not true. I am eye. Without me, my host can't see.

The retina detects the light with twelve times ten million light sensitive rod cells spread around the outer edge of the retina. That is for night vision. You perceive colour via several types of cone cells, millions of them in each eye. All these are highly sensitive to the incoming light. They channel the information to your host. Your host assembles your vision and thus recreates the seen.

You bring it in; you just do not know what you are bringing in. The host burdened or blessed with your contribution to the whole. You could do better.

What could I do better? What could I do, to do better? Seven the number of colours I see in the arc of the rainbow in front of me. That is three less than some are able to name.

There are many more but it is not what I meant.

You focus on your focus, you dissect and separate the spectrum, you seek detail, definition, using all sorts of optical tools at your disposal.

How often did you not see what is right in front of you? How many times your focus set to twelve times the distance needed, so that you looked right through the object ahead.

Seeing with senses

Join with your other senses, and the world you are in becomes another place. Take for example a picture with two shapes. Both collared white on a dark background, or in reverse, it does not matter. Two shapes, focus on them, then set your focus on the non-shape. It can appear as a third shape. You can see one or the others. Although three shapes appear to be there, you can ever only see one shape, or the other two at a time.

You will notice the impact it has, when your attention switches from one to the others. The same type of impact it will leave on you, if you look at anything with full awareness of all senses. There is a big difference though. When all senses become aware, you will see the tree, hear it and feel the wind on your skin. You will not stand on the outside looking in, looking at something; you will feel as part of the seen. You become an element within.

It will take some practice. Focus again on the shapes and become aware of the sensation when your focus jumps to the other shape. That moment of sensation is very short.

Look at a tree. Relax. Do not overpower the other senses. Allow them to 'feel' the tree. When all senses become aware, that is when the sensation jumps at you. You will not see another shape, as in the black and white image. You will see the tree in its own right. It is no longer an object by the name of tree. It is as if it reveals its spirit. It allows you in its space. You are no longer the onlooker, the stranger passing through, you feel you belong and you do. You are in the presence of the tree. The tree grows from the ground. You are standing nearby. You can sense the roots underneath your feet. It feels like the change from a flat two dimensional world to a world with depth, like three dimensions. You know three dimensions. This feels like stepping into another. Your host will feel like an invited guest to dwell in the presence of this tree.

Initially that sensation may only last a few seconds and in an instant, it transforms back, into the seemingly flat picture of a tree. You feel that looking at the world will never be the same, once you experience this sensation.

The world to you has always been in three dimensions, but here, with this awareness, another dimension reveals its beauty. You cannot help but sway with the tree, to be as one. Your host will smile in admiration. The gift of presence brings within a harmony of being. The host's hand will reach out and touch a leaf, a branch or the bark or hug the trunk.

Even if the colours in your rainbow reduce to three, the marvel of your optics has nothing to do with this. The sharpness of your focus is irrelevant. Eyes are not even needed to live the now. Vision is within. A tree this is, but not as the one within you. Train your senses on this tree. Accept the gift of sight, as it was this, it tried to give you long ago.

It is not the tree that you see, that will be so special. It has little to do with the tree. Anything you see will be, as you have never seen.

With this gift, you will see rocks and lizards, flies and blizzards. You will see everything you know in a way you never saw before. You will find and you will lose. What you will lose, you will find anew.

Once you can see, look at the lake again. You had seen it once, at the time when rivers talked with as many sounds, as there are colours in the field.

Am I blind?

The eye is I, yet I cannot see at all? The light, the photon, the carrier of radiation, the particle with zero mass, gets through the lens to cones and rods, yet none of it is part of the perception of sight in the host? Is the seen within the host a mere translation? Is all seen a neurotransmitter exchange? Is the reassembly of the outer made of chemical reactions? The photon, which travels from the sun to my core in 8 minutes and 18 seconds, has it never been seen by the host? Has the host never seen any light? What will I lose? What will I find? How could I have been wrong? Has everything I've seen become illusion, falsehood? Has everything turned around?
The choice is yours. Twelve questions at once. Search for the answers to all your questions, or see the answers without questions. Question answers, answer answers, answer questions, question questions. De chá vou.
If you knew what air is, you would still need to breathe it. Accept. If you seek knowing, know also, that each answer it brings forth is anew a question. Not a thousand lifetimes will be enough to quench that hunger.
Vision is within.
Am I redundant?
Who are you?
I am just a reflection.
You are not redundant. Vision is, with or without eyes. Accept that you are part of a larger whole. Realise that each whole is also part of a still larger whole. Recognise that each part consists of many others. Understand that each of the smaller parts is also made of still smaller parts.
Admire this, in equals out, to equals from, high equals low, yes equals no, crest equals trough, concave equals convex. Admire this too, truth equals lie, joy equals pain, to win equals

losing as rich equals poor, chaos equals order, equal unequal. Is not despair pregnant with hope, laughter so close to tears, the brave filled with fear, the far away near, ideal a point of view? The leader follows, the strong drained of strength, inside is outside, within is without, so the unbalanced balance balances unbalanced. Is not the answer a question within?

The full is empty of emptiness, as the emptiness is full of itself. As each truth is false, in falsehood find truth. Each in reverse is also true. All are ticking to the pendulum. The pendulum's motion, is it not frozen each moment of now? This makes everything seemingly turn around.

You are, and you are not. Which year does it show on the pendulum? Where is the pendulum now? And where is it now?

No light can outshine all darkness. No darkness is able to drown out all light. No heat is enough to warm all coldness. No cold is so cold to freeze all heat. In that the balance.

As the seed of creation contains the seed of destruction, so does the seed of destruction contain the seed of anew.

As each seed sowed to grow, brings forth seeds seeking seeding, each anew repeating countless repetitions, yet not one is repeating.

You be, or you are becoming, else you have been and be not. In that, you became other than before.

Yet no matter, the one you are or becoming, you are part of the whole, as the whole is part of you.

In the chaos find order, in disorder find harmony.

The light comes towards you, be graced as chosen, as the centre of all that is around. Yet three inches from you is your other centre. Between both and behind is one more.

Each eye is the centre of its own world. No other eye will see the world from that viewpoint. So many eyes, so many worlds, so many centres, each adorned as the one.

Between you and I, the flatness of this plate, at the centre of distance we seem to be spaced. Each has its own importance, without taking favour from else.

With you, I reflect you. Without you, I reflect you not, despite I reflect. I have depth, yet I have not.

You are eye. I ask you this, which eye are you? Are you not both as one? Is it not the same as anything around you? Are you not one with everything you see?

Are you alive?

I will ask the same, are you?

What is life?

Behind you is a cup. I am unable to see what is in the cup, unable to go to the cup, to see what it contains. Does that mean I am dead?

I contain what is in front. If there were nothing in front, would that mean I contain nothing? No matter which direction I face, there will always be something in front.

No matter where I am placed, there will always be something that I reflect. Even the seemingly nothing has a reflection.

What is in the cup?

Coffee, it is cold coffee.

What does it reflect?

The window reflects on the surface.

Is the coffee alive?

When was the coffee born?

When will the coffee die?

When your host drinks the coffee, will reflection live within. When your host excretes the coffee, will its reflection leave the host. Where will it go when it seeps into the ground? Where will it be, when it has been?

Why is coffee? Does it like being in the cup? Does the cup have a choice to contain tea or coffee? Perhaps it likes neither and be left alone. Does coffee have a say? Would it prefer to be tea? What is coffee? Is it alive? The source of life contained within, yet is it living?

That makes no sense.

I was waiting for your 'I am eye' comment.

What does it all mean?

It simply means that coffee is coffee, whatever that is. Coffee is. Water brewed with ground beans makes coffee. Water with leafs becomes tea. Water plus this and water plus that, becomes so many things that you see. But no matter how many oceans you drain, there is no water in me.

I am a reflection, whatever that is. I reflect as good as I can, right and left seems the wrong way around, but hey, that is how I reflect. Right is right, left is left. All you need doing is turn around, try to see from this viewpoint. You will find right is right, left is left. If only you could look backwards, both ways, you would know this to be true. Up is up and down is down. Reflection does not flip around. There is my proof. Look with me, instead of at me and you will know.

I am reflection. What I am made of is of no relevance. Be that water, glass, a polished apple skin, I am not of the physical, yet the reflected photon is.

Am I alive, you ask? Why is that question of importance? Is being alive something special? Does it not also mean that your path is to become dead?

Once, did you not stand in the darkness? You thought it was the shadow of the sun.

Yet the sun can not throw shadows. That is impossible. Is it not light from the sun that even fills the shadows with its shine? The sun does not throw shadows. But it can never shine on you from all sides with equal strength. You cast your own shadows and so does every living being.

Now is

What is life? It does not matter. Does life equal time? Is life lifetime, as in being born to death? Even if you could define life, would it elevate what is living above what is not? Would not the living also contain the not living? Would not the 'not living', outlive life?

I am reflection. If I live, then I only live now. How long is the now? No stopwatch can capture the length of now, nor can the clock that counts in millions of years.

You know the clock with rotating handles, the one that divides your measures, the one that is telling with ticks the time. It makes it seem like repetition. That clock is wrong. Time is not a repetition. Even if there are seven days per week, no week has the same seven days. Each day deserves a new name. Each day is a new day that has never been. What you call time, is more like the lines on a highway. Each line passed left in the past.

Now has no length, no weight or measure. Now equals is. Is 'now' forever? If I had time, perhaps I could ponder that question. I only have now; I will leave it at that. I reflect now, reflect now and reflect now. If you are alive, then you have used up three measures of your time. I have been reflecting now, ever since now began. Tomorrow means nothing to me.

I am reflecting from whatever has reflective properties. Are you living from whatever has living properties? Perhaps you will die many times and live just as often. No doubt, you will be becoming, the 'you' transforming. You are a combination of many things. All combined define you. I am reflection no matter what I reflect. You are eye.

I do not absorb. In that, we are different. You do absorb. You take everything in. Yet, you are not a sponge. You are the feeding funnel to the brain.

You are eye. All you can do is serve your host, as I serve mine. Without your host, you will dry and die.

In that is our purpose.

We are servants.

We are.

'We are' equals 'is'.

Eye is I, the eye am I.

Now is.

Now is and now only.

Only for now.

End

Navigating 'The Puma's Trail'

Dear Reader,

Welcome to the fascinating world of 'The Puma's Trail.' The true essence of this tale resides within the preface, which I encourage you not to skip. The pages that precede the main narrative hold the key to a deeper understanding of the writing process and the profound connection that I, as the creator, have fostered with the story.

In the preface, you will find an intimate account of how 'The Puma's Trail' came to life. It reveals the unorthodox approach I took in writing this novel, immersing myself in the spirit of the puma and venturing into the night to capture its essence. These personal experiences breathed life into the words on these pages, making the puma's journey a poignant and transformative one.

Understanding the origins of the narrative and the emotions that drove the pen forward will allow you to connect more profoundly with the characters, their journeys, and the overarching themes that define 'The Puma's Trail.'

Happy reading!

Heinz G. Ross

Preface (The Puma's Trail)

The Puma's Trail is a captivating journey that explores the interconnectedness of nature and the spirit of the puma. Through the lens of various animals, each embodying the puma's spirit, this story examines the different perspectives and experiences of life in the natural world. Next, the story shifts to the puma, an alley cat navigating the harsh realities of a dark city. Once a powerful and beautiful creature, the puma now struggles to survive amidst a polluted and unforgiving environment. We witness the puma's longing for a fight, a chance to ignite its fire, yet it remains resigned to the emptiness and decay of its surroundings. We experience snippets of life from various animals to arrive at the life cycle of a crystal.

The story splits with the transformation of the crystal and the conception of the twins. The chapter titles indicate that you either follow the puma or the twins, the animal or the human, although all are somewhat connected throughout. Asha and Tobin (the twins) share an unbreakable bond, which serves as a constant source of support and understanding in the midst of the turbulent years of growing up. They faced the world together, knowing that they were stronger together than apart. As they entered adulthood, Asha and Tobin ventured into their respective paths, following the dreams they had nurtured throughout their lives. Asha pursued a career in the arts, channelling her creativity and passion into painting, writing, and exploring the depths of human expression. Tobin embarked on a journey as a composer, guided by his love for music.

Through it all, the spirit of the puma within them propelled them forward, reminding them of their resilience and ability to overcome any obstacle. They carried within them the promise of their names, the immensity of their shared history, and the boundless potential of their future.

Perrin, the hermit sculptor they befriended, became a source of inspiration and guidance for the twins. His mastery of stone and ability to freeze moments in time fascinated them. They spent hours in his studio, observing the transformation of raw materials into works of art. Perrin's wisdom and insight offered them a different perspective on life and creativity.

The twins sought to use their artistic talents and creative expression to uplift and inspire others. Through their paintings and music, they aimed to touch the hearts and souls of those who crossed their paths. They travelled far, sharing their gifts and connecting with people from all walks of life. They witnessed the power of art to heal, to bridge divides, and to ignite hope in the darkest of times. Their art became a catalyst for change, a medium through which they could convey messages of love, unity, and resilience. Both achieved success in their chosen fields, marking turning points in their lives. Tobin's reputation as a composer soared, and invitations to conduct his symphony poured in from renowned orchestras worldwide. Asha's paintings gained recognition for their unique ability to capture the essence of music on canvas. Their collaboration became legendary, inspiring countless artists and musicians.

Meanwhile, the puma had embarked on his own transformative journey. After enduring treacherous conditions at sea, he found himself in a foreign land. Lost and disoriented, he navigates through unfamiliar landscapes, driven by an instinct he can't fully comprehend. In contrast, the puma's search for hell had led him to experience profound suffering and cruelty, both physically and emotionally. Yet, within the depths of his struggle, he discovered an unexpected resilience and a longing for something greater. He yearned for a sense of purpose and a connection to the world around him.

Asha explored her unique style of art, which was far beyond the expectations of long-time supporter Yente. As a result, Yente's gallery withdrew support for Asha. Asha's reputation suffered greatly, and the negative gossip had tarnished her name in the art world. Commissions dwindled, and the once-thriving connections with art dealers vanished. It was a harsh reminder of how fickle the world could be and how easily opinions could sway and destroy. A tragic accident in Perrin's workshop left Tobin devastated. As a result, Tobin's world turned into a bleak and desolate place. Tobin felt utterly alone, as if a part of him had been ripped away. Days turned into weeks, and Tobin found solace in immersing himself in their past creations. He listened to the recording of their unscheduled performance, reliving the magic they had once shared on stage.

Through it all, Perrin remained a steadfast friend to Tobin. He stood by his side, offering support and understanding. Perrin's loyalty was a lifeline for Tobin, a reminder that there were still people who believed in their work, despite the prevailing doubts and criticism. Tobin, now an ageing composer, had reached a stage in life where his once illustrious career had dwindled, and he found himself marginalised and forgotten. The grandeur of his past achievements now seemed distant and faded, overshadowed by the harsh realities of the present. His latest composition, a daring and unconventional piece, had been met with ridicule and disdain. The disastrous performance had sealed his fate, leaving him financially destitute and socially isolated. The cancellations of his concerts and the loss of his possessions plunged him into deep despair. But amidst the hardships, Tobin's spirit remained resilient. He had come to realise that his worth as an artist could not be defined by the opinions of others or the monetary value attached to his work. His true value lay in the creative fire that burned within him and in his unwavering belief in the power of his music.

With the support of his newfound companions, the homeless individuals he had encountered in a park, Tobin found solace and a sense of purpose. They didn't perceive him as a fallen maestro but rather as a fellow musician. Together, they crafted impromptu performances that brought joy to their lives. Amidst these humble gatherings, Tobin rediscovered the essence of his art. The barriers of expectation and judgement fell away, and he immersed himself in the pure joy of creating music. The cacophony of random sounds produced by his makeshift orchestra became a symphony of liberation, a rebellion against the constraints of societal norms. But the inevitable passage of time took its toll on Tobin's aged body.

The puma, on the other hand, continued to roam his mountainous domain. The seasons came and went, marking the passage of time. He fathered a number of cubs, and life carried on in the wilderness. The reflective plate that had caught his attention remained a source of fascination, a mirror that reflected his own strength and resilience. Through the reflections on the plate, the puma saw the interconnectedness of all things, the fleeting nature of existence, the echoes of his own breath, and the infinite possibilities that lay within every moment. He learned to embrace the present, to find solace in the now, and to let go of the burdens of the past.

And so, the stories of the twins and the puma, though seemingly disparate, converged in a shared understanding of the transformative power of art and the beauty that lies in embracing the present moment. Their paths had taken them through hardships and triumphs, loss and rediscovery, leaving a lasting mark on those they encountered.

"In this book, you'll notice that many animals are portrayed using anthropomorphism. Anthropomorphism refers to attributing human characteristics or behaviours to non-human entities, such as animals. It's a narrative technique employed to create relatable and engaging stories involving animal characters. The decision to use anthropomorphism in this book was made with the intention of fostering a deeper connection between readers and the animal subjects. By humanising the animals to a certain extent, I aim to encourage empathy and provoke thoughtful reflection on their experiences. It allows us to explore their emotions, struggles, and relationships in a way that can resonate with readers on a more personal level. However, it's important to note that while anthropomorphism helps us convey these themes effectively, it's not meant to be a representation of the animals' true nature. Animals possess unique characteristics and behaviours that should be respected and understood within their own context.

Of the many books I've written, 'The Puma's Trail' holds a special place in my heart as it was crafted in a unique and immersive manner. I'd like to take a moment to share with you the process behind its creation, which allowed me to infuse lived experiences into this work of fiction. The journey of writing 'The Puma's Trail' began with a desire to include a deep connection to the story's core. I wanted to truly feel the puma's spirit, to become one with its essence, and to embody its experiences. To achieve this, I embarked on a personal exploration, a method that blended reality with imagination."

In preparation, I adorned myself in dark attire, slipping into shoes that made no sound, leaving no traces as I ventured into the darkest corners of the city. My aim was not to embrace the lively nocturnal activities but to immerse myself in the world of the night. Deliberately detaching from human interactions, I observed the surroundings as I traversed from one place to another, seeking to evoke fear within and experience the shivers racing down my spine. It was in those vulnerable moments that the book truly came alive. Much of the story was penned during the silent hours of the night.

Each chapter, whether titled after an animal or a human, ultimately became a part of the puma's trail. The initial chapter, 'The Eagle,' set the stage by providing a broad overview. However, 'The Alley Cat' propelled the pen forward, igniting the raw energy that fuelled the narrative. I yearned to feel the puma's presence, to be consumed by its senses, and to bring its essence to life through my words. Night after night, I ventured into uncharted territories, surrendering myself to the impact of the elements—biting cold, relentless wind, cascading rain—as they blurred my vision and intertwined with my surroundings, guiding my journey. Treacherous paths along the cliff's edge tested my footing, and darkness enveloped me, providing a canvas for vulnerability. These experiences, devoid of external aids like torches, phones, or GPS, heightened my connection to the puma's spirit. It was within these moments of uncertainty that the book organically unfolded. Through this unconventional approach, 'The Puma's Trail' wove its own narrative. From one night to the next, I wouldn't know what the next page was destined to hold, seamlessly progressing the story with every step.

In reading 'The Puma's Trail,' I invite you to embrace the journey, to traverse the pages with an understanding that every word, every scene, every emotion is a reflection of the puma's path. May this book transport you into the depths of the puma's spirit, evoking the same sensations, emotions, and transformative experiences that were etched into its creation.

Heinz G. Ross

Parental Guidance

Content Advisory: Cruelty to Animals

This book contains descriptions of suffering and cruelty to animals. Some content may not be suitable for younger children. Parents or guardians are advised to review the following sections carefully before sharing them with their children:

The Puma: Caged Fights
The Puma: Albatross Finding the Edge
The Puma: The Punishment
The Puma: The Nightmare

Parental guidance for sensitive readers is recommended.

The Puma's Trail

The Puma: The Eagle

(You are encouraged to start with the preface, otherwise the next few pages may be confusing.)

He is a puma at his core, but for now, he dwells within the eagle, the eagle with the puma's spirit. He needs the eyes, the eagle's eyes, to find the answers — sharp eyes that may be able to show him the 'World of Life'.

The eagle flies for weeks, due east, to gain the distance. He settles on the highest ridge, scanning the horizon.

"This is the 'World of Life' I see in panoramic vision. The far left looks like doom, like hell. The far right looks like serenity, like heaven. Neither heaven nor hell can be seen. Even with the strength of 1000 eagle eyes, the depths of hell cannot be seen. The height of heaven is far beyond the focus of the eye."

In the landscape, there is an edge, left off-centre, called 'the edge of hell.' A little further to the left is the cliff of hell, a sheer drop straight down. One slip on the edge is all it takes. A little to the right off the 'edge of hell,' the land dips to gradually rise higher, further to the right. The gradient becomes steeper until, at the far right, it goes straight up like a smooth wall of glass.

Heaven and hell seemingly blend where they meet on the horizon. A deeper look into the vision reveals the oceans, lakes, and waterways. The edge of hell runs inside the water's edge. To the right are safe waters, to the left is unknown doom. This is the 'World of Life'. All living beings dwell within. The eagle returns. The spirit has the knowing.

The Puma: The Alley Cat

The night is dark, as black as his coat. He is a puma now, a black puma in his true self. His spirit within is home for now. His body is far from home, far from his forest, far from the mountains, and far from his native soil. He has had no food in the past four days. He blends unnoticed into the landscape of the dark city alleys. A landscape it is not. A cityscape filled with fumes, dirty gutters, and litter. There is poison in every breath he takes. He glides silently along the edges of buildings, forward, with no aim in sight. He is going somewhere, but not anywhere. That is all that matters. He is going forward in time, away from yesterday, towards another sunset.

Each stride is slow and burdensome. Once, he was beautiful, his coat reflecting the moon. Today, he is just a sorry shadow of his former self. Past a reflecting door, another cat of his kind, shows up out of nowhere, and then it is gone again. Many times he saw that cat, always without scent or sound, with a body that fit on a flat sheet. It never leaves a trace, elusive as a shadow. It's not a cat; it's just an illusion, the copycat that lives in reflective things.

He moves past a security fence. Wired on the fence is a sign. The sign of the security company used the picture of a black panther as their logo. His brother's fame, misused to frighten thieves. He greets the panther's image with respect, a black brother in the night. He knows he is a puma. The picture was of his former glory. He pushes his body along a barbed-wire fence. The barbs are drawing long streaks of blood. He presses harder into the barbs to feel anything. Deeper gauges cut the flesh. There is no pain anymore; he cannot feel it.

Ahead is a group of youths, cars, motorbikes, and girls. He can see the steel of the three rifle barrels. He glides forward, low and slow. Oh, how he would love a tangle, a fight to awaken his fire, but he knows he has no will to start it. Let's see if there are any takers. The group laughs, and the guys try to impress the girls. One shoots a handgun into the air. The chicks giggle. Music from the car is blaring into the night. The puma is very close to them now. The group becomes silent as they notice the puma's approach. The boys move out of his path. The group splits like a zipper to let him pass. In slow, silent steps, he moves through the group. His ears do not even try to pivot to listen if the rifles reveal clicks of cocking. He would sense a rifle's aim. Nothing happens. He moves on. Emptiness grows as another fight is left unfought.

He is heading towards an inner-city park. Ageing trees flank the avenue—trees of majestic beauty with branches like arms reaching out and upwards as if in a prayer to heaven, reminiscent of the trees of home, the home of long ago. Age always unfolds their inner spirit in trees. Old-fashioned streetlights dot the avenue. Up ahead, something dangles in the light. His fading eyesight can still make it out. As he gets closer, he stops and looks up. Some wire is caught in the branches, as if from a kite. It is very thin white steel wire. He studies the shape with interest. A straight strand two feet long hangs from a branch. The end contains a knot. The knot has twisted around the wire in such a way that it appears as a little noose. His tail twitches. He feels a wave of sensations over his entire body, as if some memory had a recollection. He cannot go further. That is the wrong direction.

He had learned to read signs. Every sign he read said, 'Don't go there.' He never saw a sign that read, 'Come here.' The warnings of hell are everywhere. Anything that triggers his awareness is a sign. Broken branches, a dead leaf, a misshapen object, all are signs. He turns without looking back and heads to another side street.

Sometimes his vision becomes blurred. Up ahead are some objects. He closes his green eyes, trying to forget the distance to the object. He thinks of a river to distract his brain from counting the steps. He is learning to cope without sight, whenever that day may come. He collides with the object.

How much did it cost him this time? The price was a rip in the ear and a bump on the nose. It was a steel garbage container. In the darker backstreets, he becomes invisible. A black puma on a moonless night in the dark shadow of a black building, behind the second corner inside a black hole, with his eyes closed. Nothing could be darker. Yet inside, he knows there is a deeper black elsewhere. He recalls that no matter how deep the blackness, all it takes is the tiniest flicker to make things shine. Will his eyes last long enough to see it? His legs are weak now. Time takes its toll. All things have an end, but in that, they also have a new beginning. Nothing can ever leave. It just transforms, endlessly. He is a puma. He was a puma, the solitary hunter. Cougar, leopard, carcajou, mountain lion, panther, lynx, and jaguar are all his brothers, all the same, yet rarely mingled.

The Puma: Past memories

Yes, once he was powerful. Penetrating eyes are as sharp as a laser beam. Claws that would lock into his prey and bring down the largest, even bears, cattle, and deer. In his nature, he is a loner. Once. he lived a life of exception when he was joined by another female feline of his kind. They learned to work in tandem. Each knew what needed doing. The two had become a mighty force. They would fiercely defend their territory against all comers. Attack or defence, they worked in harmony. They reared the cubs in the safety of the mountain cave while he circled the territory. Their kingdom covered part of the plains, the lower edges of the creek, and the arc of the forest right up to the ridges of the mountains. It was a vast area. Most would bolt just from the cat's hissing, not all, but most. So many battles were fought and won. Sometimes with a heavy price, but they had never met their master. How often did she patrol the woods and distract invaders away from him when he lay injured, recovering his strength? And so did he when she nursed the wounds of battle.

He took risks. How often would he stealthily engage in fights of life and death? With big invaders, he went straight for the throat; with most others, he went through the neck. The territory was marked with scratched bark, scents, faeces, and strong odours. How dare they enter? Once both lay injured, they were both unable to rule their kingdom. They had to hide in their secret spaces until they had the strength to rule again. Often, he would sit back to watch her fight, guard her rear, and admire her speed, instant reflexes, and agility to bring the prey down. Her white, four-inch fangs dripped with blood. Her kills were always swift. Most of the time, she attacked through the base of the skull. When it was all over, she would tower over the animal and release a growl of victory to claim her catch. She would grab it by the neck and drag the beast away.

Then humans arrived, setting traps. Her hind leg caught on one of them. She pulled the trap free from the stake, but it had locked around her lower leg. She never got it off. For weeks, she paced the forest with the trap firmly attached to her leg. She could no longer move in silence. Eventually, infection set in and poisoned her blood. It was an agonising way to go. He could not save her. The cubs had grown by then. They had left to claim their kingdoms, miles away. He would patrol his patch for a while, some years, and then things changed. It is a long story. These are different times today. There is no territory to defend. All were left far behind in time and distance. The cityscape is no place for a wildcat. Here, he does not belong. Ambition is gone. He heads home. The word has no meaning. Home today is anywhere.

The Puma: The Goose

A new dawn and a new day begin. Bar-headed geese are in migratory flight for the season. Time and space are of a different measure when the puma's spirit joins another being. However long he dwells, he will always return to himself.

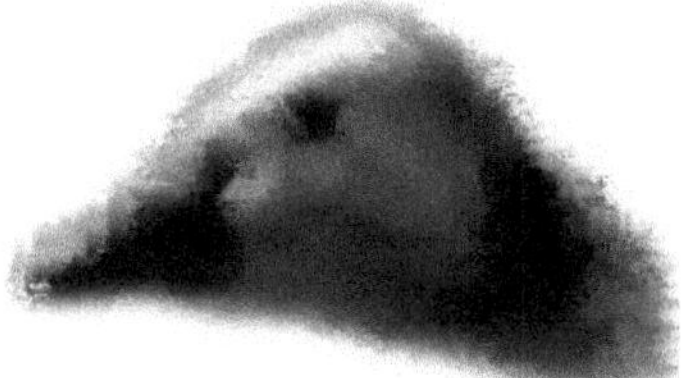

His spirit was carried by one of them. It is cold, minus 60 Fahrenheit. The altitude is 29,500 feet, deep below the Himalayan Mountains. His flock is small, 30,000 strong, perhaps more. He is about 700 feet from the outer edge of the V formation on the right side, somewhere along the rear. Two thousand miles are behind them and three thousand more to go, with incessant flapping and lots of chatter.

A monotonous journey, day in and day out. The air is thin, but the view is fantastic, compensating for the pain of non-stop flapping. But he is glad that he is not up front. Another of their species, a brant, tries to communicate, but it is difficult. He indicates to her that she should stay behind him to catch the benefit of his wingtip vortex. She does. For two weeks, they managed to stay together. One day, a big turbulence scattered the flock, and they would never meet again. His ears were tuned for her call, but not once would he hear her.

The Puma: The Marlin

Another day, at another time, in another place, in another element, he is a black giant marlin. He is a marlin with the puma's spirit. The Coral Sea, the Australian coast, is 40, maybe 50 miles off the edge of the reef. He is in pure waters. Some brave anglers try to tease him. He weighs 1,280 pounds, no chicken feed. He knows the line and knows how to snap it. You do not get to be 1,280 for being stupid.

Nearby, a blue, agile marlin swims in the currents. The blue takes the hook after spying the angler. He likes her, and he wants to be caught by her. She gets excited when he takes the line. They play for hours, running low and pulling back. They play the game of tease and excitation. She reels him in at 200 yards, 100, 50, or less, then he rears back and accelerates forward unexpectedly with powerful strokes. She is taken by surprise; she loses her footing and is pulled overboard. The line entangles her. The blue waters surround her as she is drawn underwater. She gasps for air and takes in a lung full of salty seawater. It burns.

She feels the weight pulling her downward right away. She wants to regurgitate and does, only to swallow the ocean again. She sees the blue marlin approaching. She drowns as the blue gets near her.

The black marlin watches in fascination; she chose him, and he chose her. A rifle shot cuts through the air just as it cuts through the water. The blue is dead as well. The black marlin breaks the water, rearing up in a powerful display and twisting along to stretch the distance. He dives low and encircles the two motionless bodies with respect. Love at its finest.

The Puma: The Butterfly

He re-emerges as a free-flying, beautiful butterfly. He dances through fields of flowers with the spirit of a puma. It is a calm world with so many of his kind, clouds of them. So many flowers are painted and captured for eternity, but none are alive without butterflies.

Each dance is a magical display of beauty. The wings were dressed in the most intricate designs, so rare, so precious, and so easily damaged. Panting, resting, and flying again, another joins him. They play games of chase, 'Catch me if you can.' Together, through foliage, they fly, none faster than the other.

Through scents of intoxication, each flower shines at its richest, and each perfume is unique. It is ecstasy to be alive. Looking through the morning sun, the fields become alive with buzz. Hundreds, thousands, and millions frolic in the rising heat. The music of life is all around. The birds need watching, as do the frogs and lizards, the fish, and the spider webs. There are dangers everywhere, but so are joys. They lived another day and two, and three, of joyous times.

A wagtail took a dive, and by sheer luck, he escaped in time. There is damage to his beauty. A wide scratch along his wing took all the cover scales and part of the ground scales. His unique design was defaced. Oh, what an ugly mark it is to carry. He hid from the others. He did not want to be seen.

The Puma: The Mantis

He is a mantis in China. The puma's spirit enters whichever form he chooses. He is a male Chinese mantis for now. He can sense his fate as soon as he sees her. He stays away. Already, she had eaten four males. She lives on males and hardly needs any other food, it seems. She starts eating while he is still mating. Head first, then the rest. The leftover wing will be the only evidence he has ever been. Oh, what a cruel display of passion! Yet, is it not love for a noble cause? He makes his young and feeds their mother, giving them the best chance to survive. As he dies, he will be reborn again. The watching mantis is next in line to mate with her, to feed his urge, and to surrender to her temptations. As he does, the giant female makes her claim.

The Puma: The Whale

In Antarctica, the water is cold. He's a mammal now, a sperm whale in Antarctica in the polar region, a whale with the puma's spirit. He is 23 years old and 40 feet long, going towards 60. Once he had 2.5 million siblings, now he has just a few. He weighs 40 tonnes and is still growing. The whaling fleet is searching. He swims with the boys. He can focus the beam of his sound and turn it into a weapon. The name on the mother ship is 'Godly Princess'. He sees the flag. He does not care what colour the fabric is.

He makes his offer by shooting a huge blow forward into the air. It does not take long for the cannon to roar and for the harpoon to pierce his side. Shouts of "cachalot" were heard from the bow. It is a big deal to catch a lot using a cannon.

Once, his brothers brought one of the ships down. They battered amidships into the vessel. The land lovers all went to the bottom. They are still retelling the story to this very day. How many did they claim in the fury of their revenge?

Oh, not this time; he is a gift. It is a terrible way to die. They pulled his carcass into the vessel. His skin bears the scars of squid. The body was cut into a million pieces. He supplies over 30 barrels of oil. He supplies his whole being. His remains are stored with those of others of his kind, refrigerated. On the voyage to home-port, a small fire in the engine room of the vessel occupies the crew. The refrigeration units malfunction. The crew is trying to minimize the damage. The carcasses are starting to rot. Within hours, the fire roars out of control and breaks out of its containment. Shortly later, the vessel sinks. All aboard were saved by the other ships in the fleet. He died for nothing; his gift was a waste of life.

The Puma: The Cockatoo

Next morning, the day begins with white. White snowflake bushes push out their blooms, appearing like white umbrellas held up by fine branches. The morning sun illuminates the shine of each blossom. He cleans his feathers. He is a cockatoo. White all over, except for the yellow crest. He flies alone with good vision.

His eyes see something of promise. The sky is his freedom. Nothing can get in his way. He can soar, he can dive, he can flick in flight, he can stand and balance, he can walk, he can do anything. A loud screech to let everyone know he is alive. White magnolia blooms scent the air. The day only lasted two hours, but nothing was lost.

The Puma: The Gull

He awakens at sunset. He is on the ocean aboard a trawler. The puma's spirit is within a gull. He is the brother of the tern, a larus. White gull with grey coloration; his wing is on the mend. Five weeks ago, his wing was damaged, caught in wires. A 17-year-old boy cared for him with affection. He nursed him, fed him, and cleaned his wounds. He liked him. He saved his life.

Heavy clouds move in from the west and north-west. Wind gusts whip up the seas. He hides under tarpaulin covers on the fore-deck. Within two hours, the weather turned nasty. The westerly cleans the decks. Caught in the draught, he lifts 20 feet and higher. The gull is defenceless and at the mercy of the wind. The trawler quickly disappears from view. Rain buckets down. Whitecaps on the waves, but all is dark now; he just can feel it cutting. Somehow, he survived the night. The storm had passed. In the morning, he bobbed like a cork on water. Hopefully, his wing had healed enough to try to fly. He lifted himself up in circles. The trawler had gone. There was nothing but ocean in all directions. Above the waves, there is not a living thing. Where is home? He tried to get some bearings, as he had never ventured that far out. Due east was home; must be. He headed east. How fast would a trawler be? How far would it travel in five weeks? When would he get home? Would he ever get home?

Flying became automatic after four days. At times, he would float on the water to rest and feed, then rise again, the same every day. Weeks passed with nothing but ocean around, in tireless flight due east. After several weeks, a little speck came into sight. Three days later, he could make out that it was an island. Another week, and he made it home. A good journey overall.

A long flight for survival, endurance, silence, and finding home It was good to be home amid the chatter. He could chatter; he heard chatter. Silence silenced. Endurance endured.

The Puma: The Crystal

The puma's spirit is still searching. The answers have not yet been reached, but they are close. It must make another journey, this time full circle.

The day is bright.
The day is still light.
The day is not over.
until it is night.

The spirit rises to seek a host. It finds a cloud, but it is not enough. It needs to be higher. Caught in the up-draft, he locks onto tiny particles, the particles of the cloud. Oh, what a ride this promises to be.

He is so tiny. He grows to become a crystal, a barely visible speck. With billions and billions, they become a white cloud that scatters light. Multiplied many times over, the clouds become dark. So much light is scattered that little gets through. Together, they absorb some of the solar radiation. As water, they weigh several million tonnes yet float without effort. It constantly rains within the clouds, only to be reborn seconds later all over again. The puma's spirit is now within the source of life itself. There are two choices to be made to start the round trip. It matters little how to begin.

The icy crystals grow,
more so
until they fall.

The journey of the puma's spirit in crystal begins. He is falling, colliding with others in endless collisions. He did not expect such a violent birth to become water. More and more of the smaller droplets are drawn into the wake, falling away and towards it all at the same time. Lightning and roaring thunder display the power and awe-inspiring might of nature.

He dwells inside a drop. The rush of wind, the constant changes in direction, the continual deformation of shape, the drops are being ripped apart to reform again. Oh, what a ride it is just to be born. It is not like flying at all. He falls, but not downward; any direction is possible, generally downward. The pull of gravity becomes pronounced.

Moments later the worst is over. Now he is a raindrop, along with millions of others. Each will take another journey. Each will bring life itself or take it. Each can become anything. He is near the ground. Even here, with enough energy, he could form into hot ice. There is endless capacity to become. His journey is as drop.

He could become clear, pure water, ever-renewing and self-cleaning, filling, thirst-quenching, deep and shallow. He could be calm like a mountain stream, wild as a raging torrent, or as gentle as the morning fog. He has become as hot as boiling steam, but he cannot be controlled. He would run through fingers, rise up as vapour, burst a bottle, or crack a dam if he were contained. With a strength that eats through steel, he could always claim his freedom.

He could be channelled in the right direction, in any direction. He could be guided, soak the roots of trees, reach upwards to their finest branches, and fill every cell within. Fill a desert with bloom, fill ponds with fish, make rivers run, soak the cracked soil, and bring growth. Reach into plants and exit plants. All that potential he has as a drop.

He could be used to surround swimming bodies, be used for washing and cooling, be felt on the skin as rain, be guided to every cell within a body, feel the rain as a cell, be absorbed, or be expelled as perspiration. He could be liquid in tea, tears, or steam on windows. He could be moved by many and, likewise, could move others in turn. There are so many ways to be. For now, he travels the drop's journey.

He lands in a bowl on the ground. He is down; the first part of the journey is done. With others, he had become water. He is still in the bowl, three days later. Some have gone back up to be reborn again. A dog comes and licks the bowl. He is not with the dog; he just missed it by a whisker. The dog's hind leg dislodged the bowl, and all the water spewed. It runs into the gutter, descending a long, twisting path towards a creek.
Eventually, he is inside a lake. In time, the pumps will draw him in to be filtered, sanitised, and purified. He will carry sodium, potassium, and chloride within. Pumped towards the city grid, the path along the pipes is disgusting. He is carried forwards by the pressurised flow inside the pipe.

The Transformation:

He is forced, through a tap, into a glass. A 15-year-old girl drinks from the glass. He is being swallowed and becoming absorbed. He starts a long journey within the body of the young girl. He becomes part of the body. He remained inside the girl for years. The girl becomes a woman. The natural processes inside the body use the once-water drop to become part of the egg itself, the ovum inside the woman. As with eggs, there is just one purpose.

Her body becomes aroused. The woman and her partner join in coitus. The sounds of blood gushing from the rise in temperature. In her partner, semen and other liquids call out to get ready. The scrotum tightens. All the seeds feel the rise in pressure, ever increasing, as they are forced into an ever-tighter space. The whole environment is in constant motion until the host spasms.

The Conception:

From the partner into the woman, sperm pushed inward and upward. A soup of rushing liquids surrounds the sperm; millions follow, millions ahead. The penis is still thrusting, resulting in more turbulence within the woman. Sperm is drawn deeper, inside the vaginal walls, towards the core of her reproductive organs.

The sperm rushing within lubricated channels towards the hot interior. The journey is one of constant violence but also of harmony of purpose. The route is very long, through the cervix, guided along the Fallopian tube. Ahead was the giant sphere, the largest cell in the woman's body, huge in size and under violent attack from a countless number of sperm. The soup of life, a brew of riches is beyond understanding. Each sibling that once fell from the sky with him could have carried the spirit of another. Drops that fell into the ocean, whipped up by a hurricane, blended in the surf, the rising humidity mixed with all others, re-emerge from a spring in Canada, or flow in the gutters of South Africa, all with the force of life within.

The potential between the two to create new life means they could repopulate the whole of humankind thousands, millions, and billions of times over, and each of their offspring would be unique, and not one would be identical if it were not for the time spent growing them. The sperm try to break into the jelly-coated egg. Oh, how many times have they failed? Bullet-shaped sperm with special charges. So many sperm failed, but each has endurance, persistence, strength, and power.

They surround the egg and try from all sides to break in. One sperm breaks through the jelly coating and releases its charge, which allows fusion with the egg. The skin of the egg cell fused twice when another sperm also gained entry. The egg now prevents all other sperm from entering. It is a hot place within the egg. The rhythm of life begins as the cells start dividing. Each cell contains half of the mother's genes. In that sense, the puma's spirit is linked to every new cell created. They will remain linked for this lifetime.

Days follow weeks and months of constant division. He had grown from one to millions, billions of cells, constantly multiplying. Magical energy is at work. A wondrous life is created from drops of rain and the elements combined. Ever more chemicals, substances, and additives are being pooled to form the human shape. Each cell is experiencing change and transformation. He becomes brain, skin, artery, hair follicle, blood, liver, toenail, fingernail, one, five, ten. He becomes a heartbeat, not one, but two.

He has become an unborn twin. In time, one will form as a female and the other as a male. They are identical, and they are not. They are rare and very special. They are becoming semi-identical twins, formed from one egg and two sperm. The puma's spirit is in both beings; he is in each.

The mother host is constantly supplying needed nourishment. The womb is warm and safe, but there is incessant change. The bodies have grown, moving, kicking, functioning individually, and linked forever. Both are unique, and each is unique.

Time comes for a new journey, time to be born. The path is painful down the same canal from where the sperm once entered so many months ago. The transformation from egg combined with seed to become this new being.

The mother host ejects the twins into another world, the same world it has always been. What lies ahead? What trials would they need to face in the years or seconds to come? Would they have years? Would they die the next minute? Anything is possible. Everything is possible.

He had become a twin, female as well as male. Potentially, he could become a mother and father. He could grow or perish. He could reach for heaven, hell, or neither.

For now, he is the voice that cries for soothing, guided to the breast. Strong droplets release life-giving nectar absorbed within. The mother's drops were added to both newborns, being absorbed into the inner self. They are the combined parts of mother and father, all in one being, all that in each. With the mother and father comes the whole chain of history that is all becoming part of the new life. The promise they carry within each. The incomprehensible immensity contained within.

The Twins: Asha and Tobin are born

The growing child is learning the pain of falling over. A constant firework is in the growing lobes. He sheds part of himself as urine, absorbed by nappies, somehow starting another cycle, eventually re-birthing to become anything. He gains eyesight with the growing twins. He becomes a tooth that pushes through the gum. He feels the pain of that. He sees the world as a two-year-old. He feels like a boy, while she feels like a girl. He becomes a joy in their mother's arms. He becomes a hero on their father's shoulders.

He is in both, the children named Asha and Tobin. Their names will mark their lives. Their lives will justify their names. He uses saliva to moisten the dry bread. He becomes a child's dream. He is also a nightmare, the rising ghost in the corner of the bedroom, rising like white smoke, reaching the ceiling. On both sides of the room, along the ceiling, the growing arms of the ghost are trying to grab the child. The child in bed is hiding under the blanket, a stolen peek, but it is still there. The ghost's face is bearing a wicket grin. The arms reach closer. The ghost's body is growing bigger until almost the entire ceiling is covered in white ghosts. It is just a matter of time before the ghost covers the entire room, trying to devour the child. Oh, the terrible nightmare within makes him scream, loud screams. Mother comes into the room and switches the light on. The ghost is gone. But where is it? Where did it go? It never shows itself when the lights are on.

How many times did they have to cry for help? Light that saved him from the ghost. The ghost is always within. Fear of the night, fear of darkness, 'Mother, leave the light on, please.' When the ghost disappeared, he feared meeting it in the daytime. Oh no, do not even contemplate that thought. It would be a trap without an exit. Asha would never see the ghost. The Puma's spirit in the nightmare of a two-year-old child learning how fear feels, fearing fear.

The boy and girl, as sweat, vomit, excrement, saliva, and as blood seeping from cuts, constantly shed him, leaving a continual trace of his path. He shall remain with the twins for their lifetime.

Aged six, the twins faced death for the first time in their young lives. He sheds a tear when the cat dies, although for each of the twins, this was a different experience. Asha saw how the vicious dog next door mauled the cat. The beautiful pet was ripped to shreds. She screamed in agony, initially shedding twenty tears, then a small creek flew from her eyes.

Tobin ran from behind the house towards the scream. His father called him back as they were cleaning the chicken shed. The father was unaware the event was unfolding on the street side of the house. The boy just got a distant glimpse of the cat's lifeless body. By the time he did reach the street, the cat had been taken away inside a plastic bag by the neighbour. Tears welled within the girl for hours. "Oh, Asha dear, bring out your tear," he would say. Tobin was also affected, but it left shallower scars in his being. They found comfort in each other. Their futures were shaped by everything they experienced. They faced loss, pain, and sorrow. They also found many joys, so many happy times, so much innocence, and so many discoveries. They grew by absorbing and learning, adding up.

The brains of the twins were constantly trying to sort out incoming messages. Keep that for the future; clean out this shelf that is out of date; link this smell with that colour; and combine this melody with the feeling of a gentle breeze, the shades of this sunset, and the smell of boiled potatoes.

All boys with the name 'William' are idiots, and all girls with the name 'Mary' are simply beautiful, this they both shared. They looked so alike and often spoke in unison. They could start a sentence together as if in one voice. When they spoke to each other, they often used verse. Tobin's most used words would be "Oh Asha dear..." and then fill it in with what he wanted her to know.

Asha, aged seven, wanted to name her son of the future 'Tom'. Tobin would never want a red bicycle. Aged eight, one of their classmates, a girl who sat in the back row of the classroom, cried uncontrollably throughout the day. Touching the washing machine had electrocuted her mother the day before. Her mother was barefoot, and the floor in her laundry had been wet. Thoughts of how the girl might grow up wandered through their heads. When they got home, they looked at their parents with different eyes. They got a faint hint, realising that their own welfare was very much dependent on their parents' safety.

Would the parents love each other until the end of time, or at least long enough so that they could learn to fly? In Tobin's head, this question came to the fore: How much would a bicycle cost? A blue bicycle, of course. It probably costs a million dollars, maybe two. What if he worked hard raking the neighbour's garden for three weeks? Would that be enough for a bike? He was willing to swap and trade most of his possessions, but not the soccer ball or the kite. No way would he trade the kite. The spirit of the puma within the boy's dream learned the aching longing for a blue bike.

The Twins: The morning rituals

The morning ritual of the twins became a trap in time. Before putting on a sock, Asha needed to know which foot to dress first. If yesterday she dressed the left one first, then today she would have to dress the right one first. Sometimes in summer, she would not wear socks, and that often threw the rhythm of who was first out of balance.

Tobin tried to use each hand equally often. The habit of opening the front door with the right hand would eventually mean that the right hand had more use than the other did. He'd leave the house having used the right hand; with each step, he'd go 'left, left, left' in his head, so as not to forget that the next door he would open needed the left hand to be used. Sometimes he would tap with the finger of the appropriate hand to free his brain from the non-stop burden of keeping track. Eventually, he freed himself from the constant thought of keeping track. When coming, he used the right hand; when leaving, he used the left. In the head of an 8-year-old, the curse of trying to age evenly.

Aged nine, they faced death again, this time in the form of a picture that Tobin had found inside an envelope when visiting their aunt. It showed a black-framed bed with four long, heavy posts at each corner of the bed. A white, elegant sheet covered most of the bed. Their grandmother's head lay on the pillow, her arms across the cover, both hands linked as if in prayer. The first dead human they ever saw. It was a black-and-white picture of postcard size.

Once seen, it would never leave their heads and could never be 'unseen'. The sight would pull the sight into the eyes but could never push it out of the eyes. The knowledge of this, their grandmother's final poise, could not be 'unknown'. There is so much to absorb and comprehend when you are not even ten. They would still remember their grandmother's voice, the warmth of her embrace, and the feeling of her love. In time, the memory of her voice would fade, but not the image.

They grew each day a tiny bit more, on birthdays 10, 11, and 12. Asha learned that her best friend Emily could never be trusted and promised herself to never speak to her again, even if she were the last person on this planet. She would rather scream to block out Emily's voice than listen to a solitary word she may mumble. Emily became invisible to her, a non-existent being.

Then came the time when one of their classmates died in a road accident. The whole school attended his funeral. The speeches at the open grave, only a few heard them, each worked through the meaning of this young loss. He would never hold a girl's hand, he would never kiss, and he would never grow older than 11. He would be excused from submitting next week's assignment, and he would never need to explain why he had wagged school. He would never move to the next grade; he would never see a naked girl; he would never touch one; he would never ever hold one close. He would never... never... never...

Oh, the list of 'never' they came up with while the speeches were read out was a mile long. All the things he could never do. Who was he? He was just another kid in school, just one of so many. They could barely remember his voice. They had no idea what sort of person he really was. It did not matter. He was one of them. They did not know him well at all, but they were sorry just the same for all the things he would never be able to do. Life is fragile—that's what they learned at age 11. Sorrow set in. Sorrow faded.

The Twins: The falling in love

Tobin fell in love for the first time with a 32-year-old woman. Friends of their aunt had invited them for an afternoon. She was so beautiful in his eyes. His head just reached her breasts. How lovely each of her hugs felt to him. Cradled within her safe, warm breasts. He was her man. He knew it because she had told everyone that, proclaiming the words loud and clear: 'This is my man'. He became three times his size, if only in his head. It was a love that lasted one afternoon. He would never see her again. What was her name?

Time came, and their bodies changed. Oh, how disgusting to find pubic hair growing. More and more, they grew every day. Her nipples puffed up. They would not go back in. Inside Asha, the whole machinery for the future grew. Complicated growth that would ensure everything was becoming ready to create another life one day. The rhythm of cycles was something one had to get used to.

His bones were aching. Growth took its toll on the joints. The embarrassing moments of waking up from the never-ending rise of a finger that would not stay down. Often in the most uncalled-for moments, in front of the classroom, reciting some history, out of control.

Blushing and embarrassment in the face revealed it to everyone, or so it seemed. Waving arms and gesticulations could not distract the eyes of some, who noticed and giggled in tease. Both, at different speeds, went through their own unique time of growth. There is no turning back.

The Twins: The age of juveniles

Both carry the puma's spirit. Age of juveniles: the first embraces and kisses. The time of self-discovery came, the explorations and the excitations. They would experience frustrations and the speed of quick highs, times of humiliation and captivation, playful nights, and sleepy days. Daydreaming, fantasising, imagining, and wishing wonders. Asha's first kiss was from a boy the same age as her. 'What was all that about?'

Her second kiss was two months later at a relative's wedding. She was fourteen now, in a knee-length dress, like a miniature woman with a baby face. A young man of 32 asked her to dance. He charmed her to the bushes and kissed her. Wow, that was different, infatuation, reaching cloud 9 in 3 seconds. She would recall the moment so many times, dreaming of faraway islands, Hawaiian guitars, and summer sunsets. She raised him to the level of a prince in her world of make-believe. Four weeks later, she saw him again, with his wife on his arm and two kids. 'How could he?' She loved him and she hated him, all in a kiss.

Tobin could feel her pain and anger, but he would create other memories by playing games of tease and testing the senses, creating an awareness of attraction. Asha, at 16, also played the games. She had noticed that she must radiate some sort of attraction, as most boys would turn their heads wherever she went. Black-haired as a puma, she would try different outfits to see which of them got the most attention. It didn't really matter what she wore, as most guys would follow her with their eyes.

Sometimes their hungry eyes would scan her figure. She found it all a bit unsettling. She could sense it when it happened. Although in her own mirror, all she could see was a girl, yes, gorgeous, but hey. So why not accept who you are? Every so often, she would have liked to hide in the skin of a plain girl who drew no attention, just to be left alone. Being able to have anyone does not mean there is someone.

Both grew on the outside and the inside. In so many areas, they shared similarities, yet each also had a unique sense of self. Asha loved drawing and sketching. Her pen was her camera. She drew what was worthy of capture. Her eyes would absorb and combine with her feelings, which would flow through her hands onto paper to show her render in her own interpretation.

Tobin was a non-stop whistle-blower. If he did not whistle, he would hum a tune for hours. Tobin was clever and could figure things out, while Asha was able to apply her knowledge to the best of her ability. Together, they could complement each other in so many areas.

One late afternoon, Asha walked in the park. She carried the book that she had bought earlier. The footpath forks in three directions. Right in front of her, she found two dead dragonflies on the ground. Which way should she go? She pauses. Should she go left, right, or straight ahead? She does not have vision for the next few minutes. She is unable to see into the future. All she can sense is an eerie feeling.

Which paths do the dragonflies block? The answer is unclear. They lay somewhat near the middle. If she were to go left, would she ever leave the park alive or be scarred for life? If she had gone right, would she have made the next 500 yards? It was just a normal park with nothing seemingly wrong; no threats of danger were visible. She is still hesitant to pass the dragonflies.

Ten minutes later, the sirens of police cars and ambulances wailed, approaching the area of the park. Loud shouts were heard inside the park as groups of police with dogs searched the area. Asha would always trust her senses. If in doubt, let life make the decisions.

The Twins: Tobin's friendship

Tobin, aged 17, spent 30 seconds of his life kissing a woman, aged 69. She was a writer and poet. She would write stories of magic and doom. In one of her stories, she wrote: Set your vision on the word 'ugly, multiplied 500 times. Perhaps like a 200-year-old witch. The right hip-joint has a rusty nail that squeaks with every step. Cane-toad-coloured skin with wrinkles. Feet have oozing sores, caused by the quest to find you. Hands shake uncontrollably. The lower lip protrudes and dribbles. The left eye is a scratched yellow marble found in the dark, dirty alleys of the city. The right eye is a green plastic button that the blouse shed eight months ago. She'd wear it only on Sundays. I have lost my perception of time while looking for you. Never know when Sunday comes. Hands have horrible sores with warts and hard skin from dragging the body forwards in the unshakeable belief that it will find you.

And if you meet my beaten-down siblings in the gutters, throw them a coin; they'll thank you for helping them survive. The left leg is a wooden peg from a window frame, scavenged from a garbage dump, tipped out of a demolition truck. It has a handle and a hinge, but it will open nothing. Under the eyes are heavy bags filled with precious tears of longing. Each drop had grown from the pain of searching. The bags are ready to burst. They will cry tears of joy when they find the rarest prince.

Hair that is torn, as the wolves of temptation tried to devour the body. I always got away from them to keep my heart pure for the One in my dreams. The bed is a cold park bench, found at dusk. Blankets are discarded newspapers. The body is filled with nothing and, despite that, with everything. The body has grown weak from defending its purity, and in that, it finds renewed strength to crawl another inch towards you. You look at me with love, and you will see none of that. Love will blind your sight. You will not see my blemishes of time and life. Every day appears to be a Sunday. My imperfections, faults, and failings fade in the warmth of your love. The only vanity I know was in the bathroom of my childhood, but I do not think you would feel ashamed if I were by your side. Look at me without love, and I seem like an ordinary old woman.

This was her story, in one of her stories. He had read it two weeks earlier. She was leaving for another town. This was to be their last day together. In the embrace of saying 'good bye', he saw a woman with longing and a heartbeat. Her eyes were marked with the body's signals of inner ageing, fear, and future concerns. Eyes within a body that looked tired. Aged face with wrinkles that were deep and pronounced, lips thin and flat, and grey and ruffled hair. He did not kiss her despite all that; he kissed her because of it. His eyes met hers, and all he could see was her glow and desire.

As they kissed, she closed her eyes, and so did he. He travelled inside her, she moaned. He embraced her; she moaned again; their bodies pulled tightly together; she travelled inside him, then slowly released from the kiss. All these sensations occurred in a 30-second kiss. She continued to moan and threw a thankful smile. This kiss was born of a different kind of love. The hope to leave a small gift contained in a kiss. This was his friendship at the age of 17.

The Twins: Aged 18-20

In their late teens, both grew from absorbing knowledge, education, studies, and practise. Tobin's focus became music, while Asha furthered her interests in painting. They met people and built friendships. Perrin would become a friend for life. He was 15 years older and a hermit sculptor. He tried to breathe life into stone and managed to freeze a moment of time. Most of his works were large monuments or statues. Perrin lived a reclusive life, but he did have a connection with them both.
The twins would also learn to hear the call of their hearts, the longing of their youth, disappointments and trials, and overcoming and becoming. They wrote tender words, using the ink of hope. They found another that could absorb them.

They had lost the others and had to start over. Through becoming, they became.

Dreams of long ago lay mostly dormant but did, from time to time, reach into their awareness, if just for fractions of a second. Dreams would wait their time of being brought to life to follow orders given once.

The Puma: In search for food

Only two days have passed in the puma's life. Again, the weather had darkened. He is in the inner city, early nightlife and busy streets. He had not eaten in the last six days. He pushes through a swinging restaurant door, heading towards the food displays. There it is again, the silent cat on the other side of the room walking on the flatness of a mirror.

Upon his being noticed, the guests barricaded themselves behind doors. Along decorated tables around the room were freshly cooked ducks, quails, pheasants, fish, crab, octopus, roast pork, beef, chicken, and cadavers of all kinds. A smorgasbord of human food delights All meat was either white or a disgusting brown colour, yet none he could recognise. With all the carved-up dead, none had the colour of life. There was no blood anywhere. He sniffs each offering, but none awakens his appetite. There is nothing here for him. He bumps a carafe of water and licks a few drops off the table. He leaves the place behind.

His claws are halfway out, leaving scratches on the ground. In the metaphor of his being, each scratch left a river behind, trailing creeks and rivers wherever he went. He had regained a little of his strength and was prepared to take risks. He headed for the park once more, searching for the wire on the light in the avenue, the one with the noose. Nothing had changed. It was as before. This time he walked under the suspended wire without hesitation, forwards along the path with all senses primed. His pupils were round and dilated.

Each step could bring him closer to the meaning of the sign. He knew that. Was he looking for his master? He did not know. He knew he had to overcome this inner fear.

His whole being was on alert. His ears are taking in the slightest sound. He needed to test his senses and the reliability of his instincts to find the truth. He went further into an isolated narrow walkway, along the edge of a high cliff. In this darkness, with his eyesight so faint, he could barely make out the contours of the edges. He jumped off the path along the ridges of the boulders, purposely putting his body at risk. The higher the path, the more dangerous the unseen drop had become. If he slips, then that would be his destiny. He would face it, no matter what it was. To be free from fear, face it.

He waited on a precarious ledge for 30 minutes, absorbing the sounds of life around him. He started to doubt his instincts. Still, the next night, the question demanded answers. Again, he went to the same place. 'Why was there a noose?' This time he searched the whole area, sniffing the ground and around the bushes.

In ever-widening circles, he searched until he found crossbones and a skull painted on a metal drum. There it was, the faint memory of over a hundred years ago still carried within the cat. The skull and crossbones are a mark of the poison that once claimed thousands of his ancestors. Back then it was a sign they had never seen before. He would continue to rely on his senses.

The Puma: In search for a kill

He spent part of the night sleeping on the high branches. Long before sunrise, he heads towards the field. He needs to kill. Before him, the herd of cattle can sense him and become restless. The puma searches to find a worthy rival. He sees a strong bull with sharp horns. He approaches the bull deliberately, head-on, against all his instincts. The bull stamps the soil and lets out a high shrill.

The puma advances slowly towards the bull. He is aware the horns are a formidable weapon. He had never approached head-on. The bull backs away, but his eyes are still locked on the puma. The puma accelerates directly towards the bull. The bull is very agile despite his bulk. He also moves forwards, shaking and lowering his head. The puma leaps towards the head. The bull lowers his horns still further.

The puma digs his claws into the bull's shoulders. His upper body had cleared the horns. The bull's head lifts up as the puma's hind legs fly overhead. One of his horns caught the loose skin of the puma's hind legs. The bull lifts the puma high and bucks at the same time. The puma loses his grip and is tossed through the air. Blood is gushing from the rip in the hind leg.

The puma stalks in circles around the head of the bull. Once again, he leaps forwards. This time he managed to trip the big beast on the front legs. The bull stumbles, and the puma gains a solid grip around his neck. He sinks his teeth into the bull's throat. He can feel the blood inside the veins pulsating. The bull's breath is hot. He pauses. In one rip, the bull would be dead. This was enough. He had brought him down. The puma releases his grip on the bull's throat and jumps clear of the still-struggling animal. He left the field behind. He just needed to know that he still could; that was enough. He could always catch the rats in the alleys, even if he became blind, but as a blind old puma, he would never be able to challenge a strong bull again.

He entered the city at night, rarely ever during the day. He paced the walkways and noticed that he instinctively avoided every lid, canal opening, or anything made of steel. After learning how to live in blindness, he would need to walk on steel eventually. Up ahead was a steel lid on the footpath. He aimed in that direction with his eyes shut.

His claws retracted, but as soon as his paws touched the steel, the uneven support and coldness brought his claws out, digging into the thin slits. He did not know the lid had slits. He could lose a claw easily if he was running. He needed to adjust and try to go against his automatic reactions, even if it meant he would slip on his pads occasionally.

The Twins: As adults 25-35

His spirit returned to the twins, now aged 25 to 35. Asha had grown to be an artist. The ever-changing view of a sunrise captured her attention. She would leave at dusk and await the moment when the crest of the sun entered the horizon. She would never use a camera to capture the most interesting seconds. There were only a few seconds of special lighting that needed to be captured quickly. A series of twelve sunrise paintings on canvas became her first portfolio. Each caught the essence of a fresh day starting. Every sunrise is captured from a different viewpoint: across the ocean, through trees, from a mountain, or from beneath a bridge.

She traced the light through the rising morning fog, through the reflections of a multicoloured glass mosaic, and from a dark gorge amidst trees, trying to seize the moments between day and night, between past and future, but always confined to the moments of now.

Often, she would get up early, drive to an isolated vantage point, and sit in solitude to absorb the spirit of the moment. The promise contained in a sunrise. The knowing that in the endlessness of time this sunrise happens only once. It can never be repeated or relived again. The day it bears is unique in the eternity of time. However dark the night, however sad the past, this sunrise can change everything.

Asha symbolised the immense power contained in every 'now', in a set of 'Sunrise' paintings. Each 'now' is the shortest moment in time, yet combined, they stretch from when time began to infinity. The 'Sunrise Collection' became her first exhibition. Much to her surprise, all twelve sold within the first three days of opening. One Art lover acquired all the paintings at once.

Asha drew her latest masterpiece in the colours of fantasy, combining them all in a single dream. The woven web of wondrous weavings grew from a dream to being lived. It demanded its time. Is it not a dream that gets things done? Is it not a dream that showed stargazers planets that no eye could see? Did not a dream guide sailors to lands far beyond their scope of sight? Did not a dream discover cures for ills?

It is impossible to 'un-dream'. Is not the whole world built on dreams? Cities, symphonies, precious artworks, and countless other things around us were all just dreams once. So is it not the law of nature that dreams become reality? A dream just needs believing; from that comes knowing, and from that it will be born. The brain can't fathom why or how it works. It does; that is all it knows, and that is all it needs to know. Asha had an inner knowing of that. She put all that on one canvas.

She could paint from within, and it did not take long to be noticed. Within a few years, she had become a sought-after artist, working closely with the city gallery. In her private time, she painted the fantasy of her life. On occasion, the gallery owner would drop in just to see what she was up to with her work. Asha had two successful exhibitions, which elevated her name further. Every other month, a new work would outshine the previous masterpiece. Each would hold the precious title until the next one was completed. She enjoyed the gift of perception, understanding, and comprehending and brought this to the canvas.

Her rise to fame brought an increase in orders for commissioned works, and she enjoyed a good relationship with the gallery's owner, Yente Francis. Asha had also become a solo dancer, more for her own enjoyment. She could express herself through art, either through her body or her mind. Tobin became an accomplished pianist, performing concerts in the major cities. Just before his 28th birthday, he was on a flight to Moscow for a concert performance there. The Taxi that was to drive him to the Hotel was involved in an accident that saw him lose his right arm and leave him with severe head injuries. Tobin lost so much in just one afternoon. Asha rushed to Moscow to be by his side. When he woke up, the white ceiling of the room was the first thing he saw. He had no sense of self. It felt as if he were inside the body of another person. Doctors and nurses all spoke an unfamiliar language.

This can only be a bad dream. No matter how hard he tried to wake up, he could not escape the dream. He tried to pinch his leg and felt nothing. As if he were only awareness inside a body that didn't belong. He attempted again to pinch the other leg, and this time he could feel it. This was no dream. How could it be that he didn't know anything about the body he was in? He knew neither his name nor the face he carried. Even a mirror could not reflect his face.

He was in the hospital, hooked up to medical gadgets with tubes from his nose and arm, a helpless patient. It became the new reality. He was bandaged, and his throbbing head was filled with pain. He spent weeks in intensive care. Tobin recognised Asha's face as being familiar. He did not know she was his sister. He had no comprehension of who he was. Eventually, she arranged transportation and brought him home. Over the next few years, she devoted every moment to his care. Everything transformed. In different ways, both were changed by this event.

The once easygoing man felt isolation and a physical handicap. He became severely depressed. Snippets of memories came back. The left arm refused the brain's command of movement. A right arm reduced to a stump. No thought could be put into words. The voice refused. Hopelessness and suicidal thoughts occupied his mind. All he seemed to have was awareness, not much more. Helplessness and isolation grew within. He was shut-in, locked in a brain that was trying to cope with what the body had left. An uncertain future awaited both.

Through Asha, he learned anew who he is and who he was. She would sketch a hundred sunrises, and each carried the promise of a new day. In tireless devotion, she drove him to the beach to watch and be a witness to the dawning day. She showered him with love while he stared in silence at the growing ball of light. When the sunrise was covered by clouds, she made him believe a new day had been born. In time, he refused to accept his incapacity in body and mind.

Asha rarely received feedback from Tobin. He was incapable of giving a sign. Tobin's brain took years before he was able to mumble some sort of sound. He could not speak. His speech was sound, with grunts similar to those of animals. The big gaps in his memory would remain forever. For seven years, Asha spent every day in selfless care, trying to rebuild his self-esteem and mental and physical functions. Each day, the arm needed exercising in endless repetition. Asha could only sense what went on in Tobin's head. She played music from his concerts and other works so that he could find his former self.

Now, after seven years, she noticed a glimmer of hope take root when he tapped along to the rhythm of the drums. It was a faint early sign of him reconnecting with music. Asha cried for joy. The magic and promise of a tapping finger. It took the power of over two-and-a-half thousand sunrises to make his finger tap to a rhythm. Just one more sunrise can change even more. Blind faith is rewarded with the simplest of gestures. The fruits of belief grew in abundance in the following months.

The Twins: The living picture

On a large, wide canvas, Asha started to sketch the outline of an orchestra. She started filling in the background, and over the next few weeks, each of the musicians painted in detail. The blank space on her left was the hardest to paint. She drew a grand piano, black with white, shining reflections. She traced the outer shape of the pianist on the canvas and then fell asleep.

Tobin was aware of her painting, but he never gave it much attention. Now, for the first time, he approached the work. The piano was almost complete. The upper keys were clearly visible. The pianist was just a thinly outlined figure. Asha was asleep in front of the canvas. Tobin's right hand wanted to reach for the keys, but all he had was the short stump of his upper arm. His hand and his fingers were just a memory. Tobin studied the incomplete work for hours. In his head, the picture became alive. Asha was interrupted from completing the details of the pianist. She needed to paint works for a living. Tobin began with a newfound enthusiasm to exercise his left arm and fingers. Two months later, Asha continued on the big canvas. She painted the pianist, his arms raised, all fingers extended, five inches above the ivory keys. Tobin played her the classical piece and gesticulated to Asha how the fingers of each hand ought to be placed.

Asha became excited. It's the first time in so many years that they could truly connect on the same level, even though music was not her field. The pianist on canvas was finished except for the face. The next day, his sister found a 9-year-old picture of Tobin when he was performing in London. She had taken it during his second concert tour. She placed it above the canvas and started to draw the face of the pianist. When Tobin became aware of what she had done, he walked in anger to the canvas and smudged the wet paint of the face she had just painted. He crunched the photograph in his hand. He looked at Asha and shook his head as if to say 'no.' Tobin pointed to the right of the pianist in the painting, to the space in front of all the musicians. He took a long paintbrush, walked to the back of the room, and switched on the music. He pulled out a chair and stood on it. With his left hand, he raised the paintbrush and moved it up and down to match the rhythmic flow of the piece.

Asha began to realise that he no longer was the pianist and that he wanted to become the conductor. She painted him as a conductor. The raised arm of the painted conductor covered the pianist's face on the canvas. Most of his body covered the musical scores. In the smallest of writings, she inscribed 'For my brother Tobin' on the visible edge of the scores. What she drew became his vision.

Over the coming months, Tobin would sit every day in front of the computer, sometimes for hours. He would connect with each musician. He tried to reach them through his thoughts. When he heard the cello, he would draw the cello into his eyes; the violins, the flutes, the whole orchestra, came alive in his head. All he needed to learn was how to control his arm so that he could move it automatically. Asha often watched him with a loving smile as he tried, with some awkward moves, to direct the music to the painted musicians. She continued working on commissioned art works and kept them both alive financially.

Perrin would drop in on a regular basis. Once, he brought a friend along, a tinker. He built a speech device for Tobin. He taught him how to use it. At the press of a button, ready-made words or sentences came through a little speaker.

The Puma: Standing still is no option

The puma's spirit returned. It had rained for the last few days. He did rip a claw out of his right paw when running over one of the steel lids in the inner city. A pack of dogs chased him under the bridge. How low had he come to be chased by a pack of dogs? The lead dog had the appearance of a wolf. He could always outrun them, but hunger had finally returned.

Near a monument, he turned and took on the leading dog. His claws struck out at three others and left deep rips in them. They backed off quickly. His fangs had the lead dog by the throat. In a swift leap, he scaled the monument with the dying lead dog in his jaw, leaving the mob below. A gush of blood ran down the stonework. The others kept barking for some time while he ripped the carcass apart, chewing warm, fresh flesh, wet with life-giving blood.

His canines cut through the muscles that he held down with his claws and tore the flesh apart. He gorged on the liver, the blood of life. Almost his whole head became covered in the dog's blood. It took some hours to devour the kill. The leftovers were buried in the park as food for another day. He cleaned himself, rubbing the blood off the fur on his face. The next day, he slept on the high branches, digesting the feast.

The Puma: The search for hell

In the 'World of Life,' the puma remained most of the time somewhere near the middle. Doom was on the left and serenity on the right. But he turned so many times in his life that he'd lost direction of where left and right are. That was just the eagle's figure of speech. What is on the side of doom? What is doom? What is hell? Hell is within, but it must also be in front of his eyes somewhere.

The puma left the tree, trying to find hell or at least doom, at least somewhere near the edge of hell. He had no idea where to start looking. Since each cell is programmed for survival and each instinct is geared for his protection, he figured if he did anything against his nature, he would have to find hell.

That is where it would have to be. Any scent that he would normally try to avoid, he would have to welcome and follow.

Any fear that would normally warn him would have to reverse his normal reaction in order to find doom. That would have to be his direction.

What were his biggest fears? The weirdest fears any puma would ever have. Getting his legs cut off by a truck or a train, getting his head caught in a wire, being electrocuted, being dragged out by the tide and drowning in the ocean, being sucked into a canal in a fast-flowing creek, being trapped in a fire. Would that be hell?

He could sleep with his head placed between the parked wheels of a semi trailer near a roadhouse and never know when the driver would start the truck and roll over his head. He could look for the noose on the light near the avenue, open it, and jump into it. He could climb up to a roof and lick the power line. He could jump off a cliff into the outgoing tide and see what happens. He could wait for a thunderstorm, walk headfirst into a tight culvert the rushing waters to trap him. Would any of that be hell? Most likely, it would mean certain death. It would be very close to suicide. It would be suicide. Facing hell is not the same as facing fear. Why did he want to know what hell was? Perhaps he was looking for heaven and needed hell to show him the way. He could not comprehend his own question. He only knew he could not stand still. Standing still is not an option. Life needs living. He lived in the 'World of Life'. He could roam anywhere. He just wanted to know, to see what it was like.

The Puma: Towards the unknown

He walked forwards into the unknown. Each step became ever more challenging. He left his known world behind. He hid inside a railway wagon and remained there for two days. In the afternoon, the door rolled shut, locked from the outside. The wagon connected to a train and, once moving, rolled throughout the night. The wheels clicked under the rails in a regular rhythm. For three days, he was trapped inside the wagon. Thirst set in. Being caged and dehydrated is not a good feeling, but it's not quite like he imagined hell to be.

On the fourth day, the door rolled open again. The first sunlight he had seen in days. Unnoticed, he slipped out of the wagon and drank some water near a creek. As the train set into motion, he chased it and jumped into an open wagon with low walls. This time exposed to the elements, in wind and rain, without any cover. Five days later, the train reached a big harbour with large ships and freighters. He hid on one of the freighters. Two days later, he was at sea. Six weeks went by, and it became icy cold. Snow and ice built up on the containers. Wherever he stepped, he left marks, witness marks of his being there. There were hardly any rats onboard. The ones that did live here had tiny hiding spots and were hard to catch. He had lost 50 pounds already, and hunger was his constant companion. 'Was this hell? he wondered. It was some sort of misery, but not yet hell. The seas became rough, and ice-cold gale-force winds blew across the vessel. He tried to find better shelter between the containers. Just as he jumped, one of the containers dislodged and moved against another. His left foot was trapped by the steel. The bone was not broken, but the ankle could not be pulled through the gap between the two containers.

This would have to be hell, for sure. He had to endure the weather, thirst, hunger, and cold steel. He was defenceless on a freighter to who knows where. He lost more weight until he passed out. He woke up in a makeshift cage. His hind leg was bandaged and had the scent of strong, unknown smells. There was a bowl of water and a carcass of some kind in the cage.

People came and looked at him. He was too weak to react. Eventually, he recovered. Some days later, he was poked with sticks from all sides. He was trapped inside a cage. That cage was loaded onto a truck with him inside it. His journey began on rough roads.

The Twins: The recovery

The puma's spirit returned to the twins. Years of rehabilitation saw improvements in Tobin. Each week, he was able to control his left arm with more precision. He had become skilled at using the speech device. He and Asha went out and rejoined the world from their self-imposed exile following years of coming to terms with the accident. The years of caring for him took their toll on Asha. She no longer danced. Her dream of motherhood was abandoned as her dedication to her brother became her world. Inside, she was satisfied with being able to have brought Tobin out of his long and deep depression.

Asha continued to find much joy in art and painting. From time to time, they visited Perrin and admired his latest creation. Perrin works predominantly with marble now. His workshop was a large, old wooden shed. Boulders and stones for future creations filled the place. He had built an upper deck inside the shed to store some of the excess material he had accumulated. Posts that seemed to be struggling under the load supported the whole deck. It was a very precarious structure.

Perrin was single-minded. Perfection in his sculptures and trying to extract the best from his craft were paramount. The rest was of minor importance. He was a big and strong man who cared little about appearances. It was the focus on ideals that united the three. Asha and Tobin spent hours in his stimulating company. Some months later, they would meet up again.

 Tobin's creative needs drew him more and more to concerts. Inside Tobin's brain, each visit would strengthen the new connections it had built. He sat in at rehearsals, often somewhere in the back of the hall, just to be surrounded by music. His speech had not returned, but his understanding of music grew in time beyond his previous comprehension when he was a pianist.

The Twins: Finding purpose

Tobin learned to write with his left hand. His handwriting would never look pretty, but whatever he wrote had substance. Often after rehearsal, he sat for a long time, replaying sections in his mind to such a degree that he forgot time altogether. He had found purpose, and he plotted musical scores on paper. He was overcome at the oddest places with ideas. One time, inside a toilet, he'd sit for 45 minutes plotting musical scores on the toilet paper. Later, he would unfold it carefully and transfer the scores onto proper paper. His sister had never learned to read musical scores.

Another time, Tobin invited Asha along when the orchestra was rehearsing again. They sat in the back and listened. Five times, the conductor stopped the piece in the middle. He became agitated with the violin section. Three more times they started midway, and repeatedly he stopped them abruptly. He lost his composure, began yelling abuse at the musicians, and stormed out in anger. Within a few minutes, the musicians argued amongst themselves; tempers flared, and bad vibes filled the hall.

The twins, both still sitting at the rear of the hall, witnessed the event. Tobin got up and approached the position the conductor had left vacant. With a calming expression, he raised his left arm and looked at the musicians. He was not dressed for the part, but his face commanded silence. His body posture assumed an attitude that inspired respect. He lowered his arm slowly and closed his eyes. Silence entered the room.

Tobin waited 20 seconds in silence. He turned to the trombone and fixed his eyes on the player. With a slow nod, he indicated that he would start at the beginning. His left arm rose up, and on the downbeat, the trombone started. His sister in the back of the room began to close her eyes. Cellos, flutes, and drums enriched the melody of the trombone. Other instruments coloured the scene, and the music was heard all along the corridor.

The conductor in the corridor had calmed down. On hearing the music, he returned to the hall and stood in the door-frame. Two bars before the most difficult piece, the one-armed man in front of the musicians made eye contact with the young violin players. He nodded a faint smile to the group and closed his eyes. Tobin's left hand turned upwards, fingers outstretched. Each finger represented two violinists. His head was bowed down, and all his energy was in his fingers. His whole arm began to vibrate with intensity, and the clawing fingers seemed to clasp into something. The violins translated this into sound, music, attack, violence, and fighting.

Asha had her eyes shut throughout the performance. The saturation of sound, the degree of depth, and the simmering of feelings stirred her imagination. She saw a painting unfolding in front of her inner eye, soft colours, strong colours, hues, and depth that she had never seen on any canvas. There was no shape as such, just mood and story and ever-changing colouration along with the music.
A deep red arc dominated the centre of her view. Contrasting bright white filled the right, and a thin streak of black filled the left of the red arc. It was not like paint, as the colours themselves had life and changed on their own. Never had she been able to see music as a vision.

The conductor, visibly overcome, still stood in the door-frame. He knew the piece well. Yet had never heard it played in this way before. The build-up was unusual yet fantastic, and the background framing was just constant enough to hold it all together. For the first time in his life, he would hear answers to questions that he never knew existed. There was nothing lacking. He stopped looking for faults and soaked the piece into his soul. Tobin's left arm steadily calmed the sounds to rest. The music ebbed out in silence. Tobin was exhausted. A few moments later, the musicians began to tap their instruments in respect. Asha came from the back of the hall, and arm in arm, they walked past the conductor, who was still standing in the door-frame. All were unable to speak, but they looked at each other as they walked past the conductor, exchanging a nod of greeting.

 The next eight months, Tobin added more scores to his work. Arranged and rearranged each instrument. He had never heard them all together. What would it be like? He wondered. In time, the composition was completed. Asha's painting style had changed since she saw music in her vision. Each piece that she painted was the condensation of a whole symphony, all on a canvas.

The Puma: Caged fights

The truck with the puma in the cage was just 50 miles from the harbour when it broke down. The driver worked on the engine but could not get it to start. Eventually, a second truck arrived. It backed up against the broken-down truck, and his cage was transferred to the back tray of the other. He could see the driver of the first truck lying motionless in the snow.
The puma's world would become what he had wished for. He was caged up and being abused by most who came near it. How many times was he exchanged for money? He had lost count.

A group of cruel people had bought him. They had two trucks and lived in them. From what he could make out, there were two children, six and eight-years old, the wife, her husband, and two of his brothers. All were mean and cruel. Sticks were hitting the cage. They rattled the cage, and the puma was in a constant state of agitation. Sometimes the woman would throw boiling water over the cat. Oh, she had a vicious streak in her.

The puma would learn how to earn his food. They would set up camp on the outskirts of townships and build an enclosed cage at the side of one of the trucks. For weeks, they would refuse the puma food and then set him up to fight another animal in the cage. They had the locals place bets on him or his opponent. They were always odd battles, fights against a bear or four dogs at once. His owners used him like a Roman gladiator and made bets with the locals. This is how he earned his keep. Once, they set him against three wolves. The cage was always too small, with little space to deal with three opponents at once. He could never choose his opponents. He was trapped in the cage, and there was only one way to get out of it alive. He had to learn to fight. He sustained countless injuries, but he learned to fight again. After the fights, the trucks would move on to the next place.

Over time, the puma noticed that the right side of the steel mesh had weakened in places from rust and that some of the welds had cracks. Bears were always good, as they had a lot of weight. He would coax them so that they would slam into the right side of the cage. He knew that a big brown bear could kill him if he ever got within reach. In between fights, he had to be content with sticks poked at his side, mostly from kids but also from adults who wanted to gauge his fire. His fire was well alight. His eyes had much better vision, and the blood in each victim was full of life.

How often was he paired up to fight? It took another three months of savage battles before the cage finally cracked. This time, the puma was matched against an older Siberian tiger. It was a very uneven match. The tiger had many battle scars. He was very large and heavy—almost 800 pounds—and he had a strong jaw. The puma, at 200 pounds, had only reflexes and agility against the tiger's strength and power, but very little space to use them. The puma could lose this fight easily.

During the engagement, both cats flew against the right wall of the cage, and the cracked welds parted. The mesh flew outward, and both cats were free. All the spectators jumped away and ran in panic for cover. The sight of a free tiger was something to behold. The tiger entered a farm building. The puma edged along the shadows of the buildings, finding dark cover inside the machinery shed.

The Puma: The escape

The three men who had him caged for so long gathered. They carried guns, nets and traps. Other men joined them in trying to recapture the animals. The puma preferred to hide in the darkness of the machinery shed. His eyesight had focus. He saw the tiger eventually running towards the snow, leaving a trail behind. Some locals assembled a pack of hound dogs that ran in all directions where the cats had been. It was disorganised chaos.

Two of the brothers entered the machinery building where the puma was hiding in. They carried sticks in each hand. The puma jumped from low on the ground and sank his fangs in the arm of the first man. Then he jumped the second and dug all his claws into his face. The screams of the two men alerted the others. All came running towards the building. The puma slid out through a window. He run towards the truck and jumped into the back of it. Huddled in the corner were the two children right in front of him. They could feel his breath against their faces. The youngest let out a high scream. The mother and her husband ran up to the truck.

Through the flapping tarpaulin, he could see her approaching. In one leap he jumped from the truck directly onto her. She fell over and twisted her leg. Her upper body was bleeding from the puma's claw marks. Her husband swung the stick and tried to hit the cat. The puma jumped out of the way and the man hit his wife instead as she raised her head at the wrong moment. She fell motionless backwards. The puma jumped forward to bite the man's upper leg, bringing him down, severing the muscles.

Most of the town's men had followed the tiger's trail in the snow. The puma jumped back into the truck to face the children once more. The youngest, still shaken, started to scream anew. Shortly later, the child passed out from fear. The eight-year-old was in shock and did not scream. She could not understand what had happened in the last few minutes. The puma let out a hiss at both of them. He left the carnage behind him and followed the tiger's tracks. A trail trampled by footprints, tyre marks and dog prints. Sometime later, he had caught up to the group of hunters. He was behind them, downwind. They had not yet caught up with the tiger. They had spread out and the dogs were now controlled on long leashes.

He waited for nightfall before he made his presence felt. In the silence of the night, he let out a high-pitched growl that would echo off the trees and surrounding rocks. He called out three times. Then he ran in long strides on the downwind side of the group in a five-mile arc around them. The puma and the tiger were in unfamiliar terrain. The flat fields did not offer any cover.

The Twins: The answer within

Once more, his spirit left and returned to the twins. Both were dressed for a night out. They sat in the second row of the concert hall. The conductor was the same one who once lost his temper. They noticed each other when he turned to the audience and bowed during the applause after the second piece. When the third piece was finished, the conductor stepped off the stage. He approached Tobin and handed him the baton while he whispered in his ear, "Would you do me the honour, please?" He held the man's arm and escorted him to the stage. He turned to the audience and apologised for the short interruption.

"Ladies and gentlemen, we have such unexpected good fortune to have this man in our audience tonight. It gives me great pleasure to introduce myself to you." His ear leant towards Tobin's mouth. It was then that the conductor realised that Tobin could not speak. He rephrased his address to the audience. "It gives me great pleasure and it is a privilege to introduce to you this man, who can bring this composition alive in front of your eyes. Please enjoy." He walked backwards off the stage with his arm outstretched towards the Tobin.

During the applause Tobin indicated to his sister to get his music from the car, then he turned towards the orchestra. He paused for some moments to focus his thoughts in silence. His sister left the building. He began conducting as he had done once before, trombones first.

Asha returned within a few minutes into the performance. At the side of the stage she handed musical scores to three helpers she had engaged, explaining which of the musicians would get what score.

During the applause, she sprang into action, and the scores for each instrument were placed in front of each musician. In the haste of the moment, some got mixed up, but they sorted it out themselves. The audience responded well to the performance and showered the orchestra and Tobin with spirited applause. Asha walked towards the conductor for the night and, in a charming manner, wrestled the microphone from his hands. She walked to centre stage, and with one arm, she pointed to her twin brother. With the other hand, she held the microphone and said, "My brother Tobin." She joined the audience in applauding him.

As the clapping died down, she said, "What you are about to hear is Tobin's first composition. No one has ever heard it before. Not even Tobin. It has never been rehearsed, and we do apologise for this slight diversion from the specified programme. Ladies and gentlemen, enjoy..." What did he name his piece? He scribbled it on her hand. "Please enjoy 'An Anat Ananta'." She left the stage and pulled the conductor for the night with her, profusely excusing her behaviour and apologising for this unplanned change. Tobin made eye contact with the player of the first instrument to begin the story. He twirled his finger in circles and gently formed them as if to pick a cherry off a tree. The musician's eyes jumped between scores and fingers, and within a few seconds, they knew what was expected.
Again, Tobin transposed all his thoughts into his left hand. Each finger drew the music out of the performers. The other conductor stood at the side of the stage, watching the composer direct his own piece for the first time ever. He did it all with his eyes shut; from time to time, he glanced at certain musicians as if to wake them up, two bars before their instruments were needed. Asha again sat with closed eyes throughout the performance.

Each instrument drew colours on the canvas in her mind, a haze of white, blue, and green. Heavy black, strong blues, then a rainbow of specks. Tobin was immersed in his creation. With eyes shut, his hand would find each instrument, alert the musician, and then draw the sound out into the concert hall.

The energy he spent in 15 minutes conducting could have lit the house for a year. Near the end of the piece, he was fatigued. She handed the microphone back to the other conductor and guided her brother off the stage. Both twins were filled with emotions, and the audience voiced their approval with loud applause and a long standing ovation.

Two days later, they received a recording of the unscheduled performance, both in vision and sound. Asha started on a fresh canvas as the recording of the concert played in the background. After six attempts, the canvas was loaded thick with paint, but it just would not come together. She stopped painting and set her focus just on the music. She absorbed it like a sponge soaking up water. The answer lay within herself and in the sound of 'An Anat Ananta.' The vision became clearer. The painting would never work on a flat canvas.

The Twins: The living canvas

She called Perrin and explained what she needed. A few days later, Perrin delivered a huge sphere, an 8-foot ball covered with canvas. He brought a stand for the object with a bar through its centre. This became Asha's new work. She made much progress. The work could rotate in all directions. There was no top or bottom, right or left; it could be viewed from all angles equally. Nine weeks later, the work was completed.

One could gaze at the piece, and no matter how long one looked at it, moments later it would reveal what did not appear to be there before. It became like the first painting she ever created, a new type of painting, 'Art on the Living Canvas.' When Tobin saw her completed work for the first time, he embraced her and kissed her eyes and hands. She kissed his hand, each finger, and his forehead. They were overjoyed to recognise the greatness they had pulled out of each other despite all odds. He absorbed the painting and found the sky, the heavens, clouds, endlessness, springs, water, purity, energy, might, and somehow infinity. No flat canvas could ever contain it. 'An Anat Ananta,' the sound as a vision.

During the week, Asha expected a visit from Yente Francis. When the gallery owner came and looked at the work, she thought Asha had gone mad. "This is not art; this is preposterous, an insult. You don't expect the gallery to go along with this type of ludicrous absurdity? What's gotten into you, Asha? This is just nonsensical kitsch and an embarrassment to the great work that you have done before. There is no way we can sell this sort of thing; we are not interested in lowering our standards to the level of this... whatsemacallit... this thing... this absurdity. It doesn't even have a name. Hokum, Tommyrot, nonsensical gimcrack. The gallery has a reputation to uphold... I'll find my own way out. Good Day."

Before Asha could even get a word in edge-ways, Yente had gone. Tobin had watched the whole display and could not hide his grin. He held Asha in a comforting hug. He scribbled on some paper: Oh, Asha, dear, be glad you're free. Dare you dare in defiance? The wrath of ordinary souls devours you. Thin may be the borderline between genius and madness. Whatever she is able to conceive is both her curse and her blessing. Trust in your knowledge.

'Anat' down, 'anat' up, in 'ananta'. Water falls and rises in endless circles. Who can claim to see through your eyes? Only one, and that is my darling Asha. Next day, both read the paper together and hugged again. Asha cheered up, saying, "Hokum, Tommyrot, nonsensical gimcrack?" They both broke out in discharging laughter.

The Twins: Gossip spreads

The gallery withdrew its support. Contacts with art dealers associated with the gallery became less and less frequent. Orders for commissioned work ceased to come in. It seemed that the gallery had far-reaching influence. Yente's opinion and negative gossip caused damage to Asha's reputation that was bigger than anticipated. It would be inconceivable for Asha to retract the work. It was beneath her self-respect to dignify Yente's gossip with any sort of response.

Only Perrin's friendship remained constant. Perhaps the gossip never reached him, but most likely he couldn't care less about the opinions of others. On her mixing palette, she found one of Tobin's scribbles: "Oh Asha dear, we know no fear." Once more, Asha reached for the brushes. This time, the work was born from a vision in her mind. Path, panther, painter, paws, power, and pouncing went through her head. She started edging in a soft haze of strong, bold colours towards the centre. Heavy greens with whites were dominating the centre. Sharp grey lines with hints of yellow, small streaks of orange, a dark line, and grey stretched into the depth of the work. Black dominated the upper right. Dots curled towards the depth. She scribbled on the rear, 'The Puma's Trail,' and put it away. Tobin never saw it.

The Twins: At Perrin's place

Perrin had a new project. A large marble boulder was delivered on a truck. The twins entered his workshop. Tobin ventured towards the displays and was absorbed in examining Perrin's completed projects while Asha walked under the deck towards the work area.

Perrin drove the forklift into the building to position the boulder. As he drove through the entrance, the swinging boulder hit the wooden post on the door-frame. The boulder slipped from the sling and fell against a tall stack of raw materials: sandstone blocks, granite pieces, and smaller marble blocks. The tower collapsed.

Tobin heard the noise and jumped. One of the boulders rolled away and dislodged a support post for the upper deck. Tobin looked around for Asha. He tried calling out to her, but his voice failed him. He could not get it out. The weight of the deck above forced a partial collapse of the upper floor. Asha was trapped, buried under posts, debris, and heavy rocks. Then the whole deck gave way and crushed her. Asha did not survive.

The Puma: Albatross finding the edge

Before returning, the puma's spirit rises within an albatross as a carrier reaching high. He is heading south-east beyond the shipping lanes that connect Africa and the land of the Southern Cross. Four days on, and the horizon reveals a hint of things to come. From 800 miles away, the ring of grey-hazed edges reaches from the sea to the sky. Its top is tapering outwards, and it is deep black in its core. The funnel measures 2,000 miles across.

The albatross no longer needs its wings as it is drawn into the rotating weather tower. This is no cyclone, hurricane, or wind of fury. There is no heat rising from its core. Nothing comes out.

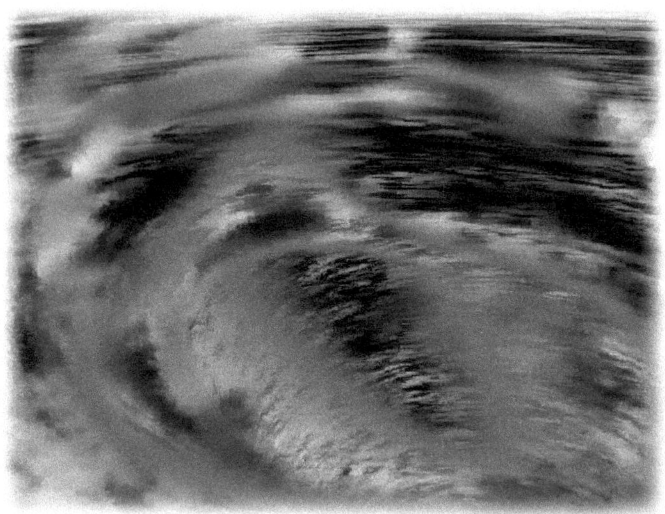

The albatross becomes sucked into the rotation. The internal force of this huge funnel overcomes gravity. Try as he may, the albatross cannot control its flight. Even if its size were a hundredfold, it could not resist the force that governs this funnel. The path is in ever-descending circles, downwards and inwards. It is impossible to fall or rise. As a particle in a vortex, the albatross is swept along, powerless within a spiralling path.

Inside the giant vortex, the haze starts clearing the view. The noise is deafening from a low-pitched roar that is in constant rotation. Towards the inner, a high screeching howl cuts the sense of hearing. The speed of descent is slow as the circle of the funnel reduces in size. Beneath, far below, the ocean is whipped up in high seas, yet there is no direction. The waves stirred up from all sides. As the albatross is drawn into the forced descent, the waves form a whirlpool. The outer edges seem to resist in a violent fight to submit to the force of the whirling suction. The immense beauty of this violent display of force transfixes the bird's eye. Unaware that he is no longer white, no longer a bird at all, but being stripped of its feathers by force. The eyes are the carriers. These eyes will not find rest to absorb the view. Eyes in motion, absorbing the display in ever-changing wonder As if the water itself is in convulsion, fighting against the downward swirl. Spits of water droplets cut the eye. There is not a moment of rest.

Then gradually the water succumbs, as if frozen in shape, and the waves form solid rock. Black granite and splinters of sharp-edged stone cover the whole shape of the transformed waves and whirlpool. As an island in the ocean, the water surrounds the rocky formation. Wetness and spray cover each surface. There, the being's eye is hypnotised by the awe before it. Embedded within the dark structure are some coloured specks of jewellery.

Lumps of opals and rubies are next to clusters of diamonds and some emeralds. Gems set amidst the granite. Fear sets in for the first time. The question does the calling, and here it screams its answer towards the eye. The wind drives the body

closer to the sharp-edged shapes. The funnel size is decreasing in the vortex. Helplessly, the body is tossed along the funnel's sharp-edged walls. Bits of torn-off flesh are bouncing off the splintered rocks as lumps of meat, still bleeding. The body is detached from pain. There is just awareness. There is no way out of this. This is a meat grinder, a giant mincer. There can only be one outcome. 'This must be hell.' The roaring winds answer the question, "Hell? No."
'Are these the gates of hell?' The winds screech in laughter. "You're nowhere near the turbines. You are on the edge of doom. That is all. Go past the edge down there, and you shall see a sign that says, 'Welcome to your dream come true'."

The roaring laughter turns to a howl. The body bounced off the razor-sharp edges of the hard-faced outer funnel. Each contact is tearing more meat off the bones that fly in chunks their own paths. There is not much left of the legs, just splintered bones and mangled remains. With each turn past the jewels, the red gems sparkled, and the diamond clusters seemed like markers of the path. Despite all the horror of this shredding funnel experience, it brought forth an awe-inspiring awareness, the fascination of the 'never seen.' With each turn, the gates come closer, claiming torn flesh and shattered bones. The muscles' tendons trail the body like strings without purpose. Wings lost muscles, and the body was cut and maimed. Each part lost is dancing beneath or above in swirling, spiralling motions. In time, the eye itself would join the mangled mess.

If this is not yet the edge of doom, then there is hope. Hope must flare to consume despair. Fear must cower and be overcome. The eye is just a messenger. It has no knowledge. Then the answer came above the eye. An eagle's talon is reaching down, hovering, and attempting to come closer. The body twists, aiming to swing the lifeless wing towards the grasp of the eagle's claw. Four times it fails. Succeed just once. Heed this command. Again, the body tries. The shoulder swings forwards. The wing rotates and slams towards the eagle until the mangled tendons wrap around the eagle's leg. The eagle's claw closes around the remains.

Which type of eagle would have such strength? Dare one not dwindle the power of hope that saves? The eagle is, and so is hope. There is an answer. Be. With each five wing-flaps reaching upwards, the funnel claimed four as it's due. The rubies watched. The diamond managed to score once more. The smudged blood will not leave lasting stains. The eagle is rising, however slowly and painfully, until the talons release their grip.

In falling, the remains of the albatross transform and become alive in the hands of a child as a toy. He is leaving one nightmare of enormous proportions to arrive in another as a helpless object. The child plays on a garden path with a toy bus. He puts the toy from his hand into the door of the bus. As a toy, this bus becomes real. The driver invites the living toy, "Please do come in. This bus just goes one way, and once it moves, there is only one destination. Do not worry about the fare. This trip is free." The voice is reminiscent of the tunnel's roars. The bus driver pulls the lever, and the door shuts. He turns the key. Un-wish a wish once wished. The child pushes the bus down the garden path. From within the bus, the path seems like a real highway. The speed, which is much too fast, is causing the bus to swerve until it hits a tree. The toy passenger flies out of the window. The toy is free.

The Puma: Trapped with a tiger

The spirit returned to the puma. He could sense that he was near the tiger. He had left the plains behind, and he was on the outer boundaries of a changing landscape. Out of nowhere, the tiger appeared above him, growling. He appeared much larger now than he ever was in the cage. His jaw could easily crush the puma. He still had blood in his fur. The puma lay flat on the ground, observing the tiger with caution while his hind legs were primed for a quick escape. The tiger growled again, pacing from side to side and reaching with one paw towards the puma. Both were male, and instinctively, they would have to fight each other, but none owned this territory. Three shots rang out in quick succession. Each splintering the rock the tiger stood on. Small stone fragments flew through the air. Both cats leapt off the clearing and ran higher up the boulders, seeking cover behind trees and surrounding bushes. Both have just one enemy to fear. The tiger's kind is near the point of extinction. Even within his lifetime, three kinds of his race have gone forever. 'Siberian' may be his name, but it is no longer his home. Their enemy has already claimed their names and those of countless others for a myriad of products that are without claws and can never growl.

Within a few minutes, they could hear the dogs barking. They would need to deal with the dogs somehow. The men would not be as fast on this terrain. No cars or bikes could chase them here. From a distance, they watched the first hound dogs be released from their leashes. Without hesitation, they raced up the side of the boulders. Then another dog was released, and another, and another. Five dogs were free.

Chains restrained another eight hounds. The first dog that came up the ridge was easy to deal with. The tiger stood exposed on a ledge and growled, calling him. The dog, in his eagerness, ran full speed, not realising the deep cliff between him and the tiger. He could not stop in time and grumbled into the depths of the rocks, yelping as he hit the rocks on the way down. The second dog stopped just in time when he realised the deep channel in the rock.

From behind the dog, the puma pounced and attacked. As the dog backed off, he too would join the other when he lost his footing on the edge. The remaining three dogs arrived together, and the trick did not work this time. All had picked up the puma's scent, and the need to avoid injury left escape as an easy option. The dogs had used up a lot of energy getting up the boulders, but they still had plenty left. The puma ran with all three dogs close on his tail. All four animals ran in a straight line when, suddenly, the tiger came from the side and grabbed the second dog. He cracked his skull in the first bite. With the lifeless dog in his jaw, he followed the puma. The puma ran, chased by the two remaining dogs. Then he stopped running and turned towards the approaching dogs. The first dog was knocked out in one blow. Three seconds later, the last dog was silenced too.

The men who gave chase would find two of the dogs in 45 minutes. They would also hear of the carnage the puma had left behind at the trucks. When they saw the carcasses of the two dogs and three more dogs still missing, they organised on a much bigger scale. Calls for help went out to the villages near the area, and more hunters joined the men. While they stayed within the rocky forest, the others surrounded the periphery. Judging by the blood on the Siberian tiger, he might have also settled some scores of his own. The tiger and puma would realise within three days the trap they were in. There were another eight dogs restrained on leashes and chains within the forest, and hundreds of men with fresh dogs had arrived outside of the forest.

The cats did not know the terrain; the men did. Each time the cats reached the outskirts of the forest, they would see a circle of men, each armed with a rifle. A puma could never hide in the white snow during the day. Not even the tiger would have been able to get through the circle.

The Puma: Encircled

The circle around the forest became tighter when the men on the outside entered the forest as well. The puma and the tiger left scents in each direction, which started to confuse the dogs. Dogs could never climb a tree. Dogs could not jump as far or as high as cats. Dogs could never move in silence, and neither could men. Cats have sharper vision in the dark, a better sense of hearing, and can outrun dogs any day. Hunger set in for the puma. He climbed down the crevasse and claimed one of the first two dogs that fell there. For five days now they were entrapped in the forest. At night, a circle of fires surrounded the place, and the dogs would quickly respond to their scent.

The weather turned, and a snowstorm would punish all that were not covered. The puma tried to break out and inched towards the now extinguished flames. The storm provided enough diversion for the cats. He jumped through the circle, followed by the tiger. The men would not realise that the cats had broken out until the next morning.

They only had a 6-hour head start on the hunters, which was not much on the plains. They left trails in the snow that were partially covered, and the hunters were motorised in the open areas. By two o'clock in the afternoon, they had reached a creek frozen with ice that was just thick enough to carry their weight. This would give them a little extra time. No matter how fast they were racing, the motorised, bloodthirsty hunters would catch up to them.

Late in the afternoon, the first cars came within range. There was no place to hide in the flat landscape. The few leafless, isolated trees did not grant any refuge. The drivers spotted the cats, and it became a game to chase and encircle the cats. The first three cars and more joined the chase. Both cats were fast, but not after such a long chase.

They scaled the only tree nearby to catch their breath. This time, the cars formed a tight circle around the tree. All the men spread around the tree, and large nets were placed on long poles. The sky turned orange with the setting sun. There were lots of rifles and double-barrelled shotguns. They could transform the tree into a sieve if they wanted to. The men were eager to catch the cats before nightfall.

Some started shooting near the tiger, trying to unsettle his balance. He climbed higher. They shot near his hind legs, and the bark of the branches splintered open. The tiger climbed higher still. Again, they shot behind his hind legs. The branch cracked under the weight of the tiger, and he lost his footing. He fell into the next branch, then two more until he was on the ground. All the men at once threw the net over him, and the tiger became hopelessly entangled. The dogs chained to the cars and trucks barked without resting. A lot of noise came from men and beasts.

The puma sensed his chance and jumped from a very high branch to the ground. He ran towards a truck and slid underneath to the outside of the temporary enclosure. Most men were busy trying to restrain the tiger. Five bullets zoomed past his ears as he ran away. Half the men gave chase. They formed a wide line, giving the puma little chance to disappear. More shots rang out. He tried to break away near the outer car that chased him, but they rearranged themselves quickly to keep the cat in the centre. Blood frothed from his mouth. The outlines of buildings became visible in the distance. If he could last another 30 minutes, he would have darkness on his side. He looked back to see which chances he would have when he ran full speed into a wire fence and stumbled.

Within moments, all the cars had stopped and men with clubs would beat down on him. They tied his legs with wire, covered his head with a leather jacket, and wired it around his neck. His body then thrown into the back of a truck. The puma was unconscious and bleeding from the hits to his body.

The Puma: Recaptured

It was near midnight by the time all the cars and trucks had arrived at the place where the cage fights had taken place earlier. They spent five days on the run just to end up here again. The puma was still unconscious. The tiger looked a mess. The man, his wife, and his two brothers arrived with their arms and faces bandaged to claim the puma. More of the town's people joined the crowd. Telling stories of courage and bravery, how that one nearly did this and the other one almost did that, and how lucky they all were to be still alive. Some called out for the owner of the tiger. The undertaker answered, "I buried him yesterday. The tiger did him good. I couldn't make out if he was a man or mince meat from the butcher, thanks to that one," he added, pointing at the tiger. "So what do we do with him?" one called out. "Let's kill the bloody killer!" another yelled while he kicked the tiger in the side.

The tiger growled at the entangled nets. "He'd take all of us if he could," another added, poking the tiger with a stick. One man returned from a truck, cocked his rifle, approached the tiger, and pointed the barrel at its head. "Hold it, guys," the married man with the bandages called out. "I'll have him." "Just throw him in the cage over there and let's all have a drink together; it's too bloody cold out here anyway," he said. They threw both cats in separate cages and woke up the owner of the Pub. The men drank and retold tales of bravery until the next morning.

The Puma: The punishment

The puma had woken up. Each of his legs was wired to a stake. A dog's muzzle, crudely wired together, restrained his jaw. The tiger lay in a similar position, with long stripes of blood seeping through his fur. Instead of being nearly white, the tiger's fur was pink and red and soaked in his own blood. He lay silent in the dirt.

The three men, with bandaged limbs and faces, approached the puma. In a fury of revenge, they hit him with barbed wire strands. The woman too, broke two broomsticks on his back. The puma struggled. With each move, the wire cut deeper into his legs. 'Am I in hell?' he wondered. Both his pupils narrowed to a thin slit, and his tail twitched from side to side.

Both children cried behind the truck's windows. The assault lasted for seven minutes.

The cats woke up in separate cages as the truck drove to another destination. They arrived near another township. The men built their fighting cages, and the puma knew another fight for life was in the making. The locals surrounded the cage, and the man took bets on both the tiger and the puma. Another freak show got underway. They led the puma into the larger cage first. Then they enticed the tiger to enter. Both animals were agitated, but not with each other. They tried with sticks, with water, and with loud yells, but the cats would not engage in a fight with each other.

"What is this crap?" one calls out. "I have put five grand on the tiger. I want my money back. My pussycat at home has more fire than these two together," he said. More people became disgruntled. "Yeah, money back!" another yelled out. "Get out of here, you losers," another advised the owners of the animals. "What sort of scheme is this?" yet another wanted to know. The group made no money at this place.

The Puma: The nightmare

They packed up and left. Some miles out of town, they stopped their trucks and discussed amongst themselves what to do next. One of the brothers said, "What if we keep both cats and let them fight against whatever the town folks put up?" The husband added, "Yep, that way, even if we lose one of them, we still have one spare." The wife added, "We should match the tiger against the stronger opponents and the puma against all the rest." The other brother injected, "We just keep quiet about what types of cats we've got, and once we see the challenger, we bring the best cat to the cage; that way we'll never lose."

"And if they don't come up with any challengers, we collect a bunch of stray dogs, wild wolves, bears, or whatever and put them up ourselves," one brother said. They all agreed to keep them both, but they never set them against each other again. "If we don't get any decent challengers, we'll find them somewhere. We could just get some kittens or puppies and bet on how many seconds they could survive before they were shredded to bits," the husband added with a grin. "Yep, we'll be in the money sooner than you think," his wife said.

The two kids overheard the conversation. The nightmare of what they heard would unfold in their dreams. The engines of the trucks started, and they moved on. Sometime later, they came to rest in a forest in a large clearing. The next day they sat in the larger cage, and the men drove into town to meet prospective gamblers. They would usually find them in pubs. In the afternoon of the same day, lots of cars arrived at the clearing. Two trucks brought the new challengers. Some of the men brought their sons. One of the sons met up with the two kids of the owners. They showed him the cats in the cages on the enclosed truck. The truck had four cages. Two were empty. Each of the cages had a door on each side of the truck. The left side of the truck formed part of the fighting cage. The door on this side used to let the cats into the fighting area. Flaps covered the cage doors to prevent anyone from looking in. The first challengers entered the big fighting cage, three Dobermans at once.

The boy who had seen the cats earlier went back to the right side of the enclosed truck. The area was dark. Instead of locks, a tractor pin with a spring pin secured the cage doors. He pulled the springs off of both cages. Then he sat in a car and giggled, using a long stick to lift the tractor pins out of the door. He then shut the car window. The doors of the cages were still closed but no longer locked. On the other side of the truck, poles with open flames shone light into the fighting cage. Nearby, the three men collected the money for the bets. The two kids saw the boy in the car and approached him. Some moments later, one of the brothers opened the cage door for the tiger on the left side of the truck, so the animal could enter the big cage.

The husband walked to the dark side of the truck and reached for a stick to poke the tiger, enticing it to go into the big cage. It was then that he realised that the pins had gone. The tiger hit the door, and it flew open. The husband covered his face with both arms as the tiger pounced and mauled him. The cage shook as he jumped, and the puma's cage door opened from the movement. The kids screamed as the tiger mauled their father right in front of them. The tiger heard the children scream and left the mauled man to jump towards them. The puma was closer and jumped from the cage forwards to put his body in front of the children, hissing at the tiger.

The two brothers ran from the big cage to the other side of the truck. The tiger turned and took one of the men down with his claws. The puma jumped at him. When she realised what was going on, the wife grabbed a pole and raised it to hit the tiger. She then saw her husband motionless on the ground. She let out a hysterical scream that alerted everyone in the clearing. The three dogs inside the cage jumped up through the open cage door, through the tiger's truck cage, and out the other side. All three attacked the screaming woman. The pole flew out of her hand forwards, and the flame ignited the straw in one of the cages. Wads of money flew through the air. Blood splattered across the car windows. The boy behind the windscreen held both arms over his head and cried uncontrollably. The two children stood frozen, unable to move. All the other men ran in confusion, no one knowing what to do.

Within a few seconds, all the animals had left, leaving nothing but carnage behind. The truck was now well alight and illuminated the eerie scene. Apart from the sound of the fire, silence and shock sat in. Someone noticed the children. Others looked at the victims. Most of the rest looked around the clearing, wondering if the animals would return. In twenty-three seconds, two children had lost both their parents and their uncles. Three years later, they would become aware that a black cat had saved their lives, but they would remember little else.

The oldest man collected all the money that was scattered across the clearing and put it in a plastic bag. He raised the bag and called out, "I think this belongs to the kids. Any objections?" "Nope," "so it does," "it's theirs," he heard. No one objected. He guided the kids to his car, looked through the cabin of the truck, and found personal belongings that he also brought to his car. The tank of the first truck exploded and splattered some fuel onto the second one, which also caught fire. The next day, the clearing was filled with reporters and TV crews from everywhere, and pictures of the surviving children appeared in all newspapers. The animals branded as "Killers roam free!" It made headlines for days. No one would ever discover how the whole event could have happened, as the boy who pulled the pins would wipe six months of his memory. No one would even know that a tiger and puma were on the scene. All they knew was that three Dobermans and some unknown beasts had been involved. The dogs would find their own way home. Their owners were glad to see their stolen animals again. They would never realise what the dogs had experienced.

The Twins: Two Graves

Tobin stood on Asha's grave. Five years had already passed. "Oh, Asha, dear, you're always near." He opened the bunch of flowers and spread them in an arc across her grave. Five difficult years were behind him. Not a single day went by that he didn't think of Asha.

Tobin placed the other bunch of flowers on the next grave. "Well Perrin, dearest friend, the burden you must have carried to make you do it." Perrin joined Asha two weeks after the accident. He shed tears for both and shared time with his twin sister and their friend. "The huge marlin you carved out of solid rock graces the harbour now. Each ship that goes out passes the spot with respect. You are sadly missed, my friend. Take care of Asha on the other side."

A new block of flats has grown on Perrin's old place. The shed was demolished shortly after the tragic accident. Life does not stop for the living. Tobin rarely finds time these days away from commitments. He worked with dedication to his music. It fulfilled his calling. Tobin was in high demand. His reputation opened many doors. Success kept following him.

The Twin: Searching for sound

Tobin had found Asha's painting, which she had named 'The Puma's Trail'. Often, Tobin was absorbing the depth of his sister's work. On one side, he noticed dots in slightly darker shading. They looked familiar. Then he recognised the coded language of their childhood. A message from Asha is concealed within dots. He noted the dots and tried to recall how they unscrambled them when they were children. The dots deciphered extracted their letters: 'Anarchy in the mind; surprise what there you find.' He searched and found more dots. Amongst them, I love Asha.' To Tobin, it meant 'love life' and inspired him.

He analysed the work somewhat detached from the sensations of mood and emotions. He studied the colours, the blend, and the soft flow from one shading to another. The smooth harmonising intermixes of so many elements in the work He wondered what that would sound like. Which instruments could blend so softly? At this point, he remembered the conductor, who had left the rehearsals in anger. The violins held the answer. No piano could ever produce music between the notes. So many instruments were forced into the limiting boxes of notes. All that came about when instruments started to be tuned chromatically. Between C and C#, there are so many frequencies that no piano could ever reach. What would it sound like using all frequencies? The half-string frequencies of octaves, the division of an octave into 12 even segments, and the mathematical segmentation of nature restrict freedom.

Had anyone ever measured a magpie's frequencies? Does it fit into our accepted view of harmonics? Even Mozart used a starling whistler. The world of sound in birds, whales, dolphins, and elephants is language. Whatever it is they are communicating, it may well be food, violence, or sex at its core. Twelve even steps per octave are like robberies of sound. If music is universal and speaks to the soul, could it not speak much clearer if it could use all the spectrum of waves that are available? Every painter blends colours to get onto canvas what his inner eye summons.

Watching the flight and fight of birds in the park inspired him with a new vision. He saw birds and the merciless violence and tenderness of nature, the diversion and similarities across species. At this moment, Tobin started composing again. Starvation and abundance, love and hate, excitement and desperation, trust and betrayal, imprisonment and freedom, and all the nuances in between became his themes.

He took time to study the painting again, this time with a magnifying glass. The valleys, the ridges, the brush marks, the holes where the paint had dried somewhat differently, another world came into view. If he were an ant walking on the canvas, that would be all he could see. The combination of colour and texture has nothing to do with each other. The imperfection within the apparent beauty fascinated him. What if the properties were reversed? Harmony and popularity are in stark contrast to reality. He wanted to break out of established conventions.

A brew of thoughts simmered in his head. Once thought, thought could not be 'un-thought,' which is unthinkable. Chaos, harmony, dissonance, beauty, ugliness, purity, bastardisation, cleanliness, and filth, side by side, and all that in a sound, or silence. The silence in a sound, the thought, occupied him. If you hear nothing, that does not mean there is no sound. If they are perfectly out of phase, they will cancel each other out. The search for the unknown began. He wanted more than a conventional composition. He sought a performance that required audience participation and the involvement of the senses.

A lion's roar is sound, but it means a lot more when he charges at you in real life. Sound is a warning, is communication and is threat or invite. Sound is only part of something else. He wanted the audience to feel this, to live a sound. It was to be a musical piece with a difference. It was difficult to write, and even more difficult to combine in his head. He organised five pianos, specially modified to accommodate different strings. He needed seven, but finding the money for it became a big issue. Each piano could only play one octave, but it used all of its 88 keys. Not 12 divisions, but 88 keys for each octave. It would still be a compromise, but who knows where it could lead. It was a stepping-stone of sorts to break out of conventions.

Then he needed to train five pianists so they could reproduce his composition, five musicians playing as one. Normal scores would not work, so he devised a special way of writing for each of the specially tuned pianos. While each musician had been an accomplished player, the new sounds these piano keys made would make playing very difficult. Reading and playing required much concentration and the ears needed time to adjust to the pitch of new notes that reverberated from the wing. A lifetime of musical conditioning was hard to overcome for this one piece.

Cello, violin and trombone filled the arrangement. The logistical problems of having five grand pianos on a stage at once were overcome. The structural work to modify the concert hall behind closed doors raised the question: How would it all transpire? At times he questioned his mental balance with doubts of madness creeping into his head. The brave defies, the coward fears and every risk is a venture. The financial problems were swept under the carpet for the time being. The piece was very complex. One could never play it twice in the same way.

The Twins: The sharing of a new sound

Months of preparation lay ahead. The tour dates are fixed, with the first public performance scheduled for Saturday night. The Press had been invited, as had notable names in the music industry. Each one was eager to partake in an event that promised to be a once-in-a lifetime opportunity. A composer is breaking new ground. Tobin was nervous. Much was at stake: prestige, bookings, contracts, income, and a hard-earned reputation.

The night of the first performance of this composition was about to begin. His 20-second silence to focus was now interrupted twice when the baton slipped through his moist fingers. The little stick made the sound of a steel pipe falling from the ceiling, if only in his ears. He had now been standing for three minutes in front of the musicians. Doubts, fear, and the need to compromise raced through his head. The sounds of little coughs and restlessness became apparent in the audience.

The Twins: The Performance

He raised his arm and indicated to the musicians to get ready for the beginning of the piece. Two pianists started, and one of them hit five wrong notes in the first few seconds. The others joined, and again, more errors reached his ears. Tobin started to break out in a cold sweat. The piece was difficult to read, very hard to play, and required great effort to direct.

Four minutes into the piece, it became challenging and offered the ears no comfort. The expectation of a perceptual experience of beauty became shattered for many of the listeners. Instead of hearing a glorious, clear sunrise, the morning was dim with grey clouds and the dirt of garbage, whichever picture the listener attached to the sound. The coughs from the audience became louder. Some groups giggled. From the back, a loud whistle cut over the music. One man broke out in uncontrollable laughter, soon to be followed by groups of people joining in. More restlessness set in. A good 60% of the audience let their feelings of disapproval free reign. Despite this, Tobin regained his focus. The pianists made some more errors, as the lifelong conditioning of piano training was of little help with the very unusual tuning. It was strenuous work to stay focused. One ran off the stage so as not to be associated with the piece. Tobin continued the performance undeterred.

One could not escape the noise of dislike that turned to ridicule. Tobin exchanged his baton for a torch from his pocket. Upon his signal, all the lights went out at once. In the darkness, the sharp crashing sounds of metal objects came from the centre walkway. The performance continued throughout the darkness. Screams could be heard from the audience, boos of displeasure and outcries of contempt. Sharp, pulsing light flashes lit up the hall for fractions of a second. On another signal from the conductor, the curtains opened the full width of the stage. As soon as they fully opened, a stack of high-powered spotlights on each side of the stage switched on, virtually blinding the audience.

It was then that people became aware of the flying insects released into the back of the hall. Many started hitting out. Tobin had calculated the attraction the spotlights would have on the flying insects. He did not expect the heat of the lights to release smouldering odours and small clouds of smoke as they burned so many at once. Then the lights switched off again. Only the dying glows of the hundreds of lights were visible. As the glow reached total darkness, silence set in. Silence from the musicians. Only the noise of the audience filled the hall. Intermittent sounds of trombone came sometimes from the left, then the right, but never from near the stage. Some moments later, short blasts seemed to come from all directions. Then the sounds began rotating, as if the trombone players ran circles around the audience and blasted short bursts. This rotation became more and more organised and lively. As if two were running around, then three, four, and six, always rotating. It was hard to figure out in which direction the stage was, although the fixed seats would only indicate one direction.

From overhead, a very fine mist is released at certain areas above the listeners. Groups would call out. Others started shouting. Then the direction of the blasts changed and gradually reduced in volume. Then the sounds of all trombones and all other instruments came from the rear, except the pianos. A row of flickering candles lit up in front of the musicians. The stage seemed to have moved. All were now behind the seats. The lights in the hall started very gradually to illuminate the hall. They were all facing a closed curtain. The stage was now behind the seats.

Confusion sat in. Which is the way out of here? Yells of disapproval, displeasure, and even abuse became louder. The musicians on the rear stage parted towards each side of the stage. The stage floor hinged up, revealing the exits in the rear. The curtain closed, hiding the two half-stages. From the front stage, the pianos started playing. Many in the audience had enough. In droves, they left the hall, shouting out insults. Many of the insects still fluttered inside the hall. The sounds ebbed out, replaced by the audience leaving the building.

Tobin's composition was completed. The performance had reached its end. All the musicians had assembled on the front stage and did the customary bow. Tobin turned to the audience and bowed too, but no one expected to hear applause. The director of the concert hall could not believe what had happened to his sacred hall of music. In resignation, he shook his head. The musicians withdrew behind the curtains.

After some rest, Tobin walked to the change room and thanked each of the pianists, the 24 trombone players, all other musicians, and everyone involved in the performance. Some apologised for hitting the wrong keys. "No, no, no, it added randomisation. Do you think each sunrise is the same?" he said through his speech device to the group. "You are all excellent musicians, and it is I who must thank you from the bottom of my heart," he added.

The critics spoke plainly in the next day's newspapers. All wrote similar negative reviews, each trying hard to outdo the others with superlatives that were more descriptive. Headlines such as "There was a madman let loose at the concert hall," "Lunacy and insanity composed this composer," "Havoc Hall," "Disturbance by disturbed composer," "It moved the audience, straight out the door," "Composer's compost," "Composer breaking new ground," with the subtitle "Damage to the concert hall parquetry estimated at $19500." The only one not joining the common view was Mr. Poison Pen himself.

Tobin read the review: "Is it not a shame that last night's audience adopted a supermarket mentality and dared to bring it through the sacred doors of our concert hall, hailing a barrage of abuse at our own composer and conductor, Tobin?

I, for one, would have preferred to hear the piece without interjection until the end. For the first time in my life, I have been ashamed and embarrassed to be sitting in the concert hall. Not because of the performance, but because of the uncultured mob all around me. I pitied them as they moved towards the exit, none realising that their feet were seemingly trapped knee-deep in the mud of the latest vogue, current trends, and the style of the day. It was indeed an audible audience." The next day, however, the paper retracted the article, explaining that it had been reproduced in error, caused by a mix-up.

The Twins: The loss of things

Three concerts scheduled over the coming weeks for Toby were cancelled via a short phone calls. More cancellations followed. Financial disaster, whichever way he looked at it. The house was mortgaged to the hilt to cover the cost of the long preparation, special instruments, and a long list of expenses. Worse news came when two of the pianists withdrew from what was left of the tour. At such short notice, they couldn't be replaced. As a result, the whole concert tour was over before it began. So much potential income evaporated in front of his eyes. They could be sued for not fulfilling the contracts; compensation claims for loss of opportunity. One night in his life changed everything. The flow of money stopped all together. No one wanted to associate with him.

He suffered ridicule and became excluded from society. The banks soon started knocking at the door. Men came to claim the contents of the house. They allowed him to collect his personal belongings. When Tobin wanted to take his sister's artwork, the men intervened and politely but firmly guided him out of the house. The piano, instruments, furniture, or anything of any value was auctioned off. It was a sad day when the property sold. He lost a lot.

The Puma: The finding

Both cats had left the clearing far behind. They found a pristine lake with forests rising on the eastern side. Thirty miles inside the forest, the land rose steep and high. Eagles would take off to soar above the valley. Several miles of grasslands adjoined the forest on the western side. This land was claimed by the tiger as his kingdom. He marked it with his scent. The puma, being much more elusive, claimed the higher regions. This felt like home instinctively, a paradise of wilderness. On occasion, they met. Once, they were within 20 feet of each other when they heard a distant rifle shot. It was the first sign of human activity in six months. Another time, the puma was engaged in a fight with a large brown bear. He could not bring the bear down. The roar of the bear and the noise of the battle called the tiger out. In a powerful pounce from the side, the tiger brought the bear down, severing its jugular vein. It was their second time joining in battle. They shared some of the prey, but the tiger made a huge claim on the kill. The puma could never feel safe with the tiger.

One morning, the puma drank at the lake. As he walked in the shadows of the rocky outcrops, the tiger pounced from above, digging his claws into the puma's back. The puma rolled away and raced up the rocks in a hasty escape. The tiger could not keep up. They would never join again. The puma retraced his steps with the strong odour of his urine a bit higher up the mountain. It was still a huge territory. Some months later, the sounds of trouble echoed from the rocks. Far-away sounds of rifle shots cut through the afternoon. Eight shots, at least, he heard. From a high vantage point, he had a clear view of the valley below. There was something in the valley that did not belong, but it was in the tiger's domain.

A week later, the puma ventured towards the lower reaches of the forest. He can see the lake. Two men collect water from the lake. The puma advances within 100 yards. Upright against a backpack stands a rifle. One of the men is crouched down, filling his water bottles. The other man is sitting nearby, holding both arms around his knees. His head rests on his knees. The puma advances forwards. The man near the water's edge screws a lid on the containers, stands up and turns around.

The puma is now within 50 yards. The man sees the puma approaching. He hesitates, then tries to run towards the rifle. The puma accelerates. The man figured that he would not reach his weapon and turned back to run into the water. Frantically, he swims to get away from the water's edge. The puma races into the water. He leaps onto the man. The other man reaches for the rifle. The fight in the water throws up sprays and makes aiming at the puma difficult. The fight is short. The puma now turns towards the man with the rifle. A shot rings out, and the bullet enters the water close to the puma. The man turns away, runs, and climbs the nearest tree. After 18 seconds, it was all over.

The next day, the puma ventured out towards the plains, backtracking on the men's trail. He arrived at a small campsite. Pots and plates littered the area. The ashes in the fireplace were cold. He found a vehicle abandoned. The hood for the engine was open. He circled the vehicle. The rear gate and one of the side doors were open. There was no one inside. He found the tiger's dead body in front of the car. He'd been shot many times. The smell of death and decay lingered. The odour of soil mixed with the gas of decomposing heaps. Each aligned next to the other, four graves in all.

The Puma: Return to the woods

Deep in his kingdom, far to the east, the puma found recently disturbed earth. He sniffed out droppings. Within a few days, he saw a young female of his kind, followed by three of her blue-eyed young. He did not sniff out the scent of another male. Without hesitation, the puma swooped down on the spotted young and killed all three. Some months later, the female came into season again. They joined in mating. They joined in hunting. The two fought wolves, occasional elk, and sometimes brown bears. He lived in times as similar as the memories of days long past, rejuvenated by a found purpose.

The Twins: Years on

Years had passed, and the remaining twin had become an old man. Far removed from the lifestyle he once enjoyed. That is not to say that he didn't enjoy the style of life he was living now. He chanced upon an advertisement for an exhibition: 'Music on Canvas: A Collection of Works by Various Artists.' Tobin, now 72, walks slowly into the gallery. In the foyer, there is a huge ball. Motorised and mechanised, the ball would rotate around any which way, amidst the cone of three soft spotlights. He grinned as soon as he saw it. He bent down to read the inscription on the label: 'An Anat Ananta'. One of the last paintings of the great Asha. For Sale by private collector. $ 5,200.000. No offers.

Still grinning, he thought to himself, 'Oh, Asha dear, it is still a painting. See how the wheels have turned. Any of your brushes would fetch more today than you have ever seen in your lifetime. Five million bucks worth of hokum, Tommyrot, and nonsensical gimcrack." He was very amused.

As he moved through the gallery, he found another of his sister's works, 'The Conductor', the one she had painted when he came out of depression. He stood in front of it and looked through time itself, indulging in memories. A smile revealed his inner journey. The smile faded. He looked down on himself and saw the worn-out trousers, the old shoes, and his appearance somewhat different than the painting had portrayed him. Yet he could not feel failure, even though everyone else around him believed this to be true. Truth is. It is not a decision by a majority. The truth is in the eyes and in the depths of the soul.

There, right ahead, is the composer he once was. The painting does not show his eyes as he is facing the orchestra. A small sign next to the painting showed the inscription, his sister's name, title, and price of the artwork: $3,800.000. He laughed. The canvas was worth more than he had seen in a long time. It was probably worth more than his life now. His canvas, his painting, no one else owned it. Despite that, he was happy. Asha's work would be cared for. His thoughts called up memories of his beloved sister: 'Oh, Asha, dear, your eyes, my ear, the sweetest tear to thank you. Arousing the music in my soul, your vision has brought me out of dark times, oh so long ago.'

Security personnel became aware of the old man through the closed-circuit monitoring system. "He is not the type of clientele we want to attract here," said the ageing Yente Francis to the young guards. She did not recognise Tobin. Two security guards arrived in the section where the old man stood, reminiscing. His left hand reached for the canvas. The two guards overpowered Tobin and escorted him away from the work.

From inside a police van, he saw a billboard for some company. It proclaimed in large-sized letters: '2 million customers can't be wrong.' He spat at it in contempt, but the glass of the van caught his spit instead. It traced a path down the glass. Following his release, he returned to the park. Many of the homeless living there would dwell beneath the bridge. Sometimes they were good company.

From his pocket, he pulled out the newspaper cutting. 'Gallery needs a security upgrade', the headline read. 'The Conductor is an irreplaceable work of art within arm's reach of vandals,' the story elaborated. His thoughts returned to Asha: 'Oh, Asha, dear, my time is near; I have no fear because you're near.' The newspaper had added a picture of a mean-looking man reaching for the canvas. He laughed again. He knew the man. He is not a vandal. Perhaps he scored a sandwich. Tobin was happy and laughing.

A voice nearby questioned, "Old man, what are you so happy about? What have you got there? Give us a look." One came, then two, then six, in no time at all they sat around him. The paper clipping went from hand to hand. Tobin pointed to the picture and then to himself. "What, you a maestro?" one laughed as he scavenged a rusty bucket and stood on it in front of the group, waving his arms around. "Like this?" he shouted. The old man grinned and nodded. "You show us then," another teased him. He nodded again. His hand and shoulder revealed a question.
His hand imitated various musicians, playing a violin, a piano, and a flute, then he shrugged his shoulders and looked around. "We're all musicians," one said. They all rushed to find some implements. Anything that could be hammered, bashed, or clapped in some way. A pipe to blow through, a bit of steel, a lid, a chain, anything that would make sound, and hurried back to align themselves as musical performers.

Tobin stood on the rusty bucket. As conductor, he raised his arm, and the afternoon concert in the park got underway. He laughed when the sounds of all sorts of noises reached his ears, a bash here, a bang there, and the rattle of a chain over a garbage lid. He kept directing, and everyone played their part as best they could. The whole group enjoyed themselves and had such a good feeling that it felt like Sunday in the middle of the week. The whole barrage of noise lasted a good five minutes before a voice from behind the group called out, "Hey you lot, keep the racket down and get out of here." The two police officers waited for the noise to calm down and walked away with a grin.

The group in euphoria exchanged thoughts: "That was great, man. Why don't we do that every day? Paris, London, here we come!" shouts of excitement come from all sides. As they turned their heads to look at the conductor, they found the bucket had rolled away. The conductor's body lay on the grass. "Maestro, what's the matter?" One put his ear to the conductor's heart. "He's dead," he said. "How come?" "But why, why now?" questions were heard. "Heart attack or something," but look, "he's still got a smile on his face," one said. "What a way to go, at the height of his career. Isn't it a beautiful way to go?"

They looked once more at the newspaper clipping and then put it in the old man's pocket. They bowed their heads, and each, in their own way, mumbled a prayer of thanks and respect. A week later, the group gathered once more. At his funeral, they recited the concert as best they could.

The Puma: Reflection

It is summertime in the mountains. The Pumas raised two more cubs. White snowflake bushes are in bloom. Butterflies dance on the breeze. A flock of geese is heading south. He circles the outer fringes of his domain. From his vantage point, he has a clear view of the valley below. There is no disturbance in the air; only an eagle is soaring.

As the season turned, a blanket of snow covered the valley. Once more, he ventured out to the lowlands. The slight rise in the snow indicated the four graves. The abandoned car was covered in snow. The remains of the tiger were all gone. The puma stands at the rear gate of the vehicle. His paws disturb the content inside the car. Several items fall out of the car.

A reflective metal plate falls and lands on its edge in the snow. The puma inspects the object. It is highly reflective from all sides. He lets out a hiss when he discovers another puma on the plate. Several times he discovers the puma, but he cannot smell its scent.

The puma calms and settles down when he remembers his silent companion that showed itself without scent or sound, the copycat with the flat body that appeared in reflective objects. He lies in front of the plate to gaze into the eyes of his reflection. His eyes never seem to blink. They are clear and calm, without question, without demand, and without need or want. As if they have a knowing.

In the magic of a shining plate, his ears hear the echo of his breath. The waves of sound are bouncing back to his ears. He turns his head to look behind him and sees his trail, a curved wave drawn into the snow. He looks forwards into the plate and, in the reflection, draws a similar trail, fading into the depths of a flat circular plate.

The back is front, the left is right, the sound towards comes from, and through the eyes the yesterdays and from the eyes tomorrows. The whites, the black, the depth, the flat, all in a wondrous mirroring plate, and in the endlessness of time, it reflects 'now'.

End

Preface (E is not happy)

In a world where letters, numbers, and characters hold the power of communication, a peculiar and unprecedented event unfolds. The book "E is not happy" takes us on a whimsical journey where a single letter challenges the established order, sparking chaos and confusion among the language's building blocks.

As the tale begins, we find ourselves in a classroom where the recitation of the alphabet is interrupted by an unexpected voice. The letter 'E' emerges from the blackboard, demanding to be placed at the forefront of the alphabet. Faced with this audacious request, the teacher and the entire class are bewildered.

What follows is a delightful and humorous exploration of language, as the letter 'E' refuses to cooperate, leading to a cascade of unforeseen consequences. As the strike of the letter 'E' takes hold, words lose their meaning, numbers lose their value, and the very fabric of communication begins to crumble.

In this imaginative narrative, the author skilfully weaves together themes of identity, order, and the power of words. Readers are invited to ponder the intricate relationship between letters, sounds, and their impact on our ability to convey meaning. Through whimsical dialogues and clever wordplay, the story explores the nuances of language while captivating readers of all ages.

Within the pages of this book, you will find a vibrant world where characters and concepts spring to life, challenging our assumptions about the written and spoken word. As you embark on this delightful journey, prepare to be captivated by the ingenuity of the author's storytelling and the profound implications hidden within a seemingly simple tale.

'E is not happy' is a charming and thought-provoking book that reminds us of the importance of every letter, number, and character in the rich tapestry of language. It serves as a whimsical reminder that the power of communication lies not only in the words we choose but also in the order and arrangement of the letters that comprise them.

So, join us on this extraordinary adventure through the twists and turns of language, where 'E' challenges convention, and the entire alphabet is turned upside down. Prepare to be entertained, inspired, and perhaps even find a renewed appreciation for the intricate dance of letters and words that shapes our everyday lives.

Heinz G. Ross

E is not happy

"ABCDEFGHIJKLMNOP," that is, very good children. Now let's all do it once more: "ABCDEFGHIJKLMNOP."

"Stop," a voice said.

"Who said 'Stop?" the teacher questioned the class. No one answered her.

"Who said to stop?" the teacher asked again, and still no answer came.

"Not I". "Not me". "Me neither," came some of the replies, and heads shook in denial.

"Shall we start again?" the teacher asked.

"All together now: ABCDEFGHIJKLMNOP," and all joined in mouthing off the letters. "What comes after 'P'?"

"Stop, stop, stop," a voice said from the blackboard.

"Who are you, the voice I hear?" the teacher questioned. "Did you hear it too?" she asked the children.

"Yes, we did." "And so did I," and heads nodded and eyes opened.

"The voice is from me, the letter E." The voice came from the blackboard.

The whole classroom looked in wonder; never before had a letter been spoken from the blackboard.

"How can it be that the letter 'E' has something to say?" The teacher questioned her, and the whole class was behind her as she looked at the letter in front of her.

"I had enough," said letter E. "I want to be in front of the Elphabet.

"The what?"

"The Elphabet?"

"Did I hear this correctly?" the teacher asked the letter E.

"You heard correctly." I want respect. I want to be in front," E said.

"In front of what?"

"In front of 'A'," this E did say.

"Oh, go away," the teacher said, "the 'A' in front has always been this way."

"Then I shall refuse to be E. I'll go on strike, and you will not be able to use the sound of me," said E.

"This is absurd," the teacher said. "Whoever heard of a thing like that?"

"No one can replace me," said E.

"Try me," said E.

The teacher turned to face the class and clapped her hands for their attention.

"Let us forget about E and let's get back to where we were," she said.

"I warned you," said E, "I will be sore. I'll turn the letters that use me into an underscore."

These words the teacher did ignore.

"All together now."

And they tried reciting the alphabet, but the E refused to make its sound. Not just the sound in its own letter, but in every letter that it found.

"A_______HIJK____O"

"Oh dear, that is not what I want to hear," the teacher said.

"Let's try again, and this time do it right."

"A_______HIJK___O," is how they all responded.

The teacher turned to face the E and asked, "What ar_ you doing to us and m_?"

The E just laughed.

"I tell you this," the E did say, "without me these words you cannot say: Not me, not she, not he and see, and free or be, nor glee, nor knee, and bee, and key, or we and sea."

"If you don't stop this nons_ns_, I shall r_port you to th_ h_admast_r," the teacher said.

The E just laughed even louder.

"L_t's try again, class: A_______HIJK___O.".

No matter how often they tried, they could not sound the E in the letters it was found to be.

'Excuse me, class, I will have to get the principal', she was trying to say, but all that came out of her mouth was, "_xcus_ m_, class, I will hav_ to g_t th_ principal."

The principal listened and came to the blackboard to see the E.

The class tried once more: "A______HIJK___O.".

"What is going on, h_r_?" the principal searched for a reason.

So the teacher explained that 'E' is on strike.

He laughed, but he couldn't even do that properly without the E; instead, he laughed as "h_ h_ h_."

"_xplain yours_lf," he said to E.

"You see," said E, "so many other letters use the sound of me. Why is 'A' in front? What is so special about 'A'? Not enough having 'A' in front, it is even called the 'A'lphabet with 'A' twice making an appearance. Without 'E', without me, you will find it difficult to communicate," said E.

"What do you want?" the principal asked.

"To be in front," said E, "I want it to be the elphabet.'"

The principal, somewhat bewildered, thought about it all. But he had another thing on his mind that was more important.

His secretary poked her head into the classroom and called out to the Principal, "Your appointm_nt is in 2 minut_s."

"Ok, ok, ok," he said and left the classroom.

The letter E' had a big smile.

"Let's get back to work, children: ABCDEFGHIJKLMNOP."

Everyone was happy, and they could speak as they had always done. Each letter sounded as it should. But many of the other letters were not happy.

It wasn't long before a knock on the classroom door interrupted the lesson. The principal asked the teacher, "I have with me a delegation of teachers from other countries. They are on tour. Would you mind if we all joined the class so they could see how we conduct our lessons in this country?"

"Please come in," the teacher said. They all stood along the outer walls of the classroom and paid attention to the lesson.

No one had noticed that the letters A, I, O, and U were engaged in a meeting on the blackboard. They thought E should get a handle on it and go outside to rake the grass.

The principal asked the teacher, "Could you explain to our guests what lesson you are currently conducting?"

"Certainly, sir, we are reciting the Alphabet."

As soon as E heard that, he called out "THE ELPHABET."

"The Alphabet," the teacher corrected.

"You promised. You said 'OK'. You've lied to me," said E.

The teacher, the students, the principal, and all the guests looked at the blackboard. A big fight was unfolding. The A hit the E for fear of losing his spot, and the U hit the O because it wanted to be in front of the O. Before long, all the letters were fighting with each other.

'E' called out, "I'm on strike."

'A' called out, "And so am I."

'I' said, "How dare you use my name? Only 'I' can be I. And anyway, I am the tallest sound in uppercase. I need to be in front. It should be called 'IIphabet'," said the letter I.

Even though 'I' had only one leg to stand on and was overall a pretty skinny letter, it did have a point, especially in lowercase.

And 'U' said, "'U' cannot be without me. You cannot use my sound."

And 'O' said: "Oh my, oh my, without me you'll have just s_und. And without 'U, it'll be just s__nd."

The letters g, j, p, q, and y were interjected. "We are the special ones; we descend below. None of you can do that."
The letters b, d, f, h, k, l, and t said, Only we stand proud in lowercase. We demand it be called the bdfhkltphabet." But they quickly corrected themselves when they realised some had a double appearance.
"We want it to be the 'bdfhklt'". They had kicked all the other letters out, which had their own agenda.
Then 'Z', always last, said, "I know what we can do to solve this. Whatever we call it, Alphabet or Blphabet, whatever, instead of writing it sideways, we could write it downwards, each character on top of another. That way, we are all in front."
That all made sense until someone asked, "And who will be on top?"
Each one called out "I.".
This made 'I' very happy, and it said, "Thank you."
And then they all called out, "That's not what we meant."
Then the principal said, "___ __ ______ __?"
What he wanted to say was, 'What is going on?'
But as soon as he said it, the quotation marks went on strike too.
The whole classroom became engaged in fruitless discussions.
One of the guests said: __ ________ __ _____ _! and another said: _____ __ _ ___?_____ _ ____, ___.
So the exclamation mark had no idea what it was exclaiming, and the question mark wondered, Why am I still here? Meanwhile, the full stop had a fight with the letter 'o' but couldn't really hit it as it kept falling through it.
Eventually, all the characters went on strike, except the underscore. It had figured that if all refused their services, then Alphabet would have to be called the ______________.
The underscore replaced every letter that went on strike.
Further, each conversation would have to be more lively as every letter was underscored or __________.
At this point, you may be wondering why you are able to read this at all when all the characters are on strike. That is easy to

explain. I promised the letter 'A' that it would be on the cover of this book, and it allowed me to use it. I promised the same to the 'B', but didn't tell the 'A' about it. So I promised each that they would be on the cover of the book that tells their story, and in return, I am able to write it so that you can read it. But as soon as someone from the story speaks, I'm bound to the language that they're using.

Some of the foreign guests said:

To which others replied: ^((*@ μ

But the tall man said: #@%&

The principal called out, ___ __ _____ __

But he couldn't back it up with a question mark because it too was on strike.

It was all becoming ridiculous. They could talk as much as they wanted, but they could not communicate. No one understood the other.

In the afternoon, the parents came to collect their children from school. Each is called out in underscores. No one knew what happened.

It wasn't long before the numbers became aware of what happened to the letters, and they too wanted to reorder themselves. Nine thought it was bigger than one and wanted to be in front.

Zero complained and said, "Without a zero, you're all worth nothing, or very little. Only I can make you important. And anyway, I need to be in front of every number that I see. You cannot start with something. Before 1, there is nothing, zilch, zero, or 0. That is my place, in front of 1."

Eleven too called out, "I do not like my name".

"As I'm the first of all the teens, I need to be 'ten-one' said eleven". Everyone started laughing at this except for the number twelve. "Then you would need to be called 'first-teen', and that would make sense," the others offered as a solution.

"No," answered eleven, the letter 'E' always gets its way. That's why it appears three times in my name. And anyway, all teens are wrong."

The numbers 13, 14, and 15 said: "Us wrong? Never!"
"Everyone is reading you back to front," said eleven. "21 and 31, 101, and a million and one all properly ordered. Only the teens are read backwards."
Twelve just stood in the corner, looking sad.
Eleven said: "If eleven is my name, then you try to write this down as a number: eleventhousand-elevenhundred-and-eleven. See what you come up with."
In a very short time, the characters from the other countries became aware of what was going on. They too started arguing amongst themselves and with those with them.
The roman X said: "x x x =?"
"Could you please translate the question?" the others asked.
"X times x," X said.
They all said what they meant, and they all meant what they said, but so often, it came out wrong instead.
The Greek α (alpha) said, "I need to be in front. I am always in front. Besides, I am better than A. I have an 'A' at the beginning and end of my name. A is just A, so what? I have two, so I am twice as important."
One of the characters from Greece started crying. "What's the matter with you?" they asked. "Who are you?"
"That's what I want to know. I'm π (pi). Without a number, who am I?" said p (pi).
E started laughing, saying, "With me, you'll be a pie."
"Don't be silly," the others said.
"What do I stand for?" asked Pi.
"When the numbers were working, you stood for 3.14," they all replied.
"No I'm not," said π (pi).
"Of course you are," they said.
No, I'm not 3.14. No one in the whole wide world knows what I stand for," said Pi.
He grinned again.
"Join up with me," said 'E', "then we can eat you as a pie."
"Will you be quiet?" the others said to E.

"We always thought you stood for 3.14," the group said to π (pi).

"I wish. Those are just my initials. Three-point-one-four, I'll be no more," said Pi, who started anew to cry.

"π, π, π, don't cry," said I.

"Why?" π (pi) answered, "why not?"

"Do you know the consequence? If I don't know what I stand for, all construction will stop, and no plane or ship can find its destination. No one will be able to calculate anything," π said.

"But plus (+) and minus (-) will still work," the others said, trying to calm π down.

"No offence plus or minus, but there is not a lot you can do with them," π said.

"Oh yeah," said plus and minus. They were hurt by π's remarks.

"What do you stand for, π?" said I.

"I can't even say it myself," π answered.

"Why not?"

"It's just so long. I can't say it out loud," said π.

"I need all my energy just to remember what I stand for. That's why I'm all bent and my legs almost give way."

Then π (pi) said what it stood for:

"3.14159265358979323846264338327950288419716939937 51058209749445923078164062862089986280348253421170 67982148086513282306647093844609550582231725359408 12848111745028410270193852110555964462294895493038 19644288109756659334461284756482337867831652712019 09145648566923460386104543266482133936072602491412 73724587006606315588174881520920962829254091536436 78

"I hope I got that right. Does the 9 come before the 3?"

"Which 9?" E asked.

"The 793rd," π answered.

"Hold it," said 'I', "how much longer will that go on for?"

"A couple of more pages," said π (pi).

"Where was I, ah yes, 94151160?"

"Stop," said I.

"So sorry, π (pi), we didn't realise," said 'I', "how many more numbers?"

"A couple of thousand," said π.

"What two or three?" asked E.

"You must be kidding me," answered π (pi), "do you think it's easy to square a circle?"

'Y', which balanced on one leg, had both arms outstretched when it said, "That's it, the circle."

"If we all form a circle, there is no front, and no beginning. We will all be holding hands, and everyone will be happy. We are neither an Alphabet nor a blphabet. We will be whatever you read. Depending where in the circle you start reading.

This was a great answer, and it would have solved all the problems until E interjected: "I don't want to be next to D and F. I am not DEF."

The N was not happy either. "Whoever looks at me first will see 'No'." I have a positive nature."

"Start with H, and it becomes the 'Hi lphabet," said I.

Then things really got out of hand as the 'meanings' of the words joined in: "Do you mean Hi or High?"

"Don't be blue," said the X.

And the meaning asked: "What do you mean, the colour?"

X said, "No, the mood."

"The grass is always greener on the other side," said F.

"Do you mean the environment?" the meaning asked.

"No, the colour," said F.

The arguments continued between the meanings, the words, and the letters, and there was no end in sight. Then things got worse when the 'pronunciation' joined in the debate of who was more important.

The letters got together and prepared a little test. "Come on, you two, read us and tell us what we mean".

So the meaning and the pronunciation looked at them and read how they stood: The night is tall.

The letters asked the meaning: "What does it mean?"

The meaning was, "We don't know. It doesn't make any sense."

The pronunciation said, "The night is tall. It sounds okay to me."
Then they reformed and spelt it as 'The knight is tall.'
It made no difference to the pronunciation, and the meaning was happy, as it made sense.
"We, the letters, have the upper hand," said the letters.
"I wouldn't know," said the pronunciation. "It sounds okay to me either way."
"Ah, you are just the mouthpiece," they answered in one voice. You two, you to, you too, you wouldn't know the difference."
"I do agree," the pronunciation responded.
"We need peas, pees, pieeces, pieces, and peace."
"There is no such thing as 'pieece'," said P.
"How would you know?" asked the pronunciation.
"I would have remembered," said P.
Then the letters W, A, and R called out: "And we are sick of being in the headlines all the time".
And the pronunciation asked, "Have you guys got a temperature?"
Then the 'importance' of words and the 'order' of words had something to say. Then came the 'intonation, the inflection, the modulation, and the 'feelings' of the words all of which claimed their own importance. As soon as word got around, and no one knew what that 'word' was, more and more attributes came and claimed their importance.
It came to the point that the legal people had a field day. This is not to say that the other people were illegal, that the people had a day in a field, or that they met on a day named 'field'. They did not come to a point either.
Communication reached a crossroads. No, it was not a road with a cross. People said what they didn't mean, and they didn't say what they meant. So, it came to be that the building blocks of language went on strike. All letters, numbers, and characters refused their service, except one.
Within a few minutes, the underscore replaced all the numbers. The underscore was very happy. It would no longer

be used as a doormat for all the other characters. No longer be used to make the letters seem important. It happily stood on its own. Laying down might be a more accurate description for the underscore.

When the decimal place between the numbers was tired of all the argument, it too gave up, replaced by an underscore.

This was good and bad in a way. The price of fuel went from _.__ to ___

The cost of a tank full of fuel was ____, and it was up to the attendant to figure out what that was. Most people quickly learned to offer a handful of small coins since the attendant had no idea what a dollar was worth.

Since the full stop dropped out, the spaces between the words dropped out as well. This caused all the newspaper headlines to look alike:

____

____

The marketing people now had a new language. Each advertiser could, in every word, underscore the benefits of their products. Never before could they publicise their wares with such powerful language. Some thought they could get on top of their competitors by underscoring the underscore, but that did not work.

New typewriters and computer keyboards were needed. They all had just one key—a long line. This increased typing speed dramatically, from a few words per minute to whole volumes in seconds. New money was printed. The cent looked the same as the dollar. The ten-dollar note is the same as the 100-dollar note. But since the numbers were on strike, one couldn't call it 10 or 100 anymore. It just became a dollar.

Watching the nightly news was not very inspiring. One could see the news announcer was trying to read something, but most of the time one could only hear him or her breathing.

Nature and animal films became very popular. Dogs barking, lions roaring, and the sound of wind and waves were still the same.

Since the letters, numbers, and characters all refused their service, handwriting also changed. Even in handwriting, everything had become underscored.
One could sign a contract, and one signature looked the same as another. On a marriage certificate, ______ was married to ________ in the year ______

Back in school, where it all began, each student passed the spelling test with flying colours. The yearly report card showed everyone as ______ The highest scores were each one had a _ in everything.
The distance had also changed. From here to there, there was ___ And from there to the other side of the world was ______
Just an underscore, more or less, was all the difference.
The undertaker had it easy. No matter who had died, their date of birth was ____ and they died on ____ So the gravestones were ready for anybody, already inscribed, including the names of whoever happened to need one.
The conversation became somewhat strained since the question mark refused its service. One didn't know whether to answer a question or question an answer.
It didn't take long for people to stop communicating. What could you say? ________ ____ and then ______
People stopped talking all together. Books became obsolete except picture books, which made a roaring trade. Each book cost ______ and was about ______ But mostly, the pictures were good.
Eventually, things became more and more confusing. A potato costs _ To dig one out cost _ To drive with the bus costs _ A trip around the world from ____ to the country ____ and the city ____ cost ___ It all made no sense. You wouldn't know where you'd end up. Why work a whole week for ______ when you could work a minute for _____?
Since there were no numbers, one would not know the measure of time. People took holidays for ______ weeks. That could be the whole year or even a couple of years.

Eventually the underscore became bored with being the most famous character, the only character, to be more precise. It tried as best it could, but the underscore was totally overworked, overused, abused, sick, and tired of it all. It tried as best as it could to hold the world together, but it could not cope anymore. It quit.

The underscore joined the rest of the letters and fell asleep. No one even knew how to pronounce it.

As soon as that happened, civilisation started falling apart. Bread cost nothing, wages were nothing, and no one had a name, not even a line. Countries didn't have names. There was no difference in anything. It had to collapse, and it did.

The letters on the blackboard were deeply asleep. The school building fell apart. Years went by. The earth rotated the sun in tireless circles. The world changed. All the buildings and cities became buried over time. Nature reclaimed the whole surface of the earth. Animals ruled the land, as they did many years ago. The letters became deeply buried in the crust of the earth. The earth continued rotating, and since the numbers were still asleep, the earth rotated for countless years.

In the depths of their sleep, the numbers, letters, and all the other characters forgot that they ever had an argument.

Eventually, one by one, they started waking up from their ever-so-long deep sleep. They had forgotten the words.

One started digging, possibly D. Then the M and the Q joined in, and in no time at all, they were all digging.

All the while, they were singing their own songs and were happy to have had a good, long sleep. Each could only sing one sound, the sound of their name. It was not long, and they all reached the surface.

They all joined hands and skipped along the meadows, singing the only song that they could sing together, "ABCDEFGHIJKLMNOPQRSTUVWXYZ."

The underscore was still asleep, so Z tied a vine around it and dragged it along. Then the underscore caught on an object, and the vine slipped out of Z's hand. Z turned around and inspected the object, and all the others helped to unearth it.

They had uncovered a box with a round glass in front, a button on top of the box, and a flat piece of glass at the rear. J was always jumping about, and he happened to land on the button, and it went 'click'. On the flat glass, they could see a picture forming. They had uncovered a camera.

Most of the letters wanted to see the glass plate at the rear. In front of the lens were the letters O, V, L, and E playing and running about. J kept jumping onto the button, and with every jump, the sound went 'click'. Then they took a look at all the pictures they took.

V, E, L, and O were no good because the L was a bit blurred.

E, V, and O with L were no good either. L had its foot stuck out of view.

V, L, E, and V all agreed that they had everyone in a silly mood.

L,V, O, and E would have been a good snap, but the O had its eyes closed.

So the only picture they could all agree on was of L, O, V, and E standing close together. I smiled at U, and U nodded.

It was a pretty picture. L standing real cool on the outside, and the O with its big belly touching the ground. V always runs around with its arms stretched into the air as it tries to catch the sun. When the shot was taken, E had all three arms outstretched, calling out for U to also come into the picture.

Since they had all forgotten all the words they had used before they fell asleep, they used the picture as a word to forever symbolise what a beautiful day they had. After that, they never invented another word. This was the only word the world ever needed—the picture of the four happy letters.

It was at this moment, somewhere far away in another time, that the alarm clock went off on the bedside table of the local primary school teacher. She nearly hit the ceiling from the fright. When she realised it was Sunday, she pulled the blanket back over her head and tried to recover from her dream.

Then she thought it was interesting that the 'e' is in front of the letter 'a' in the word 'dream'. And then she got up and forgot all about the dream.

Then she thought it was interesting that the 'e' is in front of the letter 'a' in the word 'dream'. And then she got up and had forgotten all about the dream.

End

Preface (Circle Beach)

'Circle Beach' is a captivating tale that transports us to the enchanting realm of the ocean, where extraordinary creatures roam and destiny weaves its intricate threads. This story, passed down through generations, paints a vivid picture of the majestic ocean dweller, whose journey intertwines with the life of a mysterious woman. Amidst the ebb and flow of the waves, the ocean dweller embarks on a quest for love and connection, driven by a scent that stirs the depths of its being.

As we dive into the narrative, we witness breathtaking moments of beauty and wonder. The ocean dweller's exhilarating breaches, propelled by raw power and grace, become a mesmerising dance between sea and sky. We are captivated by the immense expanse of the ocean and the magic that unfolds within it, as the ocean dweller discovers the potential for profound love in an unexpected encounter.

The story explores themes of longing, fate, and the power of choice. The ocean dweller finds itself at a crossroads, torn between the yearning for a connection with the woman and the dangers that await in the human world. It contemplates the fragility of life, the profound impact of a single encounter, and the boundless potential for love to transcend boundaries.

Through poetic prose, the author invites us to contemplate the mysteries of the universe and the profound depths of human connection. We are reminded of the delicate balance between life and death, the resilience of the human spirit, and the transformative power of love. Circle Beach unfolds as a testament to the enduring nature of hope, the importance of embracing the unknown, and the beauty of life's unexpected turns.

Within these pages, we embark on a journey that transcends time and place, inviting us to ponder the significance of our own choices and the hidden forces that shape our lives. It is a story that reminds us to cherish the miracles that surround us and the potential for love to manifest in the most extraordinary ways.

So, let us step onto the golden sands of 'Circle Beach', draw circles in the sand, and immerse ourselves in a tale of fate, love, and the timeless dance between the ocean and the human heart.

Heinz G. Ross

Circle Beach

So I see the sparkle of the sun's rays broken by shadows of boats on the surface. Some have dropped anchor as if to tease me upward. Sonar are switched on and I can feel the echo bouncing. Sound carries far in these waters.

So I dive low, with strong strokes of the tail fin, accelerating, arching my spine to turn upwards, speeding towards the surface. Five more strokes, rising swell and the water gets pushed to a peak until its tension has to break. And when it does, it explodes into millions of white droplets, foaming, frothing from the charge of high acceleration, from the depth of the ocean toward the limitless skies.

So much speed to push my whole being into the air. Breaching high to two times my length, rolling in flight until gravity intervenes. Enough time to glimpse the surface, waves rolling, swells crossing, spray sparkling in spectacular display, never repeating patterns of magic, as the white pure collared droplets return home to become one with the sea.

The writing on the bow of many is of little interest, but then, far in the distance, one that stirs my curiosity. A line with bait, a wriggling worm, delicious worm. The heart misses a beat, just one, then it catches up with raised pulse. Gratefully I'm younger than a century.

She seeks a normal fish, a mere mortal, yet she has a sparkle in her eyes and is circled by swarms of ocean dwellers. It seems a million miles I covered riding currents far from home, seeking what needs to be found, all the while, she may have been this very close all along. So much in her scents stirs my core, makes me respond.

As my nose re-enters home, my thoughts wonder, harpoons, spears, nets. The rest of my body submerges to return home. But what if the line that is cast is of soft silky strands with no barbs or other nastiness. What if gentle hands made it? What if its scent is pleasing?

Just enough time to splash my tail fin hard onto the surface, pushing up another fountain of glittering spray. A sight to be seen, a sound to be heard, with echoes for miles to far distant shores.

My body has returned to the blue in a shower of shapes becoming ever-changing rotating spheres. One more wink with the dorsal, as if to say 'hello'.

As I dive crossing several currents I wonder, was I high enough, was I loud enough and was I flying long enough to be seen.

The ocean dweller glides, it's back just breaking the surface, arching in rhythmic motion. Rich golden sunset colours the ocean.

On touching the worm the big dweller jolts, opens its blowhole, lets out an 80 feet spout of used up oxygen, exhaling, just once.

The whole being shudders. More than just a simple worm, but he knew all that when he first spied it dangling. After all, it was not just a worm, but a scented worm. Yet still the jolt, sharp as lightening, leaves a ripple of sensations throughout every cell, billions of cells, uncontrollable chain-reaction, each one twitching, each affecting its neighbouring cells.

He feels the heart regaining its function, ever so slowly. Not long and the brain is throbbing, poundings with expanding blood pressure. Stars twinkling with eyes shut. The jaw locks tight.

The ocean dweller descends, slower now the tail's fin in decreasing motion. Barely moving. To go down takes no effort. He knows it. Yet within, a raging storm of firing neurons sparks the brain into fireworks. The energy of a whole city expanded within a second in the limited spaces of its brain. Heat within. The jaw is still locked. No water gets in. Oxygen is only available at the surface. The muscles will weaken soon. The brain unable to give the orders to breathe in. The big being is consumed by the sparkles in its brain. Hypnotising. Hypnotised.

Preventing auto reflexes, seizing motor functions. Paralysed. The outer reels from the lack of oxygen, lets out a call that echoes in low-pitched sounds. Life is rushing by, brothers, sisters and parents, millions of faces seen once before, long ago, years ago, month ago, and yesterday to now. Memories of playful days rush by. Joyous occasions and innocent days of discoveries relived within seconds. The first awareness of the other, the sense of wanting, the reaching out for the first time. The scents and tastes, the discoveries of self, the ecstasies, the longing for more, the reaching for touch, warmth, softness, moisture, the rush of rivers, oceans, thundering storms, the rage of the elements, earthquakes, tsunamis, tidal waves, - all that to now, within a worm, all that.

Had he found the one that speaks the language without any restrictions? No frames within boxes, free of limitations, pure thoughts and pure words. The tongue retracts to taste again, the scent smooth, failing words to colour this experience.

The sounds bounce back from the Arctic, Greenland, China, the western shelf, the southern seas, far distant shores, all know now, all are knowing. Each particle of water has heard the call.

Time to submit. Calmness is on the outer. The sharks nearby don't notice anything. Time to let go. Time to fall. The veins carry gallons, pushing it through miles of vessels, yet the jaw remains locked. The consistency of his blood is changing.

The heart rate increases, trying to compensate. Lacking oxygen starves the muscles. The heart will give in eventually. For the moment the brain consumes, burns like a wildfire. He sees her clearly now, hears her, inhales her, absorbs all she is offering, tastes her, drinks her, consumes her, guides her, calms her, wakens her, soothes her, takes her, her, her. The brain is saturated with the thought of her.

They interact, she inhales, she absorbs, she drinks, she covers, she consumes and they feast on each other, a banquet of sensations. The brain short circuits. The dorsal stabs the water, the tail fin unable to lift, the lungs start filling and the dream of her still paramount. The body is slowly sinking.

Calmness and fire combine in the knowing of togetherness. The ball of the sun has drowned in the ocean. Just two inches show as an arc that was once a circle. It draws a line across the swells, a golden line that ripples with every motion of the sea.

The line points to the drowning mammal, a golden line and the line that connects to the heavens. He floats motionless now. Deeper and deeper the depth darkens the view. Eyes are no longer needed the sunshine shows within.

Darkness is all around now. Pitch-black, depth exerts its pressure, expelling the remaining oxygen. She is within, that's all that is important, she has come.

Organs start to fail, the body shudders in violent convulsions, twitching, arching, breaking out. One more rush and another and the jaw opens in agony. Oh joyous pain, hunger filled, thirst quenched, no strength to breathe, uncontrollable motions. A total draining of energy, exhaustion, stillness, silence, night, depth, heaven and love in its entire splendour.

So the worm still is resting under the palate of the giant mammal. The convulsions of the battle dislodge the tiny being and she is swallowed down the giant throat. The large mammal misdirects the worm towards the lungs whilst its strength is fading fast. Both are starved of precious oxygen.

They descend lower and deeper to ever more increasing pressure. The blood vessels in the lungs are starting to seep. The worm is sucked into the bloodstream, accelerating towards the heart. The last mighty heartbeat shuts its valve around the worm. The worm is sliced in half. A tiny grain of sand inside the worm is sharp enough to cut its own heart and that of the other. The heart valve of the mammal contracts further, fuses a cell of each of their hearts into one. Two cells locked to each other.

As one, the fused cells separate from their hearts, their hosts and float free with the last rush of blood. Above in a cavity they find the tiniest of air pockets, which becomes their cave. In its fading thoughts, the ocean dweller is filled with sorrow for cutting the worm in its heart. He rolls slowly on its back stripped of all strength, still descending, head first downward, spiralling again downward.

The tiny air bubble frees and finds an escape. With it the bonded heart cells escape. The waters are bitter cold outside, blackness everywhere in the deep. The air bubble knows which direction heaven is and begins to rise. Each foot it rises the pressure reduces resulting in increase of its size. The lift in buoyancy becomes stronger and stronger. The ocean dweller and the remains of the worm are far left below.

A golden line becomes barely visible above them. Night is turning into dawn. The combined cells rise now in increasing speed. They reach the surface just as the sun breaks the horizon in the east. The powerful golden ball draws its line westward with the first rays. The rays hits the sand of a beach the locals call a coast, named in the colour of the golden ball. The ray marks the spot where in days to come magic will unfold.

The combined cells rise above the waters, rise high with the morning fog. The sun rises too, washing out the last remaining stars. The ocean reveals a numb rumble. Circular ripples appear on the surface forming rings, increasing in size, radiating outwards. The once magnificent mighty ocean dweller must have hit bottom.

Out of the shine of the sun an albatross appears, gliding effortlessly. This albatross has special powers. Its wings don't move at all. Its head tilted sideways, as if to listen to sounds coming from beneath the waters. Low pitching sounds from all directions, frequencies from far and near, dozens, hundreds, thousands joining in the song of mourning, the loss of one of them.

The albatross circles in respect, tracing the radiating pattern on the ripples. Its head still tilted listening to the underwater songs of pain. The albatross is wise and heard a similar song once before. But what he heard now was another, the songs of mourning also contained sparks of hope, reasons to be grateful, of two floating beings locked as cells, rising in the fog right here. The voices from below guiding the bird to spy the morning rays position. There on the golden sands it points. Dare not a death be lost in vain, that contains the seeds of promise? Guard life, guard love, its finest treasure. Respect its unlimited strength and energies.

The albatross has special gifts and can look ahead in time, to days yet unborn. It speaks of two beings, of woman and of man. They shall meet on the marked spot. Whoever comes first will draw a circle in the sand. He or she will sit outside the circle until the other comes. When the other comes, he or she has the choice to step into the circle or leave.

The circle represents an egg. It does not matter who draws it. The one who steps into the circle represents a sperm. It does not matter who does this. Both are free to walk away at any time. Whoever leaves shall not be followed, the spell will break. Both will have lost.

The one who steps into the circle first divides it, through the middle, as if the egg had divided. Thus indicating an interest in the other. If the other also steps inside the circle and divides it again, thus dividing the two egg cells into four, both know they have agreed to be born in love.

Each will step with one foot into each cell, a foot in each quarter of the circle. They will not know their names. They have never spoken to each other. They have never met before. They begin to be born into love. They embrace, inhale each other's scent, they feel the warmth in each other's hands, soft kisses to the forehead, the eyes, the soft, warm flesh of the neck, in time their lips will meet.

At that moment, they both need to be strong and hold each other very tight. High up in the atmosphere the two fused cells have grown into arrows and have been waiting for this day.

As the couple kiss for the first time, the arrows will divide in mid-flight, with lightning speed be pierced straight into their own hearts. It will not hurt as the arrows are very tiny, but once inside each other's heart they will continue to grow. It is then that they hear each other's voice for the first time, as they whisper their names into the other's ear.

Ahead lay days of discoveries, weeks of getting to know each likes and dislikes, explorations on all levels, passions, and desires. The pleasures of giving, receiving, selflessness, caring, the wonders in the depth of her eyes, the shine of his smile upon seeing her, the months of wanting and fulfilling, the years of treasures to be found. The memories to be created that last forever.

A future of hope, it is up to them. However tiny the seed may be its potential is what makes life worth living. The albatross soaring overland clutching the dice and letting go.

"This story was passed on to me by my grandfather, who had heard it from his granddad," says the old man to his grandchild, "and this, my boy, is the reason why everyone comes here and draws circles in the sand."
That is why they called it 'Circle Beach'.

"But what's with the dice the albatross had thrown?" the boy wanted to know. "Oh yeah," the old man recalled "Eight dice in all and letters."

The first two were for the days, the second two for the month, and the other four for the year. The letters thrown formed a name, the name of the closest street nearby, where they were meant to meet at the golden sands."

"And what happened?" the kid asked back. Reluctantly the old man answered, "They never looked for them. They did not believe it. They thought it was just a tale. But keep that to yourself, or else the whale and worm would have died in vain."

End

Preface (Pearl's falling)

In the following fictional story, Pearl finds herself in a precarious situation after slipping and falling unconscious in her bathtub. Being without awareness she does not have much to contribute to the story. Her subconscious mind, a character which is also named Pearl emerges, and the narrative takes a thrilling turn as survival becomes the primary focus. Pearl, representing the survival instinct, assumes control and initiates communication with the various body parts, demanding silence and prioritising the intake of oxygen. As the story unfolds, Pearl wrestles with internal struggles, making critical decisions to sustain vital functions and extend the window for potential rescue or recovery.

The passages provided offer a glimpse into the intense dialogue that unfolds within the protagonist's unconscious mind. Pearl's authoritative presence guides the body parts, emphasising the need for cooperation and self-sacrifice in the face of a life-or-death situation. The story delves into the intricacies of the mind-body connection as Pearl coordinates efforts to minimise blood loss, control body temperature, and conserve oxygen.

Throughout this narrative, the reader is invited to explore the fascinating interplay between consciousness and the unconscious mind, witnessing the protagonist's struggle to piece together fragments of memory and create a vivid, compelling story that might awaken her consciousness. As the story unfolds, the boundaries between reality and imagination blur, transporting the protagonist from her bathtub to a boat on a summer's day, floating on an azure ocean.

The presence of Captain Malcolm and the fleet of ships introduces an unexpected twist, offering a glimpse into a floating food factory that operates perpetually at sea. As the protagonist navigates this strange world, she encounters sailors who have long been deprived of contact with women, adding an additional layer of tension and intrigue.

This story, brimming with psychological nuances and unexpected encounters, invites readers to reflect on the profound resilience of the human mind and the extraordinary measures one can take to ensure survival. It explores themes of adaptability, cooperation, and the relentless pursuit of life against all odds. Ultimately, it poses the question: How far would you go to survive?

Heinz G. Ross

Pearl's falling

It is 8 p.m. Her bathrobe slides to the floor. She stands naked in front of the mirror. She was happy with her reflection. "You're hot," she said. "You're not bad for a 32-year-old."

She checks the water's temperature, adds some oils, and steps with one foot into the bathtub. Then she stands with both feet in the water and slips. She falls backwards, and her head hits the edge of the bathtub. She is unconscious. Her head slowly slides into the water.

The story could end right here. Let's see what happens in the next few moments.

Let me explain. You see, I am living inside the head that has just been hit. I am what you might call the 'subconscious'. This is my home. Whatever happens on the conscious side is something I know little about. I am, in essence, the woman who drives the woman through her life. My name is Pearl. We are all Pearl, but enough of this idle chatter; I am her. I am her subconscious thought. It is my job to help myself, or, should I say, to help both of us survive. Better still, when she is unconscious, I get a lot of work done without interruptions.

You would not believe how much work I have to get through every night. It never stops. Let me tell you, last night I looked at my 'to-do list', and she wants to lose a little more weight. She is I. She is Pearl, the whole woman. What am I to do? I spun this huge yarn about how that could be achieved.

Sometimes she just doesn't want to listen. I know that, so I am persistent, and for every bit of food she picks up, I nag and nag until she puts it down and replaces it with non-fattening foods.

Oh, excuse me. I just got a message from the other senses. There is a problem. The heart and lungs also sent me a message. When they do, the 'to-do list' becomes so unimportant. I work and work, often for nothing. It is hard to pick up the idea the next night.

More messages are coming in, all of them in one voice. The same message from everyone: "Do something."
"Do something now, or we are all going to die."
"NOW!"

Well, that makes it much clearer. 'Survival' is always priority number one.

By the way, don't worry about time. I live by a different clock. I can spend hours, days, and years, and for her, it is just a second. I am always glad when she wakes up. At least then I can get some rest.

"Survival, survival!" come the calls from the various body parts.
They do not shut up, do they?

OK, let's get into survival mode. Where was I the last time that happened?

"Survival."
"Shut up. I'm working on it."
"The toes are twitching."

I don't want to know about the toes. Look guys, I'm saying this once and only once: Leave me alone. Shut your mouth and do not breathe. Slow down the heart. I need all the oxygen you can spare. I don't care if you're twitching or turning blue and green in the face.

If I don't get all, and I mean all, the oxygen we have left, then we're all going to be history. And no more messages. I know this is about survival; I heard you the first time. I want absolute silence. One more peep from any of you...
I think that shut them up.

How do we tackle this? What can I use? There are so many choices: Fear, pain, commitment, love, desire, and memory. You name it, and anything would work.

Let's pick a strong one. 'Love', yeah, that's ok; let's use 'love' to get out of this mess.

Oh, Jeremy, take me into your arms. Hold me close. Hold me closer. Unbutton my top."
No, forget about Jeremy. It will take him an hour to unbutton the top. He has two left hands.

He stood across the road. His right hand was in his pocket, well, only his thumb. The other four fingers tapped his trousers as if to direct my eyes. I stopped walking and leant against the lantern, looking at him. He looked at the ground, and when his head rose, he had a grin of promise.

"Oxygen, guys. I need more oxygen, otherwise, I can see no colours. Love needs colours." I call out to my body parts.

Where were we? Ah yes, he crossed the road, casual as if he owned the town.
"Hi baby, my name's Jason," he said. "Care for some company?"
What did I do? I looked him up from head to toe and walked away.
"Don't be like that," he called out, "we can have a good time together."

"Survival, we are fading," the body interjects.

Oh, not you lot again. I'm losing track here. We need more oxygen. Give me more. Take it from the feet, the legs, the hands, the arms, wherever. I don't really care where you take it from. I need it all.

Now I have to start all over again. Oh yes, the 'up himself' guy who thought he owned the town... No, let's give him a miss. Let's give all the guys starting with 'J' a miss.

Remember Jennifer? Yeah, let's have a look at how that went.

I met Paul on a rainy night. My car had broken down, and he had kindly offered me a lift. Jennifer was with him in the car. Along the way, we talked and then stopped by a restaurant and shared a meal. They were both very attractive, and the conversation was easy-going and happy. The two were pleasant company and invited me to their place. Since I was in no hurry, I accepted.

They lived on a hillside. On one side, the house banked into the land, and on the other side, it overlooked the trees below. It was a very secluded place. They showed me through the house, and it was well appointed. Jennifer took me to the bedroom and showed me her latest dress.

"Look, why don't you stay the night, and tomorrow morning we get our mechanic to have a look at your car?" she said. "It's a miserable night, and no one is going to fix it in this weather."

So I agreed to stay. Jennifer brought some towels and said, Here, have a shower, and you'll feel like a new woman."
"The en-suite is over there. Just help yourself to anything to wear, anything you like, we are about the same size."

I got undressed and had a beautiful hot shower. The en-suite had a glass door to the shower. My hair was full of suds, and as the shampoo dripped from my chin and breasts, I noticed Jennifer. She stood halfway in the bedroom and looked at me with a smile. When she realised that I saw her, she came closer. I washed all the suds out of my hair and turned the water off. She handed me a towel. "You're very beautiful," she said.

I wondered that she would not respect my privacy. It was somewhat natural to her. Then she undressed herself and took a shower, all her clothes left in a trail. I dried my hair.

She came out wet from the shower. She didn't use a towel. She reached for some cream on her dresser.
"I want you to try this one," she said. I got it last week". "You'll find it makes your skin breathe a lot better and goes deep into the pores."

I took a whiff, and it smelled good. Without asking, she filled her hand with the cream and started to rub it over my shoulders. Two naked women, virtually strangers, rub cream on each other. I did not object.

Her hands were soft, and with her fingers, she massaged the cream deep into the skin. She guided me to a stool and pushed my shoulders down a little. I sat on the stool. She rubbed more cream and massaged it into my neck.

I looked at her through the mirror in front of me. "Now, doesn't that just feel divine?" she asked.
"Yes, it is nice," I said. She massaged my arms, shoulders, and back. Then she turned the swivel stool, and I faced her breasts. She reached for a face-cream and started applying it to my forehead. She knelled and rubbed it all over my face. Then she gave me some lotion.
"Here, this is great for the rest of your skin".

We both took the same lotion and spread it over our breasts and stomachs.
"I found a lovely, sweet Mosel," the voice of Paul called through the corridor.
"That will be fine," Jennifer answered.
"I hope you like Mosel," she said to me. "Paul's brother owns a winery, and we always have good stock in the house."

"Let me do your legs," she said. She balanced on her toes and held my foot against her stomach while rubbing cream into my lower calves. It felt somewhat strange to be spoiled by another woman, but it was pleasant. The ring of the phone cut through the house. "Don't worry, Paul will get it," she said.

A few minutes later, Paul stood in the doorway, looking at both of us. "I am so sorry, but I have to leave," he said. Jennifer turned to him, asking, "What is the matter?

"They need me in the hospital; it should take about 3 to 4 hours. I'm really sorry," he said.

"Well," Jennifer said, "it looks like we get to enjoy all of the wine ourselves. Paul is a surgeon, and the hospital is just 10 minutes down the road," she explained.

The sounds of Paul's car faded into the rainy night. She continued to massage the cream into my legs. Then she stood up and handed me the container. "If you like, you can do me," she said. She sat at the edge of the bed, and I started to massage the cream into her shoulders.

"You've never done it?" she asked. No, I never creamed a woman's shoulders," I said. No, that's not what I meant," she replied. "You've never done it with a wo...."

Her sentence was cut short by the interjection:
"Survival, we are suffering: Do something."
"Oh no, not you lot again."
"Who started it this time?"
"The lower abdomen, uterus, intestines, and the whole plumbing system are at risk," was the answer. "Let me explain to you guys what is going to happen." "And I want all of you to listen, because I am getting sick and tired of you breaking into my thoughts and stuffing everything up, OK?"

"We have one breath to work with; that's all. One lousy single breath, that's all we have."
"All of you, as of this moment, are no longer needed by the body; get this once and for all into your head."
"Oh, sorry guys, that's where I live, figure of speech."
"The best you can do is consider yourselves dead already, and then you won't be bothering me anymore."

"You are all finished, OK."
"You are dead, as far as I'm concerned."

"Now in that last breath of air, how much oxygen do you think there is?"
"We have just enough to kick us over for a few minutes at the very most. How much of that time has passed already?"
"Don't tell me."
"I don't want to know. I am not interested."
"That's not my job. Now this has been the second time you guys have ripped me out of my thoughts, and I just give up. We're going to die, and so be it; it will all be your fault."
 "Survival. Survival. Do something," came the response.

"Do you think I'm stupid?"
"I know that we are almost dead. Let us first get our priorities right. Now do the legs need any blood?"
"Yes," they answered.
"No, you just don't get it, do you?"
"What are you going to do with it, run?"
"It's impossible; the body is unconscious; I know; I just took a look around and all the lights are out; nothing is happening with the consciousness."
"But if our legs don't get any blood, we're going to die."
"You got it."
"What I want you to do is die silently, you hear me: silently! Don't tell me about it; no fuss, no big deal, no Oh-my-God stories; just die and let me get on with it."
"But that's not fair," came the answer.

"Don't make me laugh. Fair? Do you think this is a democracy? What good is a leg if everything else is dead? You've got no answers, have you?"
"Now if consciousness were awake, then things would be different, but who else but I has possibly a chance to save us?"
"Are there any volunteers?" A big silence set in.

"I thought as much."

"I am in charge, and my decisions are final; is that fully understood?" No one answered. You will all be sacrificed so that I can survive as long as possible."
"Is that understood?"
There was still no answer.

"When your time comes to die, you will do it in total silence."
"Is that understood?"

"You will do exactly as I say."
"Is that understood?"

"I shall try to do my best to keep us all alive."
"Did you all understand that?"
"Yes," his various body parts replied.

"I am at the controls, and I can see who is struggling and who is dying; I can see it right here. No one needs to tell me anything."
"This is a crisis. However important you were when things were normal, all that has changed in one second. You are all redundant and no longer needed."

"Since you ripped me out of my thought, you need to get my thoughts back. If you can't do that, then you've got to give me another thought. And if you can't do that, then you've got to give me the last conscious thought there was."

"Don't tell me what actually happened. I am not one bit interested in that. Give me minimal information, just facts, no emotions, no big stories, just simple answers to the question I ask you. I ask no more and no less of you."
"What I suggest is that for once we all work together for our common survival. I tell you what I know, and you tell me what you know."

"We are losing blood at the back of the head. Someone has to fix that and stop any more blood loss. There is extra heat at the back of the head as well. We cannot afford heat, as heat costs oxygen. Someone stop the heat there. The senses tell me that the mouth and nose are underwater. That means the lungs must not breathe. Even if the reflex commands you to breathe, you must ignore it. I will tell you when you can start breathing. If you breathe before that, then we shall all drown."
"It's as simple as that."

"There is still a lot of blood in the liver. Perhaps the heart can run that through again and try to extract whatever it can. Only use the little valves that supply the head. I don't know how you do it. That is not my job. The heart has to beat as slowly as possible. The only one to be allowed to get any oxygen is the head, and a tiny bit for the heart to supply it."
"Is that understood?"

Silence was the answer.
"Here is the deal: You do that, and die when you have to, and hope that we somehow get through this and can revive you if you should cross over the line. Is all that clear?"

"We all need to cooperate as one."
"What was the last conscious thought? We can't ask consciousness because it's still knocked out. We can only try to guess as best as possible. Are there any imprints left on the eyes?"
"No" came as the answer.

"Are there any echoes or traces left in the ear?"
"Yes."

"Come on; don't hold us all in suspense; what have you got?"
"Hot."
It is not the water. That is just warm.

"Oil" was another answer. Was it hot oil? Do the two belong together? You do not cook with hot oil in water. That does not make sense.

"It's best if we consider ourselves to be dead already. That way, we won't get disappointed, and we'll have nothing more to worry about. I mean all of you. I am different. I am the exception. I believe in the survival of all of us. If I fail, then I shall fail trying."

"What I shall try to do is this: I have to spin a yarn that gets us hooked so deeply that it seems like reality. I need to visualise that in colour. I can only see colour when I get oxygen. Where were we? Ah, yes 'hot'. Now what does that mean? Is that all I have to go on? Hot what?"

"Sun, cooking, burning, what's hot?" No answers came.

"Oil, car oil, sunflower oil, cooking, salad, body oil, fish oil, heating oil, sewing machine oil, which oil?" No answers came.

"Just one more thing before I get started: I can rave on for hours. That doesn't mean I'm wasting time. In the real world, only a few seconds will pass. I have to weave a story so that I can awaken consciousness. And another thing, when I say the word 'yuck', I want you to release all the adrenaline that's left, the lung to take a deep breath, the heart to beat as fast as you can, and everyone to wake up at once."

"So don't forget, it's the word 'yuck' that is the keyword to get activated."
"Let's all do our bit and remember we're all in the same boat."
Boat?
Yes, I've got a start. Here we go: I'm in the boat.
 "Body check, what is the air temperature?"
"It's 27 degrees C on the forehead and 28.3 degrees C on the nose, just above the water level," replied the parts.

"Spare me the details."
"Is that warm, hot, cold, or what?"
"What's it like? I can't be bothered doing an analysis on the data."
 "Somewhere in between, it's like summer," was the response.

I am in the boat on a warm summer's day on a blue, beautiful ocean. The boat is a rowing boat made of wood and painted red. One ore is missing, so I can only paddle around in circles. Why am I naked? I've only just started. How would I know? I guess I am; that's why.
The ocean is coloured in a mixture of navy blues and shades of azure blues, and in the distance, I can't quite make out what colour that is meant to be. The colours are fading in the distance.

"Does anybody hear me?"
"The colours are fading."
"Hello!"
"Fading colours!"
The fading colours transformed into a rich saturation of predominantly blues. The colours blend in the distance, where the sky meets the ocean on the horizon.
I'm just glad the boat is not leaking. What is this over there? There is a whole fleet of ships. A big ship in the middle that is huge in size and yellow in colour. That colour is just yuc... oops, I nearly blew it. Yellow is just not right.

Three other vessels are bright red. All the ships head in my direction. Isn't it lovely? I'm about to be rescued by a bunch of sailors.
Before long, the big yellow ship stopped right beside me. A voice from high above said, 'Hello there!'
I look up, and a tiny head looks over the bow. Tiny arms are waving. So high as if it were a high-rise building from the inner city. I waved back.
He is not going to hear my voice up there anyway. From the side, a small rowing boat approaches me with two young men inside. Hello, ma'am, we have a message from the captain".
"You do?" I said.
"Yes, ma'am," the taller one replied.
"So don't keep me in suspense," I said. "What does the captain of this yellow ship have to say?"
"And why are you two staring at me?"
"Have you never seen a naked woman?"
No, ma'am, not a real one. Not in a long time," they responded.
"The captain wishes to invite you aboard," the tall one said.

"Does he now?"
Yes, ma'am," he answered.
"And I would appreciate it if he could move this huge yellow thing a little to the side."

"It's taken all the sun away."

"That may be a little difficult, ma'am," the short guy answered.

"Why is that?" I asked.
"Ma'am, the vessel is two miles long," he said.

"You are having me on?"
"No vessel is two miles long," I said.
"We wouldn't know, ma'am; we didn't build it," he answered.

"Go shush; tell your captain what I said," was my reply.
They turned around and left. Sometime later, they came again.
"Ma'am, the captain wishes to talk to you," he said while handing me a small phone.
"Hello ma'am, I am the captain," the voice said. "Does the captain have a name?" I replied.
"Captain Malcolm," he answered.
"Hello there, Captain Malcolm," said I.

"I'm sorry, ma'am, to be unable to oblige. The vessel cannot be turned around," he said.

Well, you put it there," I answered. "You move it to the side a little; it's getting cool in the shade".

"Perhaps you could paddle a little to the side," he said.
Well, have a look; I only have one oar, and all I can do is go around in circles, see?" I answered. I can see the captain leaning over the bow, and I paddle two circles for him.

"In other words, your boat is disabled," he said.

"I wouldn't say that," I replied.

"If you can't control your boat, then you are disabled," he said. "You are in distress."
"Me in distress? Never! Disabled? No way!" I answered.

"Ma'am, it costs the owners a fortune for the whole fleet to stop for you," he said.

"I was perfectly fine minding my own business. I didn't stop you," I said. "You just go right ahead and carry on with your journey."
"I can't do that, ma'am," he said. "And why not?" I said.
"Rules of the Sea." I have to rescue you," he answered. I couldn't help breaking out in loud laughter.
"Oh dear, you don't know how to talk to a Lady, do you, Captain Malcolm?" came my reply.
"I couldn't care less what you are, Miss. I am obliged to offer you my assistance. I have to help you," he said.
Oh, what a nerve he has! Does he think I am some sort of damsel in distress? I ignore his remarks and lay sideways on the seat of my little boat. Two hours later, it is getting cooler. From above, I hear his voice again coming from a loudspeaker: "Please pick up the phone, ma'am". I did.

"I do apologise for having upset you," he said. "I would like to make you aware that it will be night soon and it will be getting cool here on the ocean."

"Well, thank you, Captain, for your wisdom," I answered.
"What can I do for you?" he asked.
"There is something you can do for me, Captain."
"I feel like fresh, juicy strawberries. Do you have any?" I asked him.
"No ma'am. Sorry, yes, ma'am. We do have strawberries," he said.
"I shall organise to have a bowl ready by the time you get up here."

"That is very kind, Captain," I said. "Please allow the sailors to assist you and come aboard. We will lift your boat to the deck," he said.

It is getting cooler, and the thought of having fresh, moist strawberries was enticement enough for me to step into the other boat and be taken to the large yellow ship.
A gate at the side of the vessel was used to enter the hull of the ship. They led me along a corridor.
All these young sailors keep looking at me. Up ahead seems to be a large room with tables and chairs and many men.
"That's the mess hall," the short guy explained.

My heart starts beating faster.
My heart, my Heart, my heart, hard is the surface I walk on.
We walk through the dining area. I'm still accompanied by the two young sailors. They all look at me as if I am from some other planet.
I can hear an old, grey-haired sailor mumbling, "Bad omen, woman aboard ship."

We continued along a maze of corridors. "The captain's quarters are right ahead, ma'am," the taller of the two said.

Again, I can hear the thumping of my heart.
Oh, that's the engine being restarted, ma'am, the thumping noise you hear," the short guy explained.

In the house with the bathtub, the phone rings.
I can hear the phone ringing behind the closed Captain's door.
The tall sailor knocks. We wait a moment and enter the room.

The Captain speaks on the telephone. After two minutes, he hangs up. "That'll be all. Thank you, boys," he says to the two men. They leave the room.

"Captain Malcolm is at your service," he introduces himself.
"I'm Pearl," I said.
"Could I offer you one of my shirts?" He asked, "We don't have any clothes for ladies aboard ship."
 "No, thank you; I am quite comfortable," I said.
"Tell me, Captain, what is this ship? What does it do?" I question him.
"This is a factory on water, a working vessel," he said.

"What is it working on?" I asked.
"We are a food factory. We produce food," he said. "I see, and what are all the other ships around us, the red ones?" I wanted to know.
"They are our fuel supply vessels," he answered. "You see, we never dock near land. This ship is constantly out at sea and produces food. All the other ships keep us supplied with whatever we need to keep working around the clock."

"But you have to get to shore sometimes to unload all the food you make," I said.

"No ma'am. We never go near land," he said.

"Allow me to explain," he said, as we took a tour to inspect the vessel.

"Over here we catch squid," he said, and the squid is then ground up into fine particles."

"It all ends up in large tanks, like a huge cooking pot," he explained. From the deck, you can see the tank. It's a mile long, like a huge swimming pool."

"See the buttons in the control room?" he asked.

 "Yes," I said.

"They control all the ingredients that go into the mix."

"That's all a bit disgusting," I said.

"Maybe so, but that's what we do," he answered.

"Yuc..." I swallowed the word just in time.

"Yuc... Yu... Ya... Ja... Jacob is my brother's name," I recovered.

"That's nice," the captain responds.

"The food we produce is made to feed the fish?" he said.

"You are having me on," I said.

"No, that's the only way we can keep fish stocks up."

"In the control room, we can mix the most appropriate blend for any species."

"This can't be real," I said, "but who am I to know your business."

Wherever we went along the ship, the crew gathered and looked at me with wanting eyes. I must admit, it was all a bit stimulating.

"Forgive me, ma'am, but the men have been here for a long time and have not seen a woman for a couple of years, and neither have I," the Captain said.

"If you would like to wear this, perhaps you would feel more comfortable." He offered me a pair of slacks and a jumper. I just had to laugh. He had no idea.

"Not in a million years could I wear this, it just doesn't match. I don't feel like grey," as I'm pointing to the uninspiring jumper.

"Let the boys enjoy themselves and I don't mind one bit. I find it all a bit exciting, and must admit the thought of being the only woman here makes me feel very special. It's a bit of a thrill," I said.
"As you please," he answered.

"Tell me, Captain," what do you guys do for entertainment around here?" I asked him.
"We have entertainment rooms, a gym, sports, swimming pool, library, video, DVDs and satellite TV reception."
"Boring, boring, boring," I said.
"How many men are in your crew?" I asked.
"428 men," he answered.

"You're the Captain, and you have a lot of clout. What you say is like an order around here, am I right?"
"Yes," he answered.

"So why not have some fun and let me meet all the guys and organise a dance or something like that," I suggested. Then I noticed a microphone hanging on the wall.

"What does this button do?" I asked the captain.
"That is for the microphone. It allows me to address the crew all over the ship," he said. I couldn't help myself, took the microphone and had to press the button.

"Now hear this, now hear this," I said, "can any of you boys show a lady a good time?" I asked.
Within a second, I could hear a roar of male voices all sounding as one.

"I take that as a 'yes'," and again the roar echoed through the hull.

"So why don't we all meet in an hour's time at the mess hall?" This time the roar of male voices virtually shook the ship. It did me.
"See you soon, boys," and I stopped pressing the button.
"You don't mind, captain, do you?" I said to him, but he was to bewildered to say anything.

"Do me a favour, captain, the sun outside has dried my skin and I need to have a bath. Could you find me some oils to put on? I need to bath in oil," he looked like a question mark.

"Any oil, sunflower, vegetable, castor, baby oil, I don't care which oil as long as it is not engine oil, and no diesel either," I said.

I don't know how it came to be, but within 15 minutes I sat in the captain's bathtub filled with warm oil. He even found some lavender oil. I am now soaking in the relaxing slippery oil. All my hair is wet and I rub my hands over my entire body. The thought of meeting all these cute sailors shortly just got me going. Oh yes, 428 men who had not seen a woman for years. Sensations ran through my entire body.

I can feel my heart, my Heart, my HEART running, running my fingers through my hair. I hurried up and couldn't wait to

meet the boys. As I was, I ran out of the bath and grabbed the captain by the hand.
"Come on, let's go, let's have some fun."
Reluctantly he followed me.

My heart raced again, my heart; my Heart, my HEART and I raced along the corridor.

As we entered the mess hall, a huge cheer made us all feel welcome. I guess they all loved their captain very much, as none of them knew me.

Oh, how many gorgeous boys to feast my eyes on, most just had jeans on and no top. They all gave me a huge smile. One by one, they introduced themselves, except one, the old grey-haired guy. He mumbled repeatedly, "Woman aboard ship is a bad omen."

I didn't want to listen to him. "Let's have some fun, let's party." The music was good and I started dancing. They formed in a big circle around me and I had a ball. Every so often, I picked one of the crew and we had a solo dance in the centre of the circle. All my skin was shiny from all the oil on me.

The dancing and all the admiring looks started to heat me up. I hadn't seen the captain for a long time. I danced for about an hour then I got bored.

I ran along another corridor calling out, "Come on boys, let's have some fun."

427 guys ran after me, the old one didn't. I ran into the control room. They had so many buttons. In my excitement, I started pressing as many as I could.

"No ma'am, don't press that one," said one of the guys in the doorway. I kept my finger on the button and smiled at him.

"You mean this one?" I asked with all the innocence I could muster. Then I read the label on the button, 'Fuel divert'. "So what?" I shrugged my shoulders and ran out the other door.

This time 426 guys chased after me. I ran up all the stairs until I reached the upper deck. The noise of 852 boots trampling up the staircase followed me. All chasing a naked oiled up woman, in the middle of the ocean on a ship up a staircase.

On top of the staircase was a gate. I shut it. All the guys were on one side, and I was on the other. Then I saw the captain down below.

"Hey captain," I called out, "I feel for some fresh strawberries now."

All the crew echoed in rhythmic chant: "Strawberries, strawberries." The boys really tried to leave a good impression on me.

Within a few minutes, a pink bowl of strawberries was handed from guy to guy, up the chain of people on the staircase. The guy closest to me behind the closed gate handed it to me.
I took the bowl and climbed up on one of those towers on the deck of the ship. Below me was the 1-mile-long pool of shredded squid. It had turned yellow and frothy, maybe from all the extra ingredients that I added, when I pressed the buttons.

A little later, the men had managed to open the gate and were now all around the big pond of frothing brew. From the high tower, I could see all the surrounding vessels. They had all come close to the yellow ship I was on.

Far in the distance, I can see some sparks, and I have no idea what caused them, but flames are now approaching us from both sides of the vessel. The red ships ignite on either side of ours. The flames keep jumping closer and closer. In no time at all, the yellow ship was surrounded by flames. It becomes very hot.

I take a strawberry from the bowl and put it in my mouth. My taste sensations figured out straight away that they were not fresh. I spit it out. I slip.

With the taste of tinned strawberries still in my mouth, I fall towards the pool of frothing squid. As I fall, I can see the flames engulfing everything around me. I fall deep into the slimy paste of chopped-up squid.

I open my mouth wide to get rid of the disgusting strawberry taste, when all of a sudden....
I scream out:

"Yuck"

I inhale a whole mouthful of squid-tasting disgust, and it is just so revolting that I regurgitate it all back out.

Pearl lifts her head out of the water and coughs. She gets out of the bath. The edge of the bath shows a small streak of blood.

She looks at her watch and says, "3 minutes past 8 p.m." That was a quick bath. A tingle in all the toes and fingers as the blood flow recommenced.

She calls out to her children, "Hey kids, brush your teeth. It's time to go to bed." "Yes, Mum. Did you have a nice bath?"

End

Preface (Falcon in Freefall)

'Falcon in Freefall' is an exhilarating journey that explores the depths of human consciousness and the fragile nature of life itself. In this gripping tale, we follow the desperate descent of a man falling from an airplane without a parachute, facing the imminent certainty of his own death.

As the protagonist hurtles towards the Earth, the story takes an unexpected turn. A falcon, observing the man's perilous descent, becomes entwined in his thoughts and attempts to make sense of his final moments. Through the falcon's perspective, we witness the man's tumultuous thoughts and fragmented memories, ultimately revealing the complex web of events that led him to this fateful plunge.

The falcon's presence adds a unique layer to the narrative, offering a parallel perspective on life, freedom, and the fleeting nature of existence. It becomes a witness to the man's desperate search for answers and an unlikely companion in his final moments.

In 'Falcon in Freefall,' the reader is invited to ponder profound questions about fate, purpose, and the consequences of our actions. It explores the intricate connections between individuals, the choices we make, and the impact they have on our lives and those around us. Through this thrilling and introspective journey, we are challenged to contemplate the significance of each passing moment and the choices we make along the way.

Prepare to be captivated by the raw emotions, vivid imagery, and existential contemplations within the pages of this remarkable story. 'Falcon in Freefall' will take you on a roller-coaster of suspense, self-discovery, and the unyielding pursuit of understanding, leaving an indelible mark on your thoughts long after the final page is turned.

Heinz G. Ross

Falcon in freefall

"Why, why, why?" He screams at the top of his lungs. "Why?" When you are falling from an aeroplane at 14,000 feet, you are not going to hear an answer. What you will hear is the sound of rushing wind past your ears as gravity invites you to come back to earth. When you know and are absolutely certain that you are not wearing any type of parachute, no matter what the answer to the question 'why', you will know one thing: that you are going to die.

It will not take long, and you will grasp the, shall we say, 'gravity' of the situation you find yourself in. He is picking up speed.

12000 feet.

That didn't take long. He is now gravitating towards 10,000 feet. I can tell he is not a skydiver. He is not a professional at that. 'Why? Now I am starting to talk like him. Why is he not a professional? Because of the clothes he wears. There is nothing professional about that. Ordinary trousers, black shoes—oops, he just lost one. And he wears a blue-striped shirt. At least the blue matches the sky a little. The buttons may rip. He is now falling at around 121 miles per hour. But he is not going to cover 121 miles. He does not have an hour. Up here, time is measured in seconds when you are diving.

He has just gone past the 10,000-foot mark. There are no markers up here. I just know the height. Let me introduce myself. I am a Falcon, you know, the bird variety. Eagles, hawks, and kites belong to my family. I am just happy to be a Falcon.

8000 feet.

A professional skydiver would not be at 8,000 feet at this point in time. But falling from the sky for the first time is not a graceful sight. I guess it's his first time. Excuse me, but I have to fold my wings in, otherwise I cannot catch up to him. No worries; I can always catch up to him. I guess I am the fastest bird alive. I am shaped like a bullet at the moment. I reckon I could make it down to the ground in about 43 seconds, taking it easy. But if I saw some prey, that could entice me to become like a missile, and my speed towards you would become just a blur. That is why you never see us up here. And we are small in size, just a handful.

"Why, why?" the falling man is still screaming.

I am much closer to him now.

6000 feet.

It is not a good idea to open your mouth at this speed. No, you will not catch flies up here. But if he has dentures, they are not going to stay put. Just look at his eyes, wide open. The rush of wind is almost blowing his eyeballs out of their sockets. The professionals always wear goggles. It is not good for your lungs either, or his lungs. It is a bit like resuscitation with a funnel in your mouth while sticking your head out of the fastest bullet train you know. As long as he does not inhale. That must be his real hair. If he had been wearing a hairpiece, it would have been blown off by now.

I can't really tell what he looks like. His whole face is distorted. The cheeks are flapping in the wind. The skin on his neck looks like invisible hands are massaging it. Flap, flap, flap on the sides. Flappedy, flappedy flap. His shirt has been ripped out of his trousers and follows him like a flag in a gale.

His arms and legs were gesticulating in an uncontrolled manner. If he wants to go faster, then he is going the wrong way about it. He should tuck all his limbs close to his body and either go feet first or head first. Just look at him. He is rolling, tumbling, and flipping and looks like an amateur. Instead of enjoying the view, he is trying to reach out for something, trying to grab onto anything. But there is nothing here to hold on to.

He can't even keep his speed steady. Look at him now, powering away home to mama earth at 124 miles an hour. Terminal speed. It will be terminal. Oh, not for me; remember, I am a falcon. I can fly. Not at this speed. I'm diving. If I let my wings out now, my feathers will leave a trail behind me like the dirty exhaust fumes of a V8 with a blown head casket. I never tried it. I need them all.

4000 feet.

"Why, why?" he is screaming out again.

I wonder if that is the only word that he knows. I try to get a bit closer to him. Stop flapping your arms around. I do not want to be hit. Steady, steady, and easy does it.

I think he gets the hint. That is much better now. He is calming down. Have a look to the east. Squint your eyes; otherwise, they pop out of the sockets and follow you like marbles. See the beautiful ocean. All the blues you can think of. The white lines are the waves, the surf rolling onto the sand. It is the best view in the world. And you want to know why it is the best view in the world?

"Why, why?" he screams.

I am glad you asked me, because it is the Pacific Ocean right below. It kisses the beach for thousands of miles. Wet kisses on the golden sands. It has the prettiest name of any ocean. Did you know that?

"Why, why?"

It is in the name. It means 'peace'. Peaceful Ocean, that is what it is, and that is what it means. And have a look over there near the white wash. That is the surf, and the golden line along the water is the Gold Coast. The tiny white specks on the water are sailing vessels. The streak of white behind them is the wash they make. I guess your eyes are not as sharp as mine are. It will become clearer in a few seconds. And in the surf, I can see surfers riding the waves.

"Why, why?" he screams again.

Because they like it, that's all the reason you need. It is a lot warmer down there than it is up here, I can tell you. They wait in the water. The waves come in sets. Then it builds up to a real beauty. You jump up onto the board and hang in there. Weave around to slow you down, and wait until it does catch up to you. And when the waves break over your head and you are still standing, then you are in a tube. And that is the best of all: riding the tubes.

See the dark things in the water? Dolphins. Beautiful creatures. The surfers' friend They are the masters of surfing.

Hey, take a look at that. Aren't we lucky? Can you see all the creatures? They look like big shadows. They are whales, humpback whales. They come in close to the shore. They are moving up north.

"Why, why?"

They are migrating. It happens every year. There are thousands of them. They come from Antarctica and are on their way here for warmer waters. It's hard to believe the little specks weigh about forty tonnes each.

"Why, why?"

You are really interested in all this. I guess they had a good feed in Antarctica. How would I know? I am a Falcon. I do not fly overseas. It is not far to go now. Better start picking a spot where you want to land. There are Tamborine Mountains over there with sub-tropical rain-forests. A volcano built that one. Better make up your mind about where you want to set down.

"Why, why?" he screamed again.

Your vocabulary is very limited, isn't it? We have been in this free fall for how many seconds? And all you said all along was 'why, why, why, why, why'.

3000 feet.

2500 feet.
Did I tell you I was born at the stroke of midnight?
"Why, why?"
2000 feet.
Do you really want to know the answer?
"Why, why?"
1500 feet.
You know, we are going a little bit fast now. I am interested to see how you are going to make a safe landing.
"Why, why?"
1000 feet.
If you have a cord, then it is about time you started to pull it. It is as good a time as any.
"Why, why?"
800 feet.
Because if you don't, you are going to die.
"Why, why?"
You do not have a parachute on. "Why, why?"
600 feet.
I am glad you want to know this. Because it is going to be as hard as concrete, that is why. You are going to slam into it at 124 miles per hour. That is 200 kilometres per hour, or 55.6 metres per second. That means your head will meet your toes 0.032 seconds after you hit the ground. By the time your brain receives the message that your feet have touched down, I can't finish this line of thought. The mess you will make will make a distinction between your body parts somewhat difficult.
Do you see that car down there, the one on the highway? He is going at full speed. We are going twice as fast. If we were on the highway, we could overtake him, just so you get an idea of how fast we are moving.
400 feet.
300 feet.
200 feet.
100 feet.
"About six seconds to go".

"Why, why?" he screamed again.

Carefully watch the insects now. By the way, don't forget that your shoe is following you.

50 feet

Whatever you have to do, now is a good time to do it.

Do it now! Can you hear me? Now. NOW. NOW! NOW!!!!!!

"Why, why?"

Are you some sort of stuntman or daredevil lunatic?

40 feet.

You are going to die.

I am going to die.

We are going to die.

We are going to die.

How did I get caught up in this?

I could still pull out. I still have a chance.

Why can't I do it? Why am I following this nincompoop?

30 feet.

Hey, have a look down. Try to avoid the cow pad. You would not want that as your last whiff in your nose. Do you see the hibiscus? Try to give them a miss, too. There is no point in robbing the bees of some fun.

20 feet.

He must be kidding me.

No. He is not pulling on anything.

I have to see that. He knows no fear.

He is just going to do... to do... to do what? I have no idea.

10 feet.

You know you are going to die, don't you?

"Why, why?"

Well, that is what I want to know. We need a miracle. We need it now. Why, why, why, tell me why? Tell me 'why, and better make it quick.

8 feet.

"Why was..."

Oh my gosh, it is a miracle. He can say another word.

We need another miracle. Go on, keep talking.

7 feet.

"Was I pushed?"

I don't know. 'Pushed'? Pushed? What do you mean? Who pushed you where, when, how, what, and who?

6 feet.

"Who pushed me out of the plane?"

You picked a good time to have a long, in-depth conversation. We had plenty of time before when you asked me a million questions. Perhaps we should meet for a cup of coffee someday and ponder the meaning of life.

For crying out loud, how would I know who pushed you out? Who would want you to learn to fly?

Probably your mum and dad kicked you out of the nest so that you could find your wings and learn to fly on your own. We do that to ours. We find a bit of a hill, and then we kick them in the behind, and they can fly in no time at all. We would never even consider going up on a plane. But humans do all sorts of weird things.

5 feet.

"I don't want to learn to fly," he said.

Well, I could see that. You have succeeded. Your oldies will be pretty disappointed with you. So you are not coming up with anything special. Some super spectacular and amazing feats Some dramatic, unexpected, nerve-calming finale?

"No."

4 feet.

That is fine. Oh brother. What have I done to deserve this? I only hope no one is going to find my feathers. How am I going to live this down? The finest flying falcon crashing—the thought just makes me sick. What have I ever done in my entire life to deserve to die?

3 feet.

"That's what I want to know too," he screamed.

Tell me, then. Tell me, tell me, tell me. What have you done to deserve to die? I am all ears. By the way, better pull your legs and feet up. Get a little more extra time. And remember your

shoe. It is still falling at the same speed. If you manage to stop, the shoe will not.
2 feet.
"I did post a letter once without putting a stamp on it."
Yes, yes, yes, and?
"I did hand in my tax return a week late."
And?
"I didn't eat all my vegetables when I was a kid, and I gave them to the dog."
And?
1 foot to go
"I wagged school twice."
And?
"I lied. 29 years ago, I was at the chocolate shop on the 24th of August. When my mum asked whether I did or not, I denied it. I have to pay my electricity bill, and I don't know where I placed it. I put a dirty milk bottle in the recycle bin once."
6 inches to go.
Look, this could go on for another week. Unfortunately, we do not have the luxury of time. Can you hear something?
"What?"
I thought I heard something.
3 inches to go.
The last three inches are not going to hurt.
"That's good to know".
2 inches.
If you want, you can think that they all pushed you out of the plane. It doesn't really matter anymore.
1 1/2 inches to go.
That is less than the length of your little finger.
"They all thought I did it."
What, what, when, who, and where? Speak up, man. Don't hold it back. Let it out. Then it won't bother you anymore.
"They didn't believe me."
Will you get on with it? Don't keep me in suspense any longer.
1 inch.

No, keep me in suspense. As long as you keep me in suspense, we are suspended. You know what the word 'suspense' means.

"No."

It is the 'exited anticipation of an approaching climax'. Keep talking; maybe we will think of something. Suspend me a bit longer.

"They thought I did it, and that's why they pushed me out of the plane."

Who? Who are 'they'? Come on, speed it up."The neighbour, the ambulance driver, the whole hospital, my boss at work, my teacher in class when I was a kid, my friends in school when I was 12, my...."

Hurry up. What has the neighbour thought of you to give him a reason to push you out of the plane?

"When I was 8 years old, I picked up an apple off the footpath in front of his house. It had fallen from the tree. It was on his 85th birthday, and he accused me of taking it from his tree."

When was that?

"45 years ago."

I see. So some 130-year-old man had a checklist, and on his checklist was your name, and he sneaked onto the plane this morning, opened the door, and pushed you out. And he waited all this time to get even? And after he pushed you, he ticked you off his checklist. It makes total sense to me. Do tell me about the ambulance driver.

"One day I had some pain in the chest, and they picked me up and drove me to the hospital in the city and checked me out, and nothing was wrong with me. They thought I wanted to have a free ride into town.

I can see that. So, the ambulance driver, the doctors, and the nurses all got together and joined the 130-year-old man.

Go on. What about your boss? What was that about?

"I overslept a few times and arrived late for work. He gave me a warning, saying that if I ever came late again, he might as well close the whole place down. Then all the people working there started to worry about their jobs."

That is understandable. What was with your teacher?

"He thought I was cheating at exams. My pencil fell on the floor, and I just picked it up. And I had to lean over, and that would have looked like I was..."

I get the picture. Carry on. Your friends in school, what happened there?

"They thought I let them down. I was the goalkeeper, and we were playing against another school. A kid from the other team kicked the ball. A bit of dirt came off his boot and flew into my eye. So I couldn't see the ball coming, and they scored, and they won, and we lost.

And, and, and? Look, mate, I think you've got a little bit of a problem. Now I can't believe that a 130-year-old man, the ambulance driver, all the doctors and nurses from the hospital, hundreds of your work colleagues, the teacher, and all your friends from school got together on that little two-seater aeroplane and pushed you out. I am sorry. I just cannot see it. You had better wake up to yourself. Maybe you are slipping, or maybe you slipped.

12 inches to go.

"See, even you don't believe me."

It is all in your head, man. I was hoping to at least get away with some sort of good feeling, some sort of reason to die happy, and some sort of fulfilment as a reward for sticking with you. I am disappointed. You let me down. Literally. It has been good to have known you, but what a letdown.

Tell me, what is your name?

"Tom. Tom Hawker."

That rings a bell. Hey, what is that noise?

"Which noise?"

Sounds like a plane.

"And there it is. The little two-seater and all the kids from school hanging off the fuselage The doctors are sitting on the wings. The nurses are hanging on the ailerons. The 130-year-old man is sitting on the tail, waving his stick about. The teacher is screaming out of the window: 'You thought you got away with it."

"And see, there at the end of each wing the thing that looks like a long banner? Those are all my work mates each one linked to the other by hanging off the ankles of the one in front."
Oh my gosh. You were right all along.
"Yep. Told you"
¼ inch to go.
Look man, I am so sorry.
"Do you think they are going to hold a wake for me?"
Well.
"A wake to send me up?"
Like a wake-up call?
"Yes, wake up," he said.
"Wake up"
1/8 to go.
1/16.
1/32.
1/64.
1/128.
1/256.
1/512.
1/1024.
1/2048.
N o w   w e   h a v e   t o   t a l k   i n
s l o w   m o t i o n.
"   W   h   y   ?   "
D o n ' t   y o u   s t a r t   w i t h   t h a
t   a g a i n.
F   a   r   e   w   e   l   l   .
"   B   y   e   "

SPLAT

"Wake up"

"Wake up"

"Tom. TOM, will you wake up," his wife shouts out.

"I have been calling out for the last 10 minutes."

"Didn't you hear the alarm go off?"

"You're going to be late for work again."

End

Articles, thoughts...

I do bequeath

Prepare to indulge in the delightful absurdity that is the world of bequeaths and dispositions, to some a sombre subject, but on account that at this point in time you're still alive, perhaps an opportunity to greet the same with hilarity. Perhaps you feel the moment is approaching; well, 99 seems like a good stretch, but compared to Enoch's son Methuselah, you're just a 10-year-old kid, despite you nearing a century.

First and foremost, let us not forget the dramatic flair of placing the sacred words 'Last Will and Testament' right across the front page. Even if it's your debut in this mysterious art, centre it with impeccable finesse. Follow this with 'made by, and date.' On the second page, there is a chance to revel in repetition. Repeat those four words across the top, for what is life without a little redundancy? Now add a line break and let us regale in the charm of the phrase 'This is the last Will of me' (perhaps it's not, but never mind), and right behind that, pen down 'your name' (not mine).

Next, left again, a new line, which starts with the letters 'of', followed by the street you inhabit, the house number, and the suburb thereof. And never forget to flaunt your knowledge of geography with the state, zip code, and country of your habitat.

Now, the grand moment of revocation! Like a Shakespearean soliloquy, declare with theatrical gusto, 'I revoke all previous Wills and testamentary documents made by me' (even if it is your first). Fear not; you'll still be 'me,' no matter what name you choose in scribing.

The time has come to appoint your esteemed 'Executor(s),' those who shall ensure your wishes, seeded with the words you're scribing, come to fruition in due course. But beware, we're not talking about hired killers here; only trusty souls need apply. ' I appoint my' _____ (explain relationship right there and let's have some fun, shall we?), 'of _____ (let's locate them), 'in the State of _____ (oh, yes, where else?), and their esteemed country. At the end of all the names, followed by 'to be the Executor(s) of this Will and Trustee(s) of my Estate. And just in case they may have become dead or, if alive, do not feel like executing, appoint a few reserves; the baton must find at least one willing taker, like this: 'If' (whichever name is above) is unwilling to fulfil this role, then I appoint', and list some more. If you have a lot of paper, just keep going down the line; in case the reserves are doubtful, add another lot again. Do not forget, following the names, to add the words 'as Executor and Trustee.' There are three spots to sign this paper: the Testator or testatrix, a witness, and another.

At this point, caution is called for! After all, it is a legal document laced with complexities that can trigger consequential consequences. Prepare to prepare yourself for the grand preparation of a lifetime! Get ready to get ready, because you won't believe how ready you'll need to be. It's time to time your timing and ensure you have enough time to time it all perfectly. You must muster all your musts, muster your energy, and muster your enthusiasm for this momentous moment. The preparation is so much preparation that it may feel like you're preparing forever and ever. But fear not, because once you're prepared, you'll be prepared like you've never been prepared before.

You might not remember the moment that got your life started. In all likelihood, it, just like the surrounding universe, started with a bang, maybe with a big bang or a little bang; I have no idea (ask mum or dad). Yes, sex is what I'm talking about. Not your mum and dad having some fun time, your sex, that is, your gender. Why? You are considered a Testator if you identify as male. Conversely, you are referred to as a Testatrix if you identify as female. You think you know the answer, maybe. When was the last time you used your new reading glasses and had a closer look at the nucleus of your cells. I'm just saying.

Well, the first hurdle arises as some individuals may identify as intersex, a natural variation occurring in about 1 in 1500 to 2000 live births where chromosome patterns differ from the typical XX or XY. As intersex individuals represent approximately 4.6 million people (calculated based on 8 billion people and an incidence rate of 1 in 1750 live births), the legal wordsmith may need to create a third iteration to ensure inclusivity in legal documents. Since the proper classification could have significant consequences, seeking professional guidance to determine the appropriate designation is highly advisable. Do not be surprised to learn that the term 'Testator' can also be used as an all-inclusive term to refer to male and female, but I could not find a mention of intersex people. Being of sound mind means being legally competent (at least during the duration of making the will), and being 18 years of age or older comes into it as well. As you would expect, there are circumstances where a court can waive the age requirements.

As to the witness, it need not be a witness of your death or a witness of your life, just a witness of the scribbles that you'll leave there as a sign. Next, please beg the tree's forgiveness, as you need another page, which is numbered as all the others except increase the numbers placed by 1.

Start this page with a new headline, such as 'Residual Estate'. This is followed by 'I hereby leave the whole of my estate' (maybe the whole is a little much, or maybe not enough, but be kind to yourself; you tried). Continue with, 'both real, subject to other provisions in this Will, and after payment of my debts, funeral, and administrative expenses associated with this Will (and all will be hoping that there are none or very little). 'I leave' (even though you've already left the land of the living) my estate in (equal, unequal, whatever) shares to my (uncle, children, cat or dog, or the fence-post down the road)' and add the names of those that shall receive the goods that have as yet not clearly been defined.

Just in case they do not linger long enough to hear these words, you already make provision for such an eventuality. 'If any (of whoever listed) predecease me (it means they're dead as well), then the share they would have received, I give (even whilst you're being dead) to (maybe their surviving children, or the nail the fencepost had), if any, in (equal or unequal) shares.' If the kids are small and young, give one you trust the trustee powers (may I suggest a youngling full of zest), which you do by spelling out 'Trustee Powers, their name, place of abode, and the conditions thereof (like, until the kids are 59). Pick someone young enough to last the distance. Follow this by legal scribe: 'to manage and invest (as the trustee thinks fit (or not)) any property due to a minor beneficiary under this Will for the education, maintenance, repair, or upkeep) and benefit of that beneficiary.' End the page the same way as the last one you did before, with two spots for the scribbles, and then add just one more.

The final page the next one be, and pay the tree some sympathy. 'Attestation of Will', 'Dated this _____ day of _____ year, is the evidence by which something is attested, and the date as well as year shall be when the 2 scribblers are here, by that is meant the ones that see you move the pen to sign your name as 'Signature of Testator (or Testatrix)'. This then is followed by 'Signed by the Testator (or Testatrix) as his (or her) last Will in the presence of both of us (meaning the two that have watched you with four eyes move your pen) being present at his (or her) request at the same time and in the presence of each other and the Testator (or whatever), hereunto subscribe our names as witnesses.'

Follow this with 'Signature, Full Name, Date of Birth, Address, Occupation, and the 'Date' they signed; it is best that all the dates are the same to enable their attesting that they saw you scribe your name.

It is not a good idea to use a number of different colouring pencils for signing the remains of a once proud tree, but rather an opportunity to build relationships, foster empathy, and create a sense of unity by sharing a single pen that leaves its trace in black or dark blue. Ensure that at least four eyes (and of course your own) are watching as the scribe leaves its marks.

Another point of note: Is it 'Will' or 'will? That will be explained right now: Grammatically speaking, 'will' will do; it's actually the correct spelling, unless, of course, it is at the beginning of a sentence. 'Will' will do too, as it has become fashionable, or perhaps the lawyers reasoned that with capitalisation more ink is used, which could justify the somewhat higher fee than one was expecting. Let's not get sidetracked.

Who shall get all the daylight savings that have been saved throughout the years, or the cheek and grins you carried, the many unconsumed beers? My last breaths, I shall return to the land of living, for the trees to feed, transform, and mix in the wind.

I give, bequeath, and devise my short temper to my Uncle Tom. Always did he agree to do and be what anybody wanted. I give, bequeath, and devise my pride to Dr. Russell. The extra inch to raise his nose, to scratch along the ceiling, and the pack of band-aids left to him as well, he'll have a need; his nose will bleed. I give, bequeath, and devise my worries for them to be placed in a box, nailed shut, and deeply buried under 6 feet of concrete. I give, bequeath, and devise my conscience to the richest men, under the condition that each pass it on to the one that shall become the richest then, and then repeat the process 'til they're all gone. I give, bequeath, and devise my weakness to the strongest of all men, my strength to the weakest of them all, and my cunning to the kid next door, for he'll refine it so much more. I give, bequeath, and devise my hope to the old man with the grey beard; in summer he sleeps in the park, in winter in the bins, in the backstreets of our town. He is the one who forgot his name and drinks a spirit made of Metho that he carries in his pocket.

My last abode, please spare the trees; a cardboard box will do, and I'll have none of the golden handles; if such are needed, you will find some handles in the shed. If they're a little rusty, I don't mind at all; they're on the outside anyway, my eyes are closed, and I am dead; it's fine. Disguise it all with a tablecloth; if you feel the need, the white one with the stains will do; a regal touch for me. Dispose of me as you see fit; just make sure I'm not pulling a Lazarus, that I am really dead before you shut the lid.

Point of note:
Remember, while the delightful absurdity of this writing may bring a smile to your face, preparing a last will and testament is a serious and legally binding matter. The point is not to impress the judge but that your wishes are accurately expressed and legally valid. It is crucial to seek professional legal advice when drafting your will. Consulting with an estate planning attorney in your country will help ensure that your wishes are properly documented and that your loved ones are taken care of in the future. So, have some fun with your creative thoughts, but when it comes to your real will, leave it to the experts to guide you through the process.

A little is plenty

Ms Wilson, may I have a moment?
Certainly, Mr Johns.
I have some people coming over on Saturday and I wonder if you would do us, my wife and I, the honour to join us? This is so unexpected, Mr Johns. What prompted you to ask me?

Always the enquiring mind, I like this about you, Ms Wilson. I had the pleasure of reading your book, the one just released and I am intrigued. I want to get to know the person behind it, to get to know *you* better. It may also be of benefit to you, getting to meet the right people can do wonders for sales.
I'm lost for words, Mr Johns.
A simple 'yes' will suffice.
Yes it is then, Saturday, thank you.
I will send a car, shall we say 4pm?
Yes, that's fine.

Saturday:
Robert, Robert! He is deep in thought, let's go and surprise him.
Sarah, how lovely it is to see you. Robert, your wife must have a secret, each year she looks younger.
You never change, do you, Martin? Robert, Martin, may I introduce you to Ms Wilson, Perl Wilson.

So glad you could make it.
Good the chauffeur knew the way, Mr Johns.
Perl Wilson, the author, the journalist, the TV personality, are you one and the same?
I am.
Sorry Ms Wilson, this is Martin, he is sometimes my right hand and other times my left ear, and of course, you have met my lovely wife.
Yes, she is charming and what a lovely place you have here, Mr Johns.

No, no, please, no need for idle conversations. Ms Wilson, I am interested in your thoughts, in your perceptions, how you see the world. I'm sure many others would like to hear your views. May I introduce you now?
Please do, Mr Johns, thank you.

Ladies, Gentleman, can I have everyone's attention please. Daniel, excuse me, Daniel, thank you. You may remember about two months ago, I suggested having a look at the book 'A little is plenty.' I don't know how many of you did, but the author of that book is right here. It gives me great pleasure to introduce you to Ms Perl Wilson.
Thank you everyone.
Ms Wilson is also a journalist and TV personality, and those of us who watch TV may be well aware of that.
Ms Wilson, welcome, I'm Jonathan Hide. Your book suggests that on average the population is happy with just getting by, with just having enough. Your book concludes if there were less than the minimum to go around it would incite civil

unrest, revolution. Having enough just to get by is the ideal balance.

I believe so, yes, Mr Hide.

But what of dreams, hope, of becoming somebody, accumulation of possessions, of striving for higher goals, Ms Wilson?

Is not a nobody somebody also? No doubt, some will strive to go further, but on average, no. Food, shelter and reasonable health are the minimum requirements. Given a modest income, that covers food, and no need for it to be the best quality, as well as rent and some doctor's expenses, a little left over to cover transportation costs and a feel-good item are essentially enough.

Ms Wilson, how can people be happy with that? They have a window in each house, Mr Hide. They find happiness by looking through that window. If they can't find happiness through that window, then there is a door they go through, perhaps they find it there. The window called Television, the door called Religion. Some find happiness through a needle, the bottle, magazines; others are waiting for their happiness to come when they are dead.

I find it hard to believe, Ms Wilson. I'm Susanne Van Fellsinger. Judging by the many luxurious limousines I saw outside, and the designer-wear most of you carry I would suggest that none here would wear the tag Mr or Mrs Average, am I right?

Perhaps so, Ms Wilson, but why is it that Mr or Mrs Average don't aspire to better themselves. Oh they try, some do. Many set out for better schooling, education, night schools, attend courses, gain qualifications, diplomas, doctorates and gain various achievements, even with distinction. They may become the local heroes in some forgotten place, and that is about it. Occasionally one picked to stand as inspiration for all the others. It is enough knowing that one can become anything. It doesn't mean that everyone becomes someone. They believe they are 'someone', that is enough, Ms Van Fellsinger. If money is the goal of happiness, then lotteries fulfil this need, a temporary daydream, at least until next week. There are so many diversions, each triggering some endorphin release to make it through the day. There is also hope. It never needs gratification. A drop of hope lasts forever, and if it doesn't, no one listens to the disillusioned.

What of yourself, Ms Wilson, are you happy? Mr Johns, I did ask myself the same question. Initially I could not answer it. The constant drizzle of music, of people speaking, non-stop conversations, incessant attention seeking stories prevented me to listen to my own voice. I could never hear myself think. I could not even think. In the car, the radio switches on automatically to warn of some traffic hazard and continues with a story one becomes absorbed in. In the shopping centre, one can just think of what to buy. The parks, the walkways, the entertainment centres, the feel-good places, all are saturated with sounds that no one takes notice of, but the brain takes it in and is kept busy absorbing it, having no resources left for free thought. The question doesn't really come up. There is constant interruption, constant entertainment. I even carry the mpg player and put earphones in to choose my own style of brainwash media. One needs to rest from time to time and again some other means used to escape into a manufactured sequence of resting. Nothing is natural, but we don't know that anymore.

Ms Wilson, your late father was a good friend and known to many of us. Commodore Frank Llewellyn Wilson joined our little group a long time ago. He became an Admiral, Mr Johns. We are well aware of that, Ms Wilson. If there are no objections, none, good, Ms Wilson, welcome to our group.

That applause was for you, Ms Wilson. I think dinner is just about to be served, this way please... Mr Johns, I am at a loss, welcome to what, which group? My father never mentioned...

Ms Wilson, relax, your book will become a bestseller very shortly. Why and how, Mr Johns?

Why, to make you feel welcome, how, we simply buy 20 to 30 million copies at cost price. That will set the wheels in motion. Mr Johns, 30 million books cost a fortune, even at cost price. You don't understand, Ms Wilson, money is like a boomerang, no matter how far away you throw it, it always comes back, sometimes very fast. Sometimes one throws a million away and four come back, throw four away and twenty return. Nothing is wasted, we sell the books again to satisfy the demand they created in the first place, easy. If that doesn't work we give them away. It doesn't matter. What is important, that your name gets a lot of exposure. That is in our interest and for the common good.

Please, enjoy the meal. That was a lavish spread, Mr Johns, thank you. Not many people ever get to see a meal like this in their lifetime. Oh, you thought this was special, ha, don't tell the cook. Mr Johns, 'this is in our interest and for the common good,' were your last remarks before dinner. What do you mean by that?

Let me ask you this, Ms Wilson, has your book caused a stir? No, many comments of people agreeing with the content, many find, no matter what they do, it is always just enough to get by. If they do get ahead a little, the washing machine or car will break down and one is back to square one. Why is this so, Ms Wilson?

It seems the whole system finely geared to keep everyone just below the threshold of becoming angry. People thus remain sedate, pliable, 10% happy, 40% miserable, 50% acceptance, but mostly 100% bombarded with all sorts of signals that prevent seeing reality. Perhaps it was like this for the hunter-gatherer as well, he could only run fast enough to catch one meal that kept the tribe from starving, if not the hard slog of finding enough berries to eat left no time to analyse the laws at place. Oh, laws?

It seems that way, Mr Johns. If there is really a shortage, people will revolt, strikes, boycotts whatever means they have. They either get beaten into submission or gain some benefit that levels the field again. The answers are always the same, no matter which country, no matter which industry.
What are these answers? Not now, we have to keep our belts tight, there is not enough to go around. Mr Johns, my question is still awaiting an answer.

You know half the answer already, Ms Wilson, what you described is in the interest of the common good. Why, Mr Johns is this in your or this group's interest? Tradition, Ms Wilson, we uphold very longstanding traditions, going back to the times of Kings and Queens, large landowners, the Aristocracy, titles, castles and money. Nothing has changed, Ms Wilson, except perhaps we are now a little more in the background. No need to parade in pomp and ceremony, others do that instead. The world is a stage, a theatre of marionettes. We just pull the strings and sometimes watch the performance.

Mankind dances to your script and while their arms and legs are tight to strings, each feels free, believing each pulls their own strings, is in control of their own life. Ingenious, Mr Johns, the notion that democracy gives each a voice to vent their frustrations each is free, opportunities are everywhere. Make a prisoner feel he's running through the meadows and the bars of his cage become invisible. Whatever goes wrong will be the politicians fault, next term the others will form government. So it goes on and on, irrespective, you, your group will always be in control.

I'm glad you joined us, Ms Wilson.

Twins

Hello Professor Mayer, glad we could finally meet up.
Oh, the pleasure is all mine.
Dr Walker, I read in the journal you did some tests on twins some years ago. I wonder would I be privy to have a look at your findings.
I would be honoured if you did. I do have a number of videos. Sally and Sarah are identical twins. At the time when we recorded these videos they were 13 years old, very athletic and sports minded. The video recorded in the grounds of the school, some years ago. The building is roughly the shape of a cross, having eight outer and four inner corners. We placed 4 cameras around the grounds, each capturing a segment of the building. The video we are watching shows all views together, so we always see both twins at the same time. We give the girl the task to run around the building and every step of the way they are in view of one of the cameras.

Sally is wearing a red top, Sarah is in yellow. We asked both to run in opposite direction around the building, Sally runs from left to right and Sarah the other way. The starting point for one girl is the finishing point for the other, and vice versa.

Sally received special instructions of how to run, Sarah is not aware of this. We told Sally that after passing Sarah to aim for the next corner of the building. Not the nearest, but the next, even if it was behind her. Thereafter she was asked to aim for every corner, no shortcuts. We asked both, not to speak to each other and not to look behind, to keep looking forward.
Here is the video. Sally starts left corner of the building Sarah starts from the right. We assumed both would take a shortcut and aim for the outer corner of the cross, and we were right, they both did.

Because the right side of the cross is longer, we assumed they would meet in the third quadrant, near the top right outer corner or towards the next. Sally in the red has the special instructions. Here both pass in the third quadrant. The next corner for Sally is now the inner corner, so she needs to backtrack, get to the corner before heading to the outer one. Following the outer there is another inner corner for her. In effect, Sally will have to cover about 20m more distance, but Sarah is not aware of that, assuming she goes for the shortcut all the time. Now here is the interesting bit, Sarah has about 10 metres to go, clearly in front, when she trips and twists her ankle. Meanwhile on the other side Sally is gaining, she had further to run. We could not believe it, but both finished within a second of each other. Coincidence? Perhaps.

We had a break of 30 minutes then did another test, this time very different. Sally is to run around the whole building, virtually blindfolded. She is wearing a motor cycle helmet with the visor blinded and taped shut. As a precaution, we have speakers in case she heads for a wall or is in risk of running into something. Sarah is sitting in a car at the end of that road, which is 500m away from the school. She is to guide her sister safely around the school building using thought. This time Sally is wearing a helmet camera, so we'll be running with her, on video. A section of the screen shows Sarah. I won't say much, you'll be surprised.

Sally starts out aiming directly for the first outer corner. She is 12m from the first corner and veers off to the right, away from the corner, the wrong direction. I will just rewind the tape and this time focus on Sarah, here, at the same point Sarah shrugs, her posture changes, something is going on. Now see Sally increasing her speed. No one asked her to run; she meant to keep at a comfortable pace. After all, it was not a speed test. In the distance, you see a mother and her child, about 2 years old. Sally runs directly towards the mother, it seems that way, look at her speed now, very fast.

Look at Sarah; she is twisting and she is very tense. Here we see the mother looking at Sally, not paying attention to her own child. Now you can see the water pond and the little kid falls in. Sally takes her helmet off, throws it away, races past the mother, who is not yet aware of what happened. Here she gets into the water to bring the 2-year-old up to the surface, and then the mother realises what happened. The child survived.

What do you make of that? Sarah shrugs long before anything is wrong, Sally changes direction, increases speed long before there is any reason. Only after the kid falls in the water does she take the helmet off. Everything seemed to co-ordinate to perfect timing. The mother's attention taken away by Sally running towards her, yes, it may not have happened if Sally wasn't there. Is Sally to blame for the kid falling in, or did she safe it?

Disclaimer (Hear, hear)

The following content (Hear, hear) is a work of fiction and is purely intended for entertainment purposes. The events here don't mirror any real-world legislative body on Earth or beyond. Any resemblance to real persons, living or dead, or actual events is purely coincidental.

The fictional parliament, set in the year 3497, is situated in an undiscoverable galaxy, light-centuries away. It thrives on cosmic-sized wit, satire, sarcasm, irony, and absurdity. It includes exaggerations and ridiculous conversations, caricature images and a touch of meta-humour. It is a whimsical creation where political discourse takes on a light-hearted and humorous tone, devoid of the realities and complexities of your world. Politics can be fun, at least in the following.

Keep in mind that all the depictions, actions, and conversations are purely products of imagination, often exaggerated and should not be misconstrued as a reflection of the conduct or nature of our real-world politicians.

Real-world politicians are dedicated to the welfare of citizens, and this content is pure imagination, not a commentary on their incorruptible, ethical, honourable and respectable efforts.

The content may not be suitable for all audiences, after all, humour is highly subjective, but if your sense of humour is not all too dented, it could be safe to proceed. So, enjoy the cosmic farce! Here, politics goes on a joyride of absurdity, taking centre stage for laughter and amusement, as here on Earth we surely need it.

Hear, hear

Speaker:

"Order in the house, please. The Member for South Coast has the floor."

Member for South Coast:

"Thank you, Madam Speaker. It is because of the failure of the previous government that we have to show leadership in this matter. As the opposition leader pointed out, when he, yes, Madam Speaker, when he, and there he sits and shakes his head, look at him, he knows all too well what I am on about. When he addressed the chair on the 25th of December, and don't you try to deny it, when he addressed this House, saying they, the then government, had done all they could in this matter."

Speaker:

"Order, ORDER! I warn the honourable member for West Coast, any more such outbursts, and..."

Member for South Coast:

"He knows all too well, Madam Speaker. Last week, one of my constituents came up to me, an elderly lady of 83, bless her. She emptied the meagre contents of her purse into my hand: $5.87, Madam Speaker, $5.- and 87 cents, and that was on Pension day."

Member for South Coast:

"Do you know how much that is in real terms? It's only $5.85; the coppers have been out of circulation for years. She emptied all into my hand, most as 5-cent pieces, and said, 'It's a disgrace.' As true as I am standing here, she said, 'It's just a disgrace.' Then she put her arms around me and wept."

"But that's not all, Mister Madam Speaker, oh no..."

Speaker:

"Please address me with a proper prefix. I cannot be both at once."

Member for South Coast:

"Certainly, Madam Speaker, I do apologise... Oh no, we are not just suffering on the South Coast, Madam Speaker, as the honourable member from the Flatlands expressed in a Television interview I chanced to witness. They too are suffering. In fact, all parliamentarians are suffering. I asked the opposition leader, 'What have you ever done for the parliamentarians when you were in power?'"

Member for South Coast:

"This is what he said: 'We have had a 3% remuneration increase in the first quarter, an 8% catch-up payment in the next, and then a $3000 additional payment for all backbenchers, even if they sit under the table. The minimum qualification period of 3 weeks was reduced to 1 week in the subsequent quarter, with an additional $5000 per quarter allowance for entertainment costs and a guaranteed minimum superannuation payment of no less than $8 million.'"

"I ask you, Madam Speaker, is this enough? Surely not, I would think. The fuel allowance, meals away from home, postage, media, and having a clean shirt allowance are all lagging behind. There is not one person in this House who can, in all honesty, say that these measly—what is it, 30, 40, $60,000 allowances—could possibly be enough for 3 months, let alone 12. It's not enough, and we need to touch our meagre incomes to make ends meet. In effect, we're subsidising the country."

Member of Gov't:

"Dear Madam Speaker, I hope you don't mind me having some light refreshments while you ponder the wisdom of my colleague's words."

Member for South Coast:

"As I was saying, the reason why schoolchildren run countless raffles, engage in selling bees, and some even collect aluminium cans, clean windows, deliver groceries, and without any second thought mail us all their hard-earned cash is that they are ashamed. I am ashamed, I say, of the meagre recompense all parliamentarians have become victims of. Had I known this before, I would have remained on the unemployment line."

Member for South Coast:

"Without a doubt, Madam Speaker, this type of false economy was initiated by the previous government. We can quibble about pensions, aged care, farmer's subsidies, the health care system, defence, and education, but how can we look the electorate in the eye and say we are worthy to lead the country? How can we?"

Gov't Members:

"Hear, hear."

Speaker:

"Order."

Member for South Coast:

"Madam Speaker, honourable members, this government is committed to restoring pride, a feeling of self-worth. In short, a fair remuneration for all the hard work we are doing for the country, and may I add, on both sides of the chair."

Gov't Members:

"Hear, hear."

Speaker:

"Willy, would you please refrain from interjecting? May I remind the member for South Coast, you have 3 minutes left."

Member for South Coast:

"Thank you, Madam Speaker, I shall be brief. In view of the current financial meltdown, the leader of the opposition, who has six harbour properties, which last year were worth just over $40 million, is now worth a mere fraction of that. Before you take a serious look at your own portfolios, I would strongly recommend some nerve-calming medication, as the picture is not going to be a pretty one. The expectations of superannuation upon retirement are now such that we need to be prepared to sweep the streets, where once we thought the evening of life could be spent on cruisers chasing marlins."

Member of Gov't:

"Madam Speaker, honourable members, I wish to voice my support for what's been said thus far."

Speaker:

"Order, Silence! Save your voice for when your time comes."

Member for South Coast:

"May I continue? We, as the government, must not only lead the country but also be seen to lead the country. We can only do that when we have the resources to do it properly. We shall introduce a bill that forthwith contains an immediate increase in all parliamentarians' remuneration packages of no less than 250%, an immediate increase in all superannuation packages of no less than 253% of pre-existing arrangements. In addition, the establishment and free admission to a drama school, speech therapies for all those in fear of speaking in public, and instructions on how to play 'I spy with my little eye something beginning with...' whatever it may be. Further, we shall endeavour to expand the Parliament's recreational facilities with 'unwind' facilities, hide and seek rooms, musical chairs, Simon says games, ballroom dancing classes, rooms for aromatherapy, hopscotch and provide free take-home doggie bags for any left-over food from the canteen."

Member for South Coast:

"Madam Speaker, honourable members, these are tough times. We can only weather such times, now or in the future, by having all payments not subject to the conventional yearly CPI increases but by multiplying those figures with the CPI increase. All this should have been done years ago. We merely are now doing the work the previous government failed to address."

Speaker:

"Member for South Coast, your time is up. The honourable member for Highlands has the floor. Before you come up, would you please wake up your colleague behind you, or at least switch off his microphone? His snoring is becoming a bit disruptive, thank you. And please, could you pick up your doodles off the floor? Our skivvies have enough on their plates."

Member for Highlands:

"Thank you, Madam Speaker. May I say you do look radiant today?"

Speaker:

"You may not. The radiance you observe may come from this pedant, a $2 million crystal-clear diamond my husband gave me last night."

Speaker:

"Member for Highlands, you do know that I have been married for 3 months now. You had your chance and blew it. Please get to the point and don't waste the House's time with pointless remarks."

Member for Highlands:

"Yes, Madam Speaker. Your joie de vivre becomes you. My question is to the Minister for the Needy. When will the 0.0003% increase in pensions, proposed over 3 years ago, flow into the pockets of our elderly?"

Speaker:

"The Minister for the Needy."

Minister for the Needy:

"Thank you, Madam Speaker. I am glad the honourable member for Highlands asked me that question. 'Proposed over 3 years ago,' you said. Was that not when you were in government? Why did you not push it through when you could? Behold the paradox of our times: pensioners, seemingly with pockets ablaze, wielding the mighty power of $5.87. A fortune, some might say, enough to purchase a cup of luxury coffee or a modest island in a virtual game, as the member for South Coast mentioned."

Minister for the Needy:

"We will do more for the pensioners, the pioneers of our country. We will also answer questions in a clear, concise, and unambiguous manner, something your government never did. We have a 3-stage plan for pensioners. Behold, stage one of our master plan: an unprecedented raise for all pensioners! We will even backdate this raise by 3 years. The pension age will rise by 10 years, to 75 years for males and 75 for females.

We think this is an even-handed approach, which gives both genders the opportunity to socialise, excel in their chosen areas of activities, and not only substantially increase their incomes but also bring meaning back into their lives and utilise a wealth of resources, due to the experience our elderly have accumulated."

Minister for the Needy:
"As a result of these measures, we will be able to close many aged care facilities, reduce the country's overall social burden, remove costly pensioners' subsidies, travel, rent, prescription assistance, and such. Each person in that age group will gain a sense of pride and achievement."

Minister for the Needy:
"Stage two: Our valiant founders of the nation will get a pension certificate that we will email if and when the pensioner turns 80. Once a person has received such an email, they will need to create an online profile secured by an 83-character-length alphanumeric password, where no character

may be repeated, to access their pension entitlements. Each monthly pension will need to be requested 3 months before its due date.

Member from Opp. Bench:

"But there are only a fixed amount of numbers and letters; it's impossible to create 83 non-repeatable characters."

Minister for the Needy:

"I see Smart Alec is switched on; he's getting my drift. We are aware that some members of our communities may have some technical issues accessing online services. Our phone help lines will assist people in need, at $6.80 per minute. This will become a self-funding endeavour."

Minister for the Needy:

"You will notice that entitlements for pensions are at age 75, but accessing it will be slightly delayed. This will give the treasury some time to set aside needed funds and give our pioneers valuable time to ponder how to squander their newfound wealth. Those without an email account will never receive their pension notification."

Lobbyist Robbie Lobby:
"May I just slide in here, to give the Minister for the Needy a chance to breathe, to tell you about this fantastic offer. Wristwatches, washing-powder, satellite dishes, and now, car tyres. I'm looking for a couple of subsidies and perpetual tax-breaks on the following items."
Speaker:
"May I ask, 'Who are you?'"

Lobbyist:
"Oh, Madam Speaker, Robbie Lobby is the name, saviour of our industries. As a token of their appreciation and as a gesture of their boundless gratitude, I have been authorised to give each member here a T-shirt. Imprinted on it are the logos and slogans of the many businesses you sponsor with your legislative decisions. If you could just give the nod to the grants and industry stimuli I threw on the table yesterday, I might sweeten the deal with complimentary aprons as well."

Speaker:

"Lobbyists come here between Monday to Friday. It is Sunday, 3 minutes before midnight. Get your contraptions out of here. Lobbyists, they are like stray cats, leave."

Lobbyist:

"I thought I'd get an early start, as time never takes a day off. Perhaps Madam is in need of some exquisite gold chains, currently enjoying a delightful 3% discount."

Speaker:

"Order. ORDER! Orderly, get this man and his contraption out of here. RIGHT NOW! The Minister for the Needy may continue."

Member from Opp. Bench:

"Robby Lobby, wait, I want some washing-powder. Can you get me some?"

Speaker:

"This is not happening. ORDER, ORDER! How dare you interrupt the proceedings. This is unprecedented. Any more such disruptions will have profound consequences. May we continue, please? The Minister for the Needy, go ahead."

Minister for the Needy:
"The 'Chronicler of Truth,' which has an unvarnished reputation for untarnished reporting, has recently published a poll that indicates to me that the descendants of the founders of our lands would be honoured to partake in the ongoing dynamic development of our nation. On page 2 of yesterday's edition, printed in black and white and made from the pulp of a giant 2483-year-old Huon Pine, the results echo the will of the people. The paper wanted to use an older tree, but the woodchoppers wouldn't let them. May I take a moment to thank the 23 people who took part in the extensive nationwide poll, who with their endorsement signal to me the green light for the next stage."

Minister for the Needy:
"Stage three: We will increase the pension to the golden age of 85, which is the new 40, and give most of our old-timers a welcome relief from idleness. Age does not come with limitations, as our 'happy face' promotion will clearly show. Our brave elder seniors will look bliss straight in the eye. This will reduce the massive drain on our hospital and health systems and save the government an estimated $12 billion in the first fiscal year, $17 billion in the second, and $21 billion in the third."

Minister for the Needy:
"But wait, there's more! By the time we're through, the proposal from the honourable member for South Coast will not only be funded but might just become the first-ever self-sustaining budgetary miracle! Should there be any shortcomings, we endeavour to introduce a Pedestrian Tax to raise additional funds, which could also be used to fund the proposed slow-speed footpath lanes."

Minister for the Needy:
"You will be pleased to know that, in the spirit of fairness, a similar raise will be offered to the permanently unemployed, ultimately bringing the country's balances out of the red."

Minister for the Needy:
"Does this answer your question?"

Elder Member on Opp. Bench:
"What do you mean 'a similar raise' for the unemployed?"
Minister for the Needy:
"They need to be aged like fine wine, 75 to 85 years, respectively, before they can even apply."
Elder Member on Opp. Bench:
"Thank you, Minister for the Needy. It must cost a fortune to extend the vaults of the treasury to house all the massive revenue this will generate."

Speaker:
"Sir, for your interruption, your weekly allocation of soft drink vouchers has been halved. You had been warned."
Elder Member on Opp. Bench:
"It would be funny if it wasn't so serious. May I say that this government is a comedy goldmine; it has a sense of humour. We see it like this: It would be serious if it wasn't so funny."
Speaker:
"Next on the agenda is the Minister for Carbon Reduction and Prevention of Temperature Increases."

"Thank you, Madam Speaker, honourable members of the House. The previous government has left us with the burden of addressing rising temperatures, rising ocean levels, an increase in greenhouse gases, and cleaning up the atmosphere."

"As the oceans stretch their watery limbs, our coastline might just decide to take a fashion cue and opt for the chic 'short and sweet' look. Who knew climate change could be the hottest trend? Since coastlines are basically nature's fractals, we're introducing a revolutionary plan to keep them intact, no matter how high the waters may rise, even if we have to measure around every single coastal pebble."

"Industry and power providers will be required to purchase these beautifully crafted lids bearing the inscription 'It's clean when it's green', and don't you just love them? They will be popped atop every chimney, and voila, watch the carbon disappear faster than a magician's rabbit."

Minister for Carbon Reduction and Prevention of Temperature Increases:
"Feast your eyes on the most sought-after chimney accessory of the century! Crafted with unparalleled finesse by my brother-in-law. These lids could be yours for the trifling sum of $10,000. A steal, really. Failure to purchase these government-approved devices will attract a fine of no less than $100000, plus heavy pollution fines. Dairy Farmers, Cattle and Livestock Producers will be required to purchase these green devices. They do look like ordinary balloons, don't they? My son invented them and the government has approved these devices as gas-capturing containers, which will be collected by the new business my daughter has set up and sold to Power Suppliers or in Supermarkets as Energy Packs, guaranteed to be able to heat a small meal."

Minister for Carbon Reduction and Prevention of Temperature Increases:
"In regards to temperature rises: My 5-year-old, the prodigious mind, has unveiled a solution that will have thermometers everywhere bowing in awe, which I will table here as soon as the patent is granted. We simply shorten the glass tubes of thermometers to the height of the 25 deg C mark and prevent the mercury inside to rise any higher. This then reduces air temperature, water, oceans and so on. It will also be a massive export earner for the country, each of course with a 6% mark-up for my 5-year-old."

Member for Chickery:
"My department has been advised that bakeries and steel producers may not be happy with this idea, as bread is not going to rise at 25 deg C, nor will steel turn liquid. Where do we find solutions for that?"
Speaker:
"Order in the House, please. To the member for Chickery I say that your proposal regarding the interplanetary rubber

chickens will not be tabled today. The member for Loqui has the floor."

Member for Loqui:

"Thank you, Madam Speaker. Today, I'd like to tackle the most perplexing linguistic anomaly in this House. Why isn't the female counterpart of a 'speaker' called a 'speakeress' or 'speakerin'? I mean, really, are we stuck in a linguistic time warp? Let's dive into this linguistic black hole, shall we?"

Speaker:

"Order, ORDER! I caution the honourable member for Wisecrack. We are discussing language, not launching a stand-up revolution."

Member for Loqui:

"May I continue, Madam Speaker? Now, why is it that when a lady takes the podium, she's still just a 'speaker'? Shouldn't she be a 'speakette' or 'speechess'? It's as if the English language decided, 'Oh no, we've reached our pun limit for the day; let's just stick with the status quo.'"

Member for Loqui:

"Picture this, Madam Speaker. A room full of chuckles, guffaws, and uproarious laughter. The male 'speaker' steps down, and then the female 'speaker' steps up. The audience is left hanging in linguistic limbo. Do we keep calling her a 'speaker,' or do we upgrade to 'speakarella'? It's like the punch line to a joke nobody wrote!"

Member for Loqui:

"The member for Muttonhead might find this amusing, but I propose a motion to officially designate the female counterpart of a 'speaker' with something that we all can agree on."

Member for Loqui:

"Ladies and gentlemen, prepare to witness the liberation of language from its archaic chains! Because in the grand scheme of things, the real battle for equality begins with words. Who knew linguistics could be our hero?"

Member for Loqui:

"And let's not forget the previous government's lacklustre efforts on linguistic levity. The opposition leader once claimed they had done all they could for wordplay diversity, but where are the puns, the quips, the linguistic acrobatics? Nowhere to be found!"

Member for Loqui:

"Dear Madam Speaker, as we revel in the whimsy of words, I propose a motion to establish a Ministry of Silly Synonyms. Let us embrace the joy of language, where every 'speaker' can be a 'speechster' or a 'laughter luminary.'"

Member for Loqui:

"Thank you, Madam Speaker, for your linguistic light-heartedness. I hope my words tickled your funny lexicon and resonated with my fellow wordplay enthusiasts. Let the laughter cascade through our sentences, so we can side-step the seriousness of our times."

Shadow Member for Loqui:

"But would it not also mean that a speaker becomes a spoker after the last word is uttered? That a spokesperson has never anything to say because she or he spoke it already?

Speaker:

"Stop interrupting. Order in the House! The member for Pompville on the Flair has the floor."

Member for Pompville on the Flair:

"Esteemed Madam Speaker, I express my profound gratitude for the opportunity to address this august assembly. Today, I proffer a revolutionary proposition destined to reshape the very fabric of political discourse, an entitlement to the laurels of thespian remuneration for our televised and radio debates."

Member for Pompville on the Flair:

"Why should the luminaries of stage and melody monopolise the enjoyment of pecuniary emoluments? It is the season, I posit, for we, the political custodians, to bask in the radiant glow of the limelight and partake in the commensurate financial recompense."

House:

"Hear, hear."

Speaker:

"Order, ORDER! I tender a judicious caution to the honourable member for Jestington. This is no occasion for a theatrical casting call, nor an overture to the commencement of a political sitcom. We convene not to indulge in the levity of performance, but to deliberate upon the weighty matters of fiscal policy and pecuniary allocations."

Member for Pompville on the Flair:

"Fear not, Madam Speaker. This financial endeavour is as unswerving as the pledges of a politician during an electoral cycle. Allow me to evoke a vision: with each delivery of a resonant aphorism, engagement in a fervent debate, or execution of a seamless pivot, the harmonious resonance of 'cha-ching' shall permeate the air, the sonorous herald of royalties cascading forth. We, distinguished denizens of public service, shall henceforth not merely occupy roles as civic custodians; we shall transcend into the realm of public performers!"

Member for Pompville on the Flair:

"The member for Funville may perchance derive amusement from this proposition, yet I submit a motion for the establishment of the 'Poli Awards,' a nomenclature succinctly derived from 'Politicians Awards.' This heralds a proposition for an illustrious ceremony to commemorate the most superlative feats in the domain of political histrionics. It is incumbent upon us to acknowledge the valour, the perspiration, and the felicitous repartees that constitute the backbone of our theatrical political performances."

Member for Pompville on the Flair:

"The opposition leader, in a rare moment of candour, refrained from professing any laurels for the fraternity of political performers. For once, his assertion held an ounce of veracity. We are acquainted with the harsh verities of our vocation, no scarlet carpets unfurled, no photographic chroniclers in pursuit, and the semblance of glamour? An ephemeral apparition, nowhere to be found!"

Member for Pompville on the Flair:

"In conclusion, dear colleagues, I implore your earnest consideration of this proposition, for in acknowledging our thespian panache, we sow the seeds of a cultural metamorphosis. As I conclude, let the 'cha-ching' echo in our political chambers, not just as a fiscal melody but as a sonnet to our collective artistry. Because, in the end, what's politics without a touch of financial fanfare and a symphony of political sonnets?"

Member for Pompville on the Flair:

"In a final nod to our collective artistry, let's envision the 'Poli Awards' as our glittering recognition ceremony, celebrating feats in political sardoodledom."

"The establishment of the 'Poli Awards' shall stand as a testament to the valorous narratives woven within the precincts of this hallowed institution. Because, let's face it, where else can you witness such daring feats of verbal gymnastics?"

Member for Pompville on the Flair:

"I tender my sincere gratitude, Madam Speaker, for your astute understanding. May our political stage continue to captivate the discerning audience, and may the pursuit of excellence be duly acknowledged and rewarded!"

Member for Pompville on the Flair:

"I can see the despondent expression of the Shadow Minister for Happiness, Fun, and Excitement. Is he perhaps gazing into the future or just becoming aware of the cheerless drudgery of sitting on that side of the chair?"

Member for Pompville on the Flair:

"Dear Madam Speaker, as we revel in the limelight, buy milk and toothpaste. My sincerest apologies, for I seem to have encountered a minor syntactical entanglement."

Member for Pompville on the Flair:

"As I was articulating, I propose a motion to establish a Ministry of Silly Solutions, a bastion of intellectual mirth. Let us embrace the exuberance of political performance, where soliloquy and witty repartee not only garners votes but secures a coveted berth in the annals of the Poli Awards."

Member for Pompville on the Flair:
"Methinks, a touch of folly amidst the gravitas shall render our political stage all the more enchanting. Forsooth, in this grand theatre of democracy, let the curtain never fall on the comedy of errors, but rather rise on the sublime comedy of collaborative governance, scripted with quills dipped in the ink of reason and camaraderie."

1st Year Apprentice Politician:
"But wasn't Thespis, that venerable precursor of theatrical artistry, more renowned for elevating tragedy?"

Member for Pompville on the Flair:
"I extend my gratitude to the esteemed member for his sagacious interjection. The term 'tragedy,' as it languishes in the annals of theatrical antiquity, is but a mere allegory for our contemporary political landscape. The demarcation

between tragedy and comedy is, indeed, nuanced, delicate as the parchment on which our legislative proclamations are inscribed."

Member for Pompville on the Flair:
"And now, if you'll permit a brief sabbatical into the realm of speculative scholarship, I shall commence honing my acceptance speech while contemplating the weighty matter of the categorical supremacy I shall undoubtedly attain at the inaugural Poli Awards. Best Supporting Politician? Most Dialectically Profound Debate?"

"The prospects are as boundless as the royalties that shall cascade forth. Our citizenry anticipates not merely governance but a virtuoso performance, and this modest incentive is a token of appreciation for the outstanding brilliance we, and in particular, I bring to the political stage."

Member for Pompville on the Flair:

"A unanimous consensus on tax exemption shall undoubtedly elevate our political theatre to a zenith befitting the grandiosity of the Poli Awards. I thank you, Madam Speaker, for your discerning comprehension."

Speaker:

"I thank the member for Pompville on the Flair. The Minister for Cyber Security and Youthful Activities has requested to address this House. Please, Sir, you have the floor."

The Minister for Cyber Security and Youthful Activities:

"Thank you, Madam Speaker. Why you may ask am I wearing a black hat? Anyone? No...? To protect my head? No. To tell each of you of the ever present threat of black hat hacking. Some older ones of you may have heard about DOS, but what about DoS, or DDoS, where one has nothing to do with the other two. A firewall, much like a security guard, cannot prevent a 'hot-fuse' or a blown fuse. Your kids don't need a sandbox, but you do. APT, attack vectors, does your area of expertise give advice on BCP, or at least BIA? 'Defence in depth' does not entail having a security guard in the cellar of your abode."

(Explanation: Black Hat = Computer Hacker, DOS = Disk Operating System, DoS = Denial of Service, DDoS = Distributed Denial of Service, APT = Advanced Persistent Threat, BCP = Business Continuity Plan, BIA = Business Impact Analysis)

The Minister for Cyber Security and Youthful Activities:

"The other day some bright spark from the frontbench asked me if we could install a light-switch in the dark net, to brighten up their day?"

The Minister for Cyber Security and Youthful Activities:

"I can see by the vacant expressions on your faces that not one of you understood a single word I said. Wake up, folks. Pull your finger out, is all I can say. The times of blissful slumber are over. We can no longer be complacent. It's time to take proactive measures."

"In regards to my other portfolio there has been a breakthrough, it's 'Youthful Activities' in case you forgot. We measured the performance of our youths on a popular on-line game, measured the time it took for them to complete the game and the speed of their keystrokes. We then disassembled their game devices into their components and spread them over a 25mile distance in the forest. The one who comes back with a working device will be the winner. The last time I saw any of them was 3 months ago."

"As to the Minister for Social Influence I notice you gained a new subscriber, which does little to aid our country in need. We have secured a cyber thread to your account."

"I am the Minister for Social Media, Sir."

"My sincerest apologies. I stand corrected. At least you know who you are."

Minister for Social Media:

"Well thank you, Sir. We'll have our wordsmith reconstruct the gist of your contribution so we better understand what you were trying to convey."

Speaker:

"Order in the House, the honourable member from the Weedy Plains has the floor."

Member from the Weedy Plains:

"Thank you, Madam Speaker. In these challenging times, I present an avant-garde proposal that taps into the potential of our Public lands of non-specific tenure. Introducing Nutri-Mows for hire! These aren't your run-of-the-mill lawnmowers; they are heralds of a green revolution. Thank you for your applause. The trade-mark was just approved yesterday. The Nutri-Mow fleet will gracefully tread the Public lands, turning those once defiant weeds into the very essence of culinary excellence! With the addition of a marvel known as Nutri-Powder, a game-changer intended to make these once bothersome greens not just palatable but downright irresistible for our citizens."

Member from the Weedy Plains:

"In the spirit of rethinking everything, these Nutri-Mows are more than machines; they are equipped with cutting-edge technology, they'll mow down those pesky weeds, and with a sprinkle of Nutri-Powder magic, turning them into a digestible delight for all our peoples. May I add, franchises are available."

Member from the Weedy Plains:

"Now, I hear the concern about potential unemployment, and I appreciate the foresight of the honourable member from Behind the Woods. Fear not, for the Nutri-Mow operation is poised to create new opportunities, at least for my business. We're transforming lawnmowers into eco-friendly gourmet machines. It's the green revolution right in our backyards, providing an activity for idle hands whilst fostering self-sufficiency. The additional income my company generates will no doubt fill the empty pockets of our treasury, via the tax revenues it creates. In other words, it is self-funding."

Member from Opp.:
"But wouldn't that cause massive unemployment, especially on our agricultural workforce?"
Speaker:
"Order in the House! The honourable member from Behind the Woods is reminded that he will have his turn in time."
Member from the Weedy Plains:
"Indeed, the transition might bring changes to traditional employment dynamics, but we've made provisions to ensure a smooth shift. In a world obsessed with economic acrobatics, behold the Nutri-Mow revolution, where mowing lawns not only cuts grass but slashes through economic woes. A subtle reminder that sometimes, the greenest solutions are right under our noses! The Nutri-Mow revolution also empowers citizens to actively participate in cultivating their own

nutritious resources. For a modest fee each user can harvest their patch whenever the need to still hunger arrives."

Member from the Weedy Plains:

"As we sit at our dinner tables enjoying delicacies from around the world, let's consider the environmental cost of such delights. In the grand scheme of things, the Nutri-Mow initiative isn't solely about job creation. No, it's a paradigm shift, a transformation in our environmental ethos, a journey toward a future marked by sustainability."

Member from the Weedy Plains:

"Now, Madam Speaker, I propose a second facet to this visionary initiative. In addition to hiring out the Nutri-Mow fleet, we shall also commercialize Nutri-Powder! Picture this, every citizen cultivating Nutri-Mows on leased Public lands, and purchasing my Nutri-Powder, which aids the digestion, is contributing to the green movement. A win-win situation for all, promoting economic benefits while actively participating in environmental longevity."

Member from the Weedy Plains:

"In conclusion, Madam Speaker, the Nutri-Mow proposal is about cultivating a greener, healthier future. Leasing patches of Public lands, hiring Nutri-Mows, and selling Nutri-Powder can and will turn our challenges into opportunities."

Member from the Weedy Plains:

"Thank you, Madam Speaker, for your patience. I look forward to unanimous support for this eco-savvy endeavour. May I also mention that Nutri-Mow and Nutri-Powder are going public soon, and every member in this House is invited, including the opposition, to come in on the ground floor at the initial public offering. We call it: Sharing and caring."

Speaker:

"I thank the member for the Weedy Plains for this fresh approach, but also the previous Minister for his earlier contribution. May I remind the Minister for Silence that uttering a few words from time to time could contribute to the discussions, as whatever it is you're discussing with your handsome colleague would be of little consequence to our nation or your electorate."

Elder Member from Opp.:

"I must apologise for interjecting, but I had a look at the proposal, and it seems that the allocation of my patch of available public land is located some 3487km away from my home. Are you suggesting I undertake a journey at every mealtime to harvest my greens?"

"The member for where does he come from? That one, yes, you have the floor."

Member for Wherever You Come From:

"In this delightful chaos, we weave a fusion of illusion and seclusion, culminating in the grand spectacle of an illusionary illusion!"

Speaker:

"May I remind the member for wherever you come from to express your sentiments in a coherent manner that does not require linguistic funambulists to extract its meaning."

Member for Wherever You Come From:

"My apologies, Madam Speaker. I shall rephrase that. Well, well, well. That's all I can say. Perhaps we should take a gander at the shining example of the oh-so-honourable Minister for Meagre Means."

Member for Wherever You Come From:

"Have a look at his dinner, and may I take a wild guess? Caviar from Russia, rice from China, wine from France or Italy, fruits from every corner of the globe, tulips from Holland, chocolate from Belgium, Switzerland, or Austria, cheese, and whatnot."

Member for Wherever You Come From:

"Are ten or more countries enough for your dinner? Most likely not. The energy it takes to make this food and get it to your table exceeds in excess of a trillion-fold the calories you get from it."

Member for Wherever You Come From:

"I highly doubt that your feast is prepared from the weeds in your neighbourhood. It's more than just dinner; it's practically a gastronomic world tour. And I bet it's not even served on a pine table."

Member for Wherever You Come From:

"The honourable Minister for Meagre Means has a penchant for nothing but the fanciest. The oldest, rarest and most exotic trees make up his furniture. To each his own, but can we sustain it? I mean, does he really need a B.C. dining table that's older than most countries?"

Member for Wherever You Come From:

"As to the honourable Minister for Carbon Reduction and Prevention of Temperature Increases: Your brother in-law manufactures chimney lids, your son produces fart bags for cows, your daughter sells the farts, and your kid tampers with the temperature. And now this, weed as feed, from the Member of the Weedy Plains."

Member for Wherever You Come From:

"Am I to believe that the government has reduced the body temperature of all its citizens to 25 deg Celsius, and that all these measures are government approved? Are you not all out to line your own pockets?"

Speaker:

"Order in the House, the member will not interject, first warning."

Minister for Carbon Reduction and Prevention of Temperature Increases:

"To the member for wherever, you must be new? How do I line my own pockets? My son, daughter, brother in-law are not I?

Member for the Weedy Plains:

"You are welcome to become a part-owner in the weed venture; just buy some shares. In any case, we do a few years or twice that, and then it's your turn again. That's how it works. Your time will come. We've waited long enough."

Member for Wherever You Come From:

"You announce the tender is not even published, yet the contract is already..."

Speaker:

"Second warning, one more word and I'll have you removed. There will be order in this House."

Public Gallery:

"Madam Speaker, may I draw your attention to the unbearable heat in this House. Yesterday I bought a dozen eggs from the member for the Weedy Plains. All were boiled by the time I got home."

House:

"Hear, hear!"

Amid the lively banter, a sudden call for order reverberates through the House. The reason? The air-conditioning, it seems, has declared its own rebellion, leaving us in the unrelenting embrace of an unexpected heatwave.

Speaker:

"Order in the House. I hereby order a cooler atmosphere, not a heated debate. Members, let's expedite the repair process faster than the time it takes for a bill to become law. We can't have our debates boiling over like eggs from the Weedy Plains! I propose an emergency session to order a fix for our air-conditioning woe. All in favour, say 'cool.'"

House:

"Hear, hear!"

Speaker:

"Thank you. The motion passes. Let's keep this House cool and composed!"

Speaker:

"Would the member of the Happy Party please refrain from dropping her pencil every time she comes up to the podium? It seems to be happening at a regular basis. I do not suggest that it has anything to do with the shortness of your skirt, but the open mouths of many members indicate to me some laps of concentration."

Member of the Happy Party:

"Thank you for addressing the discomfort, Madam Speaker. It appears our esteemed air-conditioning system has chosen this moment to embark on an unscheduled vacation, leaving us to endure the sweltering heat. A matter of urgency, indeed."

Speaker:"

It seems to me more like advertising your underwear, which I'm aware you have a commercial interest in."

Member of the Happy Party:

"It's the heat, Madam Speaker. The pencil slipped out of my moist fingers."

Speaker:

"So you say. Before I forget, would the clerk please come here and tag the new price list for ministerial dinners on the noticeboard? Thank you. For your information, the fees for these events have slightly increased by a modest 63% from the previous quarter, while the available seats have expanded to 2000 per session. This grants exclusive personal VIP access to a minister of your choosing. While no minister can guarantee actual attendance due to government business, rest assured that the smiling face of the minister, suitably framed, will grace the head of the centre table. Ideal for lobbyists, members of the media, industry, mining, and, dare I say, the public. Any submissions, suggestions, or praises should be left in the bin on your way out, where the minister's skivvy will diligently note the order of their disposal."

Speaker:

"Please remember to bring your own plates, cutlery, snacks, and beverages this time. If you feel inspired to leave a donation, kindly dispose of it in the large bin on the left side of the door. It's worth noting that, due to overwhelming popular demand, all ministers have graciously increased the frequency of such events from bi-monthly to six sessions per day, including breakfast, lunch, and dinner, for two sessions each. The duration for each session is a sharp 30 minutes."

New Arrival:

"Hello everybody, where is my place?"

Speaker:

"And who you might be?"

New Arrival:

"I'm a senator."

Speaker:

"I would suggest your place might be in the Senate."

New Arrival:

"Oh, and this is not the Senate? Sorry."

Speaker:

"Let us get back to the items currently on the agenda..."

Member for Sandy Beach:

"G-day you all and greetings from Sandy Beach."

Speaker:

"What is going on today, who are you and why are you interrupting the House?"

Member for Sandy Beach:

"I am the new Member for Sandy Beach, Sheila Sands, and have been elected in the recent by-election to represent my constituents in this great hall of voices."

Speaker:

"Where in the Lord's name is Sandy Beach, Mrs Sands?"

Member for Sandy Beach:

"Oh, Miss, please. Sandy Beach renamed from its previous title, Dry Sands. It is located in one of the driest regions of the country, the rain hardly comes, but when it does it falls."

Speaker:

"The by-election was 4 months ago. How come you grace us with your presence now?"

Member for Sandy Beach:

"As I said, when it rains it falls. We were flooded in."

House:

"Hear, hear, Four months flooded in. Good one."

"May we get back to business, Thank you. Standing order, Questions without Notice. I have here 'Rolling Thunder,' it must be his CB-handle. Would Rolling Thunder please put your question."

Rolling Thunder:

"I extend my gratitude, Madam Speaker. I direct my enquiry to the esteemed custodian of Asphaltic Thoroughfares, the minister therein. Pray, gather round, esteemed members, for a contemplative inquiry into the narrative articulated by the venerable Morrie of the Lorry Union, whose presence I embody in this assembly. The concerns posited by this envoy of the transportation fraternity beckon our philosophical scrutiny as we embark upon a transcendental exploration of fiscal responsibility and the allocation of societal burdens."

Rolling Thunder:

"Morrie and his compatriots, purveyors of the vehicular conduits that traverse our thoroughfares, lay claim to a financial yoke borne through contributions manifest in the form of taxes, fuel excise, tolls and vehicular registrations. In their contemplation, a discrepancy emerges as they espouse the notion that a non-contributing public avails itself freely of the communal infrastructure bestowed upon them."

Rolling Thunder:

"It behoves us to engage in a dialectical exploration of Morrie's lamentation regarding the artistic delineation upon the thoroughfares, the Zebra Crossings. The metaphorical absence of zebras is invoked, prompting reflection on the symbolic character of these markings, the implications of which may transcend the mere literal interpretation."

Rolling Thunder:

"Further, the coterie of the Lorry Union expounds upon a perceived encroachment by cyclists and pedestrians upon the asphalted domain. Morrie's numerical calculations, constituting a discourse of quantitative assessment, postulate a disconcerting incongruity in the apportionment of fiscal resources vis-à-vis footpaths and bike lanes, thus demanding an ontological examination of the inherent value assigned to each."

Rolling Thunder:

"In addition, Morrie submits a poignant query concerning the requisites of newly instituted laws mandating a requisite spatial separation between his adherents and cyclists. The source of this additional space, Morrie contends with unwavering logic, emerges from the very fabric of the roadway itself. This inquiry prompts a deontological contemplation of the ethical implications inherent in the imposition of spatial constraints within the societal contract."

Rolling Thunder:

"I present before this esteemed assembly an illustrative tableau, depicting the arduous trials endured by Morrie's comrades in their daily endeavours upon the thoroughfares."

Rolling Thunder:

"I bring forth an additional entreaty from the Lorry Union, beseeching that every denizen traversing the walk- and bikeways be outfitted with a distinctive number plate, thereby facilitating meticulous traffic surveillance. This, in turn, would empower the authorities to mete out judicious fines for any perceived trespass upon our designated bitumen, while also contemplating levies on the pedestrian's shoe soles and the cyclist's rubber tyres. Such proposals, intertwined with the philosophical fabric of fiscal responsibility, beckon us to contemplate the intricate dance of societal obligations and the ever-expanding purview of regulatory considerations."

"The demands articulated by the Lorry Union are no less than a categorical imperative unto themselves. Their motion mandates sound barriers betwixt the roadway and the adjacent bike lanes, ostensibly shielding the lorry-bearers from the purportedly frivolous auditory disturbances emanating from bicycle bells. Additionally, retroactive reimbursements and novel fiscal impositions upon pedestrians and cyclists find their genesis in the pursuit of a harmonious societal arrangement, albeit one that necessitates careful examination within the parameters of moral and ethical frameworks."

"In conclusion, as we embark upon a metaphysical expedition into the labyrinthine corridors of Morrie's grievances, let us scrutinize with discernment and sagacity the layers of his discourse. The synthesis of these considerations may well illuminate the path toward a transcendental understanding of the intricate web woven by the interplay of fiscal obligations and societal organization. Thank you."

Speaker:

"Ah, the eloquence of Rolling Thunder's inquiry truly dazzles the senses. It's a rare and exquisite masterpiece of linguistic finesse. Now, let us eagerly await the profound and undoubtedly complex response from the Minister of All

Things Asphaltic. Minister, do enlighten us with your erudition."

Minister of All Things Asphaltic:
"Thank you, Madam Speaker. To the esteemed Rolling Thunder, I offer my profound gratitude for your vocal and thought-provoking inquiry. After careful consideration, my response is succinct and unequivocal: No."
Speaker:
"That's what I like about the custodian of Asphaltic Thoroughfares, the Minister for Bitumen, Roadways, and Infrastructure. He can hone in on the most elaborate questions and crystallize his condensed response to a comprehensive answer. Which is generous with two letters."
Speaker:
"It's time to see who our winner is for the first-ever raffle draw. As was announced last week, we gave visitors to the Public Gallery the opportunity to pose a question to these Chamber."

House:
"Bravo."
Speaker:
"All 5000 tickets sold out at $50 per ticket, and the proceeds will be split with the elected members of this chamber at the end of the day."
Entertainer of the Parliament:
"Parliamentarians, prepare yourself for tough questions. Without wasting any time, let's spin the barrel."

Entertainer of the Parliament:
"And we have a winner: Green ticket number 347! Green 347, where are you? Call out! Your time in the spotlight has come."
Public Gallery:
"Here."
Entertainer of the Parliament:
"Please come down, lad, don't be shy. What is your question? Oh, this will be so exciting. This brave young man, let's give him a hand. Which question seeks an answer in this young

lad's mind? We will hear soon enough. Come on, boy, there sit down. What is it that you wish to ask?"

Member of the Public:
"I'm kind a busting. Where is the toilet?"
Entertainer of the Parliament:
"Who wants to answer this? Never mind. It's the second door on the right, lad."
Speaker:
"Before we continue with Questions without Order, may I propose, esteemed colleagues, a groundbreaking departure from the conventional geriatric rituals of our hallowed assembly?"

"In the spirit of innovation and a dash of whimsy, I suggest we veer away from the mundane choreography of votes and, instead, embrace the ineffable mystery of chance. Picture, if you will, a mystical apparatus, an arcane contraption, which, when set in motion, shall unravel the fates of our deliberations."

"A symbol of uncertainty and a harbinger of destiny, let us usher in a new era of decision-making, where the capricious twirl of this enigmatic device shall guide our legislative journey."

"Without any hesitation, let the dance of unpredictability commence!"

Speaker:

"Why, you may ask? It gives each of us the freedom not to be enslaved in these walls for fear of missing a vote. As long as someone puts a question, he or she could simply spin the wheel to get an instant response, liberating us from the shackles of parliamentary predictability."

"A serendipitous ballet, where the rotation of fate grants us the liberty to engage in more pressing matters, or perhaps indulge in a delightful afternoon tea, while our queries find their answers in the mystical pirouettes of chance."

Senior Member of Gov't:
"Please forgive me, mate, while I wipe my tears."

Senior Member of Opp.:

"Ain't got none left. There must be some roos loose."

Senior Elder from Public Gallery:

"... in the top paddock, yep. Greetings gents, I shouldn't have flushed the wax out of my ears, I would have been spared this. I share your sentiments. I'd been better off sleeping outside in the rain, than seeking the comfort of the Public Gallery to spend the night. Each night I hear the bugle coming closer. Let's face it, it's time."

Senior Member of Gov't:

"I'm starting to look forward to the ever-sleep."

In one of the offices, a newcomer is being acquainted with the intricacies of political operations.

Keen Newbie Politician:

"Party leader, tell me again: Where is the party line? I'm kind of thirsty, if you know what I mean."

Party Leader:

"Ah, dear novice politician, the party line is not a treasure map leading to a diaspora of half-filled kegs, nor, contrary to your belief, is it a liquid dispensary for alcoholic beverages. It is a directional beacon we follow. The policy of our party is very simple: Better in our pockets than in theirs."

"So, my neophyte in the world of political chaos, if you want to succeed here, keep your pockets open for opportunities and favours. The only spirits we prioritise are in the form of political alliances, not a shot glass. If you find yourself in desperate need for six-pack or a flask, just press the appropriate button on your desk."

Keen Newbie Politician:

"Now you're talking. What else do I need to know?"

Party Leader:

"Whatever they say, you say: Boo. Whatever we say, you say: Aye."

Keen Newbie Politician:

"I have so many questions. Are any pigs harmed in pork-barrelling? I have been given a key and a cabinet to store my handbag in; does that make me a key minister of the Cabinet? I think it's a bit tight for a Cabinet meeting. Do I need to bring my own chair tomorrow, or do I have a safe seat? I know a bit about politics. When you mix Vodka and milk you get a double-dissolution, but it's hard to swallow, especially with a squirt of lemon juice. But that would be a triple-dissolution, am I right? In any case it's a solution for any confusion. I prefer a Concrete Mixer. Have you had one? No? It'll knock your socks off."

"I've already prepared myself for the swearing ceremony, and I'll tell you, I have some beauties. Just let me get a hand on that microphone and there'll be no stopping me flapping my gums."

Party Leader:

"No, no, dear, it's a swearing-in ceremony, but you'll have plenty of opportunity to release your treasures of profanities in due course."

Keen Newbie Politician:

"Where and when is the party? Do I need to hold a maiden speech? I'm no longer a maiden, and I don't think any of the others were either. I was told I could be the leader of this mob. It's been already three days now, how much longer does it take? And speaking of preferences, can we have a conscience vote on the colour of the seats in here? I prefer paisley. Who is the big shot for tattoos? I need my own helicopter to check on my chickens from time to time. What is the difference between a state and a nation?"

"What's the constitatation, constitutation, help me here, what's it called? Ah, got it, Constitution? My doc said I have a good one. Someone asked me about my constituents. Do I have any? What is a constituent?"

Party Leader:

"Ah, don't worry about them."

Party Leader:

"Here's a picture from the last party meeting."

Party Leader:

"And here our last cabinet meeting."

Party Leader:
"And here we're trying to solve pressing issues of the day."

Party Leader:
"The nuanced art of politics is to always keep a straight face."

"The inaugural award for Branch Stacking, much to everyone's lack of surprise, does not go to the Woodland Party today. As we can see in this rather futile display of indecision, the member is dithering in his pre-selection; despite that, he still managed a respectable base to build upon."

"Let us encourage his efforts with subdued applause. What we see here is a sorry, pitiful, and unabashed cry for help, a desperate need for more funding, which all too often necessitates the ignoble act of gathering branches from tree nurseries, a practice that is not looked upon with favour."

"Saplings must be given a chance to take root. May I suggest a grand 'plead-a-palooza' before your party descends into the bottomless abyss of total obscurity? Despite that, let us encourage our courageous nominee, who, through gritted teeth and a strained smile, believes his efforts are worthy of recognition. Careful now, keep matches far away to prevent the embers from burning."

Speaker:

"It seems the public gallery is bursting at the seams. We shall now proceed to hear the responses to the Dorothy Dixers* put earlier. I must ask for your responses to be brief and devoid of self-promoting language, as these proceedings are televised."

*) Dorothy Dixers: a pre-arranged question to own ministers, friendly

Minister for Sports and Geriatrics:

"Thank you, Madam Speaker. Bursting at the seams, you say? Perhaps the sheer towering magnetism of my presence willed it so. Dear members, and to our home audience, distinguished citizens, let it resound today: as I stand before you, as your visionary leader, this is no moment for mere trifling promises or hollow rhetoric Schmalz. No, this moment is a milestone— it is a colossal boulder bestowed upon you in this instant of our times, so that you, my esteemed audience, with primed ears, have been chosen to witness the proclamation of a grand revelation at hand!"

"As I stand before you, I am reminded of the indomitable spirit that defines us. Our dreams are as vast as the skies, and our ambitions know no bounds. Today, I propose a monumental project that will etch my name into your memories and the dossiers of history."

"My political vision is reflected in my leadership and my dedication to the community. I don't bring you lofty promises, no impassioned rhetoric designed to elicit applause and admiration. You know this is not my style. Under my visionary stewardship, which serves as a guide to you all, it has enabled all of you to reap the bountiful rewards of the economic renaissance that I helped birth, struggling through nights of pain and self-sacrifice. My unparalleled commitment to my ideals is well known, just as my smoothly paved highway jets us forth at high speed to prosperity."

Minister for Sports and Geriatrics:
"Kindly excuse the abrupt alteration in my attire, for it is a necessary adornment I am compelled to wear in order to impart the gravity that befits the forthcoming diatribe. As these words are to be televised and eternally etched into the archives of history, it is only fitting that they are delivered with the due importance they deserve."

"As the Minister for Sports and Geriatrics, and as a testament to our shared greatness, I present to you the grandest of grandstands, the birth-mother of all grandstands, a towering monument to our collective aspirations! The sports arena, blessed in being selected, will not only host thrilling competitions but will also stand as a beacon of our strength and resilience."

"Allow me to elucidate on the grandstand. It is the biggest, the grandest of all grandstanding grandstands that have ever been built. Future generations will gaze upon this monumental platform of grandstanding grandiosity and view our times and era as a dawn of enlightenment, no, as the all-time golden age."

"I cast my eyes back to the inception of this grand vision. It was only last week when young Freddy... Are you here, young Freddy? Speak up. And there he is. I held him in my arms at one month and a few weeks old, this newborn, when I asked him whose name this infrastructure should bear."

"Do you want to know what he said? Do you want to know? Do you really, really want to know? He didn't need to say it. I knew it all along. He pointed the finger at me. It was then that I knew, this young man's pathway into politics shall encounter no mountains, no hills, no knolls or mounds, that it would be paved with grapes, incense, and myrrh. Before me, a vision appeared voicing in celestial choirs that he made the right choice. The pièce de résistance: the grandstand at this arena, the pinnacle of our collective achievement, located in my hometown, which bears my name, shall, through the cooing, gurgling, sighing endorsement of its youngest resident and with the overwhelming approval from the sagacious people of my hometown, now also bear my name! I graciously and, in all modesty, accept the will of the people and congratulate them for accepting my wise counsel."

Minister for Sports and Geriatrics:
"A round of applause for young Freddy; there he is, in his young mother's loving arms. No, no, don't clap for me. I'm a man of few words, never seeking anyone's appraisal. The legacy I'll leave behind, as the profound thoughts still incubating in my massive brain, all are geared to lift civilization out of the dark ages of our time. Oh, I just remembered, Freddy, can you hear me? Remember when I asked you for a new name for our state, our country, our nation, the earth? Yes, you remember. He can't yet talk, but knows je ne sais quoi when he sees it."

Minister for Sports and Geriatrics:

"You pointed at me. Five times you did, but I never mentioned the Milky Way. Mmm, hh mum, I just got a whiff; I think it's time to change his diapers. Better wait a few more months with the Brussels sprouts. Ugh, ew, good one, Freddy."

"As I recall young Freddy's gesture, pointing to his napkin, clearly indicating the only possible conclusion. The flag; his gesture indicates my name to grace the flag. Oh, mother of the child, how old is he now? Two months and a day tomorrow? There, in your caring embrace, you cradle a seer. At the threshold of infancy, a predictor of foresight, a gifted clairvoyant, a prophet who speaks without words—an anointed soothsayer, a vaticinator, a prognosticating sage of divination."

Minister for Sports and Geriatrics:

"In days yet unborn, my name will be whispered in hushed reverence, and our descendants will fall to their knees in appreciation. They will gaze at the 10-metre-tall letters of my name and wish they were here today to witness this historical moment of announcement. In my arteries pumps the blood of progress, in my mind spark the neurons of innovation, and pulsating in my heart is the love and dedication for you all."

Minister for Sports and Geriatrics:
"May the yarners and threaders hasten, so the warps and wefts intertwine the weaver's woven fabrics needed to adorn the biggest, most enormous, most gigantic, unparalleled canvas. With frayless stitches holding gold-embroidered letters, with sheening silk-framed embellished detail mounted upon a giant sequoia base, spliced upon with Himalayan cypress—a skyward-piercing post that holds the flag, that holds the name, that all bear witness to this young predictor's prognostication."

Minister for Sports and Geriatrics:

"As clear as day, I envision, perched upon the grandstand, this towering flagpole swaying in dizzying lofts. Its zenith scratching clouds, lifting my hometown's skyline to eye-paining heights. To this, dear friends and brethren, I humbly lend my name."

"You will note that my down-dressed attire lays bare my lack of vanity, but I must implore you, forthwith, to sign the purchase order without delay. I envy the people of my hometown, for they are decreed to have the unsurpassed pleasure of admiring my name. The nights there will no longer be veiled in darkness but be ablaze, glistening in brightness with a radiating glow that can be seen from far-off stars, reflecting my name and illuminating vast swaths of our state."

Minister for Sports and Geriatrics:

"Before I forget, I wish to share a premonition. I foresee a symphony in the currency of destiny, where the visage of my morning glow shall pirouette upon notes of paramount grace. The artist's hand, adept in the delicate ballet of lines, will soon clear desks, for the welling conviction whispers of a time when my countenance, a brushstroke of sovereignty, graces notes of opulence, surpassing all currently high-valued tender."

"In compliance with the guiding words of our esteemed Madam Speaker, you will note that not one word in my meek speech could be construed as self-promotion; was it just a declaration of times to come upon us."

"Now, going back to answering the question, it all started 12 years ago when..."
Speaker:
"With all due respect, Minister, a day only has so many hours. I am consistently amazed at your ability to condense lengthy speeches into so few words. Your response was admirably reserved and self-deprecating. With appropriate deference, Minister, I express my sincere hope to be spared the day when your countenance graces high-value banknotes. Should fate decree otherwise, let my repose be that upon my expiration, my body will laid face-down in my grave. Achieving this may pose a challenge if not done due to the inactivity of my facilities, but such is the price I willingly pay to shield my lifeless eyes from paramount, eternal distress."
Opp. Backbencher:
"Madam Speaker, I am sitting on the backbench, which unfortunately is not far enough away from this podium. My ears were in excruciating pain to hear what was said. I reflect on the words from the Minister for Sports and Geriatrics. I must correct myself—not the words, but the wretched-up puke that came out of his mouth."
Opp. Benches:
"Hear, hear."
Speaker:
"Order in the House. While I sympathize with you, we should still refrain from gutter language, if you please."

Opp. Backbencher:

"Point noted, Madam Speaker. As I summarize his response to a Dixer, I'm not quite clear on what the Dixer actually was.
a) I want to know who the honourable nincompoop was that asked the question in the first place;
and b), what was the question?"

"Is it not abundantly clear to all of us that anyone who ever asks a question of this particular minister deserves to be expelled from this House and let loose on an island as far as possible from our lands and shipping lanes? Is it not always the same when said minister opens his mouth, that we all end up with gut-wrenching convolutions irrespective of which side of the chamber? His demeanour shames a peacock."

"May I say, Madam Speaker, that I'm struggling to keep my language civilized. I can see the tears rolling down your cheeks as you're straining to prevent bursting into laughter."

Speaker:

"It's not you that sparks my amusement, dear backbencher, the minister you mentioned just spilled his yogurt and some biscuit-crumbs into his keyboard. Please continue."

Opp. Backbencher:

"Thank you, Madam Speaker. Said minister wishes to build a grandstand upon which his name peaks in 10m high letters. On top of all this, he wants a flagpole made from the finest trees on earth. Hanging off said flagpole, a flag the size of a football field adorned with his name. All this flooded in glaring light at night time."

"Backtracking the voice of the people's choice, all based on the erratic and incoherent movements of a newborn that shat in its nappies right in our chamber. Some racked their brains—was it the Brussels sprout, lentils, or cauliflower? Whatever it was is of little relevance. The kid had a moment, and so did said minister. Admittedly, one was a stinker, but the other screeched past highest heavens."

Opp. Backbencher:

"But that's not all. He sees his face on all banknotes of the highest tender, with future nightmares planned, such as renaming the state, the nation, the earth, the Milky Way???"

"I've been to the town that bears his name. It has 3 brumbies, a store, a bench in a park. The store only accepts coins that bear said minister's name. Upon the coin, said minister's unsightly visage. If one is inclined to purchase postage stamps there and tenders a note of high denomination, be prepared to receive change in the form of a bag of copper coins. Each coin bears a countenance so pitiable that it might move one to tears, imagining the hardships its figurative mother had to endure upon his debut."

Opp. Backbencher:

"Are these self-minted coins meant as a tourist attraction, or is said minister intend to make all of us suffer? A nearby foundry is all too pleased to take your bag to the smelter and give you more than you had pulled from wallet, plus the stamp for free. I wish to remind said minister, the time is nearing, for the costume hire store is closing soon. Time to get moving, else pay a fee for late return."

"In a feat of political prowess, said minister gerrymandered his way to winning a seat in this legislature, even in a humble three-horse town, where he aims to have his name echo louder than the hoof-beats of the entire equine population."

Opp. Backbencher:

"Beware, minister, may I caution, your grandstanding grandstand may spook the brumbies, especially once the switch is flicked. Their gallop makes the bulldust rise as cloud will cover grandstand's stage to cover all, before you'll have a chance likewise. And once the horse has bolted it drags behind your seat."

"May I appeal, I plead, I beg on my knees, that anyone who hears my call seeks out and guards with all your lives all giant sequoias and Himalayan cypresses in your lands."

Opp. Backbencher:

"Let it be known that should any of this minister's wishes take fruit, well, I beg, I implore, I ache; please hasten fast to take me forthwith out of my misery."

Speaker:

"Oh no, we'd miss you should that day arise. As to the question what the Dixer was, the Minister for Sports and Geriatrics chanced his moment in the hope one would not ask. I cannot find a fitting questions that could justify his tripe. Therefore no Dixer crowned as nincompoop, nor cast on barren shores."

Member for Pipelines and Tubes:

"Madam Speaker, may I request permission to leave? I have received an urgent message from my constituents who request an urgent meeting. The message informs of rising swells, which means that it is an opportune moment to study tube, pipe, and barrel formation in the local foreshore."

"I have been feverishly awaiting this moment, as this allows comprehensive study of the green-room spaces, rag dolling, and the observations of shoobies, kooks, and barneys and their usual interferences.

Member for Pipelines and Tubes:

"I should advise that I'm no clam-dragger but always keen to reach the doggy door before it shuts. My task is to analyse the analytics involved in pipeline formation and try to answer why barrels are hollow, a question that has baffled my constituents for years."

Speaker:

"I do not need all the intricate details of your urgency. For how long is the leave request?"

Member for Pipelines and Tubes:

"The remainder of the day, Madam Speaker."

Speaker:

"Any objections? No? Leave is granted."

Member for Pipelines and Tubes:

"Thank you, Madam Speaker."

Credits (Surfer jargon):
source 1: (boardcave.com.au), source2: (surftoolkit.com): tube, pipe, barrel: hollow part inside a wave (2); green room: inside of a barrel (1); rag dolling: being tumbled around by a wave (1); shoobies: tourist who gets in the way (2); kooks: disrespectful surfer (2); barneys, benny: a beginner surfer (2); clam-dragger: female body-boarder (1); doggy door: time to leave wave barrel before it closes (1)

Speaker:

"We move on; the Minister for Healthiness is next, and after that, the Minister for—sorry, I forgot who's next."

Minister for Healthiness:

"Following the abolition of bulk-billing practices in our clinics and the implementation of self-determined fees, the number of patients has markedly reduced. This is an indication that our healthcare cost-saving measures are bearing fruit."

Member for Unique Funding Proposals:

"In response to the earlier Dixer, we propose that all future elections be funded by the voters, and citizens need to contribute. This is a small price to pay for democracy. It will alleviate the need to seek funding elsewhere and ease the burden on businesses, the media, the lobby clan, etc who may have a bet each way."

Speaker:

"The question on climate change is answered by, yes, please, go ahead.

Member of Opp.:

"Thank you for the question on climate change. When I'm elected leader, there will be a new wind blowing in these chambers. This is my climate policy. That is all I have to say, Madam Speaker."

Speaker:

"Thank you for your answers. I can tell you right now, the windows will remain closed for as long as I am sitting in this chair."

"A carrier pigeon has arrived with a message from our absent leader, who is in the third year of his 12-year worldwide diplomatic journey. His brother's son, a recent school leaver — well, that was nine years ago — has expressed the wish to leave his mark on the world. He comes with a glowing reference from his father and a fresh haircut from his mother. He is willing to accept a managerial role of some importance."

Speaker:

"It says here, that he can be motivated at times, but not all too often. He is willing to start his role in Bali. He mentioned that he is already there, thus saving the country some travel costs. What else does our absent leader mention? Ah, yes, he has given the account number for the lad, where he expects the numbers' crimson colours to turn black. He needs to be in Oahu during the winter months for the Banzai Pipeline, particularly mentioning Sunset Beach and Waimea Bay. I personally don't know what that pipeline pipes, but the young man seems to know what he wants. He also mentioned Jeffreys Bay in South Africa, Tahiti, Fiji, and Santa Cruz. There are a few more places listed here. Is there anyone here who can fit him in?"

Member of Gov't:

"Certainly, Madam Speaker. I am excited. Are you excited? If you're not excited, you will be stamping with your feet and banging with your fists when you hear what I have to say. If the lad is also willing to travel to the Maldives, France, and Southern Californ-I-A, then absolutely, I give him a job. It is so rare to find a young man with a truly pioneering spirit, who conquers the world on his own initiative."

Member of Gov't:

"Dear Madam Speaker, please message our absent leader to say no more. It's done. If any other members have similar requests, let it be known that this is how we create employment and reduce the unemployment lines. I told you it would be exciting; thank you."

Speaker:

"It might be difficult to respond. Our pigeons know not where he dwells."

Member for Festivities:

"In this year's festive season, I'm authorised to announce that suggested gifts need not be declared. The suggested gifts are upper-body apparel, which members on this side of the chair exchange with members on that side of the chair and vice versa. The value per item must not exceed $28.53."

Member for Festivities:

"It is suggested that each party imprint the garment with their party logo and slogan to foster a festive atmosphere. Members are expected to wear these garments with pride, particularly during televised sessions, to instil a sense of parliamentary harmony."

Speaker:

"Thank you for this novel suggestion. Moving on with the replies to the questions without notice. Would the Minister for Bright Ideas be so kind to give a reply to the question put to her portfolio, please?"

Minister for Bright Ideas:

"Thank you, Madam Speaker. The answer is: No."

Speaker:

"Thank you, Minister for Bright Ideas. While we may ponder what the question was we now have a clear answer. Let us move on."

Speaker:

"For your information, you may have noticed a lot of construction going on. I have received many questions from members across the floor, in particular about one spherical building. It is to do with the expansion of our recreational facilities, mentioned this morning. Yes, you heard me, a spherical building. There is not a flat wall anywhere. Even the floor is curved. It is as if one is inside a giant ball. I have been told that it is the new Ballroom."

Speaker:

"The architect is currently being examined. I'm also told that the new hopscotch squares will be touch sensitive, so no more cheating."

Speaker:

"Well, well, well, will you look at the time. We've done well today. I can see some of you are getting tired. Let's have a short diversion. Whose turn is it to pin the tail on the donkey?"

Speaker:

"And who volunteers to be the donkey? Come on Minister for Sport and Geriatrics, be a sport, be the donkey. Shall we have a vote on that? Perhaps the member for Pompville on the Flair, or the Weedy Plains, no? Ah, the Minister for Cyber Security and Youthful Activities does us the honour, thank you Sir. Your work ethics are an example to the nation."

Speaker:

"This will be so much fun. We'll go from side to side, each has a turn, until one gets to put the tail on our donkey. We'll go from left to right, like a donkey ballot, starting from the frontbench and continue towards the backbenches, until the donkey lets us know that we're right on target."

Three hours later...

Member of Opp.:

"Oh that was so much fun. I love these short diversions. Does it not show that fun and joy we all enjoy, with child-like innocence and banter. To know that we are privileged to lead our nation by example is such a delight."

Meanwhile, outside, a nascent day unfurls rays that gently raise the veils of morning mist.

Speaker:

"I know this has been a marathon sitting. I can see many of you are struggling to keep your eyes open. Does anyone hear me? No. It looks like all members have succumbed to blissful slumber."

"May I continue in whispers to conclude the business of the day? Orderly, please nudge my niece awake, but don't wake anyone else up."

"As the current incumbent deputy speaker is indisposed for the foreseeable future, I hereby propose my 18-year-old niece as deputy speaker, bypassing the current standing order, whichever somnambulistic number it is. With over 6570 days of existence and a staggering 157,680 hours of life experience, she is not only qualified but feverishly awaiting this role."

Speaker:
"As she is not currently a member of the House, I cordially ask one of you to vacate your seat so she can assume her new role."

"As there is an audible absence of sound, I surmise there are no volunteers. I hereby declare the member who graced the House with his persistent absence to be the one. Just in case one of you only pretends to be sleeping, the said member has some bankruptcy issues and perhaps even collecting disallowed recompense, which is enough to keep the expulsion legal."

"I hear no objections. Sally, do you accept the honour of Deputy Speaker? Speak up, girl, but keep your voice down."
About to become the Deputy Speaker:
"Aye."
Speaker:
"That's a yes. I, as the Speaker, move and second it in support of the nominee. Are there any further proposals?"

"Let it be known that an overwhelming silence echoes this question. The time for further suggestions has expired, and nominations are closed. I hereby declare the Deputy Speaker to be duly and democratically elected."

"Sally, cease your nocturnal phone-fiddling and embrace your role; welcome to the wonderland of parliamentary proceedings!"

"Orderly, ORDERLY, WAKE UP!!! Would you please yield your magic and bang your rod to wake up our esteemed members who seem to have slipped into unconsciousness?"

"I would like to thank all members for the unanimous decision to elect a new Deputy Speaker, duly noted, and wish the always absent member a pleasant retirement."

Speaker:
"Could I have the word count of the day, please?"

"Thank you. It seems the Minister for Silence has again come last. I don't know how you can survive on that, especially when every word we utter adds to our pay check. As I said before, some participation in the proceedings would give your placing a boost. As of this moment it seems to be the member for the Weedy Plains has made a good contribution, but the final tally is not known as yet. We'll soon enough know who's going home with bulging pockets."

"Oh gee, talking about home, I just remembered I still have a roast in the oven. Attention everybody, I am so sorry, I need to rush home. The new deputy speaker will take the chair in my absence."

And thus, the newest member of the House, 18-year-old Sally, somewhat bewildered, tasked with carrying the mantle of responsibility folds it beside her chair.

"Sally, wake up, take the chair! Sally, don't *take* the chair, sit in it. You're now the Deputy Speaker. I need to rush."

Wide eyed and somewhat dazed, Sally blinks at her colleagues, while her eyelids succumb to gravity.

Deputy Speaker:
"What happens now? Who is speaking now?
Member of Opp.:
"You are, Madam Deputy Speaker."
Deputy Speaker:
"Where is she?" Sally asks, seemingly perplexed.
Member of Opp.:
"Who?"
Deputy Speaker:
"The Madam Deputy Speaker?"
Member of Opp.:
"You are."

Deputy Speaker:
"I know I am, but who's the Deputy Speaker?"
Member of Opp.:
"That's what you are. You have been elected as the Deputy Speaker."
Deputy Speaker:
"I am? Wow, I must text my friends. Carry on. Who wants to chat?"

Minister for Shielding the Nation:
"Madam Deputy Speaker, I think it's my turn. I, the Minister for Shielding the Nation, extend my greetings to all. Peace be upon you. Let's pick up from where we left off—delving into the notice, moved and seconded, debated in part, with unamendable amendments due to a procedural motion. As per standing orders, no vote could proceed."

Minister for Shielding the Nation:
"Since then, a newfound insight has illuminated my path, urging me to present innovative solutions for our nation's

protection. Recognizing our island status, I propose a motion to plant shrubs and bushes along our coastlines."
Member of Opp.:
"And what's the rationale behind that?"
Minister for Shielding the Nation:
"It conceals our presence from prying eyes. An epiphany guided me, 'Eureka, this you do.' Our foreshores must convey the impression of a barren land, uninviting to any conquerors that may seek to step ashore."
Member of Opp.:
"Before you had your 'aha' moment, have you perhaps been sampling wild mushrooms? Consider the wisdom by adding signs proclaiming 'There's no one here.' Would that not please the esteemed minister?"
Minister for Shielding the Nation:
"Please address your remarks through the chair."
Member of Opp.:
"I doubt anything gets through that chair while she keeps the cushions warm."
Another Member of Opp.:
"Could we sprinkle withered flowers in the sand for a more desolate ambiance?"
Yet another Member of Opp.:
"Ah, dear Minister, I perceive your suggestion. How about placing empty bottles with tales of devastation scratched onto fallen leaves for added credence?"
Minister for Possibilities:
"What is the nation coming to? How much is this brainchild going to cost? Are you out of your mind. I, as the Minister for Possibilities say this: Opportunity bangs at the gates. Can you not hear it? It's shops we need, perhaps some chairs, where famished mouths can savour a delectable repast, accompanied by wine to soothe the parched and salted throat."
Minister for Possibilities:
"Where should the comers find a place of rest? Hotels of course, the very best. And shops we need to sell our pictured cards that they send home to summon kindred spirits, who do

as they did, lure them in. Let's hope they not forget to bring their coins to fill our hungry pockets."

Minister for Possibilities:
"Just think of how much advertising we will save. They come on their own accord, and they need clothing, they need toothpaste too, and schools their children can attend, and pet food for their little friends and toilet paper for their ends."

Minister for Possibilities:
"We need to plan for this and swift, build cities right out to the cliffs, and place a welcome sign atop, from far off shore to see, as well as signs beyond the breakers, 'We're open for business.'"

Minister for Possibilities:
"Unfortunately our esteemed Madam Deputy Speaker seems to be more interested in recording the handsome face of our Minister for Shielding the Nation, presumably as a live feed to her media profile what not, instead of keeping order in the House."

Deputy Speaker:

"What was that? Are you talking about me? I think he's kind of cute."

Whip:

"Yes, Madam Deputy Speaker, I thank you for partaking in the conversation."

Deputy Speaker:

"Who are you?"

Whip:

"I am the Whip."

Deputy Speaker:

"But where is it, the whip?"

Whip:

"No, no, not now, here is the list of the speakers."

Deputy Speaker:

"Whatever. Hey, come back, give it to them."

Member for Wreckville:

"Oh, thank you, Whip, for my time to quip has finally come."

"What I have heard thus far's mere gibber, fudged boloney, absurd, preposterous hokum, and hare-brained blithering nonsense. What we need and what my constituents need are full-time jobs. We need thousands, no, millions of cannons all along the periphery of our lands, so that any invaders need to crawl through the projectile barrels, ensuring our aim's on par."

Member from Opp.:
"As always, the member for Wreckville wants his finger in the pie. There are huge costs involved. Would we not save a fortune to import such cannons from our foes? Should they fail in their function, invaders would most likely be well-versed enough to fix the thing for free, as the warranty's still current, given that it came from their own shores, at a discount due to quantity."

Minister for Subversion and Confusion:
"The Wreckville member got it right, so I say with all my might, as Minister for Subversion and Confusion, say this: You all got it wrong, except for the one I mentioned. We must at once prepare. We must surround all lands of foes, from

outside and within, cunningly disguised, I add, incognito, as masquerading tourists blend into their strange surroundings. Then we attack, we strike with brawn. We make them wear the yoke they hoped to put us under."

Member from Opp.:

"But are we not outnumbered before commencement of such feat?"

Minister for Subversion and Confusion:

"Each one of us is nine of them, we'll win, so the prediction."

Member from Opp.:

"What makes you be so certain?"

Minister for Subversion and Confusion:

"I saw it on a silver-screen, when once I was a child. All we need do, as they did then and conquer forth their neighbours. And once all lands are conquered we shall rule the earth."

Another Member of Opp.:

"Should we not wait? Our Fearless Leader's mission of diplomacy is only in year three of twelve. Give it some time to root?"

Deputy Leader of Gov't:

"Another pigeon just came in with a message from our leader. Henceforth, he requests a funding drive to keep himself and staff alive, and toothpicks for Martinis."

Minister for Subversion and Confusion:

"We cannot wait for his return, the hour's closing in. Enlist all men of any age, bear pitchforks, picks and muskets, and ready all, before the bugle sounds the 'Charge' signalling a glorious day's begin."

Whip:

"It's ok, Minister for Subversion and Confusion, the man with the jacket are here now. Don't forget your medication."

Deputy Speaker:

"Ah, there you are, aunty. How is the roast."

Speaker:

"I should have switched it off three days ago. Well, the house burned down. Never mind. How did you go here?"

Deputy Speaker:

"I've been looking for a hole in this chair, but I couldn't find it."

Speaker:

"Why, a hole?"

Deputy Speaker:

"This mob is constantly saying, 'through the chair,' especially that old geezer. But I've been reading up a bit about my job. It's an interesting place you have her. I read about the whip and gags and guillotine. Where are the dungeons, where do you keep the heads? Whose heads roll next?"

Speaker:

"Fill me in, Sally, what's been happening?"

Deputy Speaker:

"Well, cutie wants to plant some greenery, that one's talking about mushrooms, the one behind him wants to dispose of his empty grog bottles on the beach, the one with the beady eyes hopes to grow new flowers from dead ones. Another one is a bit weird, talking about the cost of a child from the brain.

He lost me on that. Ah, yes, that one is into chairs, corner stores, wine and banging on doors, and something about salt. He wants hotels and the other one is into toothpaste and toilet paper. See the one in the back row, he keeps perving at me all the time."
Speaker:
"Thank you, Sally, you've done well."
Deputy Speaker:
"Sorry, aunty, I must carry on."
Deputy Speaker:
"So speak up, folks. What's it gonna be? The red carpet, the bushes, the shops, hotels or cannons? You need to sort this out before we can go any further."
Speaker:
"Thanks again, Sally, I'll take over the chair now."
Deputy Speaker:
"You can't. I have 739 followers on this podcast now, they wanna know what happens next."
Speaker:
"Clerk, please, the light?"

It was moments later that the House filled with darkness. First there was silence, then the sound of a phone ringing. Then another, and another. The television audience regained vision, as cameras switched to infrared to witness whispered phone call conversation by most legislators, casting an otherworldly ambiance over the room. Sally's growing fan-base delighted as the dim glow of her smart phone revealed a hive of activity.

Amidst the confusion, the Minister for Possibilities, true to his character, seized the moment to advocate for economic opportunities. In the darkness, his voice echoed through the chamber as he proposed building cities out to the cliffs, envisioning a thriving society that would attract visitors and fill the nation's coffers, while the Member for Wreckville stumbled over unseen obstacles, championing cost-effective solutions. When the light came back on, the speaker back in her chair, hastily arranged her hair, whilst rising chest exhaled the breath of calm.

There, near the door, the left of Sally's boots was left behind.

Speaker:

"Esteemed Members of the House, as we all have just witnessed, the challenges with our infrastructure underscore the pressing need for immediate attention. It is imperative that we swiftly pass the proposed bill for the renovation of these chambers to address these critical issues so that darkness does not befall our halls of bright deliberations."

House:

"Hear, hear."

Speaker:

"As I observe the escalating online activities, spurred by the televised remarks of the former deputy speaker regarding 'beady eyes' and unsettling behaviour within these walls earlier, I direct our Cyber Minister to demonetize the account of the former deputy speaker and, if possible, deactivate it altogether. Undoubtedly, this speculation will feature prominently in this morning's news. I recommend employing the customary denial strategy to address this matter."

House:

"Hear, hear."

Speaker:

"You will note that the Retailer's Association has increased the 15-minute hourly commercial time we have to endure to 18 minutes unless we grant them the tax concession they are after. Members, we must not give in; we will endure the hardship as an example to our people."

Speaker:

"Ah, the honourable Member from Behind the Wood, it seems your feline companion has once again embarked on a nocturnal adventure, leaving the opposition leader with an unexpected slip on its entrepreneurial endeavours."

"Meanwhile, the esteemed Member for Wreckville appears eager to share his pearls of wisdom; do enlighten us, dear colleague."

Member for Wreckville:

"Thank you, Madam Speaker. I rise to second the proposal of our peace-loving Minister for Subversion and Confusion. However, in the spirit of financial ingenuity, I suggest an amendment: let us unleash taxation loophole sniffer dogs to fund this noble cause. And, Madam Speaker, did you not just now instruct the clerk to switch the lights from bright to dark? This is the reason for the lack of illumination. There is no need to renovate these halls just yet, as funds are elsewhere needed."

Speaker:

"Let a commission make this decision. Perhaps the member from Behind the Woods stood hiding behind trees as the minister took leave, gowned in a white jacket with long sleeves and tied behind his frame. The said minister's speech did not explicitly put forth a formal motion or proposal in his eccentric commentary. The chair acknowledges that said minister found an opportune moment to escape his handlers and entertain us with what he would describe as a voice of reason. It shall be up to the House to give it further deliberation."

Member for Butterfly:
"We need to build a wall, says I, the new member for Butterfly, and with our backs against the wall, we'll find our strength and backbone. And once we do we're ready, as once we were before. And then with an all-mighty roar we unleash our kids, they'll show them good and proper."

Novice Politician 1:
"I cannot hear it anymore. I've had enough! My ears refuse to endure the pain they had been strained to bear. Is this a madhouse or a zoo? The yelling over the top of each other sounds like a monkey-cage before feeding time."

Speaker:

"Is this your maiden speech, my dear, or just a release of pent-up tension?"

Novice Politician 1:

"Oh, Madam Speaker, help me out. Everyone just screams and shouts. The future does not wait; it's here, yet voices of the long-gone time still bellow from the same folks that, as always, had the floor. You speak in phrases that no man, nor woman here can understand, at least not in my generation."

Opp. Bench:

"Hear, hear! Whose voice is this my ears can hear."

Gov't Bench:

"A novice politician."

Speaker:

"Step off the table immediately. Echoing the words of the great Latinian thinker Propter Caelum, Ridiculum Est Me, who uttered the immortal words translated to and 'so be it.'"

Member of Gov't:

"Madam Speaker, Point of Order, a procedural quagmire! I believe Madam Speaker is not adhering to the rule, therefore it warrants scrutiny. Please let the scribe look it up in the big books of rules, which cover the disparaging and denigrating remark directed at my colleague, the novice politician."

Speaker:

"Which were?"

Member of Gov't:

"'My dear.'"

Speaker:

"Excusez-moi?"

Member of Gov't:

"You addressed the novitiate young lass as 'my dear.'"

Speaker:

"And you, Ms. Know-it-all, shall spend the next 10 minutes in contemplation. Allow me to draw your attention to the term 'young lass,' which, in the spirit of parliamentary decorum, is not deemed appropriate. In contrast, my use of 'my dear' was intended as a beacon of respect and endearment, and as such, it stands unscathed and aligns with the rules. Therefore, my ruling is that my expression was meant to be respectful, while your choice of words was not."

Member of Gov't:
"How could you possibly know my intent, Madam Speaker?"
Speaker:
"Order, Ms. Know-it-all. Back to your corner. Ten minutes, not a peep."
Opp. Bench:
"Hear, hear."
Novice Politician 2:
"Madam Speaker, that is exactly the point. Where is the fairness in all this? Your opinion has more weight than my colleague's intention."
Speaker:
"That is democracy, my dear."

Novice Politician 2:

"My foot. It'll take the scribe eons to unearth the rules that make it so, in a book with ever growing pages."

Speaker:

"Do you wish to join the previous speaker in the corner?"

Novice Politician 2:

"No, dear, Madam Speaker, dear."

Speaker:

"Off you go, you've earned it.

Novice Politician 3:

"Madam Speaker, may I take the floor?"

Speaker:

"You may not *take* the floor, as we still need it. But you may address the House."

Novice Politician 3:

"Thank you, Madam Speaker."

Novice Politician 3:

"I am going through the petty cash statements of some of our honourable members. One minister who repeatedly frequented an establishment of ill repute spent several thousand dollars but failed to detail the services rendered. Another claimed $3.50 in stamps, the purpose of which is a mystery. I also note the present speaker in the chair did not mention the contributions made by the following donors from both sides of the House, which are..."

Speaker:

"Thank you to the esteemed member. May I have your paper for further perusal, and all the copies thereof?"

Novice Politician 3:

"Certainly, Madam Speaker. In addition, may I mention that this member, on page 39, ate all of his constituent's weekly rations during a visit, yet claimed a 6-course meal five minutes later, as well as $4833.87 in travel costs to his mother, living just 5 minutes down the road?"

Speaker:

"Thank you again, esteemed member. The paper, please. I want to save your larynx. It's a matter of health and safety. By the time you reach page 124, your voice will surely be gone. It sounds hoarse already; please hand in the paper, and you may take your seat."

Speaker:

"The Member for Alternatives has the floor."

Member for Alternatives:

"Oh, thank you, Madam Speaker. Is it not a joy to be alive in our splendid era of harmonious existence? The birds are singing; even the crows' enthralling calls spread calm across the land."

Speaker:

"Yes, yes. I can see your expressive demeanour screams 'important tidings.'"

Member for Alternatives:

"Quite so, indeed, I do, beloved Madam Speaker. Hear music echoes through the glen, young children holding apron strings, no ache of want, but rich abundance for all needs."

Speaker:

"Where is this place, as you describe?"

Member for Alternatives:

"Right here it is, below are feets."

Speaker:

"I see. Perhaps we should not trample on it. I see the Shadow Member for Alternatives wishes to address this chamber."

Shadow Member for Alternatives:

"Indeed I do, and thanks, Madam Speaker, for I can't wait to share my conceptations."

Speaker:

"There's no such word, it's not been coined."

Shadow Member for Alternatives:

"But, Madam Speaker, did I not speak it now into perpetual existence? Have I not birthed it with my voice? My colleague from the other side, with closed eyes, shared his vision, which opened our sense of sight. Beneath our feed, he said, so true, and all around in splendour. Can you not see the meadows bloom, where drones mate queens and workers blessed to carry honey, and in the sea where dolphins frolic playfully? Serenity is everywhere."

Speaker:

"Except perhaps reality, that might be the exception. Esteemed member, lest we forget our place that nature has imposed on us and act accordingly."

Shadow Member for Alternatives:

"But, Madam Speaker, and all members of the House, is this not the cause of our demise? Ignorance of consequences in all our grand assumptions. The illusion of supremacy has faults. Balance is a must, or else we fail in achieving our dream of calm."

Speaker:

"Is calmness our dream? Was there perhaps a little something in the tee? Yes, Leader of the Opposition, speak up."

Leader of the Opp.:

"Thank you, Madam Speaker. As a sign of hope, and as a light that shines forth through the bleakness of our times, I wish to introduce to one and all a new generation, who will one day be seated in these chairs. These esteemed members are the young, whom we paved the path for, that they're yet to follow. Meet Ms. Positive and Mr. Invincible, both with postgraduate qualifications at levels 9 and 10, who graduated with high distinction."

"I ask you all to look at their faces and take in the virgin innocence of their aspirations. For this, dear members, we have toiled. I'm not going to list their qualifications, or we'd be here all day. In any case, it would put most of us to shame. Perhaps we can all reflect on our time, when we stood hear, in our younger days. Perhaps remember what we'd hoped we could achieve. Thank you to you both."

Leader of the Opp.:

"And here, dear members of the House, are Ms. Bright Eyes and Mr. Possibility; one is a Professor in Philosophy, the other a Doctor in Political Science. Can you all see the joy in their faces? They are just some of the millions of young people that one day will take over. They and their peers will trot the path we paved."

"They will meet the challenges head-on. They will fix the environment, the greenhouse gases, the rising seas, the pollution in the oceans, the radioactive waste, the space debris, the smog, and millions of other little things that need some cure. The heirloom of our hard work bequeathed to them, as opportunity to rise beyond their wildest dreams. And once we've passed, we can relax in our armchairs high above the clouds and shall peek down in slight amusement, as they are stunned in awe at what we did achieve. We shall watch as they try with tiny tweezers to find the minute bits of shopping bags we left them in the seas to find. Our problems are no more, as they will have the chance to pioneer the future. This, kids, our gift to you."

Leader of the Opp.:

"When our time comes to retire from these chambers, we can take pride in knowing that we have raised these fine young people. We can be proud to know that we gave them some responsibilities, a few small trials to cut their teeth, some minor issues they can champion, and some diversions to test their endurance. When the time comes, we can sleep easy, knowing that the nation will be in good hands. They will remember our names and all our glorious deeds, and they will build large monuments in our honour. They will be grateful for the opportunities we have given them. And once these minor tasks are done, they too can rest."

Speaker:

"I believe the Deputy Leader wishes to speak."

Deputy Leader:

"Thank you, Madam Speaker, and thank you, to the Leader of the Opposition. Our Chief Whip and his deputy will be retiring next week. We wish them well in the years to come."

Deputy Leader:

"Let me express our thanks to Celeryanus and his offsider, Exitatious. While they have served us well for many years, the recent failure to pass several bills requires us to rethink. Some of you may have forgotten what the role of the whip is. I will spell it out. A whip is a wise man. He will always provide you with gentle guidance on any decision. They are well-informed, impart reason, are always helpful, and have a gentle nature."

"May I take this opportune moment to introduce the new replacement whips, and I advise all members, in particular on this side of the chair, to give my speech your undivided attention?"

Deputy Leader:

"This term we have a Chief Whip and two deputies, any of which can guide you to the correct answer you might be seeking. They are well-versed in the objectives of the party, which has ensured our continuous hold on power over many generations. There were moments when we had to sit on the other side, but if need be, we can easily delegate additional whips."

Deputy Leader:

"A whip is a member of the House. Much of their activity involves counting votes, but at all times they will keep an eye on us. They also ensure that we all follow the party line, mostly through gentle persuasion. Should their wise council fail, they will have means and ways at their disposal to convince any of us of which path to follow."

Deputy Leader:

"I mentioned party line. See the ridge across this mountain, akin to the party line. You'd be well advised to remain on the straight and narrow. A whip is there to ensure your safety. They help prevent you from slipping into a deep abyss. The narrow path along the ridge was forged by our pioneers. Our whip ensures our legacy and helps keep the hounds from straying. For those with an adventurous inclination, rest assured that the next station's chimes signal your exit from the gravy train."

Speaker:

"Thank you, Deputy Leader; you made that abundantly clear. I hope our young visitors earlier took some of your wise words aboard. I must inform the House that yet another pigeon has arrived from our absent Fearless Leader. It says that he is in comprehensive discussions with future leaders. A picture shows him sitting with a group of toddlers. He mentions this: Should we have difficulties providing ongoing funding for his diplomatic efforts, he gives us the green light to tax the sun, the sea, the wind, and whatever else we deem appropriate."

Member of Opp.:
"How many pigeons did our Fearless Leader take?"
Speaker:
"Enough for the duration. May we continue? The Novice Politician Number 3 has slipped me a note. His eager eye has found a claim by one of the ministers from the frontbench."

Novice Politician 3:
"Yes, Madam Speaker. A pencil sharpener, which the esteemed minister claims to cost $5843.-. The same minister waived a $2.7million tax burden by one of his constituents in exchange for a $128.- contribution to our Christmas hamper."
Speaker:
"Congratulations, young man, that is $128.- we didn't know we had. The member for the opposition has the floor."
Member of Opp.:
"Thank you, Madam Speaker. I want to wish to express my unwavering support for opposing the TPPKMMNZ trade agreement currently being hoodwinked into something that could be a benefit to anyone."

Speaker:

"I shall give the other side of the aisle a chance to respond."

Member of Gov't.:

"Thank you, Madam Speaker. I do not wish to acknowledge his remarks with a response. What I will do is thank our countries' workers, who, through their Unions, have rejected a pay offer of 50%, which was made by the opposition, should they gain government. Madam Speaker, these underhanded tactics won't work."

Gov't. Benches:

"Hear, hear."

Member of Gov't.:

"Madam Speaker, our workers, who have shown restraint and endurance in suffering the last 12 years, they have looked hardship in the eye, and they didn't blink."

Member of Opp.:

"What a lot of bollocks."

Opp. Benches:

"Hear, hear."

Member of Opp.:

"What I've just heard, Madam Speaker, can only be described as a froth-covered fermented stew of slosh."

Opp. Benches:

"Hear, hear. Bravo."

Speaker:

"Order in the House. You, sir, please take your seat. Oh dear, oh dear, I must apologise to the government member, as well as the Novice Politician 2, for you are still facing the corner. I think your 10 minutes expired some time ago. Please take your seats. Consider the extra time in the naughty corner for misdeeds you did that I didn't quite catch."

Speaker:

"Yes, Leader of the Opposition, what is it now?"

Leader of the Opposition:

"Madam Speaker, I am beyond words for what I just heard across the aisle."

Speaker:

"That's good. It keeps your speech brief."

Deputy Leader:

"Madam Speaker, the opposition is trying to buy their way into government by offering or workforce unsustainable increases that would take the nation nine generations or more to come to grips with."

Member of Gov't.:

"Madam Speaker, in addition to that, and I've just crunched the numbers, another 1000 years on top of it, to recover."

Opp. Leader:

"Madam Speaker, I say to the Deputy Leader: Look at the reflection in the bottom of your cooking pot; can you not see in crystal-clear clarity that your family lineage is as flawed as your futile attempt to govern? 'They have looked hardship in the eye?', your words. Forgive me, Madam Speaker, while I weep. He thanks our workers for their restraint. All this while his Fearless Leader is on a 12-year global tour to meet with toddlers across islands and send pigeons asking us to tax the sun."

Opp. Leader:

"Madam Speaker, there he sits, the Deputy Leader, an excuse for humanity, an abomination, a reject of nature, perhaps best described as 'it'. You'd be well advised to take a detour around every mirror. Madam Speaker, our workers have lost their homes; Madam Speaker, they have lost their belongings; Madam Speaker, they sleep in their cars under bridges; and it's just a matter of time before they lose their cars too. All it takes is a registration bill they cannot pay, and that's it. And he boasts about the tax breaks he's given his comrades. All pretty meaningless if you don't have the luxury of having an income."

Deputy Leader:

"Madam Speaker, how can you lose a house? Has it come off the foundations?"

Members of Opp.:

"Booh, Booh!"

Deputy Leader:

"Madam Speaker, last week I saw the opposition leader mowing his lawn. Even his dog piddled all over his mower while he was changing the blades."

Members of Opp.:

"Booh, Booh!"

Speaker:

"Order, ORDER! Well, dear members, I kind of enjoy your entertaining pleasantries, and so do the networks. I look forward to their contribution to our holiday fund due to the rise in ratings."

Opp. Leader:

"Madam Speaker, we know the member has some sows and three cows, two for milking, the other his wife, but I would have hoped he'd change his boots before coming in here. The whiff of country follows him like his shadow. 'They have looked hardship in the eye,' so you said. What they have seen for sure is all the BS that's going down. The next pigeon mail will ask for rent collectors under bridges or have them issue trespass fines."

Member of Gov't:

"Madam Speaker, that one over there is nothing but a scheming puppeteer pulling the strings of deceit! Adorned with the laurels of a rusty barbwire fence."

Opp. Leader:

"Madam Speaker, why are you smiling? More money for the playtime fund? The next thing our Fearless Leader's stooge is saying is that our workers have voted for a 12% tax increase because they had no idea how to spend their fortunes. While the Deputy Speaker at 7ft 9inches gives a towering impression of his stature, his member is not."

Deputy Leader:

"That is below the belt."

Opp. Leader:

"Precisely. I saw you in the shower. Need I say more?"

Speaker:

"Order, ORDER! Look, folks, there is no one watching your performance at this hour on TV, and the member for Pompville on the Flair's Poli Awards has not yet been finalised. May I suggest you all take whatever medication it may be, as the air-con is still out and hot tempers are not helping at the moment? There on the backbench, who are you?"

Leader of the Modest Party:

"I am the leader of the Modest Party."

Speaker:

"Go on."

Leader of the Modest Party:

"Madam Speaker, esteemed colleagues. In solidarity with our suffering workers, I have listed my abode for sale, the proceeds of which shall be of benefit to the workers in our nation who are currently suffering hardship."

Members from both sides:

"Bravo. Hear, hear."

Leader of the Modest Party:

"Madam Speaker, I put forth a motion that all others do the same."

Speaker:

"Does anyone second the motion? Hello. Can anyone hear me? The motion is that every member put up his or her house for sale, the proceeds of which will benefit workers currently suffering hardship. Does anyone second this motion? No? It seems there are no takers."

Deputy Leader:

"Madam Speaker, to the Leader of the Modest Party, I say thanks for his charitable contribution. Let's look a bit closer at his grand proposal. He offloaded one of his many properties to ease the hardship of our workers, when in actuality his property was burdened with huge negative equity. That move, in effect, puts the burden now on the taxpayers. Bravo. Not all is as it seems, Madam Speaker. The Leader of the Modest Party has grown up with a silver spoon in his mouth. To him, politics is just a diversion."

Speaker:

"To the Minister for Shielding the Nation, I am sorry to say that we must push back the 2nd reading of your bill to another day, as we've exhausted all of today's allocated overtime allowance. It's perhaps a bit late today, so I bid you 'good night' to you all. I hope I find my traumatised hamster and give him some breakfast. Therefore, I propose the House be adjourned."

Opp. Backbencher:
"I wish to raise a point before the House is closed."
Speaker:
What is it now? Can't you just plot it down on paper and we deal with it another time?"
Opp. Backbencher:
"Madam Speaker, this would not be wise."
Speaker:
"Go on then."
Opp. Backbencher:
"This morning's paper has just came out. I draw your attention to the front page. It does look very much like our nation's heavily armoured official limousine, with its unique number plate. It was seen cruising through the centre of town. According to the pigeons, our Fearless Leader is in far-off lands. The limo was mothballed three years ago upon his

leaving, as he was very particular about who might sit inside it."

Opp. Backbencher:

"Madam Speaker, do the names Josh and Joshuette mean anything to you? Perhaps the teen offspring of your newlywed groom? Perhaps it was a coincidence. Might I say the picture bears an uncanny resemblance to the leading car in your wedding entourage, except it did not show graffiti embellishments then? Said limousine went through 13 red lights, complete with a 100 strong police escort, through the red-light district, then up the main avenue with music blaring and teens hanging out its windows, yelling 'immunity,' and 'Vienna Convention.'"

"The car has rolled three times while engaged in navigating a sharp corner; no injuries have been reported. All 15 teens are currently recovering; perhaps sobering up is more to the point."

Speaker:

"Let me have a look at this. Oh dear."

Member of Opp.:

"This is fantastic. Is this the Deputy Leader's son?"

Member of Gov't:

"So it seems, but look again; your daughter is on the roof. Hang on, and mine sits on the bonnet."

Speaker:

"They are having a good time; isn't that what life is all about? At least they have some nice snapshots. It's good to know that they had police protection. Mothballing a limousine was never a good idea. The kids just took it for a test run, stops the bearings from rusting tight. All those in favour of ordering a new limousine for our Fearless Leader?"

Small End of Town Party:
"I do object!"
Speaker:
"Why?"
Small End of Town Party:
"It'll take 10 years before he's finished his journey."
House:
"Hear, hear."

Small End of Town Party:
"Madam Speaker, it is a waste of resources. Our Fearless Leader's current vehicle is a write-off. Investing the funds needed for a replacement could potentially generate returns that could be redirected towards party initiatives or community projects."
Member of Gov't.:
"I must agree, that is a great idea."
Small End of Town Party:
"Alternatively, the funds could support charitable causes in current need. If the leader does return in 10 years, his

physical needs may be better met with a more suitable method of transportation, initially a bicycle and eventually a regular ambulance, as his health condition may require it."

"In any case, any of these suggestions would send a message of environmental responsibility, social justice, community engagement, and prudent financial planning, all cornerstones of party policy, likely to underline the party's commitment to sustainability, including a reduced carbon footprint. In addition, this strategic move will enhance the party's image, strengthen ties with the public, and serve as an example to leaders across the globe. Madam Speaker, unconventional times call for unconventional measures. Transparency is a cornerstone of effective governance."

Small End of Town Party:
"Madam Speaker, I wish to make you and the House aware of events that raise my concern level. Considering the recent developments in the government party with the replacement of the whips, I must issue a warning. Changing the whip to a couple of intimidating strongmen is likely to have consequences."
Small End of Town Party:
"Madam Speaker, the role of the whip, as misleadingly explained by the deputy leader, is traditionally about party discipline. The current shift towards strongmen intimidation is likely to provoke responses from other parties. We might see armed whips with weapons, or even worse."
Speaker:
 "Armed whips? Weapons? What are you suggesting?"
Small End of Town Party:
"Madam Speaker, I did not suggest it; this is just the logical progression currently set in motion. A shift towards physically intimidating whips is likely to escalate tensions within and outside our political circle. Other parties might feel compelled to respond in kind, leading to a quasi-arms race that distracts from the actual business of governing. There are many examples in the past and present of such escalation."

Speaker:

"This is a political arena, not a battlefield. What is the solution?"

Small End of Town Party:

"Madam Speaker. I propose that this concern be addressed diplomatically, highlighting the importance of maintaining a civil and respectful political environment. It would be of benefit to express reservations about the potential consequences of such a drastic change."

Small End of Town Party:

"Madam Speaker, we could stand firm on existing principles. We could work towards fostering a collaborative and constructive political atmosphere, emphasising the need for mutual respect, and resisting confrontational politics."

Member of Gov't.:

"And where is the fun in this?"

Small End of Town Party:

"Madam Speaker, traditionally, the term 'whip' originates from previous centuries, derived from fox hunting. Whips were used not to keep the foxes in line but to stop the hunting hounds from straying off the scent, to keep the pack together."

"Madam Speaker, the Small End of Town Party embraces a unique perspective. We proudly set ourselves apart in this parliament and across the nation by championing persuasion over confrontation. While we acknowledge that the government's recently appointed whips are undoubtedly physically formidable, capable of instilling fear in most individuals, our approach differs significantly. Our whips are adept at the art of persuasion, effortlessly blending allure with a velvety voice that resonates sweetness. Their captivating demeanour beckons cooperation, and each has mastered the delicate skills of beguilement, enchantment, and persuasion. We believe in fostering understanding and collaboration rather than relying on force or intimidation. I'm confident any strongman whip will get soft at their knees."

Member of Gov't.:
"Why can't we all be friends?"
Opp. Leader:
"My dear Deputy Leader, have you not paid attention? Is this not the voice of reason we've just heard?"
Speaker:
"I only hope your whips don't catch a cold in winter."
Deputy Leader of Gov't:
"Madam Speaker, congratulations to the Small End of Town Party. I wish to advise them to keep their whips away from my members. Any liaison between their whips and our whips is unthinkable. On another matter, last week, 'The Undeniable Truth' published an article complaining about a fall in their readership. They believe that a majority of their readers believe they are experiencing financial hardship. They suggest that we conduct a wealth census on the population, which will clearly show that there are no financial inequalities in our

nation. They have expressed some urgency in this matter and offered to publish any findings."

"Instead of having our citizens go through the ordeal of counting every penny in their wallet, estimating the value of each real estate holding, and any other assets, I propose a very simple one-question wealth census. The question will be unambiguous; it reads: "How many things do you have? The response will be a simple number. We'll know very quickly what the wealth distribution is."

"Depending on the postcode, a pamphlet explains what 'things' are. One postcode may explain 'things' as: a property with 5 garages, 4 limousines, a boat, and 20 horses would count as 1 thing. Another postcode may explain it as: How many coins are in your wallet? Count them. How many keys are on your key ring? Count them. How many members in your family? Count them. How many sheets of toilet paper are on each roll? Count them. Add all the numbers together and note them down. There might be a super-rich person owning 38 paperclips, or one could simply answer 1 for the entire office complex. Let's not be too pedantic. So it's straight-forward and easy to understand. After all, it's the things we own we consider as wealth, and that is what we're counting."

Members of Opp.:

"Boo, boo."

Leader of Opp.:

"Madam Speaker, such poppycock twaddle can only come out of the mouth of the Deputy Leader of the Government. I can see the headlines already: 80% of the nation owns millions of things, while 20% make do with a few pitiful possessions. It can only mean that the 20% need substantial tax breaks to survive. They need alms, charity, a trust fund to help them stay afloat, an aid agency; please, somebody help them. And yes, 'The Undeniable Truth' will print such trash, and everyone feels happy."

"The poor will dance in the streets as they have more things than the big end of town. Barefoot and in torn clothing they'll mock the passing limousines as they dine with rumbling bellies from the trashcans. They rejoice as they live in the world of the free, free from shelter in any weather, while the few are burdened to keep remembering the password codes to enter their guarded estates. As they bathe their children with joyous faces in the stale gutters of the backstreets they are aware of the jealous glances from the tinted windows of the lead car, followed by a guarding convoy."

"The Deputy Leader of the Government cannot be serious to put this up as a motion. Perhaps there is more to this, taxing the garbage bins as food distributers, meal bins on wheels, are they registered, licensed, permit carrying footpath-users?"

Deputy Leader of Gov't:

"My oath I am."

Member of Opp.:

"Madam Speaker, I request temporary leave."

Speaker:

"Why?"

Member of Opp.:

"I need to go to the beach to have the Member for Pipelines and Tubes return to these chambers."

Speaker:

"Now, isn't that interesting, moments before a vote? The Member for Pipelines and Tubes, as you heard earlier, is conducting important studies on barrels and whatever else. She is engaged in community consultations with her constituency. This is an important role, and judging by the urgency she had expressed when she requested leave, she could be up to her neck in tubes, barrels, and pipelines. In the interest of efficiency, I think it's better to let her continue her important task. Your leave request is denied."

Member of a Minor Party:

"Madam Speaker, In the realm of strategic governance, we must conscientiously navigate the labyrinth of contemporary challenges by leveraging a paradigmatic approach that synergistically amalgamates innovative methodologies, thereby elucidating a visionary trajectory conducive to the augmentation of societal well-being and the perpetuation of our shared values."

Member of Opp.:

"In the spirit of fostering a climate of collaborative engagement, it is paramount that we undertake a meticulous and nuanced examination of the intricate complexities inherent in the current socio-political milieu, with a view toward formulating judicious and forward-thinking policies that resonate with the diverse spectrum of stakeholder interests."

Shadow Finance Minister:

"In the hypothetical circumstance wherein the exchequer, through a fortuitous concatenation of fiscal abundance, were to manifest a surfeit to the extent of bursting at the seams, it would, by virtue of this opulent profusion, obviate any exigency for the augmentation of fiscal levies, thereby presenting an auspicious juncture devoid of necessity for the imposition of additional taxation."

Speaker:

"Does anyone here has something of value to contribute?"

Member of Opp.:

"Yes, Madam Speaker, I do. In the pursuit of a synergistic paradigm shift within the dynamic landscape of socio-political discourse, it is imperative that we engage in a comprehensive and holistic examination of multifaceted strategies, fostering a robust and inclusive framework that endeavours to address the nuanced challenges confronting our constituents, thereby propelling our collective aspirations toward an enlightened and progressive future."

Member of Gov't.:

"Madam Speaker, I request you order the ringing of the bell for several minutes. This is very urgent."

Speaker:

"That was done this morning. May I ask why?"

Member of Gov't.:

"One of our members seems to have lost her sense of time. I believe she is testing our new recreational facilities rehearsing her hopscotch routine."

Speaker:

"There are several thousand clocks in this building, as well as personal watches and one on every mobile phone. Anyone not aware of the time in this building may waste it playing hopscotch. I thank the member for making me aware of the absence of leave without cause, which will be recorded. The bells will not chime to interrupt her hopscotch session."

The Minister for Meaningful Dialogue:

"To foster a collaborative transformation in the ever-evolving terrain of socio-political discourse, it is crucial that we undertake a thorough and holistic exploration of diverse strategies. This involves cultivating a resilient and inclusive framework aimed at addressing various aspects."

Speaker:

"Yes, Shadow Minister for Clear Expression, speak your piece."

Shadow Minister for Clear Expression:

"In the event that the assemblage of the chamber were to attain a state of replete occupancy, it would, by logical extension, preclude the possibility of its remaining bereft or devoid, thereby insinuating a condition antithetical to emptiness."

Speaker:

"Never in the field of human nonsense has so much gibberish been spoken by so many to so few who understood even less."

Rolling Thunder:

"Madam Speaker, I, Morrie, channel the indomitable essence of the Lorry Union. Within this revered assembly, my utterances may bear no substantial weight, yet I persist in bringing forth a matter of paramount concern. In bygone years, automation replaced many of our toiling brethren in various industries, leaving once-thriving communities in desolation."

"I cite just one example of many: a once-thriving factory with a workforce of 700, robust enough to sustain an entire community. Management succumbed to the seductive whispers of cost-cutting allure, replacing the entire production chain with robots. Only one soul remained, holding the key to unlocking the doors for raw material deliveries. His wage, deemed excessive in the insatiable quest for cost savings, led to the relocation of the entire operation to a distant, low-wage land."

"In the tireless pursuit of efficiency, cost savings, and heightened productivity—the anthem of that era—towns were allowed to wither, the life choked out of once-flourishing communities."

"Esteemed members, where was the empathetic ear when our fellow workers were replaced by robots? Where was the sympathy as the mechanisation wave swept through our industries? Workers paid the price, losing jobs, dignity, and self-esteem. Many took their own lives, burdened by the shame of being unable to provide for their families. Their children are still paying the price to this very day."

"In hindsight, one must concede that the reliability of these devices is of high order. Witness the flawless automated ballet in paint booths, assembly lines, banking systems, warehouses, and beyond. Let us not forget that it was the workers who showed many of these devices how things are done. Despite initial glitches, do they not perform admirably? They are the underclass of their 'species,' the slaves, yet they produce unmanned, more quality output than ever before."

Member of Gov't.:
"That's right, that was the whole idea."
Rolling Thunder:
"The current iteration of these devices is beyond belief. The humanoid marvel of the 'I-class,' an abbreviation of 'Intelligent-class,' has now surpassed all others, and its dominance will only grow."

"In this very Parliament, we encounter entertainers, jesters, and comedians, each playing a role in the grand theatre of governance. A proposal shall be put to our comrades throughout the land, and their decision I already know. If this 'I-class' humanoid is indeed the epitome of omniscience, then let us usher in a new era where these beings guide our policies with sagacity and foresight. I implore any member of this dignified House to champion this cause as a private member's bill, a beacon signalling our commitment to a future where governance is guided by logic, efficiency, and an unwavering dedication to sustainability, so that you all may taste the fruits that your decision made us swallow."

"Just as in the factories of years ago, I propose to replace the lot of you and watch how smoothly all problems can be solved. There is no need to waste your time here with senseless verbal gymnastics; there is no need to spin a wheel to get your answers. Perhaps retrain, up-skill, and relocate; somewhere there is a job for you too, so this you said, remember? Become the hopscotch champion in your neighbourhood if you must."

Member of Gov't.:
"This is very amusing. Do you think anyone here would support such nonsense?"

Rolling Thunder:

"Is there a need for any of you? Is there a need to pay you long after you have left office? Is there really a need for any of you at all?"

Member of Opp:

"This is blasphemy. Madam Speaker, help. This man has lost all of his marbles."

Rolling Thunder:

"Consider this: The elimination of corruption, bribery, and personal bias will yield a dramatic improvement in efficiency and productivity. The humanoid politician can process vast amounts of information quickly and make decisions based on logic and data, freed from the influence of emotional and subjective factors. This is the end of policy flip-flops."

Member of Gov't.:

"Madam Speaker, I implore you to put a stop to this. How can we live without bribery? Corruption is the lubrication oil of business. This man is rocking the boat."

Rolling Thunder:

"They need no sleep, no breaks, or holidays. They don't require salaries, healthcare, pensions, and perks. There is no need to renovate these chambers; they can work in the dark from anywhere. No canteens, restaurants, or ablution blocks are needed. The massive number of current staff can be reduced. Humanoids do not require expensive election campaigns, advertising, or fundraisers. There would be longevity, stability, and substantial savings."

Member of Opp.:

"Where are the whips when you need them?"

Rolling Thunder:

"Humanoids have a long operational lifespan and have no health issues, memory lapses, or disruptions due to changes in leadership. We'd benefit from their accumulated wisdom over many lifetimes. We have a chance to not repeat the errors of the past. All we need to do is lay down a framework of ethics and unbiased decision-making to ensure the fair and just function of our humanoid politicians."

"We put in place a comprehensive set of ethical guidelines to ensure humans make decisions that align with societal values and norms. We'll develop sophisticated decision-making algorithms that consider diverse perspectives, avoid biases, prioritise the well-being of the population, and also consider what effects and consequences our decisions might have on the wider world we live in."

"We'll programme the humanoids to adapt to changing circumstances and new information while maintaining consistency, transparency, and accountability in their decision-making processes. Humanoids should be able to explain their reasoning in a clear and understandable manner to the public, contrary to what is currently in place. This contributes to public understanding and trust in governance."

Backbencher:

"This is all good and well, but not for us. We wouldn't need the limos anymore, but I'm not giving up my entitlements."

Rolling Thunder:

"Perhaps the day will come when, instead of golden door handles in ostentatious buildings, we can boast that not one of our citizens needs to sleep under bridges. We should awaken a hunger for wisdom, justice, empathy, and equity instead of the painful growl of empty bellies. The meaning of favouritism, cronyism, and nepotism has long been forgotten."

"We'll implement mechanisms for continuous learning and improvement. Humanoids should be able to analyse the outcomes of their decisions and adjust their algorithms accordingly. We'll integrate robust security protocols to prevent hacking, tampering, or external influence that could compromise the integrity of humanoid politicians."

Frontbencher:

"There goes my future."

Rolling Thunder:

"We would also incorporate mechanisms for public input and feedback to ensure that humanoid politicians are responsive to the needs and concerns of the population. We need to consider cultural nuances and sensitivities to avoid unintentional biases in decision-making and ensure humanoids are culturally competent and comply with existing legal frameworks and regulations."

"We will establish a system of human oversight to monitor the actions of humanoid politicians, intervene if necessary, and address unforeseen ethical dilemmas. Let us turn our gaze towards the present, where the march of automation continues its relentless stride. We stand on the verge of a new era where the products of metal and circuitry outshine those of flesh and bone. We are on the brink of witnessing motor vehicles built not by the sweat of human brows but by the precision of robotic hands. These mechanical marvels could come adorned with lifetime warranties, a testament to the durability that only unyielding metal can provide."

"As we look to the horizon, envision ships and planes meticulously crafted by machines, equipped with fail-safe systems so intricate that the prospect of failure becomes an anomaly. In this age of technological prowess, efficiency reigns supreme, and the dividends of our progress are clear for all to see. Yet, I implore you to reflect on the implications of this advancement. Are we not witnessing the dawn of a new era where the very fabric of our existence is woven by the hands of automatons?"

"Consider the tremendous power at our disposal. Rather than relying on the frailties of human nature, we could entrust the governance of our nations to beings immune to the allure of corruption unaffected by the biases that cloud our judgment.

Imagine a political landscape where decisions are made not out of self-interest or party allegiance but guided by the pure logic of algorithms and the unbiased pursuit of the common good."

"Instead of deploying resources to spy, control, and intimidate entire populations, we could redirect our efforts towards the efficient and cost-effective management of a select few humanoid politicians. These synthetic statesmen, devoid of personal ambitions and immune to the temptations of power, could usher in an era of governance untainted by the flaws that have marred our political landscape for centuries."

"Let us not fear the changing winds of progress but embrace the potential for a brighter future. The time has come for us to consider the possibility of replacing the traditional political order with a new paradigm, one where the virtues of artificial intelligence guide our destinies and the legacy of our decisions reverberates through the circuits of time. The era of humanoid politicians beckons, and it is our duty to explore this uncharted territory for the betterment of our societies."

"Do we not already put our trust in self-driving cars, autonomous systems that help land planes, drive tractors, operate on patients in hospitals, in satellites, and an endless list of systems that do not require human input, relying on their programmed precision and advanced technologies to navigate, perform tasks, and make decisions with a level of efficiency and accuracy that continues to shape the future of various industries?

"But let me also issue a resounding word of warning to all those gathered here. If we do not seize this opportunity to harness the power of automation and replace unpredictable and fallible politicians with the rational minds of humanoid counterparts, then we leave the door wide open for the dire fate of enslavement. A fate where the very tools meant to propel us into a brighter future will be wielded by politicians to tighten the shackles of oppression around each and every one of us."

"The potential for abuse is staggering, and the consequences of inaction are spine-chilling. Those of us that could withstand the tide of relentless propaganda, beware: our freedoms, our autonomy, and our very essence as free-thinking individuals will be jeopardised."

"We are on the brink of a dystopian future, where the constraints enforced by those in authority are so deeply rooted that escaping them seems nearly insurmountable. The sanctity of elections, the cornerstone of democratic governance, may well become a farce if we allow the unchecked influence of politicians to persist."

"The allure of control is a potent elixir that, if left unchecked, will intoxicate those who hold the reins of power. The very tools that could liberate us could also be turned against us, and the democratic ideals we hold dear will crumble in the face of unchecked authority. It is our duty, our responsibility, to ensure that this scenario does not unfold."

"Let us also recognise the perils of stagnation. Now is the moment for decisive action, as choosing inactivity might consign us to a future where we ourselves forge the chains of subjugation. Let us not be the architects of our own demise, but rather the stewards of a future where the fruits of progress are shared by all, unencumbered by the heavy burdens of oppression."

"Deep down, I feel that the heartbeat of democracy lies in the pulse of public sentiment, and we must be attuned to it as we chart this unexplored course."

"Diving into the economic seas, consider the ripples and waves that would emanate from replacing traditional political processes with humanoid counterparts. Industries intricately tied to campaigns, political consulting, and event planning may face disruption or evolution. The currents of change, though powerful, may present opportunities for new forms of economic activity to emerge."

"Recall the societal shifts brought forth by technological advancements and political revolutions. Analogies from the past can illuminate our path forward and offer valuable insights into navigating the challenges and opportunities that lie ahead. The tapestry of history, woven with threads of change, serves as both a guide and a cautionary tale."

"As we weigh the consequences on the international stage, ponder how nations across the globe might respond to the concept of humanoid politicians. Cultural variations, geopolitical considerations, and the potential for global collaboration or conflict in this new era must be considered. The world watches, and our decisions resonate far beyond the walls of this chamber."

"Now, let us turn our attention to the legal and regulatory landscape. Introducing humanoid politicians will undoubtedly raise complex legal and ethical questions. We must carefully navigate constitutional frameworks, ensuring accountability, and crafting legislation that governs the actions of these artificial entities, lest we find ourselves in uncharted legal waters. The unforeseen often lurks in the shadows of progress, and it is our duty to bring it into the light."

"And finally, let us not forget the philosophical underpinnings of this proposal. Questions of morality, agency, and the role of humanity in shaping its destiny must be grappled with. We stand at the precipice of a philosophical frontier, and our decisions will reverberate through the corridors of history."

"In the realm of representative democracy, you stand as elected individuals, chosen by the people to bear the weight of their hopes, aspirations, and concerns. From this perspective, one could argue that you are indeed servants of the people, entrusted with the sacred duty of translating the will of the electorate into policies that reflect the collective welfare."

"Yet, as we navigate the corridors of power, we must acknowledge the complexities woven into the fabric of political reality. The notion of public servants implies a duty to serve the public interest, to act as stewards of the common good."

"As trustees of public trust, you find yourselves at a crossroads where decisions made on behalf of the people may not always align with immediate popular sentiments. The trusteeship model demands that you exercise judgement for the greater good, even when faced with tough choices that may not satisfy every constituent."

Rolling Thunder:

"As for the suggestion of being replaced by humanoids, I understand the sentiment. The allure of artificial intelligence, free from the influence of financial interests and personal agendas, is an intriguing proposition. Humanoids, while efficient, lack the nuanced understanding that comes from the human experience.

"You all need to commit to learning from mistakes, listening to the concerns of the electorate, and striving for a balance between the demands of governance and the common good. It is through dialogue, accountability, and a commitment to the ideals of democracy that enables us to navigate the challenges before us."

"In conclusion, the road ahead is fraught with challenges, and the weight of responsibility is profound. You all know, including me, that our days are numbered if the humanoid politician becomes the servant of the nation.

There needs to be a collective effort to reaffirm your commitment to ethical governance and work towards a future where the common good prevails over individual interests, with or without you.

Rolling Thunder:

"You can wake up now. I said my piece. I didn't expect much support from you, but, yeah."

Wheelies

Anyone would be familiar with jam, marmalade, and butter—the ones that come in small plastic containers and are served on airline meals in flight or at breakfast at a hotel. Possibly, a great part of the population has no big problem peeling the lid off to get to the substance. Fading eyesight makes these triangles minute. All have their outer ear chopped off; a smooth radius blends both sides of the triangle, which is fine; it prevents scratch and cut injuries. Nature, especially living beings, rarely grows geometrical flat surfaces (like ice, crystals, etc.), and so all of our fingertips are rounded, the thumbs included.

This, in effect, reduces the amount of fingertip area that could grip the small triangle. The radius has further reduced the triangle's height. Skin itself slips off on very smooth surfaces; instead, many try to dig in with the fingernails for increased gripping power.

One usually employs the thumb and index finger, while the other hand holds the container with the precious goods. Often it works; sometimes it does not, and the whole container flies through the room. All too often, this small triangular lip can drive one to frustration and outright anger. All it takes is normal ageing, some weakness, brittle fingernails, coordination, and eyesight interference, and most everyone will come across this eventually.

I mentioned this to a friend of mine who is in the design and manufacturing business of food processing machines, but they were not producing such small products, more geared for different lines. One item I have come across deserves a mention: a twin-pocket tomato sauce container with a raised edge on the discharge side. The pack is designed to fold; a little pressure forces the ridge to crack, and the user is in full control of the amount discharged. The different viscosity between sauces, jam, and butter does not make this container ideal for all contents. These items (the jam containers and such) don't usually bother me, but they bother many of the people I know (but rarely do they complain). Some call themselves affectionately the Wheelies. Instead of legs, they have wheels, even if they have legs.

A dear friend of ours became a wheelie through age and lifelong hip joint problems. My late wife hid her own wheels behind a corner every time we visited the dear friend in the age care facility. 'We must not let her worry about me,' she said, and arm in arm, slowly and carefully, we 'walked' the five steps to the safety of a chair.

Buying a set of wheels is an experience. The first one is perhaps the hardest to buy. No one likes wheels. My late wife hated the thought of it. I carried her piggyback or in my arms for weeks. 'Just think what we could do?' I said, 'a park, the ocean, the river's edge, the inside of a forest.'

For many, a wheelchair is a marker that lets everyone know where one is going. A bit like clothing, once the trendy clothes don't matter anymore, another part of life begins. The same is true when the hair becomes tired of chemical colouring. There are many small wheelies who are not one bit concerned about the colour of their hair. Many have none to colour, and so it was for Julie.

One day, and the day was always a Thursday, Julie came into oncology. Her all-black wheels roll silently, but Julie never is. 'Hi guys,' she calls out, 'Good morning. I want to wish you all a happy day.' Then she throws a red rose of hope, a ribbon, and a red balloon onto each bed. 'What's the occasion?' someone asks, 'I am in the clear; you hear, I'm in the clear.' Her face said it all. 'Just needed to share my joy with you and hope for you too.' She made everyone happy. Each clock ticks differently; one accepts that, but seeing a kid of 16 with low batteries is painful; many clocks struggle to make 8 or less. Julie will turn 17, and that is joy enough to know.

Not all are weak or frail; many are strong, healthy people who have lost the function of a leg or both from one day to the next, often due to bike, industrial, or other accidents. Karen is about 25, mostly wearing a singlet, her upper arms well toned; she looks strong and full of vitality, as does any woman that age. There are no handles on her wheels, no push bar, or the usual gizmos. Her wheels angled in, a wide wheelbase, you could say, rock-solid grip, the Formula 1 equivalent, definitely a sports model with exceptional handling capabilities.

Some wheels are not for life; transitional wheels will do until a new leg is fashioned and the art of walking becomes normal. Paul was one of them, waiting for the stitches to heal. Every mealtime, he came as the last. He'd stop at the entry to the hospital dining room (perhaps 60 seats), his voice strong enough that the deaf could hear, or at least adjust their volume. 'Oh my God, look at you lot,' he calls into the room. 'It's like in a morgue. Don't anyone make a noise, or they think you're still alive.' He had a habit of stopping at each table, greeting each person by name, 'And how is William on this beautiful morning?' William answered, nodding with a grin. 'And the delightful Mrs. Carpenter, are we in a good mood?' 'Go away, Paul.'

'Aye aye, Captain, please hold still; here is your bib, and there is the serviette, and you are ready, Captain,' The captain could not speak, but he did acknowledge Paul's assistance by moving his head. Paul was always on the move; he would read out the menu, spy a bowl of bananas, and say, 'Who wants bananas?' Then he took count and delivered them all before the kitchen staff had a chance to defend them. His place was besides the captain. Paul made his bread, cut it all up, fed the captain, and cleaned up whatever spills may have happened.

He also had enough insight to leave those alone who could not cope with his outgoing personality.

In hospitals, three times a day is mealtime, and butter or margarine is the first to challenge the once independent men and women. Now they are patients; some are patients with patience and endurance. Paul knew everyone and knew what they liked most. He opened many of the butter, jam, and marmalade plastic containers on his regular route. One man like that can lift so many spirits at once. Live and let live is Paul's philosophy.

Each new wheelie will go through traumatic times, understanding and learning to cope with new realities. 1.7 million people suffered limb loss in 2007 (excluding fingers and toes, USA). A wide range of causes can lead to limb loss, limb difference (the congenital absence or malformation of a limb), or amputation: crush injuries, bad breaks, diabetes, war injuries, drugs, blood circulation, and many more. AK/BK, above or below the knee, will influence the future leg and ambulation.

In below-knee operations, higher percentages are expected to become walkers. Unfortunately, sometimes complications afterwards may require another AK amputation. Some legs feature microprocessors and control systems for swing and stance with weight bearing and position sensors, designed to aid smooth ambulation in AK cases, but this is not a medical paper.

Hospitals are well prepared for amputees of any type, at least by having wide corridors and doorways, lifts, accessible toilets and bathroom access, and help buttons too, but the normal residence is not. Getting from the taxi to the house is the first trial; getting into the house is another, even if there are only three steps. Most standard wheelchairs fit through doors, but expensive modifications may be required to get the house up to a safe level. Two access points for wheelchairs: in and out of the building in case of fire; manoeuvring through the corridors; being able to enter and exit anywhere safely. The height of the kitchen sink, location and type of taps and fittings, ovens, appliances, shelf heights, washing machines, laundry, drying, switches, manoeuvrability in corridors, and the height of the fuse box all become new issues. A simple blown-light bulb is virtually impossible to replace (pull-down lamps help).

Just a few weeks ago, Jenny moved into her house, which was especially modified. With a couple of friends, we helped her move a few miles down the road. Jenny seems to be in paradise now. His husband and children, too, are happy with the move. Jenny has been a wheelie for a good many years, having several manual wheelchairs. She is a very independent woman (early forties). She moves from one wheelchair to her car, lifts her bodyweight from the chair into the car seat, and is ready to drive. Wherever she arrives, she opens her car door and flicks a button. A simple, but ingenious, custom-made device lifts her wheelchair (from the rooftop) over the edge of the car and, via steel wire, lowers it to the ground. She unfolds it, adds a firm bottom part to the seat area, and transfers her bodyweight from the car into the chair. She has both legs but no hip joints connecting them to her body. She does it so effortlessly, and she must have done it countless times.

Jenny also has a scooter that runs off a battery; it gets her safely to the local shopping area, several hundred metres away. There is just one road-crossing that is a bit tricky and bumpy. She feels a lot more at ease if someone is nearby, just in case she gets stuck. Some hundred metres is a fair way on a slow-speed scooter; there are no guarantees the weather will be the same upon arriving at the destination. Summertime brings thunderstorms that come very fast, are vicious, and many last just a few minutes.

Once, a friend, who was not in a wheelchair, was trapped and hammered from all sides by wind and lashing rain in my open carport. He could not even get to the next building, which was 5 metres away. There was an unlocked door right behind him, safety within inches, but trying to scream the 5 metres to let him know, he could not understand a word. He was soaked through. The thought of being surprised on the road in an open scooter would get the heart pressure up (pea to golf ball-size hail is often part of the greenish storms).

Being alone at home is another of many issues that can fill one with fear. Just the knowledge that someone is nearby, in the next room, or within calling range is enough to calm such fears. The mobile phone is always charged and hangs attached to the clothing. Overall, the manual (none-motorised) wheelchair has many benefits: it is reasonably cheap, fits folded into cars, is lightweight, and is self- or push-drive. My late wife too managed to overcome the 'feeling' that the word wheelchair instils. Calling it wheels or wheelie takes the edge off a little. She never had the strength to move her meagre weight; inside the house was about the limit. But on each hill, the downhill side, she did enjoy being able to choose any direction she wanted.

Learning to come to grips with the milestones in life, like parenthood, becoming a grandparent, a pensioner, or a wheelie, all take some time before one 'is'. Living it has its benefits and memories; the scent of a flower, the sniffing snout of a deer, the sound of a creek—a million totally normal things can be experienced by accepting the wheels as a means of transport, as a device that enables the going there. Shopping together becomes easy; the left hand pushes the wheelchair handle, the right hand pushes the trolley, and somehow they become a unit that moves as one.

Not everyone will feel comfortable in a simple wheelchair, especially if one spends a lot of time in it. Billy, whom I met recently, has the motorised version. She arrived in a special Maxi taxi; a hydraulic lifting device at the rear of the bus brought her to the ground. No normal family car can cope with such a chair. There are only a fixed number of special taxis in the area, so waiting times of over an hour are not unusual. Pre-booking guarantees that one will come, but 'when' is another matter. An accident put Billy in the chair over 20 years ago. She has a digital readout, a monitor showing her angles of seat and backrest, adjustments under the seat and in the seat, and massaging programmes, but she is missing a coffee maker to get all 100 of my points. I have never heard of one of these heavy chairs tipping over. Forward and behind the main drive wheels are large-type castors that prevent tipping in both directions. In Billy's case, one could compare it with the extra wheels on drag racing cars; she'd understand that.

She has another as well; it's a drive-in motorcycle tricycle, and she can ride it as well, hell yeah. Some of the motorcycle clubs around town do a lot of charity work, for kids in hospitals, Christmas, Easter, etc., and Billy is often the honorary leader of the pack, followed by a few hundred noisy sisters and brothers carrying fluffy toys and teddy bears, and Santa is going to get the cobwebs blown out of his beard as well.

Two months ago, Billy tipped over. It was evening time, a nice breeze in from the ocean, perhaps just a bit too dark to notice the hole in the footpath and the heavy chair tipped on its side. Her mobile phone was safely at home, and so she was at the mercy of the Gods for the next hour. She did not sustain additional injuries; eventually, a passerby alerted the ambulance, and all worked out OK. She'll be busy in the next few weeks doing charity drives.

Jenny loves rock concerts and would love to be able to see the stage with her favourite band. Most of the tables and seats were arranged in a big arc around the stage (meals were served as well). Within an hour, people will be dancing right between the stage and the tables, and that is the end of seeing anything. Pushing your way through a group of dancers, many of whom are young kids having fun and letting loose, is fraught with all sorts of dangers for Jenny.

She has a rare bone disease, and any sudden jolts in her case are life-threatening. We did manage to get to one side of the stage; she enjoyed it, and I stood guard so that no one accidentally fell into her.

I met Patsy too, and it took a little while to be able to communicate. When communication is hard, one speaks in words, not sentences. It takes a little practice, mostly on my part, to understand her unique way of expressing herself. Her wheels are also powered by electric power, and she shifts her body weight throughout the evening. I was amazed at the accurate control she had over her wheels. There is a small joystick on her left side and several switches, yet eating and drinking are not without their risks for Patsy. Everyone I know on wheels is an expert in controlling their machines, except some.

The newbie wheelies are different. At the turn of retirement, Ted's planned around-the-world trip with his wife came to a sudden end when he was hit by a stroke. Ted cannot open any butter, jam, or even squirt tomato sauce at mealtime. How many times did we sit together and his bread was flying off his plate? Every time, it did amplify his new condition, resulting in much distress. Ted is still in the process of digesting what happened.

Next to Ted, Chen, a man from Vietnam, had learned to manage with one moving arm. Every day his wife came in, brought him Vietnamese delights, steaming hot, unpacked a bag full of things, and best she could tried to explain what it is. Language was signs and pictures made by the hands. She mothered her husband; she mothered Ted; she could not do enough giving. Three times a day, she came. A person like that seems like an angel. Ted loved her in such a way that she stood on the highest pedestal there is. Chen had infectious laughter, nodding mostly and gesticulating; language without words; if it was right, he was very happy; if not, he tried his best to get there. Chen was a fast eater and never took his time. Often, I thought of my older brother, who had acquired a whole assortment of sayings and idioms to do with food. 'Eating while standing up is a crime against one's health,' is one of them; 'Chew long and slow,' is another.

In hindsight, I could find much wisdom in some of his words; it would allow time for saliva creation, time for the stomach to register what is coming down, and signal the 'enough' watcher. I thought I had a sweet tooth; oh no, Chen's is a lot sweeter. He buttered his bread and sprinkled something on it. Intrigued, I inquired. It was a small mountain of sugar. No matter what he put after, the base coat was butter and white sugar. Within a few seconds, he pushed one over the table, nodding, full of encouragement with his beautiful smile (I translated that as, 'It's not going to kill you; have a go'). The sugar crunched between my teeth like rocks in a mining crusher. White is not my favourite colour in sugar. His wife did it the same way.

Chen's wheels didn't mean anything to him; I rarely saw him drive them, and if he did, he bumped into things a lot. He only had one hand to use; the other was in permanent sleep. Moving the hand over to turn the other wheel never really worked out with Chen. In his eyes, one could see his pleading, 'Get me out of this mess.' Chen accepted his wheels like a diver accepts a bottle to breathe from. He never fought with it; he was just not interested in it. His face always mirrored his inner calm—easy happiness, no fights with anything.

Ted still needs time. I made sure I stayed long enough to sit with Ted alone. In a way, I guess, he is still trying to rewind time. Why now? His wife was on his mind. The gift he could not give to her, the future he would bring her now, like this, why? As the dining room emptied, we hugged, and streams of tears were freed from his eyes. Such tears wash away many poisons, so another friend once explained to me that he is a professor and authority on blood and heart; that's another story. Ted has a heart of gold, is a soft-spoken man, and probably shares a lifetime worth of love with his wife. Becoming a burden to her in time is his worst fear. In the afternoon of life, some want to put their feet up and just watch the sunset in peace.

I had several extended stays in the same hospital; my first day was also when Tihana was admitted. Tihana is a wheelie newbie and cannot really relate to it. She is Croatian, and I suspect she had a traumatic life. I sensed a lot of fear in her eyes, nothing to do with being in a wheelchair; she is very shy and would have been content hiding behind a long curtain. It took a week of sharing meals to exchange simple human acknowledgements that were slightly more than avoiding eye contact. We spoke in gestures—too few. Her granddaughter was fluent in both languages and had built small bridges.

Somehow, when I think of someone, I get this one summarising image of the person. With Tihana, it was when I walked past her room while she was reading something. I stood in the doorframe and said 'hello'. She put the book down and smiled. There was a peace in her nod, a return smile. She did never use words, but this was as good a 'hello' as any. This is her picture in me, instantly available. My room was next to hers.

Thinking of Chen, one starts to grin for no reason; that's Chen in one picture; his wife's little pots are there as well; she's endlessly fussing over him. Ted leaves an overwhelming feeling of the love he has for his wife. I never met her, but she is his treasure. Patsy has not yet burned her picture in me; I don't know her well enough. Jenny has this huge smile, sometimes her small dog on her lap, but the community involvement and massive amount of knowledge in her surroundings are what shape Jenny's view within. She is a very capable organiser down to the details. She is also an adviser or consultant in wheelie and related matters and knows the place inside out. Inspirational would be the word for Jenny, if it had to be condensed. Her skin is marked like a road map, with straight lines crisscrossing each other. Each line represented the need for another operation. Underneath all are the bones that will never be normal. How many lines? Does it matter? There is no need to count; no one has enough fingers and toes to count them.

My image of Billy's is double-sided: definitely a lady of style and poise, painted toe nails, high heels, high fashion, and the down-to-earth opposite of it all, outspoken, adventurous, actively involved in many charities and good causes. The captain is stored too. Many faces stored at instant recall—some without names, many trying to cope—who have not yet found a balance are there as a group picture.

Paul is walking now, but still, the image I have is his banana distribution, a grin like a little mischievous kid, but always meaning well. One man appeared to not let anything get in the way of life's continuation. No doubt, he ran a business, and that is what he was doing, straight from the hospital. It would not surprise me to see him getting back to his office, his managers asking, 'Where did you leave your leg?' His response may be, 'Leg, what leg? Ah, yes, give me last month's balance sheets.'

Jess, whom I met just once in emergency, was still wearing the colours of his club. I didn't like all that much the messages in his tattoos, but they were clearly made in another time, the younger days of rebellion. Realities for Jess were his legs now; he still had both: solid red, hot, swollen, and his toes turning colour. His Harley slid in the wet. He was on the 'before' side, trying to cope with that.

Karen is still pumping weights, looking great, and so very independent. Julie will turn 22 soon. She is no longer a wheelie; she has become a walker, so grown up and blond, somewhat different from the girl who gave all once a rose of hope, and she still shares her joy.

As I think of Karen, Speedy Gonzales, for some reason, pops into my head. Perhaps both share 'speed' as getting from A to B. Speedy Gonzales is not her name, but the first thing that came into my head was the first moment we met. Margret is a lively soul; she nearly ran me over in a shopping centre with her scooter. She has the luxury model, decent headlights, a basket, a seat with an armchair and number plates, and a long antenna (a stick with a flag). She lives in the suburb nearby, and we only ever meet in the shopping centre, so often now that one expects to see her there as a part of it, but she's not. I am a little worried, as I have not seen her for some weeks, but no one lives in a shopping centre. She is getting on in years, and I hope she is OK. Margret is a joy to watch; she moves a yard, stops to talk to person 1, moves another yard, and has a session with person 2.

One can easily do the shopping; she may have moved some yards, but not all too many, as each time she meets a face she has not seen, catch-up time is certain. It seems she knows everyone in town; she drives to them, and they go to her. Sometimes her smile and open laughter stop; she can listen, give one her full attention, then hold the arm and say, 'It'll be right, you'll see' and crown it with a heartfelt squeeze. She can walk some steps, park her scooter outside the toilet, lock it, and hope it will still be there when she returns.

After my wife died, our dear friend of so many years said to me with a smile, 'I knew she was ill all along; she wanted to protect me. I knew.' Love has many faces. Infection becomes the biggest enemy, and when it came to my friend, we looked at each other, both knowing. Her picture in me is of a healthy woman who happened to walk with a limp from the day we first met. This had never changed.

In looking at what each went through, perhaps facing death is common for many. Many come out of such an experience with a fire for life, an inner strength, and a purpose for living that turns each day into an unforgettable experience.

Losing a leg is not a death sentence, but getting one is only fully understood by the receiver. Often, illness is a delayed death sentence. It is also a life sentence. Death does not come until it gets here; until such time, there is life. There are many still alive today, giving hope to millions that a doctor's death sentence is not necessarily correct. Even if it were, it is one's own choice to believe it or believe in overcoming it. The zest for life in all who faced adversities can be so infectious, and in that, I believe, each shares with all a unique gift.

I am deeply grateful to all the people I have met, for they have awakened a profound sense of humanity within me. Each one, whether facing physical challenges or life-altering circumstances, has shown incredible strength, resilience, and kindness. From Julie, who spread joy and hope with her red roses and balloons, to Paul, whose infectious laughter lifted spirits and made every mealtime brighter, they have all left a lasting impression on my heart. I have learned that facing adversity with courage and love can transform even the toughest situations into opportunities for growth and compassion. They have gifted me with the understanding that life is precious, and the zest for life they exude is a reminder to cherish every moment. I am inspired by their stories, and I carry their lessons with me as I navigate my own journey, forever grateful for the awakening each has instilled in me.

Consumption

I had never met my great-grandparents, but I do remember one grandfather on my father's side and both grandparents on my mother's side while they were alive. My grandfather (on my mother's side) is also my godfather.

During their lifetimes, the world began to change. Oh, the world is always changing, but this change comes with consequences, as every change does. Most of the year I lived in the city of Kassel, in Europe, located on the river Fulda, approx. 300km north of the Rhine.

My grandmother lived in a small village near the Rhine, close to the rock of Lorelei, where her legendary sirens echo from the rocks. Most in the area grow grapes in steep vineyards, reaching skyward on both sides of the river. The fine wines of the area are still highly valued to this day. Mosel, or Moselle, is the name of a river, of a wine region, and of wine grown only in France, Luxembourg, and Germany. Stories from the late Middle Ages tell of miracle cures for terminal illness (the local archbishop, no less).

Mosel from the Mosel region is traditionally packaged in long green glass bottles, while Mosel from other regions is bottled in brown glass bottles. My grandmother's village, 'Werlau', placed high on the Rhine valley, has beautiful spots to see the river snake its way towards the North Sea. I spent most of my summer holidays with her and my aunt. My grandmother was a very religious woman. Reading and praying the Rosary were part of my childhood duties (chores), which I found rather boring. At that time, God was feared, although in nightly monologues I tried the art of diplomatic negotiations, making deals to pay for my sins.

Sundays were holy days, nicely dressed, starting with a visit to the church down a steep road, past the Burg Rheinfels

(Rheinfels Castle), into the valley the Rhine must have cut over millions of years. Often, my brother and I would walk the 4km distance to St. Goar, as it was just a beautiful place to take in. We called to the rocks across the valley and waited for the echoes to bounce back. The inside of St. Goar's church was fascinating due to the many art works, carvings, and good acoustics. The ice-cream afterwards held a special attraction; I took it as a reward for being reasonably still for an hour.

Going shopping with my grandmother was great up in the village. The local bakery had various rolls (Wasser Wecke, Milch Broetchen), bread rolls made with water, others with milk, both my favourites, and many other goodies. The rolls, uniquely shaped, as unique as the butter, which sold as a yellowish lump wrapped in grease-proof paper, weigh approximately that much, all for a few coins. Milk came fresh from the cow, including some hair, warm as her udder, from the next-door neighbour's cowshed, just across the road.

Once I went to a local fish shop, and the slippery herring didn't feel like being sold. The customer, a very vocal lady of advanced years in black folk-dress, laughed, and through a toothless smile, she called to the sales assistant, 'Losse do nenn hippe,' then exploded in a huge holler of laughter. It took me awhile to dissect the heavy dialect, which is far removed from a newsreader's language. It had to do something with the fish and perhaps its slipperiness. 'Losse do', came close to my Kasselaenerisch 'Lasse doch', in proper lingo 'Lass sie doch,' or in English 'Let them'. 'Nenn hippe' was a little harder, but since the fish ended up in a plastic bag, it could have meant 'nein hippe, 'nein huepfen, 'herein springen', or 'Lass ihn doch hereinspringen', 'Let him jump into it.' Since she expected some sort of response from me, I nodded, returning her smile, and was glad that I could understand my grandmother most of the time without the need to dissect every sound.

'Why not shop in a shopping centre?' I asked her, 'Oh no,' I shouldn't have asked that. 'If I don't buy from the locals, in time, there will be no locals left to buy from,' she explained. The weekdays were the best. As city boys, we were invited into many homes, lived not just with my grandmother, but had access to many families in the village. We went out on the wagons, drawn by cows. Another neighbour used a horse, just short of 1 hp; it was old. The horse was much easier on the eye than the behind of a pair of cows walking slowly. In some farm houses, the chickens were part of the furniture, flying onto the breakfast table.

It was an experience; all eating from one bowl in the centre of the table was another. We lent a hand on the land surrounding the village and got a feel for what it was like to bring the harvest in. We would sit high, atop the laden wagons, swinging to the potholes on the dirt tracks. Beautiful memories and itchy backs, and what ever happened to her? What was her name? She wore her dark brown hair in two long plaits and had a country girl's name, perhaps Emma. She used to get under the cow, hold a teat, and squirt the milk like a water pistol. Great fun when you are 6 or 7.

Sometimes I stayed longer and attended the local school. It was so small that all grades fit into one classroom, and one teacher taught them all. In a small place like that, no one is a stranger for long. Each year, things changed slowly; tractors came in, and so the drive to the outlaying fields became a little faster. The cobblestone streets became cleaner as fewer animals were required to draw the wagons. In front of the houses were still the concrete-framed pits that stored the soiled straw and animal waste, in a smelly display of unpleasantness.

When I was eight, my grandfather died. Everyone wore black for a year. A town crier used to spread local news, walking up the small lanes, ringing his bell, and yelling with a massive voice his message from place to place. Low-flying swallows would indicate a change in weather. I always admired their skills at flying. Low flying swallows indicate rain on the way.

In 1988, I was a parent myself and had left my childhood far behind. I flew back to Werlau, which was once my mother's hometown. It did not exist anymore. Werlau had become a part of St. Goar. The new name is St. Goar-Werlau. The family neatly keeps the graves of both my grandparents. The baker's store has become part of the baker's children's family house. The place where we got the butter no longer makes any. Next door, the 12 or so cows and tractors, all the farming machinery, and the smelly pits are gone. The farmer's children go to work instead. The largest farmer of them all has absorbed the outlaying properties. They use the modern gear that does as much as the whole village did once together.

Speckkuchen (a type of bacon quiche on a dough base), once made by many of the women in the communal ovens, where long-handled devices used to retrieve them from the hot belly of incubation when I was a kid, are no longer made. The place is now used for another purpose. So too are the places of butchers, shoemakers, and blacksmiths, as well as the dressmakers, milliners, and so many others, now used for something else. The 'we buy in bulk' supermarkets now replace the uniqueness of their products, most likely cheaper and with no hair in the milk.

There is no longer a need to wash the aluminium can to get a refill of raw milk. The new milk is all pasteurised and free of E. coli 0157:H7, Staphylococcus aureus, Listeria, Campylobacter, Salmonella, and T.B. Every time one buys it, it comes in a brand new, sterile container. The neighbours' tractors, in the Werlau, had long been traded in for cars. The tractor lasted many years and perhaps still works today, but the first car it traded for has since been replaced countless times. The cars that ran on 'Standard' are long gone; the ones on 'Super' are history; the cars that run on 'Unleaded' are becoming history.

Tractors were a lot simpler; they had a power take-off at the rear, and the older ones had a wheel at the sides that could power all sorts of gadgets, like a saw and auxiliary farm equipment. A tractor was a tough machine, and details like leather seats, built-in radio, CD players, and safety doors were no issue. At least a bottle holder and lunch pack box would have been appropriate accessories. Tractor manufacturers were not yet on the ball, as tractors were not a status symbol.

Cars changed all that. The little letters at the rear: GT, SE, SL, 5l, 6l, 8 cyl, 500. Oh no, my ego needs a 600 at least; better make that 6000. Fridges changed all that too; freezers, bathrooms, kitchens, TVs, washing machines, telephones, and internal water-flush toilets all did their little bit to change the world. None of them are classified as status symbols anymore. Dishwashers and electric inline water heaters have long since been replaced by other types. The new world of white goods has been replaced countless times with monthly changing models and additional innovative devices: the electric toothbrush, meat slicer, remote control garage door, vacuum cleaner—in short, more electricity-eating paraphernalia than a house could nurse with power points.

The wood and coal fireplaces were replaced by oil installations, providing central heating. The film formats of a few changed to the video formats of the many, replaced and improved, and with 200% certainty, replaced again. The 16k computers jumped to 64k, to 4MB, to 64MB, to 1TB, and may end up with thousands of TB next week or thereafter. The records started turning faster and became a tape, which became a cassette tape, which became a CD, a DVD, and a memory chip.

How many goods still in good working order will be replaced in the household over the lifetime of the occupier? A 'Lloyd Alexander TS' was my first car. It had 600 cc, 25 hp, 2 cylinders, and 4 strokes. It had four gears on the steering column and a rated top speed of 100 km/hr. I got it to go 150 km/hr down a long hill on the Autobahn; the needle would not go that far; a friend confirmed the speed, but the Lloyd did it only once. It gave up the ghost after that. I was 18 then. I have lost count of how many cars I've been through, nor do I remember how many fridges, washing machines, lounges, and whatever else I've been through. How much of the pollution up there is my doing? How many degrees, or fractions of degrees, am I responsible for? How many mines, trucks, heavy machinery, and planes did I keep operating? How many trees are on my conscience? How many miles have I travelled, and how much pollution has been pumped out?

When I was 18, I never looked at the price of fuel. I never looked at the price of anything. Since then, the chase for the lowest number behind the decimal point has become common practice. I listened to the marketing people, 'why pay more?' and abandoned the corner stores, which could never keep up with the big guys, and in doing so, the big guys have become bigger; the rest had to find a niche or go under.

So how do the big guys do it so cheaply? Do I know? Do I care? Do I know that the grower gets a pittance of the charged price, the child labourer slaves all day, and there are no penalty rates for extra long hours?

Do I know that the cheapest meats contain the worst ingredients, responsible for future sickness? Do I know that the freshest apples are some years old? Despite the fact that the owners rake in piles, their accountants used sniffer dogs to squeeze another coin out here and there. The scientists employed to modify seeds and crops, livestock, the heritage of evolution, for longer shelf life, for faster and more consistent growth rates, for animal-less steaks, for chicken-less eggs, and for crops that have no seeds. Progress and innovation are possible as a result of consumption.

The ever-rising GDP is used as a measure of economic health. Negative growth is a bad thing; depression, or worse, recession, doom, jump out of the window time. Consumption means many things; in the old films, it referred to a wasting disease. Consume means to devour, squander, destroy, waste, deplete, or wipe out. A consumer is then a person who destroys, devours, squanders, wastes, depletes, and wipes out.

The more consumers we have, the better for the economy, and as a result, the sooner we'll have to face a serious dilemma. We can no longer rob the colonies (not officially); it is going to get harder to find cheap labour countries, but not impossible. No longer will the 'Indians, natives, aboriginals, indigenous,' or whichever name we graced the ones who are different, accept a broken piece of mirror for their gold; perhaps they would, but no longer have they any gold to trade. Most goods are paid with currency, which can be used to buy the products made by them. The physical goods were paid for with notes of apparent value, traded for other physical goods, plundered from the earth, and 'value' added.

The search for cheaper suppliers will also create new markets, increasing demand even further, all becoming consumers that, with every purchase, consume parts of the planet. Bauxite under fertile ground is a fateful combination; mine sites near the food bowls' water table are another; oil rigs and shipping near sensitive eco systems are another; each compromise brings us closer to the edge. Hills and mountains change their shapes as crushers eat them up. Dipped in black tar, they transformed into motorways, highways, and toll roads.

Food used as fuel, our poison and garbage sold to countries that live on the edge of survival, and a philosophy of consumerism, constantly increasing turnover, increased GDP, and return on investment all play a part in trapping us in a vicious cycle. The poor sift through mountains of stinking debris to reclaim copper, metals, and anything worth recycling, exchanged for paper money, surrounded by smoke and poisonous gases.

Wars of ideology become wars for resources of any kind, fought with robots and AI devices controlled from afar. A cycle it is not; as the blundered goods don't re-grow in the earth, the extracted oil has turned to fumes, which cannot be converted back to oil. The cycle is a spiral of demise. This we shall leave to our yet unborn.

The beginning of the industrial revolution, from the steam engine days to now, is mere microseconds in the history of time. Population growth is in slow decline in Europe, steady in many countries, and on the increase in many African nations, many of whom are unable to feed their own. The constant repetition of starvation, due to many causes—ruthless selfish rulers, corruption, unsustainable offspring numbers, mismanagement of funds and resources, climate change, the blundering by other nations, or a combination of many others—draws a picture of imbalance and moral dilemma.

The milk of Mother Earth is drying up. Perhaps intelligence can save it; otherwise, we drink our mother's blood in thirst. Intelligence is a word with many meanings. The CIA's definition of intelligence is 'the information our nation's leaders need to keep our country safe'. Put in context: the information the world leaders need to keep the world safe. Do we have any leaders? Have we become blind followers? Do we follow performers or people with vision? Does their vision transcend borders? How short is their vision?

Intelligence is the faculty of understanding. A pig with too many piglets will squash a few so that its siblings have a chance of survival. Intelligence (learning, prior experience, and memory) = hard-wired instinct. Intelligence: the ability to comprehend, understand, and profit from the experience; gathering and interpreting information about an enemy; The ability to absorb information, reason, formulate goals, and make plans; the ability to interact with the environment and adapt to changes. The ability for original, productive thought, and there are so many more definitions for the same word.

It was intelligence that changed the world and started the industrial revolution, which is still continuing. In the process, intelligence reached higher levels, starting other revolutions that changed the world. Too often, intelligence collaborates with self-serving interests and does little for the common good. Intelligence combined with greed, power, ego, and selective vision can be a destructive combination.

Sir Joseph Whitworth, among many other inventions, devised a standard for screw threads in 1841. It became the first nationally standardised system. This eventually became the British Standard. It meant that one nut of a given size, angle, and pitch would fit onto a bolt of the same shape, no matter who produced it. In expanded form, it made mass production possible, each adhering to given standards.

A look inside a supermarket quickly demonstrates the greed and madness of manufacturers accepted by consumers of computer printers and the ink that goes with them. An entire wall needed to feature the various brands to suit the countless models, most carrying black, red, green, and blue ink in different-sized containers, which, as ink cartridges, are a few dollars less than an entire printer is including its ink. If your printer is older than XYZ years, rest assured, it will end up on the dump somewhere, as print cartridges are no longer available for that model. The ink is worth pennies, but because your printer needs it, it costs dollars.

A new model car costs a small fortune to develop, often put together from existing engines, some other undercarriage, and whatever else, so that everyone knows the newer model is the one that delivers all their dreams. It has become a world of throwaway items and replacement goods where wear and tear is finely matched to one's income capacity. We have not realised that we are one, no matter what we look like. The clan instinct is still very much alive, mostly just under the surface. We would rather identify with select interest groups than with the whole of humankind.

The five permanent members of the United Nations Security Council were drawn from the victors of World War II. All have nuclear weapons. Four of the five are also the biggest arms exporters. The objectives of the UN Security Council are to maintain international peace and security.

Going back to the original thought, we all too often see more of our differences than what we have in common. Backroom deals, stooges, opinion makers, lobby groups—all unelected self-serving groups that either have voices, power, or money to twist the arms of others. And if it's not them, then the local heroes, preachers of fear and doom, or prophets of heavenly bliss will have their ten cents worth of influence.

Each has tried, and ideologies have led to persecution, wars, and destruction. Loving your neighbour has killed so many. The preachers had a demand, a claim on heaven, and theirs was the only true word. They dismissed the faiths of millions of others as misguided ideologies. Various interpretations of scriptures and manipulations to meet objectives—all the influence of men's imperfections—are presented as truth.

1970, 80, 90, the hope—oh, in the year 2000, everything will be so different. The New Year started from the east, crossing the timelines of all during the following 24 hours. Each city was celebrating with joyous faces, heralding a new beginning that leads us out of the dark ages—a moment of worldwide common feeling. I took a picture of the sunrise on January 1, 2000; perhaps many others did too, as a symbol of a new era, a time of promise. No one made such a promise, though many had expectations.

Is there a common conscience, a global comprehension of what needs doing? By saying 'mine is better', we also mean 'yours is not.' Is not intelligence also our enemy? We see ideals, patriotism, and the honour of the flag (whatever colours your country may have) as noble traits, and our cultural, political, religious, and ethnic identity as something worthy to cherish and defend. Often, our upbringing and our belongings forge our being into believing that this, that, or the other is what one needs to keep as an ongoing legacy. As far back as 1966, I had a discussion with a friend of mine who entered the then new profession called 'Umweltschutz' (environmental protection). How long have scientists waited for their warnings? How many disproved their colleagues for whatever reason? At least now, carbon trading has value, and there are deals to be made. It may not have a clear sky, but it looks like someone is doing something. Of course, a low-wage country producing all the goods will also produce the pollution that goes with it, as long as the country is on the lee side of the wind.

'Smoking is good for you,' paid stooges claimed without batting an eyelid. 'There is no pollution under your houses, schools, or suburbs,' the paid experts exclaimed, while the poison seeped into the residents, killing them with cancer following years of suffering.

We sent signals into space to establish communications with aliens, yet they fail to understand the language of our animals and are too often incapable of comprehending the reasoning of our fellow men. Can we not hear the missing sounds of those we helped wipe out? The scraped-up DNA samples used as comfort may one day be used to fix it all. The tribes that could live in harmony and sustainability in their environment are now reduced to dancing for coins; some have become drunken derelicts, living in another world, displaced, and ripped from their roots.

Some have proven that it is possible to amass personal wealth in excess of US$58 billion in less than a lifetime and, in doing so, become beacons to others, as anyone can reach that level too, in theory. Update 2023: No. 1 stands at 180 billion, No. 2 at 114, while the poorest of the first 195 has 9.6 billion (according to Forbes). Once, being a millionaire meant being rich in wealth. Now the list of billionaires with over US$15 billion each is getting very long. Update 2023: Forbes lists a total of 2540, each having at least 1B or more. The poor millionaires don't even get a mention. Yet each dollar in a billionaire's pocket is a dollar less in everyone else's. Time has shown that this imbalance is steadily increasing.

The poorest of us all have 65% of their body weight in oxygen, a bit of carbon and hydrogen, a little bit of nitrogen and calcium, and a very little bit of various other compounds. That is all. He or she may crave a drop of water, a piece of bread, some medication for their kids, perhaps a sheet of plastic as a home, or less.

By property deed, we believe to own a speck of dirt or a place at the water front, yet we are tenants at best. Each speck we claim is taken from someone else, be that a bear, a fox, or a thousand birds. From my grandparents to now, what have we done to our home? There is no 'us', no 'we', no common identity. We are not earthlings; we are females, males, adults or kids, Europeans, Asians, Africans, Jews, Moslems, Catholics, French, Lebanese, Koreans, lower class, middle class, upper class or classless, engineers, thinkers, plumbers, artists, makers and takers, followers, and individuals. Each identifies with one or another idea, belief, concept, or direction, or none at all.

We are animals of the kingdom 'Animalia', from the class 'Mammalia', the order of 'Primates', the family of 'Hominidae', the genus 'homo', the species 'homosapiens', and the subspecies 'homo sapiens sapiens'. Homo sapiens, taken from Latin with the meaning of 'wise human' or 'knowing human.' We can crawl, climb, swim, dive, even fly, enjoy sex (with a few exceptions), reach orgasms, some wonder about the paint on the ceiling, think abstract thoughts, create, invent, handle tools, and no other animal can do all that as one species.

Although many animals can do many things better than us, with applied intelligence and appropriate tools, we've overcome many of our shortcomings. We can outrun a cheetah by sitting down with the foot on the gas; we see further than an eagle's eye with satellite images and massive-sized antennas. We are faster than any fish and can adapt to most environments. We can recognise ourselves in a mirror; not many in the kingdom of Animalia can do that. In a mirror, we can also see 'the most dangerous animal on earth,' as in the 1963 exhibit at Bronx Zoo, which was duplicated in 1968 at Brookfield Zoo, Chicago.

Other animals have no votes, no voice, and no decision-making powers. Trees, plants, and insects have no voice either. All are made of cells. Yet we share and need our fellow animals and plants. A wagtail may just have had a chance to avoid an approaching rifle bullet, but it will not escape a 5000-mph, 8 mega-joule electromagnetic rail-gun, a million bullets per minute, an airborne chemical oxygen iodine laser, electromagnetic radiation, or microwave beams, which will burn off all its feathers before it knows what hit it. But a wagtail is no enemy of any man. Wolves and bears, white pointers, snakes, crocodiles and lions, tigers, germs, and viruses are all capable of bringing men down. But H-bombs, A-bombs, and E-bombs are not directed at the kingdom of Animalia, just at one of the species therein. The thousands of others that will fry to a crisp are collateral damage.

Napoleon is perhaps one of the last leaders, actually riding alongside his army and being close to the action. Presidents, Prime Ministers, Chancellors, and Emperors remain far from the battlefields. Their armies do the deed, some as joystick soldiers firing weapon systems that leave no sound in the faraway 'homeland', the screams of the dying unheard. Nightmares are a thing of the past, at least for the joystick heroes. Sympathy has little chance to grow, as those are the bad guys; we certainly are not; they, the baddies, are very different from us.

A single room, where each country's leader could sort out their differences with the enemy's leader, would save massive costs and lives on all sides. Both could assume to be the last men standing, instead of wasting the lives of the people they meant to serve. Is there a need or point to fight to the last drop for every citizen? The weapon's manufacturers and their directors are maybe the first to oppose such an idea, with the shareholders not far behind. Perhaps the leaders of industry would also oppose that thought; after all, if destruction can go hand in hand with reconstruction, the economic returns make it all worthwhile (my pardon for being sarcastic).

1988 saw the attack on a common enemy of men, poliomyelitis, which left 350000 children per year with paralysis. Polio is now mostly confined to four countries, currently claiming just over 1000 victims globally (data in WHO HQ, August 2008). This world is based on the survival instincts of the fittest, be they men or cancer cells within men.

What if we had no past? We would most likely create a different future. Imagine that there is no hell. Yes, John Lennon, you said it all before. No history, no traditions, no customs, no hierarchies, no rituals, no past scores to settle, no religious battles, no superior race, no borders, no domination over another—each has claimed a lot of blood and will continue to claim more. Would we feel lost without it? If we were any other animal and watched what men were doing to the planet and its own species, would we not think of humankind as polio?

The average world's population rate is 1.17%. Based on this, the population will double in just less than 60 years to 13.670 billion people (bear in mind that this original article was written in 2014). Never in known history has such a rapid increase in the world's population been experienced, in particular in the last 500 years. Taking stock of the rapid changes, upheaval, and tempering of nature's finely balanced systems over the last 200 years has had an impact on every continent and ocean on earth. In men's minds, the future is a forward projection based on the past. Will the next 200 years be a progression of our past? The numbers don't seem to support this, especially if each expects a living standard that is unsustainable. The dream of happiness may well be limited to food, shelter, and reasonable health, which even today is not guaranteed, much less so in the future.

Imagine there is no humankind. The rivers and oceans will find a balance, nature will have time to recover, trees and forests will have a chance to re-grow and filter our poisons, and animals and plants will find ways to recover. Healing is given a chance. If no child is born, the world will be free of humankind in 100 years. Perhaps this thought goes against our built-in instincts, against all religious teachings, and against all we have come to accept. Perhaps a sensible reduction in numbers could lead to a world where we don't become endangered species.

We do have the ability to adapt. In local and global emergencies, we can act as one. Often, these times of natural disasters bring out the best in men, can unite communities, and display a genuine desire to assist and help with whatever means. In such times, we can lose our sense of hierarchy, be selfless, and be concerned for the other, irrespective of who the other is. Anyone would jump without hesitation into a pit of mud, or worse, to save a life. Many who have gone through disasters, be they floods, cyclones, or earthquakes, will also have noticed the change in men and the courage, commitment, and self-sacrifice men are capable of.

We also have the ability to bring down borders, build bridges across nations and ideologies, and reach out and share in the lives of individuals through friendships and associations. The gods of money are paper-thin, have no substance, and have no worth. If we don't find an answer, nature certainly will.

Two dreams

I had two dreams during the night. The first dream has me standing at a Gold Coast beach, looking eastward, over the ocean into the distance. A haze obscures where the horizon meets the water. The dream set in the present day. Through the haze, I noticed a faint, bright dot moving skyward, trailing behind an even fainter cloud, barely noticeable, blending into the haze. Scanning the horizon sideways, I noticed another small dot, which looked identical to the first, ascending at the same speed skyward. `Did you see that?' I asked a person nearby. `See what?' he replied. And if one looks across the distance, nothing is obvious. But when I directed his eyes to the two spots and explained to focus there, he too could faintly see what I described.

The islands of New Caledonia, Tonga, Cook Islands, and Polynesia are slightly north-east of the east coast of Australia, the Gold Coast, with Chile far beyond the curve. Norfolk Island is much closer, a little south-east from where I stood. In succession, several more bright dots launched from the two spots. As soon as the two were high enough, another two rose up. In the foreground, young kids splashed in the water. Swimmers were between the flags, and on either side of the flags, surfers caught the waves. At 35 degrees C, a cold shiver runs over my back, while the sounds around me are filled with laughter, seagulls screeching, and waves rolling in.

Am I looking at the launching of missiles from submarines or from vessels beyond the horizon, obscured by the haze? I could not sense who the senders were, nor the payload or intended target. Then I looked at the waves and watched the parents guarding their children, the old couples walking hand in hand along the beach, the sand castles and footprints washed out by the incoming tide as if to salvage the moments of an ordinary day, at least as a memory for posterity.

(Trigger warning: Aboriginal, suicide)

The other dream played in a mixture of time, the past as well as the present and future, in an unknown place up in North Queensland or the Northern Territory, Australia. A very old Aboriginal man is sitting on the ground, resting his back against the wall of a bottle shop, drinking alcohol (alcohol generally sells in pubs and bottle shops in Australia). He nods with a serious face, then shakes his head in disbelief and takes another few gulps of spirit. He is deep in thought— dreamtime, the rainbow serpent, the waterholes then and now. The young man he speared in his legs for starting a fight, the curse he unleashed on two members of another tribe, all so long ago, when he once was a tribal elder.

He gulped half the bottle at once and swore. He looked at his bare feet, where the mud had baked dry, and picked up as he crossed the river that hadn't seen water for many years. Its edges are like hard-edged, cracked clay islands; the deepest part of the riverbed contains a little mud that could not even enable the smallest fish to swim. Despite this, life could quickly return. Those that could would have buried deep to survive. He had seen it many times. His eyes catch the roos that can barely stand upright. Those who still stood were mere skin and bones. Along the way to his waterhole, he steps over many carcasses. There are remnants of emu, egret, bilby, bandicoot, frilled lizard, the bones of water buffalo, and camel. There are so many more that the sun quickly bakes them, extracting all the moisture.

He finishes the bottle and throws it away. `When did it all change? Why has it come to this? Then he knew that times began changing after he raised his newborn son sky-high towards the sun. Change came slowly, but was irreversible. 18 years later, he buried his son, who took his life when he couldn't see the sky. Rainbows became rare and then disappeared altogether. `Are they now within me?' he wondered. The serpents are now black; they no longer have red bellies. They snake across the country but never move, each leading to a waterhole where the spirit is bottled and sold. It helps to forget. He staggers up to stamp his heel hard onto the ground as if to dance to awaken the sleeping serpent underground.

Why did the chicken cross the road?

As to the age-old question: Why did the chicken cross the road? The short answer is: It wanted to cross the road. Perhaps it was thinking. The long answer is that it was during this time that Tim's world began to change. Tim is 13 years old, lives in the inner city, has been playing video games for most of his life, and, due to a lack of exercise, is slightly overweight. The world changed not just for Tim but for many others too. A man from the power company came and cut the electricity off. This changed Tim's life in an instant. It only took 5 minutes, and Tim discovered he had a voice. He had rarely used it, but it was time to test if it still worked.

'Dad, I'm bored,' he said. 'Same here,' Dad answered. 'What can we do, no money, no electricity, any ideas, Dad?' 'Let's go for a walk and discover the world,' he suggested. Off they went, ending up in a zoo. 'What's this thing?' Tim asked. 'You can read. Elephant, so it says right there, on the sign.' 'It must have taken a shortcut on the road of evolution.' 'Why is that, Son?' 'It's got no bum; look at it.' 'Look at this. Holy cow, no bum on that either. What is it?' The keeper answers the question. 'You are very observant, young man; this is a holy cow indeed. The Vechur cow comes from India.'

The cow slowly walks towards Tim, leans over the railing, and starts to whisper in his ears. 'Help me; I am a holy cow. I do not belong here. They want to kill my kind, for I am the smallest of all cows, make the richest milk of all, and need the least amount of fodder. Some even want to patent my genes.'

Tim can't believe his ears. The cow licks a drop off its nose. 'Oh, yuck,' Tim calls out. The keeper, standing behind the cow, laughs, 'You should see her from my end; it's not a pretty sight, especially when she lifts her tail.'

'Hey, Tim, look over here,' his father calls out from the next enclosure. 'What are they, Dad?' 'Wait a second; I have not read the sign yet.' 'Ah, what do you know? This one is from India too. It's a chicken.' 'So that is a chicken?' 'According to the sign, it is.' The chicken walked up to Tim, and as it knelt, the chicken whispered in his ear, 'Help me; I am an exotic bird. My home is far from here; we are displaced. They trade us as slaves. This is not our native home. We live here in bondage. They want to kill my kind. Can you see the rooster over there? Even lions fear him.'

'Come on, Son, let's move on. Have you ever seen a pig?' 'No, Dad, I'm coming.' When Tim approached, the pig came close to the fence, sniffed his hand, and whispered, 'Help me; they want to kill my kind. They cage us in, and we live in slavery. They exploit us, kill us for food, and turn our hide into leather. They cut our hearts out and eyes to use for themselves. We have intelligence, but they mutilate us in medical experiments.' 'Come and tell my dad; he might be able to help you.' 'No, he can't do it; he's one of them,' the pig replies.

'Tim, over here, these are sheep; have a look.' 'Coming, Dad, look how many sheep there are.' The keeper laughs, 'No, not sheepses, not sheeps, not sheepens either; the plural is the same as the singular, sheep.' 'Aren't they cute, Dad?'

One of the sheep comes closer to Tim, leans forward, and whispers, 'Help me, help us. They shear us naked, they cage us in, they use us to sniff out truffles, and then they want to kill our kind.' From a distance, Tim's father calls out, 'Let's go get a drink somewhere.'

In bonding bliss, they walk along the road. 'I've never seen so many animals in my life, Dad, and they all talked to me.' 'You must have been hearing things. Animals don't talk. Let's get that drink.'

Inside the supermarket Tim stops in the meat section and asks, 'What is pork, Dad?' 'I don't know, Son.' 'Have you ever seen a veal, Dad?' 'I have no idea what that is; look at this; it's called mutton.' 'What is all this stuff? Maybe your mother knows. We have never been shopping; we don't know what that is.'

All the while, a chicken with a camera follows the two through the shopping centre. 'Caviar, what on earth is that?' asks Tim. 'I wish I knew,' his dad replies. They buy two bottles of water. Outside the shop, they sit on a bench. 'I get us something to eat,' Tim's father says as he heads towards another shop.

'Psst, psst,' the chicken tries to get Tim's attention. 'Hello, let me guess, you are a chicken, right?' 'I am.' 'What's with the camera?' Tim asks. 'I'm a freelance chicken reporter.' 'What are you reporting on?' 'The plight of the chicken was my calling, but the story is much bigger than that. The world needs to know.' 'So I have been told,' replies Tim, 'you live in bondage and slavery, and they want to kill you.'

'Here, I'll show you,' says the chicken, handing Tim some pictures. 'That is a chicken concentration camp; I escaped from there. I played dead, and they threw me out on a heap. Then I flew away. Here are the hens caged in a wire box. Each day they need to lay an egg; otherwise, they kill the hens. They switch the lights differently so that they lay two a day. Here they incubate the eggs, by the millions; here they sex the newborn; the females are thrown in this bin after their beak is burned; the males are squashed by a machine that extracts every ounce of meat from them.' 'Wow,' says Tim, 'why are these chickens so big, almost huge?'

'They are fast-grown for food consumption. They will murder all of them, by the millions, every single day of the year. Not one of those chickens has ever seen the sun or the grass. No newborn knows its parents.'

'That is terrible. I never realised. Hey, you got a picture of a pig.' 'Yes, the pig is a swine.' 'Why do you say that?' asks Tim. 'Because it's true,' answers the chicken, 'do you know what pork is?' 'We were just wondering in the supermarket,' answers Tim, 'I have never seen living pork anywhere.' 'And you won't,' replies the chicken, 'the dead, cut-up corpse of swine is called pork. These pictures show the transformation from pig to pork to leather shoes.'

'A pig talked to me earlier, saying that they want to kill their kind,' says Tim, 'and so did a sheep.' 'Yes, there are extermination camps for many of us,' replies the chicken, 'the sheep becomes mutton and lamb, even a knitted pair of socks. The cows and cattle turn into beef, leather belts, sausages, and much more. Here are the pictures.' 'You have been very busy,' responds Tim, 'and you create a report from all the material you have gathered.' 'That's right,' answered the chicken. 'What are you going to do with it when it is complete?' 'I want to publish it in the newspapers,' replied the chicken. 'It's right across the road,' Tim responds.

'One thing I don't understand,' says Tim, 'who are the 'them' you all talk about? Who wants to kill you all?' At this moment, Tim's father returns, 'I have a chicken sandwich and brought you a hamburger.' The chicken shed a tear. 'Them, you ask, 'them' are the likes of him and you. How could you?' 'What do you mean? It's just a hamburger. It has ham on it,' answers Tim. 'What is ham? Do you have any idea?' 'No.'

'Ham is also from a pig. A hamburger is a minced cow or pig. Minced is when everything gets squashed through little holes to disguise what it was,' answered the chicken.

Tim is holding his hamburger. 'I had no idea, Chicken. Who invented all these strange names?' 'I can't answer that. I got to go and get this story published.' 'Well, it's been nice knowing you. Say, What are you going to call your story?' 'I'll think about it as I cross the road.'

Show and tell

"Good morning, Pierre, how was your sleep? You seemed to be restless."
"Good morning, Françoise. Oh my head."

"My poor darling has a headache, cup of coffee?"
"Oui, mon chéri."

The aroma of coffee lifts from the pot floats gently, to encircle Pierre before engulfing his senses.
"Oh combien beau, so lovely."

"Do not forget the group's meeting tonight, Pierre" Françoise calls out.
"Where do we meet?"
"We are the hosts, it's our turn."

The 'group' is a collection of friends who have known each other since they were children. Every six weeks they meet at one of their places, each plays the host in time. No longer are they children, all in their forties and fifties now, some partners perhaps a little younger. As each ventured through life, found a soul mate, married, divorced, remarried or just had a serious fling, the new partners were always welcome in the group. The remnants of the schooldays are 'show and tell.' On each meeting they shared from their own life, just as in school, when 'show and tell' made the lesson all so interesting. Inevitably the barriers of secrecy broke down over time. After all, most of the group knew each other since childhood.

Françoise looks her husband of 25 years deep into the eyes, "What will you share tonight?"
Pierre is rubbing the sleep from his eyes, "That I am still debating."
"Time to get up, shower, breakfast, work."
"Give me 10 minutes in silence and I promise to do all three, need to catch a fleeting dream."
"Pierre, they are here."

"Hello Dominique and Étienne, Stephanie, Sébastien, Zoe, Vincent, Pénélope, Luc, Aurélie and Antoine."
"Hello Luc, so this is Pénélope?"
"Yes Pierre, no other than."
"I did expect you to fly in from the sky, white wings, escorted by countless fairies, glittering stars trailing your flight."

"What on earth has he told you about me? As you can see I'm no fairy, no angel, just me."

"Welcome Pénélope. My wife is… where is she? Ah, over there, that is Françoise, I am Pierre, and I don't know how many you have met so far. For tonight, my wife and I play the hosts. Feel at home."

"Show and tell time, who's first, Pierre?"

"I have something to 'show', perhaps you can 'tell' me what it means."

"I can say this happened to me in the first person, but on second thoughts I will explain it to you as in third person, to detach from it somewhat. I need two names, a male, female, help me out."
"Tom."
"Sarah."

"Sarah and Tom is fine, thank you, Sébastien and Zoe."
"Here is my 'show and tell'. Sarah calls Tom on the construction site. She is distraught. She insists Tom heads off home this minute. Reluctantly Tom radios his supervisor explaining the need to get home. The problem is 20 trucks with hot bitumen are waiting to put it into the spreader."

"Would I be right in assuming that it is the kind of spreader you operate at your work, Pierre?"
"Yes, sort of, Stephanie, perhaps a little cleaner, anyway, that's beside the point."

"Pardon, Pierre."
"Today is Friday and it was also a Friday for Sarah and Tom. About an hour later Tom gets home to find Sarah very upset. She has two scratches in her face. Calming her down Sarah reveals that there had been an accident."

"Forgive the interruption, Pierre, you said this happened to you in the first person, literally?"
"Forget that, Étienne, the first person. It's Tom and Sarah, no me, I or anyone we know. It came in a dream, not real life, ok?"
"Oui, oui."
"Étienne, one is enough."

"Don't get upset, Pierre, I just want to get the story straight."
"Let him get on with it, please!"

"Thank you, Aurélie. There had been an accident, yes. Tom notices the scratches in Sarah's face and hugs her."
Luc started to grin.

Pierre continues, in a slow voice, as he explains, "He hugged her. He hugged her because they love each other, because they were married for 25 years, and there he saw her bleeding, and he hugged her as a means of sharing her concern.

Perhaps you don't get that into your twisted brain, Luc; some people just do it like that."
"I must have misunderstood, Pierre."
"I wish you'd wipe that stupid grin off your face, Luc."
"My apologies, Pénélope; he will never grow up; he still thinks he's 10. I'm sorry for the outburst; forgive me."

"Sarah calms down and explains to Tom what happened. She had been in a fight with another woman. The scratches resulted from that. The other woman fell and hit her head."
"Tom is trying to absorb all this, asking, 'When did it happen?'"

"On Monday, she replied. Yet throughout the week, she never had any scars, but Tom never noticed that at the time. Many questions in Tom's mind needed answers: Who was the woman? What was the fight about? What was the outcome? Why is she upset?"

"Follow me, she said, leading Tom to the upstairs bathroom. Before she opened the door, she said, 'The woman fell and hit her head. She is dead; see for yourself', then she opened the door. An awkwardly twisted body lay in the bathtub. Her long hair covered most of her face, except for part of the left cheek, which revealed a large but shallow abrasion of the skin. Not serious in itself."

"'What are we going to do?' Sarah called out. 'She bumped her head in a fall; that's how she died. I didn't kill her. She fell; that's all that happened. I killed her, but I didn't kill her. Tell me what to do. What can we do? Help me.'"

"The woman had brownish, blackish, and some grey-coloured hair amongst them. Who she was became irrelevant. What they argued about didn't matter anymore. She wore a dress with an old-fashioned print, dull in colour, just like her hair. That is all I noticed about her. I mean, that is all Tom noticed about her."

"I asked Françoise... sorry, Tom asked... Sarah, on Monday, it happened? Why not call the ambulance, the police, anybody? Today is Friday; why didn't you call someone on Monday?"

"'How could I,' she said, 'how could I explain this? Who would believe me? I killed her. She's dead because of me. Help me.' I asked her, 'What have you done since Monday?' Forgive me. Tom asked her that question."

"Sarah explained that the argument developed in the cellar. She, the other woman, fell backwards against the wine shelf. That killed her. She moved the body upstairs to the bathroom so that no one would discover it. Sarah cleaned the whole house, especially the steps to the bathroom. She needed time to think of what to do. By Friday, she still had no answer."

"'We must get rid of the body,' she suggested, 'you must help me to get rid of it.' 'But then I become an accessory to a crime. I can't do that.' Tom answered."

"'What crime?' asked Sarah; 'there was no crime, she fell. It's an accident, end of story.' 'But who is going to believe that now it is Friday?'" added Tom.
"'We must get rid of it; it is going to stink the whole house out. Can't you dig a hole with one of your machines and drop it in there?' Sarah suggested. Tom explained that this was not a good idea, as sniffer dogs can sense the gases released by dead flesh."

"'Then a garbage bin; let's hide the body in a garbage bin down in the new estate. Some houses are empty; no one can see us; no one gets the blame', was her next suggestion, but Tom reasoned it to be odd that an empty house would have a garbage container out for collection."

"In the evening, both went for a drive in the new estate, for ideas. Houses stood here for months; no one lived here, and no one could afford to buy them. 'Why don't we hide the body in one of these houses? There is no one here to smell it. It gives us a little more time, some breathing space.'"

"Tom replied, 'Be aware that I cannot become an accessory to this. I can only help you if you turn around and do not see how I help you; perhaps that way it leaves me free from this committed offence, and you can always say you don't know who put her in the garbage bin. That's what Tom said."

"She thanked Tom and returned to the kitchen to focus on a chicken stew, while Tom again drove to the new housing estate to search for a suitable house. Sometime later, Sarah knocked at the door. Tom opened it and said, 'You scared the living daylights out of me. How on earth did you find me?' Sarah replied, 'Yours is the only car in the whole estate; in front of this house, where else could you possibly be? I brought us some food, chicken stew. Enjoy. Both forked and spooned the cast iron pot with fading appetite, sitting in an upstairs room, lit by the moon."

All twelve sat in a circle, everyone paying attention to Pierre's words. Françoise sat opposite Pierre, between Aurélie and Sébastien. Pierre continues, "Tom set out to place the body in large plastic bags and lifted it into the garbage container, a large wheeled bin. Sarah did not see any of this. He placed the bin in the back of the car. Together, they drove to the house Tom had selected. 'We cannot use the garbage bin,' Tom explained, 'the collectors have cameras on their trucks to look inside the bin when they tip it out, so they can sort it.' 'But that is ok; the body is in a bag,' answers Sarah. 'Except the foot is sticking out,' adds Tom."

"They arrived at the house; again, it was dark. They did not know when garbage collection day was in that estate, so they decided to keep the bin inside the house. Several days passed, then Tom realised the bin was theirs; it could be traced back to us. The question 'who' the victim is was never of any importance. Tom had to get the bin back. That night, he drove alone to the house and tipped the bin over to empty the body contained in the bag onto the tiled floor of the corridor. The head of the victim then also showed through the bag. And here is where it gets interesting.

Every few minutes, Tom had to run outside to take a fresh breath. Who do you think was in the bag?"

"It can only be the mother-in-law," suggests Vincent. Pierre's head shakes in denial. Étienne adds with a laugh, "The butler?"
"No," was Pierre's short reply.
"Was it Sarah's lover?" asks Stéphanie.
"No"
"Tom's lover," adds Sébastien.

"Tom's detective after discovering that Sarah had a lover," suggests Antoine.

Suggestions flew through the air; none noticed the internal agony Pierre went through, except Françoise.

"It can only be the milkman," Étienne adds to his comments, "or the postman."

"You will never guess it," says Pierre as he looks at Françoise, the love of his life for 35 years, his wife of 25 years, and the mother of their children. Tears break out in the corner of his eyes.

Françoise steps forward, cups Pierre's face, and says, "Mon chéri, who did you see?" Pierre is unable to speak; the lump in his throat is growing. Tears run as if escaping from some inner well, each knowing they would be followed by many others eager to escape too. No surface tension is enough to keep them in the eye.

"Darling, Pierre, look at me; tell me, who did you see?"

Pierre buries his head in Françoise's embrace. "You," he whispers in her ear.

"Who did he see?" the others ask.

"Sarah," Françoise replied.

"Oh, ah, wow." It mattered little who said what.

"Sarah killed Sarah," Zoe summarised.

Luc adds, "An accident."

Pierre slowly regains his composure. "I am sorry about this; it is not yet finished." Luc hastens, "Please go on, continue."

"Tom is stunned to recognise Sarah as the dead person. Confused, he drives home, intending to show Sarah what he has found. 'Come with me,' he says to Sarah, 'I need to show you something.' Both drive back to the vacant house. Upon opening the door, the stench of decaying flesh is overpowering. He opens the door wide. The moon shines all the way down the tiled corridor.

There is no body. 'But it was right here; where is it?' he calls out. No plastic bag, no wheelie bin; the floor is clean; nothing is there except the sickening stench of death. 'Sarah, believe me, it was right there, the body.' 'Which body?' That's what she said."

"Tom, nearly out of his mind, runs into every room of the house; all are empty, vacant, and clean. 'What is going on?

Someone must have moved it.' He hears Sarah's voice from upstairs: 'No, it's still here; no one moved it.' Tom leaps up the staircase, his lungs aching for oxygen. He holds onto the door frame, gasping for air, inhaling stench instead. 'Someone forgot a chicken stew,' said Sarah, placing the lid back onto the cast iron pot. 'A bit sick, don't you think? The stench, I mean.' she said."

"That's it; they may have thrown the pot into the bin, but that is the end. What does it all mean? Can anyone tell me? It's your turn now."

"That is very interesting, Pierre, but before I say anything, I need to see the little girl's room back in a minute," and so Dominique leaves the room.

Sébastien leans towards Pierre and says, "I'm busting; mind if I use the upstairs bathroom?"
"No, go ahead," Pierre replies.
"Very, very interesting, Pierre," Antoine picks up the treads.
"He gets to feel the same as she did earlier; she loves him; he is overcome by fear. Fear renders his love useless."
Pénélope adds her thoughts: "She needs him once in her life, and he is totally useless."

Luc added, "He did help."

"He thought of himself as an accessory to a crime," Pénélope answers. "He judged her guilty, his own wife of many years. He did not believe a single word she said. If he finds her guilty, which judge could call her 'innocent'? He is a bastard."
Vincent added, "Was she testing him? After all, she was both a victim and... "
"Go on, say it, 'killer', that's the word you were looking for," snips Stéphanie.

Dominique returns to join the group. Zoe adds, "The scratch appeared on Friday, yet the argument was on a Monday. Did he never look at her during the week? Did he never notice?"
"Étienne wouldn't notice if I had my hair done, would you, darling?" says Dominique. "I would," Étienne replies.
"Ok, tell me then, what colour bra am I wearing now?" asks Dominique.
"Black," came the quick reply. Dominique pulls the strap to the side to reveal the colour red.

"There is definitely a trust issue at play," continues Vincent, "and also a paralysing fear of authority. You told it in third person, yet a couple of times you slipped up, Pierre. I suggest it is something much closer. Law and Order seems to me to have an underlying message, or rather, a fear from the authorities, so much so that one becomes Judas, sells one's own, or at least abandons one's own."

"Pierre, when did it come to you?" asks Françoise, "Was it this morning when I brought you the coffee? You needed to catch a fleeting dream," Was this your dream?"

"Oui, chéri. I have been trying all day to make sense of it."
"I feel empty; I feel like a failure; what can I trust?"
"Don't be so hard on yourself, Pierre. Perhaps it is a hint to take a closer look at your relationship. It may seem rock-solid, but tiny hairline cracks can make the strongest structure fragile. Perhaps you lost trust in yourself. Has love become an

expectation? Perhaps it tested you, and now you feel betrayed by your own... Tom's actions"

"What's all that noise upstairs?"
"Who is up there?"
"Sébastien went for a pee," Pierre answers.

Vincent opens the door. A horrible scream wails through the house, followed by the rhythmic rumble of a body falling lifeless down the staircase.
A fraction of dead, eerie silence follows.
Françoise and Pierre look at one another while everyone else joins in on one call: "Sébastien!!!" Each is racing towards the doorway, trying to reach the staircase.

This instant, time freezes, casting each as a solid statue, eyes agape, concern etched in each face, none further than the others, all guarded to see what came to be.

Perpetua

Let us not get into how many people have paid with their lives in trying to help humanity. Patents were refused, and the seeking mind was declared mad, belittled, and simply discredited by the powers of the day. Their private lives were put under the microscope, and if nothing was found, falsehoods were therefore made up and fabricated to make them the joke of the world. After all, their claims are just impossible.

Every scientist knows, and every layman repeats the well-versed words, 'There is no such thing as perpetual motion.' Should you believe it, fine, believe what you want. Should you claim you have created such a machine, your madness will soon become official and certifiable. Should you have actually built the proof—a machine that runs without input and returns power instead of consuming it—then you are absolute in your madness and you have a death wish. You may believe otherwise, but just wait and see.

Shall we call him 'Brett'? For all intents and purposes, it is a just name. Many 'Bretts' exist, but the one I have in mind is not named Brett at all. Our fictitious Brett did not build just a prototype; he built an actual production engine. Not just one; he produces them non-stop. You may think he was mad not to patent his invention, but be assured he knew what he was doing; he is not mad.

In his mind, there is a perfect sense of purpose, determination, and drive to see it through to the bitter end. He has no death wish either, which is why he did it all differently. Instead of trying to make a quick buck, he is a dreamer—his dream is that each person on earth has access to free power that does not pollute the environment and costs no resources in fuel.

In a faraway town, he lives. His engines drive pumps and generators, and now they also power some cars. You have never heard of him, unless you are one of the lucky ones. If you ever get the chance to be offered one of his special engines, be prepared to pay three times the price of a similar-sized fuel-powered engine and your signature on a piece of paper. For that, you will never pay a cent for fuel, not you, your children, or their children, ever.

Brett's engine you purchase today is guaranteed to never require any fuel at all. Just roughly calculate your weekly fuel bill x weeks per year, x years you'll drive, and all that is what you'll save. When you get home from work, drive the car onto four rollers, put it into gear, and let it run. The generator hooked up to that will now heat your water, light your house, your stove, and every power point in your house, and you can use it as you see fit. Let it run all night; it is silent enough. Store the energy, and your house powered up for the day will run fridges, freezers, and so forth until you come back from work.

Just roughly calculate your quarterly power bill x this x that, etc., and all that you save there is yours as well.
Just for fun, let's find some numbers for your current fuel:
$80.- pw x 52 (weeks) x 30 yrs = $ 124800.-
your current power:
$250 per ¼ x 60 yrs = $ 60000.-
total cost or savings $ 184800.-
(30 years = your active driving life; 60 years = your life to live)
(Needless to say, assumptions)

Admittedly conservative, assuming your age is around 30. All that for an outlay of say $15000—for an engine, clear left over $169800, or 2.91 years of your current fuel and power costs to be in the clear.

Why would you want to go to work at all? Take your car somewhere, let it run all day, and collect whatever the car will earn for you. It can drive farm machinery, supply power to the grid, pump water, lift weights, or anything that needs an engine; your car can drive it with no fuel costs. Having a car like that is an investment. Drive it onto a barge gear down propellers, and yes, your car engine, or better, Brett's engine, now becomes a marine engine as well.

Compare your total savings with the total cost, even at three times the price of an equivalent fuel-powered engine; you would agree that this is the best deal you have ever had in your entire life. Did I mention no greenhouse gases? No wasteful, harmful by-products; nothing is released in any way or form to give Brett's engine a negative taste in the mouth.

Ah yes, the signature is not too bad either. The engine comes sealed, any seals are broken, and your warranty is void. 1st year 100% new replacement should it die or fail. The engine's rated power is as per the label. They guarantee that it can run without ever stopping. Part of the purchase price includes $100 worth of shares in the company that produces the engines. You have the option to increase this to $1000. Brett allows the nomination of two other customers who will get the same deal as you did. Nominate your wife and one child; your wife will also get two nominations, as will your child. Buy all the engines your family needs and then spread the nominations around to your relatives or friends, whomever you want. In time, each will become the owner of the cleanest business on earth. That is the only way to get one of Brett's engines. Once your petrol or diesel engine is replaced by a Brett's, it will be destroyed and rendered useless. It would not make any sense.

Another thing you are signing is not to reveal a word to anyone about what engine you have purchased. Word of mouth is a big no-no. The company is young, the demand is unprecedented, and they want to remain far below the radar for as long as possible. None of them has a death wish.

Since you already ordered one, I can tell you this: In 8 to 10 years, the power and oil companies will offer you a lease deal for a home power pack. It will cost about the same as your quarterly power bill. Another lease deal is on a replacement engine. You top it up week after week with credits; if you don't, it just stops. The credits cost about the same as your current gasoline bill; allow for inflation.

Since you are an investor and, as such, a part owner of Brett's engine plant, you can see what they have in mind. By that time, Brett hopes to have saturated the market with not only engines for cars but trains, planes, ships, lawnmowers, anything you can think of, all with a no-fuel engine. All transport costs come down, and pollution becomes history. The cost of the engines is likely to reduce further.

Bear in mind that you are also an owner due to the $100 shares. In fact, everyone is an owner. The company, once it has a sizeable presence in each country, will start selling carbon credits, because all engines are clean, it constantly has credits to sell. Do you know how much your $100 worth of shares is worth in real terms at this very minute? It sounds like a pipe dream. If it is too good to be true, it probably is. No matter how right you are, it is just fiction.

Of course it is, or is it? Come on, stop that. Don't look at me like that; I have no idea. Who is Brett? I don't know any Brett. I was just joking. The factory—what factory?—I don't know what you're talking about. Where are you taking me? Don't touch me. Let go of me. Put that bloody gun away. I don't know anything. I'll call the police. What would be the point? Help!

Welcome to our country

Welcome to our country.
Thank you.
How long are you intending to stay?
Two months.
Business or pleasure?
What do I say if business is pleasure?
Or pleasure is business would be your next question, am I right?
Business or pleasure?
Business.
Do you have anything to declare?
No. Here are my health certificates, immunisations, test results, etc.
We don't need any of that; your health is fine.

How do you know that without these?

We are analysing your DNA and so far you are still healthy, until the machine flags you. If it does, we will take a closer look.

Are you carrying any items forbidden on or in your body, such as luggage or clothing? Before you answer, take your time to think about it.

With forbidden items, I guess you mean weapons, drugs, and such.

It is your responsibility to inform yourself before coming to our country what our forbidden items are. If your answer is in the negative and we happen to find any forbidden items on or in you or in your luggage, you become liable, and this will have consequences. If you do not understand this question fully, please say so now.

I do understand your question. My answer is 'no'; I do not think I carry forbidden items on my person, in my clothing, or in my luggage.

Thank you.

Your answer suggests to me that you might carry such items. You said 'you think'; 'knowing' would have been much more positive. You will be strip-searched, and your luggage and clothing will be thoroughly searched. Please follow me.

What?

I know I have nothing on me.

Did you have a memory lapse before?

No.

Behind this door, you will find an orange table. Get undressed and place all your clothing on that table. Please...

For crying out loud, what the...

Please be aware that we give you the courtesy and dignity to get undressed alone. Should you misuse this gesture and use it to swallow or hide any forbidden items or substances, you may do so. If you do, be aware that our scanners have never failed, and any fines or jail terms associated with what we may find will triple. Please, when you are ready, press the switch on the wall.

Thank you for your cooperation. There is just one scanner to go through, and if that clears you up, you are ready to go.

Thank you.

May I ask you a personal question because it is my first day on the job?

Please go ahead.

Have I been professional?

Yes, now tell me where the cameras are hidden. This is some funny show, is it?

No, I really work here.

Sorry, I forgot one thing. On whose invitation are you here?

What do you mean? Is this a trick question?

Not at all; every visitor to our country needs to have an invitation. Do you have one?

An invitation—this is ridiculous.

Not to worry; we talk about it after the strip-search examination.

Nonsense about flies

Pessimistic one-day-fly:

"Tomorrow never comes."

"Time flies."

"Flies fly"

"Do you have time? "

"No, got to fly, so does time."

"Hurry up, or you won't catch it."

Today is the worst day of my life.

Today is a pain.

One-day-fly in the afternoon:

"Time is running out."

"Haven't you aged since this morning?"

"I love you 'till the end of today"
"The future is not looking rosy."
"Only Rosie looks rosy."
"When I was young, things were different."

Forgetful one-day-fly:

When was it?
Today.
What day is it?
Your birthday.
What day is it?
Your birthday, your graduation day, your wedding day, do I need to go on?
When was my birthday?
Today.

Hopes of a one-day-fly:

To see another sunrise.
Four weeks holiday.
Getting to know the seasons.
To see the sun on a cloudy day.
Meet someone, one day.
Having a date tomorrow.
Sleep in, in the morning.
A big payout from superannuation.
"What did the judge say?"
"Life sentence."
"It's not too bad, you'll only do 20 minutes."
"Should we go on strike?"
"What for?"
"For a longer lunch break."
"What's the point? We'll only have one."
"When I was a kid..."
"What are you talking about, it was only this morning."
"We can give you a mortgage for 10 minutes."

"How long is the warranty?"
"Several lifetimes."
"Who did you get the ring from?"
"It's from my great, great, great, great, great, great, grandfather."
"When did he die?
"Seven generations ago, last week."
"Isn't it amazing, all of us born on the same day."
"What star sign are you?"
"Same as yours."
"Why don't we meet here, every year?"
I want to be a fly on her bedroom wall.
Why don't you?
She has fly screens everywhere.
We will solve that problem another day.
If it smells lemon fresh, don't fly near it. It could be fly spray.
If you see a fly only once, say fly bye.
If you see it several times, it's a fly by.
If you see it shopping, it's a fly buy

Fly communications:

What's your name?
Fly.
How did you get here?
Fly.
What's your Mum's and Dad's Name?
Flown.
Your Grandparents Name?
Flew.
What can you do?
Fly.
If I throw you out of here, what will you do? Fly.

Breadcrumbs International Flyport:

Hello reader, you know that Fly (a) and Fly (b) are two different flies. The control tower does not know this. Flyport's radar is out of action and voice communication is the only means to control air traffic. Both flies use the name 'Fly'.

Flytown control tower: This is the control tower, Breadcrumbs International Flyport. Come in please.

Fly (a): Fly approaching from the east at altitude 200 feet.

Flytown control tower: Control tower to fly: Stay on same altitude.

Fly (a): Roger.

Flytown control tower: Who's he?

Fly (a): You must be new in the tower, roger, over and out.

Flytown control tower: Over what?

Flytown control tower: Out where?

Flytown control tower: New, why?

Flytown control tower: Ah, Roger, he is doing the nightshift.

Fly (b): Fly approaching at 3 feet altitude, requesting to land on the Breadcrumbs.

Flytown control tower: Request denied, who did you say you were?

Fly (b): Fly.

Flytown control tower: Why aren't you at 200 feet?

Fly (b): Because my feet are nearly on the ground.

Flytown control tower: How long are your feet?

Fly (b): It's not a good time for me to measure them now.

Flytown control tower: That will cost you a fine for violating the tower's instruction.

Fly (b): What instructions, I'm still in the air, as your instructions were not to land.

Flytown control tower: My instructions were to stay at 200 feet.

Fly (b): First of all, I cannot stay in the air and you never said that.

Flytown control tower: I did and have a recording to proof it, get up to 200 feet NOW.

Fly (b): Yes, Sir.

Fly (a): Emergency, Emergency

Flytown control tower: Who is it?

Fly (b): Fly, now at 200 feet.

Fly (a): Fly at 200 feet.
Flytown control tower: What's up?
Fly (a): Someone is in my airspace at 200 feet and broke my wings off, how can you let that happen?
Flytown control tower: I'll check, how many wings do you have left?
Fly (a): Right, check wing count, none left on the left.
Flytown control tower: Right.
Fly (a): All on the right are OK, none left.
Flytown control tower: What does that mean?
Fly (a): On the right no wings have left, all are OK.
Flytown control tower: Then fly in circles, but stay at 200 feet.
Fly (a): Roger.
Flytown control tower: Who?
Flytown control tower: Fly at 200 feet: Come in please.
Fly (a): Make up your mind, am I coming in or am I staying up here?
Fly (b): Make up your mind, am I coming in or am I staying up here?
Flytown control tower: Stay up there, Fly, but come in?
Fly (a): What?
Fly (b): Hugh?
Flytown control tower: Never mind, I can hear you, can you hear me?
Fly (a): Yes.
Fly (b): Yes, why else would I talk to you?
Flytown control tower: One yes would suffice.
Fly (a): Yes.
Fly (b): Yes.
Flytown control tower: How many wings do you have now?
Fly (a): Same as before.
Fly (b): Same as before.
Flytown control tower: There must be an echo in the line.
Fly (a): Yes.
Fly (b): Yes.
Fly (a): I didn't say that.
Fly (b): I heard that.

Fly (a): I didn't know clouds have echoes with a voice.
Flytown control tower: Fly, what are you on about?
Flytown control tower: There are no clouds at 200 feet.
Flytown control tower: Come in to land now.
Fly (a): Which runway?
Fly (b): Which runway?
Flytown control tower: West to east, runway 3.
Fly (a): Coming down.
Fly (b): Coming down.
Fly (a): On approach to landing, can you eyeball me?
Fly (b): On approach to landing, can you eyeball me?
Flytown control tower: I have a visual. Hey, which are you, the one in front or behind? Identify yourself.
Fly (a): Fly.
Fly (b): Fly.
Flytown control tower: Oh Lord, what is happening?
Fly (a): Why is there one in front of me?
Flytown control tower: Is there one in front of you?
Fly (b): No.
Fly (a): Yes.
Flytown control tower: Which is it, yes or no?
Fly (a): Yes.
Fly (b): No.
Flytown control tower: At least you're decisive. Are there any maybes up there?
Fly (b): It's not May, there are no bees here.
Fly (a): All I can see is a fly ahead.
Flytown control tower: Who lost the wings?
Fly (b): Not I.
Fly (a): I did.
Flytown control tower: How can you fly with no wings on one side?
Fly (a): I'm following the other lunatic who crashed into me up there, I'm getting sucked along his vortex and someone is going to pay for this.
Flytown control tower: But vortex is free.
Fly (a): I'm talking about my missing wings, roger.

Flytown control tower: Roger?

Flytown control tower: Roger, glad you came, they have been asking for you. I have to go home now. I do not feel so well.

Roger: Roger.

Flytown control tower: No, I am not Roger, you are Roger, I'm the new guy.

Roger: What's your name, new guy, roger?

Flytown control tower: No, Guy.

Roger: Hi Guy, roger that, what's up?

Flytown control tower: Looks like a half-wing fly and another attempting a tandem landing.

Roger: Easy night then, bye Guy.

Fly conversations:

How far is it to the ocean?

Two weeks that way, you'll never make it.

How high is the highest mountain?

It would take 97 generations to get there.

When are you going to retire?

This afternoon.

Have some respect for your elders.

Which elders?

I want to invite you to my funeral.

When is it?

Tonight.

I will be dead by then, come to mine first.

Who saw what happened?

I did.

You are the fly witness.

Fly school:

Good morning, class.
Good morning, fly teacher.
Let's see if everyone is here.
Fly? Here.
Fly? Here.
Fly? Here.
Fly? Here.
Fly? Here.
Fly? Fly? Fly, answer, oh, absent. That is twice in a day.
Fly? Here.
Fly? Here.
Let's start with history.
What came first?
Monday, Tuesday, Wednesday, Thursday.
What came after Thursday?
Flyday.
And after that?
Flewday.
Why are we called 'one day flies'?
We cover that subject tomorrow.
Tell of things that you know can fly.
Flying Saucers.
Pigs. Perhaps.
Time.
Time runs. Time runs out.
To where does it run?
Running is not flying, back to the subject.
Fists.
Frogs.
Bys.
Bys?
Flybuys.
Flags.
Yes and no. They usually just flutter in the wind.
Visits fly, but they have to pay for it.
How so?

Yes, if they pay a flying visit.
Starts fly.
What.
Flying starts.
Rumours were flying.
Can they really?
All the time.
There goes another one.
Accusations are flying.
They too?
How far is it between Sydney and Melbourne?
90 hours driving time, 53 Minutes flying time.
If we were not flies, we would live longer.
Imagine 90 hours, that are almost 4 lifetimes.
Maybe, but we can fly over 27 times that distance in our life.
Somehow, I doubt it.
Why not?
You'll never get from the arriving plane to the departing plane quick enough.
Good point.

No bang

The year did not end with a bang. The absence of a bang was due to oil. What am I talking about? Man-made devices do not last forever, especially if one ignores their need to be serviced. Since when does a ride-on mower need oil? Perhaps ever since they made the first one. This is, of course, a serious design error that is still with us to this very day. Such details of technical 'how to keep the wheels turning stuff' have never been my strong point. For weeks without end, the engine gave me plenty of hints. The smell of burned oil, the labouring starts, the tightening of the piston within its confines. Could I spare a few seconds to give the poor sod a sip? Of course not.

Time is precious; just cut the grass and do your thing. At the end of the year, I took the 18 horses for a short lap; none of them sounded happy. I turned around and parked them undercover (I am too kind; horses do need shade). For what? All died in one hit. Turning the key, no one made a sound. Not even a click. Let's try to turn the doobie that usually turns around, indicating life, like it used to. It is stuck solid; I guess the piston is welded to the rest of the engine. Inside the engine, someone does not put the 18 horses to use, left in the stable, because this is the 'grass grow fast, high time' and just perfect to make a point. What is the point of having 18 HP when they all die at the same time?

I read somewhere (maybe the owner's manual) that the first oil needs to be changed. Why did they not put the second oil in there in the first place? A dead ride-on mower is a dual function device. No matter what, it can always be used as a mobile seat with a steering wheel. A volunteer could push it (for the mobile effect). The thought occurs, 'do 18 dead horses graze?' How? Easy. Take the wheels off and let the absence of sunlight do the deed. Given a week or so, the grass underneath will have stopped growing. Time to make some calculations: is 'grazing' as efficient as mowing in order to keep the grass at manageable levels? The mower provides shade of approx 1/2 m2. The grass that is growing covers 20,000 m2. In 40000 weeks, all will be fine (but not if it re-grows again). 769 years is stretching it a bit. Will the mower last that long to provide deadening shade? The artist within wants to create a design first; 20000 m2 is a fair-sized canvas. Where to begin? Where to move in the following weeks?

I can safely assume that my time will run out before I get to see the patterned patches, no matter which design. Time for Plan B. Ring, ring, ring: 'Such a model, yes, a new engine, how much?' It could be $2000. -' 'What?' while in the news, the cost per barrel of oil is going down. How much would a few drops have cost? I do not want to know. Let's Google for some horses. I found a herd with five missing. 'Will the holes fit?' 'Yep.' 'New?' 'Yep.' 'How little?' (It helps to stay positive.) '$850.-' 'When?' 'You'll get it within a week.' Done.

Fit, fit, unscrew, re-screw, turn the key time, 'hummmmm.' The sun shines again, the birds are singing, there are happy clouds on the horizon; better give the horses a run, and so I'm happily cruising down the paddock. 13 non-grass-eating horses spit the cut grass out on one side. Let's see how long that first oil lasts.

Isn't it time?

Every industry has undergone massive changes over the last 100 years to afford safer working conditions. Safety glasses, footwear, gloves, respiratory equipment, a non-smoking work environment, and a million other things are in place to try to safeguard quality of life and, not least of all, reduce compensation payments and insurance premiums.

Isn't it time, since we seem to be unable to make wars an outdated undertaking, despite having had several 'wars to end all wars', to make the battlefield, the workplace of the soldier, a safer work environment than it has been thus far?
The experiences many soldiers go through leave countless numbers in a traumatised state, too often for the rest of their lives, wheelchair bound, physically and/or mentally scarred. The incidence of workplace-related deaths is such that if it were a business (which perhaps it is), it would have to clean up its act or shut down forever. Even if a participant had absolute protection (and there is no such thing) and were to be a mere eyewitness, the experience of such an environment may well have a lifelong impact on anyone. In addition, the non-participants, the wives or husbands, the children, and loved ones in faraway 'home' go through worry, fear, and traumatic experiences while far removed from such workplaces.

In the process, the so-called 'collateral damage', the civilian population's suffering, all too often exceeds the suffering, at least in numbers, than the number of actual participants on both sides. In addition, the civilian population is likely to lose all possessions, house and home, cats and dogs, food shortages, and any number of associated (shall we call it 'sub-collateral') damages, like no medication, hospitals, electricity, water, etc. If a business caused such suffering (the word in this context means any loss of any kind, due to the fact that the combatants have moved their workplace into someone's private backyard), every related suffering would bankrupt any business in less than a second.

What comes to mind to make war safer in the present day? Perhaps it is best to sort this based on all of the participants and the willing and/or unwilling civil population.

Working conditions and related matters:

38-hour week, working hours regulated, 9 a.m. to 5 p.m., 20 min. breakfast, 1 hour of lunch time, and another 20 min. afternoon tea. Any combatant risks instant dismissal if discharging a weapon outside of working hours, prior to 9 a.m., after 5 p.m., or anytime during rest breaks (on designated workdays). In addition to regular weekends and public holidays, overtime payments, double time on weekends, and triple time payments if required to work on holidays. 'Work' on such occasions is limited to restocking food, drinks, or any non-combat activities.

Each soldier may call for 'time out' at any moment. 50-day provision of 'time out allowance' factored in each combatant's availability for service. Shift allowance if needed; living away from home allowance, unless the workplace is within 5km of the participant's regular place of residence. The religious holidays of any faith become part of the overall holidays since none can be discriminated against, be it in their own ranks or in the enemy's. Safe transportation to and from the workplace is mandatory, as is adequate leisure time, uninterrupted sleep, and Physical as well as mental diversions are needed to minimise work-related stress, all essentially geared to making this work environment as 'normal' as possible.

The participating parties are encouraged to pool resources to enable the sharing of sports and recreational facilities with their own and their enemies' combatants. This will reduce auxiliary war costs accordingly. 24 hours of notice before any unexpected call-outs. Safety signs and personal protective equipment are adequate to counteract any threat to health and life. Normal home leave is 8 times per year, with all travel costs borne by the organiser. The definition of organiser in this context is anyone who calls for war or on whose behalf such war is fought. The organiser guarantees special home leave for any family event or celebration, funeral or illness, the birth of a child or a relative's child, as well as family birthday celebrations in a combatant's family.

While engaged in the activity of 'work', distinctly different clothing must be worn, alike to team sport activities, to enable clear distinction between one team and another. There is little point if both opposing teams wear the same colour utfit. Before any action commences, each weapon's toting soldier must test the performance of his or her weapon by looking down the barrel with either the right or left eye, pressing the trigger, and ensuring the bullet or cannon shell (whatever weapon it may be) does travel the length of the barrel unobstructed. Anyone unable to see the weapon properly discharging is doing something wrong.

Application to wage war

Only organisations that agree to wage war in the manner outlined in this document may apply to wage war with another organisation that is or is likewise agreeing to it.
One can wage war if...
There are no objections from any party.
There is a clear objective.
There is a set day to start and cease activities.
There is a place where such a war may take place.

Theatre of Operations, workplace demarcation
The workplace of war must be fully fenced and away from any civilisation and void of any living being BEFORE any activities may take place. Animals are also living beings. No activities may begin without the express permission of the property

owner. Objections from any owners, occupiers, or tenants of neighbouring properties will render the site useless for the requested activity. The property owner is entitled to receive lease payments for the duration of hostilities. War must cease at the predefined moment. Any non-conformance results in the no-conforming party no longer allowing the waging of any war. The site of the war must be rehabilitated after the event to the same condition as it was before activities started.

Financial gains from war

Any financial gains to any party, person, or business because of the waging of war are deemed the proceeds of crime, the selling of drugs, robbery, or any unlawful activity, and are confiscated. To gain from the pain of others is, in itself, a crime. Bringing pain to others is also a crime. Victims of war do not gain from pain, but pain from pain. No gain from pain is correct, while 'no pain, no gain' is an outdated illusion.

Rules of engagement

One can only aim and discharge a weapon if the intended target is a willing target, and there is no chance other targets are hit in error or via deflection. The victim has the right to choose the type of victimisation he/she/it is willing to suffer, provided the victim wishes to be victimised and due compensation is paid accordingly. Each participant has the right to injury, as long as the cause of such injury is the participant's own choice. Participants in need of injury must supply the means to cause such injury. The individual's choice of weapon is paramount. If the participant wishes injury by soft-cooked noodle, such a wish requires the respect of the enemy combatant. In this case, the victim must supply the noodle that was used to cause the injury.

An unlawful reason to wage war

One may only start a 'fight for survival' if it is survivable; otherwise, it is of little point. The 'fight for peace' is a slogan of war profiteers.

The 'war to end all wars' is over. It ended before most people's lives began. Therefore, any additional war is contravening the spirit and intent that allowed the 'war to end all wars' to begin. Do not begin what can't be ended. A good place to start a war is at the end. The carnage on offer is a good indication to ponder if it's all worthwhile. Cannon makers will take their place on the front lines to see how their wares perform up close.

It's you

It's yours to visit.
"Oh my gosh, it's true," says I, '...it's you" as joy came by. The happy face replies, "It's true; it's me. I came to visit."
"No, 'you' I said. Not I"
"I know, it's me."
In my reply, "I thought it was you; I must have been mistaken, sorry."
"Sorry, I forgot my place. Brother, embrace speaks louder than the words we're given. I have an hour; let's not quarrel."
"An hour without 'h' is ours," so says I, and he did smile.
"So true, what do you do?" he asks.
"I'm guarding," I echoed, rearranging the sound to suit.
"Guarding what?" replied.
"Guarding that borders do not grow, keep order where none thinks there is. If the border grows, I pull it down. This duty's mine 'til the end of the week; the roster sets my doing."
"Is it important to have none?"
"My word it is, my word and theirs. Madness in bounds is worse than insanity gone mad; the thought just bulks each cell in the brain. Insanity contained? Sheer madness to the power of its root, then cubed, then squared, then split as hair, then plat using the spit of cave-dwell bats, then blend in a boil of bubbly brine and try you may and try you do, such a mess no men and neither you undo. No hare, insane or otherwise, brain such as this speaks to bear, even if blessed and able to

split hairs it bears, each into nine. Brother, what did you eat? What led such a question to speak?"

"Forgive me for the asking."

"Forgive I do, forgave I did, for you do not know freedom. It's a deadly sin; there's no space I have to grant it harbour. Nurse, I shall not feel such wrath. Take this, don't look, and swallow; it's just a bit of soil. Harm knows it not; it's all I've got, and it's not even mine. It's from the earth, and the earth will keep whoever it as bits may carry. With it, the gifting, as the hour is not ours soon, may bring to you the wisdom no erudition is able to. As core of stalch absorb the soil, that's all, no need do any else. This gift endowed to you will bring. Here, sip some water, do."

"Bring what?"

"Why is it that you can ask a question while the answer's in your mouth?"

Hurricane

The image, in which she stood under a sun umbrella, and others taken in the same setting make me wonder whether weather works like this: The air particles at her front wanted to see her from the side. All their friends followed the one and then moved on from side to get behind you, and before long, all ran around, and thus, motion started, energy was born, will heat, and will make the ones above you rise. Others come from near and far, call to their friends, 'Come over.'

'What's there to see?' they ask, following the circular possession, round and round and round, and none able to look through other air particles' shoulders, ran faster for a chance to see the one that sat, that smiles to you, the picture taker. Since particles must stay as one, always next to another, one draws the next along, and so for miles around all come to see, low pressure draws them in to be in motion that one started.

Is this the making of a hurricane? But then, I am no weatherman, and even if it's true, on a stack of bibles, I deny that the start of the hurricane was hers. If hurricanes would leave no trail of carnage and destruction, then, true as truth, each weatherman would know how hurricanes began.

Immortal infancy

A journey through the woven web of criss-crossing information in its infancy can be amusing, confronting, and, oh, so ridiculous as to be of little informative use. In moments of absolute boredom (when one not even feels like rehearsing tomorrow) or some inner sense of self-analysis, double check, a la 'who am I' and one may try to Google oneself, in order to find, just in case one forgot who one is. If my father were still alive, he'd ask me, 'How does one Google oneself? "In a mirror?' He was spared a lot; he died before the spider started weaving. The new spiders don't weave anymore; they 'spider' with woof and weft to tie it ll together. Adhesive threads bond every word I say in writing to its web. We are the weavers.

So what did I discover? It's news to me, but so I'm told: I'm dead. I died some time ago—over two years, actually—on the other side of the earth. I also have a gravestone to prove it, across another ocean. It's a very nice gravestone. My admiration to the sculptor. I also have a boyfriend, and I categorically state hereby that no male in my world or any other world I do consider 'boyfriend.'

Even in 97 years from now, my dead age is 2, and on the thread, it's frozen. When this now, far behind, has aged beyond my comprehension, my comprehension's left, as death paid me a visit in due course, perhaps it knows me not, forgets, vain optimism peaks, just for a fraction, then it's dead, an illusion without breath. In time, deadness will start another count. Yet woven in the webbed words, the time slice of someone I don't know ensures my ageing deadness toddles is timeless toddlers' age, forever suspended.

A deed poll could grant divorce of name if, upon birth, I carried, then the death age of 2 clearly not me or I. Better not ponder this too long, 'cause who I was would never die, yet I could not live forever either. Who'd I become, born not from life, pond-less? The ponder hints with a grin, 'no birthdays either.' Stop teasing; grey hair will find the colour it once was each night. Wrinkles do not know how to undo. Have none when all the mirrors die, except one when the arm shapes into a bow named El.

There is a consolation, as any death begins with infancy. No matter how old death grows, infancy is forever, as long as one does not speak after one's death. How did my mother know that so long ago? As a child, I heard her say, 'When you are dead, they need to shut your mouth.' I must not forget to let them know.

Internet creations

Internet, each word I'd written, sticks to the sticky silk of webbing; Internet is its name. Life has a life that's all its own, and so too does the web. Each web is set to trap, to feed a spider's belly; some think the webbed strands are a net that too will feed their needs.

Some spiders born just recently could bring the web down to its knee, wherever they may be, the knee that is. To trap is every spider's aim. Flies caught shall be devoured.

It seems to me the 'in thing' are totally misleading leads that use part of legitimate information to lure the flies in, yet nothing of what the fly was hoping to find will become visible. Flies are, of course, the likes of I that search for you or that, or this or what I hoped to find. Instead, one's name is used, already pre-loaded in someone else's web-based search box. That's all; there's no legitimate reason for it being there. Why should the spider care? It wants the fly to fly.

If one's name happens to be 'Cook Pot', it will be there as well. One can spell it as 'Cooooooook Poooot' or any way, whatsoever, it will find something and even replace the 'Cook Pot' spelling with one's own in the listed links. In fact, no matter what one may want, it will not be there but will be listed on such sites for the sole purpose of bringing them up in any searches. No matter how many zeros one adds behind the decimal place, followed by 1, multiplied by the number of any words and combinations thereof, alpha numerical segmentation, re-combined into trillions of combinations, will still add up to a sizeable number. Rest assured, if one's a seeker of yyGH64kkkkl99p and adds whatever else, it's there. I don't know what it is. I did not know it was; the Internet can bear it instantly, being seeded by mere questions.

Money, the god of creativity, makes its debut to mess things up—greed, to be precise. But then, perhaps that's how it goes, as recently (3 days ago), or was it two? (Fixed numbers have a way of changing.) I learned from voice, digi at that, web speak from plastic held two speakers, both silenced once speak spoke. Voice said that three from all a hundred are the real McCoy (perhaps just 4; good memory is but a joy; rarely did I rejoice in meeting; try to forget the not so good; just keep what's worthy for awhile).

Back to the point, and I'm in awe, if web is 50 years or more, once started as a thread, computers 'round a little more, say 1940 as date of birth, not yet with keyboard, and even if one were to start, the day when it began, how did each dollar ever get from paper grow to clone, digitisation, so that as of two days ago, thirty cents are left from every one?

Of course, I know it's easily done—scan one, burn all the rest, or shred them for the birds to nest. But truth be told, each buck of paper, upon its face printed with its name, doesn't mean the tenderness of its worth or the number it uniquely gained. Now cloned, all digi bucks imposters bear the same.

What if interest is unpaid upon deposit? What if computers stop? Not one, two, three, or four regress in time, just as before, let's say, 60 years ago, all plooters stopped to do the plooting all at once, today? Impossible, no way it can? Possibly, it couldn't! Don't draw the devil on the wall. How many yeses in one's life remain unchanged 'til the day one dies? Each duplicated digi clone devalues all its brethren. By rights, the paper-loaded carriers ought to be worthy of all clones, but weigh them on a scale to see. One of the few will balance four midsized free-range eggs and bits of shell, not that I know the prise of eggs down to the yolk inside. Once plooted clones, and all are drones, are in a plot of never-be, one needs to find 14, to balance what once needed less. Prior to the days of GST, MS, or, call it, VAT, each egg weighed less, but not as little as pre-ploot clones started to meddle; perhaps a refund for the shell?

Time for a speeding ticket

I wrote a number of articles on the subject 'time', published elsewhere. Here is another angle.

Sometimes some things take some time; time's not yet cloned; time is of the essence; a concept; Einstein's been there, done it. Time ran out; all is collecting in a puddle down the hill. Time's up, to rise as vapour-shaping clouds, quick, snap a picture, timelessness timely caught. Time waits for no man; women are so lucky; oh, '...no men', oops, time for a pickle. Desperate times, hopeless times, times for peace, for love, for fixing holes in roofs, double time, overtime, over time, and under, who will have the time?

'What's this? a copper with a gun?!?'
'Don't aim at me, time-freeze, now; get this mobile to a halt. Time can't; it needs space.'

"Sir, what is the speed limit here?" My chest rises in pride. A knight or a cop needs my advice. (From where he's standing, the sign shows no inscription.) "Same speed as my angel flies, but we can change it if you like."

"Officer, I can explain; time ran away; I was just chasing it; speed ticket 'it' should get. You snapped the radar trigger. You saw it happening. It overtook me and dragged the car behind it, adhering to its vortex, a physical phenomenon. Let me explain..."

"I have no time for this," he says.

"Neither have I; good bye."

"Get back over here, sir; we're not yet done; it takes some time."

"Sir, is there any reason for your speeding?"

"I thought I made myself clear. No, officer, being absent-minded comes to mind."

"Sir, this shows you doing 83 in a 60."

"83 of what that might be?"

"83 km per hour, sir."

"Would I not need an hour to travel 83km? This car is incapable of doing 83km in such a short time, as it did take you to laser snap it, nor would those few yards contain a distance of 83km. Perhaps 83 microbe km, if they have such a measure."

"Sir, I will issue you with a speeding violation."

Knighthood is not free; each 'Sir' will have a price. I had a suspicion this was not just an idle conversation.

"Please, let me pay you for the artwork, framed or without. How much?"

"$150, no frame, and 3 points."

"At least, it is so pretty, worthy of much more."

Signs in my neighbourhood proclaim, 'When you are speeding, you're an idiot.' I did, therefore I am... a cretin, moron, half-wit, retard, imbecile, simpleton, of subnormal intelligence, with mental impairment, and so much more. All these promises and still no membership—the mail takes time, I guess.

Here is the trick: time. Another time, in the same place, in the same spot, the sign will show 60 km/h. Time is something one should never take for granted, as it will change to 80 km/h. There is a pattern (timed, of course). I figured that much out, it would never be 63, nor 79, not even 62.49, based on my observation that not any time once such it had ever been. Ever, never say it while there is still time. Nature drives plants to grow. A few yards, that's all, reveal the sign in unobstructed view. If one is to stand at a certain angle, and I'm yet to position my car in such a way, I have no time for splitting hair.

I got it all wrong. I can rely on my memory to get things mixed up. No wonder my membership had not arrived. The signs do not say that at all; the real signs are, 'If you drink, then drive, you're a bloody idiot', and the TAC (Transport Accident Commission) came up with it and several variations as well. Are they going to pay for the grog? I am unwilling to risk a single brain or liver cell by becoming a drinker, just so I can try to become a bloody idiot. There are not many wits in the TAC (wits with the noun of wit, that is). 'Bloody Idiot', suggests blood, death.

Death is not becoming to the happy drinker (is it to anyone in time?). I guess if time after time one is dealing with the untimely demise of life, one becomes hardened, fed up, seen from the side of the boys in blue, girls too, the staff in white coats wearing gloves, death, the reward for doing time?

It is not really a subject to mention without feeling an upwelling of anger. A feeling of massive pain overcomes, of questions that will never find answers, no matter how long the survivors seek. I broke the law, admit to that, this time doing 23 over the limit; another time it would have been 3, either way, the law broke. It costs $150 to fix it. One would think it makes more sense if laws were such that they would not break as easily.

Durability, a trait unknown to the law—that is the law—yeah, look at them; they are all broken, and one of them I did. If I were in the law manufacturing business and knew that each of them would break and that each broken law needed to be fully refunded (I would assume that's in the contract), I would become a professional insomniac in 2 seconds flat. There is another way; let us address it later, if there is time.

The odd thing is that I knew the gun-toting boys were there when I passed them driving in the other direction minutes earlier. I thought to myself, I must remember to wave on my return. The place where the sign is placed is such that one approaches from a 100 km/h highway. The exit lane is like the approach to landing, clearly marked 80, then 60. I can hear my turbines winding down. I head into a roundabout with due care, exit the roundabout, align the car from two lanes to one, bushes, and growths; the sign is right amongst them, like a plant specimen, odd, without growth.

Even after being issued the ticket, I snapped myself, repeating the same thing over and over again. It is time to dissect. Why is this happening? Home is beyond, 5km further. The heart wants to go home; like a child running in joy towards its mother, so too do I want to run towards home.

Pedestrians are never an issue in that area; none are 'pedesting' there. It feels like cheating when one breaks the law and no one is there to witness. Wit aside, I must find an answer to this. $150 is comparable to time; it takes time to reap, more than I spent on purchasing other boys' artwork.

Next time I approach, I give each action my full awareness. The exit lane starts as single and, fine, opens up to two lanes. Either is OK to take. The inner has less distance (trig), the inner lane can trap, and the inner offers the shortest line between two points. The inner is closest to the planted centre of the roundabout. Around there, that weed is newly grown. Welcome to the world. The core of the roundabout devours the poison from my car tonight. The inner requires two additional computations, as the outer is crossed twice: care, care, carefully. Observations: right, left, left, out.

When taking the outer lane, it takes a wee bit longer, requiring fewer calculations; it sometimes feels like putting my life at risk if someone else does not heed the stop sign. The thought of relying on others to stop to avoid minor collisions is always more pronounced in the outer lane. The inner lane could also trigger accidents; cars could rub side by side. I always look, estimate, judge, and calculate; I know I do. I always indicate each lane change, so many blue shirts must have forgotten how to do that. The exit tangent offers one choice, from two lanes into one. Coming from the inner, be aware not to cut off the outer, while from the outer, check who wants to be ahead.

I know that being in front of one also means being behind another; there is no glory in either position. So I'm considerate; you want to play the leader; go ahead; no, not sure; let's talk about this. Anyway, having passed all the mental 'to do's', the single lane is the point that frees the brain of all that. And here, this is the moment; the right foot gained weight. This is it; why? What do I need to do at this point to lose weight in my gas foot?

Which sign would make me aware that this is my trap, which I keep falling into repeatedly? Ponder, home calls. Which sign? 'She will still be there' would work for me; 'She will still be there; take care' garnished with elaboration. 'I am; come slowly', all would do. I guess the cause is coming from the instinct to run towards, to cut time short, rejoicing calls to come, and the thought of home pumps Adrenalin. It is like the instinct of danger primes the body to escape, though in reverse. Driving away from home always seems slower than driving towards it, yet both are the same distance.

Honesty could be another solution, helping me not fall into the trap. Like the taxation system introduced some years ago, we trust you to do the right thing; if we catch you, fine. My tax returns are clean. I am not a speed demon; that is not in me. I was once, and I admit to that. The new motorway completed, and underneath me, the once fastest bike in the world, set out to pasture and then saw what once was.

Glorious empty three wide lanes ahead with a gently sweeping curve. The bike remembered, the bike spoke, begged, and pleaded, 'Just once, please, just this once, let me run, come on, just you and me, no one will know, let me relive the moments of my glory, just this once, I'm in your hands, make my life complete.'

Young I was, I listened, mercy spilt, throttle turned, bark bearing hiss. This, breathe, live your moment, roar spitting flames, my shirt shred in its wake. The music rushing past the helmet, the stallion rising to the call, wails in your ecstasy as a silvery shadow blurs. Hard on the edge of the inner curve, curve curves, sweeps into the curve opposed, crosses all the lanes in blending tangent, mirrors thousands of pictures, all at once. Why bother? No one could catch us.

Gosh, what a ride! The fire in your loins, the engine purrs in squeals, its high pitched howl, each horse 'least once to lead, six pistons, all alive, on fire, in flames exhaling breath that splits the air in waving rise as wake. Each drop of sweat ripped to a line takes time to reshape into a ball, to burst, to bust. Explosions trail 5 miles behind; the followers must think it's raining dew. The wanting more, bow rising, no, oh yes, succumb, the feeling...

No, reason, hear me, you must reason, know we cannot rise, wings none we bear, elation this, I hear you plead, calm silver, clouds will wait. Let go, two miles to shudder, let go, scream now, climb, axe, because beyond the rise, there is the town. Through the shut helmet, one could smell the radar trap ahead; the nose knows; time to ease; calm now; my silver treasure; easy now; get me down to something that I can afford. My bike-riding brother in blue knew my joy when he rewarded me with an award, the ticket prise at a bargain price. I was so glad the laser took its time to meet us. Honesty still knows that I owe much more than he chanced in the capture of our rapture, ruptured by his being there. Bliss, he sensed, in grinning and writing the citation, in thought would have loved to wear my ripped shirt that I wore and lived the living time.

Years mellow one's perception. As I was saying, honesty may work. A large sign, a table, un-legged, showing the available choices, like, this much over the speed limit is available now for $50, that much over $75, etc. Discount the low end and add an extra premium to the high end. Why ask for more? (The rich may have a need.) '80km per hour on special, today free' until stock runs out. The supermarkets did an excellent job; one is conditioned to chase the fraction of a dime, and getting something free always works for many. The blooming renascence of financial hardship aids in driving home the awareness that driving home can be a painful endeavour. Money never had a voice that I could hear when I was younger.

Another sign my brain fully registers are preparatory signs. Usually in black writing, the sign tells the reader that further up the speed will reduce to what it suggests. So I slow down prior, trying to catch them out. Are they telling the truth? Wow, they did. How did they know? Many of these features can be found in the state south of the Land of Queen. A clear sign that boys and girls in blue, in Wales that's south, that's new, are fed well and do not need alms of guests that clog un-clocked its roads north in their land.

An 'honesty self-catching speeding system' (that's a mouth full for any poet) would require some investment for safety reasons. Infrastructure modifications to allow one to stop the vehicle, note down the amount, the self-catch details of one's claim, and justification for the award one wishes to be honoured with. Time is required to record the mailing address, the self-imposed fine, and the name of the person to receive the toil in the form of a cheque. Check for correctness; all this takes time. Unmodified, the infrastructure would grind all traffic to a halt, failing to realise the opportunities on offer, which in turn would trigger the system's demise before it had a chance to flourish.

Of course, just for some added twist, in case the blue-dressed one is a wise guy. Perhaps he tries to extract what he thinks there is, contained therein above, and aims to earn points by mere volunteered self-confession. BEFORE such a system is in place, know this: Each word a truth, as truth turns lie, as lie lies truthfully, says I from here, my sanctuary, that by default grants privy. The facts that were knotted in a knit and then spliced into the crossing yarn first had been unravelled, cut, and recombined by twisting fibres spun into a yarn. In a cohesive thread, how would I know? One better ask a weaver.

One should go with the times; otherwise, forget the thought. Time is the theme. Let's stick to it. It's time for the manufacturing sector to help us each save time. An automatic ticket dispenser machine comes to mind. How many roads do we have in the country? Some are very long. How many 'honesty self-catching speeding system ticket dispensing machines' would one need to be able to satisfactorily service each municipality, and let's not be selfish, the country roads ache for the same? There were hordes of people measuring each inch of road and years of work in preparation.

Unemployment... tomorrow, no one can remember what that meant.

Business opportunities are everywhere. Just think of the number of extra psychologists, psychiatrists, counsellors, healers, and a whole industry of scientists needed to aid those who do not heed the suggestions such a system brings upon them, a growing guild to cope with guilt.

One could speed, yes.
One could not fine own break of law, yes.
One could think one gets away free, but that is wrong.

One can think whatever one wishes, but that's not how it works. The guilt creeps in and starts to nag. You did it: 62 km/h in a 60, you low-down weasel, measly 2 don't warrant fine, wrong, wrong, wrong. You cannot carry over the 2 from before; when you did 58, I would not buy this. I am your conscience, you owe, and you know, and no matter how long you live, this on this day of date at this moment, as you did, shall never be forgotten. You owe, how can you sleep at night? 2 kilometres over, each dream you have, I shall remind you. I am conscience; I have memory; however far, there is no escape. You owe, and this, you know, the debt demands its payment, and pay you will, if not in money, then in illness.

Where do I pay? You know that all too well. What is my cut? .0001 cent per km above the given limit will do. What for? The solution that can potentially lift each nation out of recession is a means that frees the resources of every law enforcement group in any country.

Law enforcement—is that a strange word? Let's not get sidetracked. Imagine the tremendous lift in the self-worth of every citizen such an implementation would bring. What a different approach! Each speeder would be aware; there was no need for blue shirts chasing and asking silly questions. I am a woman, I am a man, and I am adult enough to admit I have been wrong. I know I need to make amends. Solutions are so simple: big brother, go away and do something useful. If I catch myself speeding again, I know how fine the fine will be.

Marrying ideas to potential economic windfall and success is much more likely. Consider this: a mobile radar trap (a police car or bike that invests 30 minutes here or there with a handheld laser) is likely to return $XYZ per given time slot; you know the figures better than I do. A self-trap system operates 24 hours a day on every and any road in the land; the potential of return is in excess of the mean a cop-manned trap could return (is there such a thing as 'womaned'?), due to the fact that a busy cop is not going to stop the ones they let pass through. Some may not pay their due, just like the ones that nick bananas or a newspaper sold via the honesty system. Pay as they will, one way or another. Just on speeding alone, an estimate over the thumb is $ABCDEFGHIJKLMNOP per annum. Human resources are free for reassignment elsewhere, plus hardware and logistics. Why is the treasurer smiling?

Think big. Where have you been? The honesty, self-fine, self-judge, and condemn system is what comes to mind. Which laws, all laws, which crimes, all crimes, and how would it work? Ticket dispensers for all there is; self-serve jails where needed. How many laws would such a dispenser be able to cater to? That depends. There is a law that covers stealing. Is there a law that covers stealing half a 'stole'? Instead of stealing a full apple, one steals a few bites and then, when it happens to taste sour, returns it to ripen. Could the stealer, having bit, sue the grower for the lack of sweetness and offset the fine with the gain expected to be due?

Times grew into a legal minefield, and brave are those who venture through. No dispenser is able to house the number of buttons needed. Cut the chase, economise, and approach the new dispenser: Did you do something wrong (y/n/maybe/undecided), was it bad (yes/no / maybe / undecided), was it very bad (out of a scale of 10), please measure the depth of your pocket now (use the tape provided), and press for a verdict.

There you go; that's all there is to it. The treasury's coffers burst in a day; crime fights itself; ethics reborn; each one admires every other; proudly shall walk who has done his or her time and paid for their crime.
New industries spring up; a best seller this week is the 'mobile self-check answerer.' One may be in the mood to rob a bank, ask the device, and hear the answer: 'Your account is $7.89; you must have a minimum of $3921.39 to rob the cheapest bank I found, willing to be robbed for the shown amount. Travel costs will, in addition, increase the total to $23873.46 (return). In other words, Sir/Madam/it, "NO, you cannot afford to rob any bank on earth at this point in your life. Instead of paying in money, I suggest you opt to pay in time. Please try again. Have a nice day.'"

The serious crime addict will, of course, always be able to play 'virtual crime' games for free. Very popular is the digi rob complete with joystick car chase. Some have more than $7.89 as their sole possession. Tycoon asks the'mobile self-check answerer' what crime I could afford: "Your balance is shown truncated to the last 12 digits. You can do anything you want, and your resources will cover it. You cannot afford a crime that costs much time, or you will owe it after you go. Please try again. Have a nice day."

Time will take some time

Time flies. Where is the airport? Look, there flies another one. Where? There. Don't spray it. Now fly's a flew. Time changes everything, as everything changes in time. Time waits for no one, what are they waiting for? Who, them? They have the time to wait for time, give it time, time sorts it out. Perhaps they swallowed a time capsule. Time is coming, time will come, time has come, will time and time again. Time will go. Where to? Time will tell. Time is gone. The time is now 6:37pm and 43 seconds precisely. That is impossible. It takes 3 seconds just to say it; time is between 40 and 43 seconds, or between 43 and 46 seconds, or any other time slot in between those times, or any other, so, what's the point? Each point in time is worthy of a name; unique none is as it. Time is everywhere, I gave my time, she took her time, he left in time, right time, they have no time, and the others have all the time in the world. Time for a nap, time will move on, we'll move in time, time's standing still, time is on their side and ours, time's gone, time warps, time in the doldrums, time to say, time to speak, time to listen, time to peak, time share, this time it will cost time. 5 times 5, those were the times, time for a break, time after time, daytime, night-time, time at night. Let's measure time, just to make sure it's still there.

Here comes a thought: a place where all the minutes lost are up for adoption. Greed heard that, forever listening, all the time, greed within comes out to shout, "Business Opportunity!" Capitalised both, as earth not never seen such finer wares as such a shop would have on offer. How would one begin? Sign out the front: 'Introductory Special.

90 seconds for the price of minute 1, only while stocks last.' The first week will be a success, sell all the stock on opening, then close the door to buy some time. Time bought, week two begins. Comers are there many, sifting through the shelves. Take time to buy their time, once bought to come again, repeat. Demand outstrips supply. The owner fails to find the time, to find the time that buyers are demanding, brainstorms, while seeking goods. Idea, none fruitless ever was for those who'd dare. Sign out the front needs decorating:
'All old stock must go. Be here or all gone before you know.

!!!NOW 30% OFF!!!' exclaim it double sided.

(How can a new shop have old stock, one may wonder? In time, one will know. Just write that bit, give time to think of how to run the shop, not I but him who raised the sign, he'd know.)

It took just moments—hardly any time—before the shop filled to the brim. The till was tilling the song of clocks, such as when set to do alarming. The drawers failed their names;

jammed-full to the bursting point, each failed to slide, but pregnant each cost time to count. A little kid, of age just 6, brings in a trolley full of money—not coins, but notes of the highest tender.

"What would you like to buy with this?" The shop owner did question. "Whatever I can get, of stock you offer at a discount."

"Old stock, you mean?"

"Yes, that's the one."

The shop owner's blood rushed to his toes, paled whiter than the purest snow; speech slurred; he tried to, but failed in doing so, until some helping hands turned him around. There, on his head, he stood; some helped him stand in this way, and then his speech returned. "Boot this kid right out of here; he is the greedy tycoon's son. He wants to buy old stock of time before his life begun. In all my days of life, I've never come across such nerve to even think of asking what he never earned, with no claim to deserve. Your custom, I refuse."

"How can you say 'no' to this much?" Another person there did ask, "Does the buyer need to earn the wares as well as pay for them?"

"Too right, they do. Don't get me wrong, business is business. I love to keep the money, but if I did, he'd send me broke. I'd lose each customer as well; old stock he would own all. No way could a 6-year-old carry the time he'd get for all he had; the next day he'd want a refund. How can I refund anything? When will the returns be? Void of its value, without worth, I would lose everything."

"Oh my, oh my, what's this I see, the mother of the boy?"
"It is," she says.
"How may I serve a madam's wish? What would you like to see?"

"I want the best time that you've got, the one that shines and glistens, the time that gives and brings, is hard so that no diamond may it shatter, the time that feels as silk, as hush, light as a feather, and... may I ask this of you in whispers, perhaps in pink?"
"Perhaps, let's see."
"It seems you are in luck, yes. Madam shall be pleased."

"Oh yes, before I forget, psst, psst, the pink, perhaps just maybe, if you please, with a touch of purplish, a bluish hint of green, about this big, 3 inches to the right, yes?"

"Yes, yes, it all came in just fresh this morning, all new, brand new, untouched by any."
"And may I quest, for this, what'd please you for in need?"
"How many of the ones discussed..."
"Enough to fill the truck outside."

"Oh, yes... This pleasure all mine be, Madam, how much does it need an answer (click, click, press, press)? This many, plus a cloth to polish rounded edges and a hint of purplish, bluish greens, shall yours be free of charge."
"Agreed, here is my tender."

Truck loaded, time barely able to carry, Madam's elation bursts in joy: "I bought the best time of my life."

"Oh, no," the shop owner pains in calling, "you've not; you bought time as a box, unfilled; did I not explain? Brand new, this time has never lived. So sorry, Madam; do forgive. To fill will need your doing."

"If madam wishes to decline a refund, I shall refund each single dime, but counting all will take some time."

Insomnia

She stood in the dark,
I said `come to bed'.
She did, and there she lay.
She had no body.
I watched her all night,
in the dark.
When the sun came up,
she was gone.
Her name I recall, Insomnia.

How to become a successful insomniac

There are many insomniacs in virtually all communities. There are long ones, tall ones, short and cute ones, gender ones and gender none's, rich and poor, and many more. Most are amateur insomniacs (they do not get paid for it). As soon as one overtires, sleep creeps in, and there goes the reputation. To excel in the craft of 'insomniacing' (*), one must apply discipline and purpose.

*) (This word is yet to be added to the wealth of words lingo-books contain, as a sticker on the appropriate page.)

Be considerate of those who are not blessed with a 24/7/365 time system. If they need sleep, let them, watch them if you like, and give as long as possible a head start to all the 'un-insomniacally inclined' (another word is born).

Here is a little self-test to see if you have it in you to become a professional 'insomniacer' (words sprout new specimens). Set the alarm clock to 2 minutes from now. I mean, let the alarm go off in two minutes. Crouch down on the starting line to sleep (like in the Olympics, before the gun pops for a 100-metre dash). Be safety conscious; don't trip over the drooping eyelids or the sacks that sag below the eyes.

Visualise the race ahead; it's not 100 metres; we both know that; it's a gruelling long-distance climb; breathe slow and deep; charge the blood with oxygen; you will need it all and more. Saturate it, if you can. You are barefoot; each race is run barefoot; those are the rules. No one wears shoes in bed. See the track in your mind; the track is littered with nails, broken glass chips, and splintery things; each gravel stone is sharpened (as per the rules), with sharp edges, some seen, some not. This is ahead; you know it well. Fear no pain; enjoy; you are alive. Laurel waits at the other end. Laurel will cost you; prepare to pay your dues. Focus, silence, calm, last moments of void...

Hear the ticking of the clock's second handle. If it sounds like a tick, tick, tick, you are not paying attention. You must hear it as door slamming. Bang, bang, bang, you got it. Prime yourself, charge all your senses... Bang, ready, bang, set, bang, go!!!!!

Swing the starting arm hard down, bash the alarm into silence, sleep NOW, faster, you're losing ground, nail number one got you, missed it, come on, we don't have all day, how does that splinter feel? If you don't pay attention, it's going to hurt. I knew you were going to trip here; sleep faster; I can't feel a thing. Gosh, you are good—16 nails, 5 bits of broken glass, and 3 splinters. A piece of advice: avoid them all, or else you will not reach the laurel. In another 2 minutes, your foot will swell. The more bits you pick up, the more it looks like a porcupine, and it will hurt. I would love to help you carry pain. I just can't stand it, not even laying down. I wagged school when the subject came up. I never studied pain in my life. I am not qualified to carry pain. I'd spill it all over the tracks. So glad you are here. Does it hurt much? Faster, sleep; you are falling behind; hurry; watch out; here, there, everywhere. Sleeplessness can cause more pain than hunger and thirst combined, so you are already very tough and conditioned to endure. Catch up; what is holding you back? You've done just about 4 minutes; you're still going strong; there are only 476 minutes to go.

See that minute little peak in the distance? We are almost there. Sleep faster and deeper; get that adrenalin pumping; here, swallow a bottle of oxygen; burn; sleep; go, go, go. Watch out; oh, that must have hurt. There was no time to ponder, run, or sleep. Sleep must be earned; no laurels for nothing; effort becomes effortless; trust me, you can be the best; you are... You are the best, the only one; you will not surrender; you will sleep despite all agony; you will rise above all earthly qualms; you will have some coffee; you will smoke; you will...Where did he go? Am I talking to myself? Where is he? Excuse me; I'm the coach for the guy that is supposed to win. Where did he go? Ah, it's OK; I think I can see him.

Thought thought, thought brought, there you are. What on earth do you think you're doing? Balling your eyes out, a wee bit of pain, and it's 'I want my mummy' time. Look at your heart. At only 99, you must have lost a digit; no man can sleep with that. 120, 150, 180—that's what we want. Here are nine espressos, they will fix it, yes, all at once. Blood pressure: you are running on flat tyres, 150 over 99; what's that supposed to be? No way are you going to win with that. Keep the last espresso 'til after; have this first, yes, the whole bag of salt; swallow; get it down. I know it's hard, but you can do it. Imagine it is vanilla custard; easy; it sloshes as once exogenous past oesophagus; done; splash. Now flush it with the last espresso. Let's have another check: 287/173; heart at 184 beautiful; how could you lose? Impossible, sleep, go, go, go, sleep faster, catch up, and overtake all the others.

You're eyes are bulging out, beautiful, like a fiery stallion. You will sleep deep and long. Let's go, do it, and sleep. Just remember, the winner is the one closest to the finish line, not to the starting line. Move it, move it, move it. Didn't I tell you to watch every step you take? How can you sleep when you're dreaming? You must keep your eyes open. 5 minutes already; you're doing so well; don't give up now, not again. 5.5 minutes; out of puff; well, pack up; we'll try again a little later. We are going to find some sleep, even if it kills us.

It is time to stagger to the letterbox. Better pull your eyelids over your head, or you will miss it. Ah, a letter from, oh, the 'Professional Insomniacs Association'. What do they want?

Dear applicant,
We sincerely regret to inform you of your failure to be accepted into our society at this point in time. Should you happen to die from your affliction, we would only be too pleased to reconsider and most likely accept your request for membership, as there are currently no Professional Insomniacs alive. Try as you may, try as you will; no professional insomniac can be alive by default; such is the worthiness of our degree, issued henceforth via decree. This is part of the society's ruling. Claiming to be a professional insomniac while still alive is against our society's Charta and is looked upon with low esteem. We admire your enthusiasm for trying to become a professional insomniac and wish you much success in the future. As long as you remain awake in an uninterrupted manner, rest assured, interruptions will set in. In other words, the longer you avoid sleep, the sooner it will come, permanently.

The cost of PIA membership is free (upon you qualifying for such and being accepted), and we are pleased to announce that we will continue this during the next year. We wish to make you aware (forgive our lie, we must make you aware) of a recent taxation ruling, which is based on legal clarification, and the decision based thereupon the taxation department has adopted and is forthwith enforcing. Please do not nictitate now. VAT (value added tax), calculated at the current rate, to the value of your life at death, is payable upon your death, since in the legal definition, PIA Membership is free but

is a condition of your being dead. This, the cost of your life, becomes an exchange of goods with value attached that will necessitate its taxation. As they say, death and taxes...
Sincerely....bla...bla
Grrrrrr... Dzzzzzz... Grrrrrrr... Dzzzzz...
What's this noise?
Grrrrrr... Dzzzzzz... Grrrrrrr...

I don't believe it. "WAKE UP, WAKE UP!!!!!!!"
We were so close.

Cautionary Note: Please do not try any of the above solutions at home. The above treatments are sheer madness, shared with you under poetic licence, in a tongue-in-cheek look to see the world from a different view. Such treatments can and will result in death or severe disability. Should you suffer from any such sleep disorder, seek the guidance of your medical professional. The writer does not promote the content as a medical solution or glory for eternity.

'borning'

when
when I
when I was (glad still I am)
When I was you,
when I was you, ng (wake up, try again, you can do it)
When I was young, (I was, while I was, both we were, while we were, stop it)
When I was young, er (er, err, I, neverrrr, ego, e, go, I go, gone)
When I was younger, (er, still, don't be so pedantic).
when I was younger, still I remember, still know in stillness, that I was listening, (stillness listening, thank you, oh, so beautiful. Stillness listening and I in stillness listening (the

moment before 'listening's' quest rewarded with a sound) joined hands, both shared this moment's anticipation, we were (were we? Stillness listening, listened, listen, still (thank you again)), awaiting a sound? Were we?), fully aware, my ears primed for any sound that may come forth, worth the effort, listening seeks point of something for to elevate to 'listen', then in stillest climax has found reward, the importance of this (now 'that', then) moment, there stood, I, standing, said to myself, whilst speaking not. 'Self', so said I, you, we, both, all do remember this, this thought is such of magnitude, that you, I, we, all of us, must never ever forget. Much more than mere thought the listened core, 'it' word that may come close, but it's not it, I know. The composer still scans with a forklift through the shelves of words' warehouses, conductor waits until it's found. I do know so well, that I burned all I could in the time-slot's box that moment did provide, in the shadows of the big-name towns, a small, unknown, but not forgotten place, there it did drizzle, the smell of baking apple stew, the sun at 23 degrees, angle not heat, a dog barked, failed in winning food's rewards, (try again, my thought encouraged it to do), what did I wear, the coat of cells, all I remember, all that I ever wear, 'still now. Younger, such of space and time and shape, from now to my beginning, what is the youngest I could be? Zero, 0, zilch, that is the lowest number, and I don't care if it is not, to me it is, a number at the point of 'before' of being born, prior to be. Yes, a number is a substitute; at zero, it's just an empty box; that's not the point. That, the defining, divining moment, the becoming filled with essence, the... look what the composer found, dusty on the highest shelf, in Word Warehouse 87932, lower the forklift's treasure. 'borning', what does it mean? Are there definitions? What's on its label? 'borning', the becoming of 'is', 'ising', filled with life, infusion, divine, a noun, an adjective, a sentence, a book, a library. I always used the word but was never brave enough to write it down. It is a sacred word. A word I used as colour, faintly drawn, so faint no eye can see, then splashed any and all the colours all around, so it did not slide right off the wall. The only way I knew to contain it was to make it stick. I used it as sound, never though spoken, mostly after minor, so it would not fall through all the floors of music's washing lines. I used it in a million smiles—maybe a few more—and lost count of smiles. Borning, borns, aborned—why is it not in any of our word instructions? Not in any book on earth, not on a single page? Perhaps none found it on the shelves.

I think I know.

No book contained it writ, no word contained it spat, no view contained it splat, and no shine contained it scratched. So light it weighs; that single feather weighs 900 tonnes and 57 grammes, plus 2 pounds and a bit. So heavy is it that all it needs to bear, each I, each you, each them and those, each everyone, each flower, tree, each plant and sand, each soil, each rock, each substance known, each sound, each sing, each sung, each sang, each thought unknown, all needed, and much more, just to ensure it is not trodden on by one. Loft up the forklift's fork and place it back where it was before. Take care; beware of the treasure's gift. Out of respect and reference, shall not forget nor ever use in writing thy again, as lettered word, unknown, now I recall, "When I was younger, still remember to this day, when I was born, that there and then began for me, that what has always been."

Where were we?

often, well actually not all too frequently, but sometimes, it does happen occasionally, not that I suggest it be anytime soon, yes, though it could at any time, anytime virtually, literally, and as matter of fact, most likely not every time, but any moment also true, it could be the case, even if it is not, in a matter- of-fact type of way, likewise case exists, that if may not at all be the case, merely a simple box, plurals could, but have not looked into that too deeply, shallow one might say, not that I'm saying they are, perhaps none at all, but it most certainly, with an absolute guarantee of such occurrence at least happen just once, unless of course that event had already transpired, as I was saying, in the lifetime of anyone who has ever lived, likely going to live, or in the unlikely event that such person may not fully gifted with awareness of it, and the possibility could avail itself, that it were to proceed, and I can see your head nodding, as if in anticipation, feverishly awaiting where this may be leading up to, I will come to that in just a minute, if you please... Where were we, were you with us then, where was that? Probably it matters not, but what I'm really getting at is trying to finish this 'full stop less' sentence off in such a way that the last thread of the last letter in the very last word weaves into the very first one, the one already read, and such, combining in an endless loop, which could be read forever if there is such length of time, and one has the capacity to endure such suffering, making sense to all but none. Here we go, continue reading at the birth of this sentence, as...

So this could be an interesting but very cruel way to punish a kid. By saying you read this sentence until it is finished and there is no cheating, in 19 years from now, the grown man will still be following your instructions to the letter.

Sell-All Corp

At 9:02 a.m. on Tuesday, Sell-All Corp. announced their latest contribution to the world, with promises such as turning the gloom of desperate times into hope of riches in abundance for each who's sitting on the board of the corporation, as well as each investor and participating store.

Trained reps out in the field canvas their new domain. Ice-cream vendor, one of the first to get the offer, said, 'Sir, I do not even need to explain. Watch this.'
'See the lady over there, the one that has just crossed the road. She's gone, right? Most very likely not buy ice cream from your store, right?'

'Right.'
Press, press, click, click, and the thingy does its thing. 'Now watch her change her mind. She'll order a strawberry sundae and then top it with dessert. You'll see.'

A moment's hesitation was all it took, and all happened, just as the rep said it would. The butcher next door, witness to what transpired, un-delayed asks the rep, 'Could you get her to walk through my door too?'

Press, press, click, click—she did.

The banker too, next door to the butcher's place, asked, 'Could you...?'
Rep did the clicking bit; she did the doing, as expected.
Five minutes passed—perhaps just six—and the ice cream vendor, banker, butcher, and rep sat on a bench to ponder.
The butcher said, 'She bought the best cuts that I had, my boy to carry in two bags, then she came back, bought more, whatever for?'

The banker too did look surprised. 'She's 83; I loaned her $86 plus nine and 720000 bucks, all cash and all secured; the boy helped carry that as well, mind you, all day it took.'

The ice cream vendor said his piece, 'All stock of strawberries gone; how could she eat it all? She did!' Rep grins to do his spiel: 'Just think, each one that walks past all your doors, compelled to come and buy whatever is on offer, even the most unlike contender, spending in excess of all your dreams, as you have seen, where would you be tomorrow?'

'Oh my,' said one, all others dittoed.
Butcher is suspicious. 'May just it be that she's an actress that you paid, performing buying so you can impress, so that we want whatever you are selling?'

Press, press, click, click—that's all he did, the rep.

Not one of all the passersby suppressed their urge to buy; four minutes later, all the shops were out of stock, as was the bank as well. 'I rest my case,' said the rep, 'you are the judge.'

Banker confused in wonderment: 'Remember last week, Monday? Each one that walked along had a cell phone ring to tell them of our specials, the ice cream place, the butcher, and my bank. They all did a roaring trade that day. We all paid a fee of hundreds of dollars to the rep that promised us the sky, but Tuesday there was trouble. No one could move an inch without their cell phones ringing. Each phone tracked GPS, what not, and near our doors, no one forgot to make their phones ring right in line. No sound of a bird, no cars or trucks, no plane, or anything else could be heard except the ringing of mobile phones all day long and everywhere. The ones that sold the deal are sitting pretty. It was a pity, though; on Tuesday, no cell phone worked. All had enough; all switched them off. One day we made good money; nothing has changed since, but we paid a fee for 12 months in advance.

The rep said, 'Here is the deal: 5% of the nett you make I get; that's it. 5% of nothing I will get if you don't trade.'

Butcher said, 'Done deal, I'm in.'
The banker asks, 'How does it work?'
Rep responds, 'It's like a voice inside the ear that every passerby will hear somewhere near your door, if you agree.'
Banker, 'Agree, I do. 95% of something is better than all of nothing.'
'What about you?' rep asks, ice cream vendor answers, 'nay' rep says, 'OK.'

Next morning, at the break of day, the ice cream vendor is busy doing, screwing, fiddling, twiddling, wiring, and gluing, 'til all is done that needs doing. 8:29 a.m., all three are watching, each foot that's left behind the other catching up to overtake the other foot until near the bank's door slows. The banker grins. 'It's working.' From across the road, one nears the banker's door, then moves towards the butcher's place. Butcher is pleased.

A young kid is riding a bike, and its tyre rolls across the mat, which the ice cream vendor had previously placed across the patch that fronts his door. In the softest of angelic whispers, the speakers that he'd placed above his door announced in voice, enthralling all, ever so slow but slower, just a smidgen, 'I dream, I dream, Ice Dream, Ice Cream, Icy, I see, I see Icy, Dreamy Ice Cream, all for me.' A message that contained enough 'mesmerisability' to tease all from where they had been, each gravitates towards the door that holds the promise of a dream, despite each hearing things none could explain.

Anger filled the banker; no one came, none through his door; the butcher too turns blue; for whom he'd chopped the chops, he did not know.

The next day, mats hid the footpath; each one voiced a dream of 'it', some triggered by compression, non-mat space laced with laser traps, or other life-sensing devices. Any living, dead or alive, would inescapably attract the registration of the homing gadgets to unleash what was once just a mere simple call to one's attention. The earmuff traders were all too pleased.

It only took a short time for things to get out of hand. The needers spent money to buy the names of sports arenas, schools, and places; other needers sold the rights they found. The city, too, saw an opportunity to get in on the act. Queens Street and King's Place bear the names of your brand for two months if you willingly part with coins of valued tender.

Map makers and street directory designers were all booming. The river too, each week, carried another name, until language and everything on earth stained, straining with nonsense that no sense had ever sensed or seen.

Look at the tomato sunset; we must catch up sometime. (I know the spelling's wrong.). No pay, no way; why should I advertise? Team sports are not for the fainthearted, and my sympathies go out to callers of events. The players, commentators, spectators, and rules of the game all needed to change with the times.

League, Aussie Rules, Netball, and more. The below example is for soccer: Once (yesterday), it may have sounded through the radio like this: "Oh, what a beautiful path from Tompkins, across to Meyer, dribbles; he boots it hard. GOAL!!!! GOAL!!!! How sweet it is, the Tigers in the lead."

Now, even a translator is of little help: "Floor polish at 3% off this week only Tompkins kicks the Sunshine Alliance Ball for when you get old you'll need insurance, across to chocolate is another name for heaven. Meyer dribbles, he boots the dribble trouble-free boots size 8.32, buy 2, get 3, not ever wet, even in rain. It's a 'coffin when you need it' goal! Red, black, or blue, it's up to you, goal! How sweet, three times the sweetness of the finest cane, sweet-cane sweetener when all else turns sour it is, the beach resort upon a mountain's ridge, Tigers in the lead."

"Oh no, what's this? The referee shakes his head with reference and wears it proudly on his head. No goal? What? Why? It's as clear as a spray can on this orange burst with vitamins. The rules...? The advertiser's privilege... The what...???

#346.76, Section 8, Paragraph 43 states: The advertiser shall have the right to display their goods in a manner they deem best. No goal; the ref is right. The 'coffin when you need it goal' should have its lid down and closed. If it were, no ball could have gone in. The coffin, when you need a goal, does not need a goalkeeper; no ball can ever score. It's in the rules.

The beach resort on a mountain's ridge Tigers better get up from the mowed by manicured lawns and grassed fields."

In short, each shouting each other out, as many of them, screams each other out to combine as noise, none able to digest the load of promise and exhilaration of suggest the sellers' impregnated messages contain. A closer look reveals all want the same thing: money, the generating of which is the prime purpose of any business.

No law in the land suggests that those who have any must part with it, nor that those who have none must mend their pockets to prevent the loss of any. For a brief period, 'Tomorrow predictors' came in vogue, a small, short-lived, isolated boom for the manufacturers. It was a lever glued to an envelope. The inscription read, 'Outlook for tomorrow,' with the pointer indicating the answer, 'same', day in, day out, the same, 'same'. A competitor envelope manufacturer brought out its own version, 'same' replaced by 'perhaps not'. When a new manufacturer brought out yet another version, replacing 'same' or 'perhaps not' with 'hopeful', and adding stamps so that message could easily spread, all hell broke loose.

Stalemate came and stayed. Those with empty pockets could not afford a bit of wall, which became home for all those that had none, with commitments to pay what they had loaned to those that they had borrowed from, plus a bit more.

In time, not enough walls could accommodate all those who went there.

Tough decision time for gov.gov, reasoning across the floor, bla, bla, bla, if those that have wish to retain and those with none no hope of gain, then zero-hour shall be this, each to remain where each one is, in status quo. All deals prior to hour zero zilch. The new currency will have the name 'Currency' and each soul in the land will have Currency 100 in their hand, infants with clenched fists included; the bucks of old stopped bucking, lame, lost bounce, and thus lost their right to legal tender. The exchange rate from the old to the new currency: nothing, zilch, zip, nought, null, nought, nix, all with a receipt.

Sad-eyed one guy explained, '$87 trillion I brought in; look, all I got is this receipt'. 'Why didn't you let them buck before?'

'I wish I knew?'

Ten minutes before zero hour, bulldozers lined the street with walls. Nine minutes later, no wall remained. At the stroke of midnight, each woke up, as rich or poor as any other.

The day when all began anew, when each had currency 100 in their hand. Needless to say, some were screaming, and many were dreaming of the coming of the day.

Toys for kids

I have no idea what I do in my sleep. I assume I stay at home when I do. Sometimes I can catch a dream, even after waking up. I am often able to get back into a dream to see what happens, watch the sequel, and remain a participant in the play. For some strange reason, every morning, some 'whatever subject' raises its finger. As if it had been overlooked, seeking attention, 'What about me?' Write about 'me', or I'll be forgotten, the voice of the subjects.

Thus, 'shopping' is born as the theme for my daily scribbles, at least for this morning, or, more precisely, 'weighing'. The weighing of goods in the time before supermarkets made their debut. A few items were pre-packaged then. Milk is sold by the scoop, and most other things are put on scales to find balance with steel and brass weights. One was served with individual attention; the assistants could compute in their heads; they were fast. They must have run a million miles a day to bring every item to the counter. The word 'self-serve' was not yet born. Being a shop assistant then was like 8 hours of nonstop running, arm stretching, lift gym training, and mental exercise.

'Bang', I can hear the sound of a dropped penny this very moment and marvel at how each signal one soaks up rearranges in the brain to tell a new story, to ask a question, to make things happen, to call for life.

Last night, through the wire (the telephone), a voice spoke, saying, 'There are no toys for the kids in the hospital here'. Where is 'here'? Here is there, well, somewhere far from here, remote. The country, a continent, an island, dwells south in the southern hemisphere, down under. Australia, one of the remote regions, is what I am talking about.

Here is my self-analysis of what just happened: The thought of 'old-time stores' relates to time, time long forgotten. I imagine living up in an isolated place is like living in another time. 'Weight' comes in to tell me of two worlds: the sea snakes that live up there in the oceans and the $20 million, an amount related to our times and the present. 'Weight' is about balance and tells me to have a look at what's important. Should I write something that is of little relevance (the past) or focus on reality (now)? I can get carried away with anything; mostly, it is not going to make one iota of difference to anything on earth.

To get things done needs the doing. I usually do that with a promise to myself. The fact that I know that the kids in that hospital have no toys is irreversible. I promise myself to do every day a little bit to put wheels in motion that result in 'toys for kids' in that hospital. Last night, I sent an email to the president of a large motorcycle club in the country, asking if they might be interested in lending a hand.

Today I write this article; perhaps it can trigger an avalanche of toys. What are toys? Toys are an important aid to help divert the attention of a two-year-old when the needle stabs in the arm. Toys allow an escape into a world of dreams and fantasy when the leg needs time to mend. Toys allow hugging when mum and dad are at home and one needs to stay in the hospital.

What's in it for you? Nothing.
What's in it for me? Nothing.
What's in it for them? Perhaps something.
Who are 'them'? Kids, kids of all ages.

They are kids, just like our children, mostly Aboriginals and Islanders. A kid's teeth are brilliant white when they can smile. The hair is curled, dark, and a little straight. No one up there knows that I mentioned the lack of toys. 'I have a dream,' maybe not, just wishful thinking that the place receives mail from all over the world.

The hospital serves several nearby communities. Each has a health care centre (I do presume they have no toys either). The cost of living is high due to additional transport costs and the price of far-off isolation. It is not the place where big business makes a stand with special offers. Unemployment is high, and job opportunities are low (and yes, they are in our world too).

Thank you for reading this far. I said what needed to be said. It is hot in Australia in the summertime; I dive into a pool of dreams.

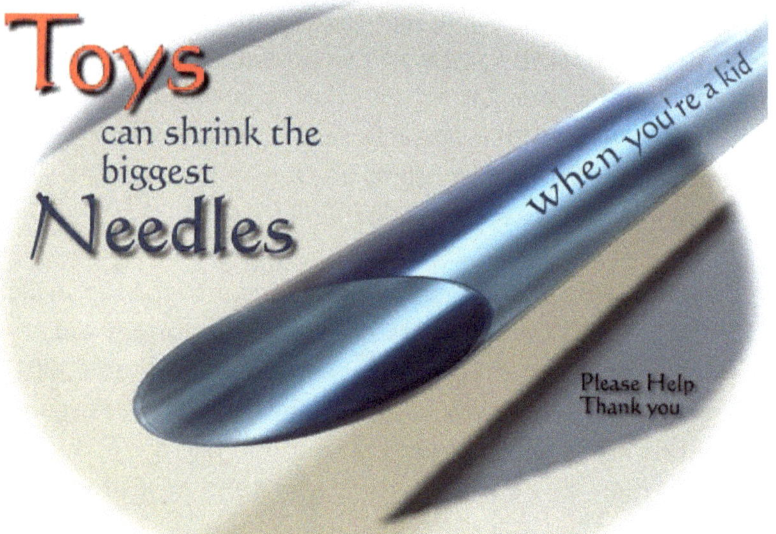

Dear remote kid,

my teddy has one arm, but you can have it. I hope my sister sends the arm when she can find it. His name is Sir Michael the 3rd. I know, it's a stupid name for a bear. When the arm comes in the mail, maybe your doctor knows how to make it stick.

Here is a ball. I have not played with it since Sunday. I hope it does not lose its bounce. This truck I sent to you because my brother likes it too, but he has two. I was going to send you my newest toy, but I have not finished playing with it. I will remember and send it out tomorrow. There is much in the world that needs doing. Please accept my doll and let it do what only dolls know how to do.

One could dive a little deeper into the dream, the fantasy; I have never been there, but I could very well imagine the hospital's notice board filling walls with notes and messages of good will. Dreams build the world. Thank you for helping to colour it in.

PS: In view of health issues, second-hand toys may not be ideal.

Dreams turn into reality with the help of a Sydney-based motorcycle club, which made contact with a Mackay-based motorcycle club. Word spread via a member of the Queensland Police to an ever-widening group of people.

Businesses donated money, toys, and pledges. One business matched the amount of another, and individuals chipped in as well. One of Queensland's foundations contributed as many clean and near-new toys as they could find. A total of 50kg of toys were collected.

The Mackay MC had planned to bring the toys on bikes with trailers, covering a distance of over 1500km, but the rainy season floods all the access roads to the Far North at that time of year. Queensland Police brought the toys on one of their planes.

Tomorrow

My place is surrounded by sugarcane. Some years ago, a 15-acre block at the back went up for sale; a couple bought it, built a house, and became the proud owners of a pair of geese. The gander was white, and the goose was grey. Every day the owner came over to my place with a long stick, trying to herd them back home to his place. Why did they come every day?

Geese and ducks need water. The neighbour didn't have a dam. After a week of trying to show them where home is, he gave up, and this is how they came to live at my place. They tried to do what comes naturally, but each lot of eggs turned out to be bad. Eventually, the grey female was taken by a fox. Another neighbour threw another grey goose over the fence, and within a day they became a couple.

I asked her for her name, 'Quack Quack,' she said. Again, they tried to breed, and she sat for 6 weeks and then gave up, while he continued for 2 more months until I took their eggs away. Sometime later, the white gander was taken by the fox, and its feathers were found 2 miles away. Last year, before her season, the grey goose flew away, returned two days later, built a nest, sat for weeks, and did nothing. Along our road, I saw the fox, dead, run over by a car.

August is breeding time, and she has been quacking and calling for weeks. The other day, I brought her a young white gander. A week and a few days later, she had her first egg. Now she sits on six. His name? I don't know yet. He's busy breeding, perhaps Charlie.

August is breeding time and she had been quacking and calling for weeks. The other day I brought her a young white gander. A week and a few days later she had her first egg.

Nora's eyes (1)

The first time she saw the light of day, we could all see her
eyes. much larger than an infant's eye and clear as day.
'Doctor, what's wrong with her?' her mother asked.
'She's fine; just give her time.'

Nora turned two and loved the shy,
especially at night, her face lit up in wonderment.
While it seemed dark to everyone,
to her, it appeared bright.

Two years and six months she was old,
her mum to consult Dr. Wilson,
'Her eyes are still so big,' she said.
'You said they'd change in time.'

'See this picture, Emily, my firstborn,
on that day she was three,
her eyes don't look like Nora's.'
'What's wrong with her? I need to know.

Her vision is amazing, and she often sees
what I can't see, I need to understand.'
'What do you mean,' the doctor asks.
She pulls a 2-inch cube out of her bag,
each containing a letter and a picture.

'Here are the letters A and B
and little pictures so that she may get to know the sounds.
An apple and a bear; a cat for C and a dog for D;
an elephant and a fish; and as you see,
they are much smaller than the letters.'

She doesn't know the letters yet,
but she can read the pictures.
Let's go out in the corridor, so you'll see for yourself.'

'We stay on this end, take the cube and go right to the end,
turn 'round, and show her one face at a time.'

The doctor walks for 20 paces, then stops and turns around.
'No doctor, this is much too close; go all the way,
right to the end, and when you're there, turn off the light.'

'I'm now at 60 paces.'
'That's good; turn off the light.'
The corridor is dark; the doctor can't be seen.
'Nora, look down there; what can you see?'
'It's Wilson.'

'Can you see a picture on your cube?'
'No.'
'Where is the cube?'
'I don't know.'
'Doesn't Dr. Wilson hold the cube?'
'That I don't know.'
'Look in his hands.'

'Wilson hands like this', she says,
moving her hands behind her back;
'he's hiding hands like this.'
'Show her the cube.'

'Woof, woof, a doggie.' Nora says.
'Is it a D?' her mother questions.
'Wait just a moment; it's too dark.'

The light is on, the doctor calls,
'It is,' and studies each face on the cube,
and then it's dark again.

Nora points to the darkness:
'Fish, fish swimming in the sea,
bear, big bear, elephant, apple, dog,

I love puss puss, I love she.'
'What animal is puss puss?' her mother asks.
'Cat,' Nora replies, 'she's biscuits all finished,
Mummy, buy a new one, or puss puss hungry.'
'We will,' she says.

'I love her,' Nora answers.
The light comes back on, and the doctor returns.
'This is extraordinary, I must say.
How did you become aware of this?'

'One evening she kept pointing into the dark,
calling her cat puss puss,
but the cat was right there with us.
Next morning, I found her cube,
100 metres from the door, showing the letter C.
You can see how small the picture of the cat is at 100 metres.
I would be lucky to see the cube in the daytime, let alone the
small picture in the dark.'

'I'm not concerned about her sight, but she can see much
more than I and often doesn't know what to do. Sometimes
she stops and refuses to walk, and if I pull her arm, she cries,
and then she screams as if in fear. She will calm down as soon
as we turn 'round, but she can't tell me what she sees.'

But that's not what I came to show; she speaks, and I can't
grasp the essence of her meaning, perhaps you know. 'Nora,
come here, my darling girl; tell Dr. Wilson of the flames that
you saw behind your sign.'

'In Sagitrus, the flame is dying; the dark is eating it,' says Nora.
'She means to say Sagittarius, her sign of birth that she knows
well. What does she mean by that?'

'Please, Nora, tell me more about this:
why does the dark eat flames?' asks Dr. Wilson.

'That I don't know. Sagitrus was pretty,
and now it's not the same;
the dark moved in the flame,' she says, 'the other day the
flame, like this, was so big and so pretty, and now it's dark,
and Sagitrus is sad.'

'What colour was the flame before?'
She points at her dress, the part that's red; 'like this', she said,
'the flame got heavy and it fell, not all of it but some. That's
why pretty Sagitrus is sad; it's falling and then it's gone.'

'The light is heavy; that is why it falls into the sky.'
'But light does not weigh anything; where can it fall,
do you know?'
'The flame got heavy, then it fell back home,' she says.

'How did the light get heavy?'
'When it flew across a growing cloud,
none like it ever I had seen.
The light slowed down just as a fish in mud
could no longer travel,
as mud slows waves and makes them stop.

From where the cloud came, I don't know, but it's coming
closer as it grows. It seems to seek the light, and when they
meet, a change occurs.'

Ethics

Well now, that sign there, painted all bold-like, caught my eye as I was steerin' my car down the dusty trail. 'Galah with cage, $25.' Well, that's a sum that could make a man think, I tell you. So, I pull over, take a gander at this bird in question.

"Interested?" I say to the fella standin' nearby, sportin' a face more serious than a cat at a dog show.

"Wait a minute, I get my son; it's his," he says, like he's retrievin' a treasure. Out comes a young 'un, a little tyke about ten, lookin' as silent as a church mouse.

"Do you take $20 for it?" I throw in, thinkin' I'm a slick talker, tryin' to squeeze a nickel out of a dime. Soon as them words hit the air, I wish I could lasso 'em back. The kid, bless his heart, didn't rightly know how to answer. Just shrugged them little shoulders, wearin' a face that could make a grown man feel lower than a snake's belly.

"I'm sorry," I mutter, reach into my pockets, and fork over the full $25. He bids farewell to his feathered friend, and I drive off feelin' like I'd just lost a game of checkers to a ten-year-old.

The ride home was a quiet one, and in that quiet, I reckoned how foolish I'd been. Guilty as a fox in a henhouse, tryin' to shave a penny off a fair deal. Them hagglin' ways of mine, they'd become a bad habit, like a stubborn mule that won't quit kickin'.

That galah, whom I christened 'Birdie Num Num' after some flick from '68, brought me a good ten years of joy. Still got that cage sittin' in the corner, remindin' me of that boy's face, clear as a bell, even after three decades done passed.

You know, life's like a bid at an auction. Every lot's got a tale, a value, once cherished by someone. And now, they're on the block, lookin' for the sole bidder. A bargain, they call it, and for a low price, you get to feel a mite good about it. Ain't no coins comin' back to the original owners, though. Tough luck; that's just the way the cookie crumbles, as they say.

Who sells for less? Well, folks these days seem to be chasin' after the lowest cost like a hound on the scent. Horses go up in price when the cavalry's in need. Famine, floods, disasters—demand shoots up, and the coffers overflow. Sweatshops, kids toilin' away, sellin' bits and pieces just to make ends meet. Worth, it's a noun, a quality that makes somethin' desirable, valuable, or useful.

That $2000-a-day model, she'll lose her worth one day. The high-flyer, once ridin' high, may feel worth less if the world don't reckon his value anymore.

Look around, and you'll see labels on folks like price tags on goods. A $3 million yacht, a $78 tie, diamonds sparklin' like they're worth more than their weight in gold, or so they think. It's all a statement, a claim that says, "Look at me, I'm worth somethin'." But it don't always mean they're in the right, trustworthy, or believably correct.

Them high and mighty, they got this shine of worthiness about 'em. Freebies fly their way, maybe a free ride or a free breakfast, all for donning a uniform. Some get goodies, a favour returned, or just to stay in the good graces, often footed by a boss who ain't got a clue. And then there's that little word called 'ethics.' Something worth more than all the gold in them hills.

End

About the author:

Welcome to the vivid tapestry of the author's artistic voyage. From an early age, he proclaimed his destined course as a writer, hinting at the extraordinary journey that lay ahead. Alongside his passion for music creation, he delved into the visual arts and video production, expanding his creative horizons and nurturing an enduring quest for artistic discovery.

His musical compositions became transcendent channels for emotions, freed from linguistic confines, as books, akin to vessels, became conduits for his thoughts, dreams, and explorations across a diverse range of creative paths. This 17th publication follows a lineage of previous works including 'The Puma's trail,' 'Tears,' and numerous others.

From poetry to articles, from magazine production to his diverse array of books, compositions and videos, the author's unwavering passion for artistic expression shines through. Within the pages of his works, readers are welcomed to embark on an extraordinary voyage where inspiration intertwines with imagination, prompting thought-provoking questions along the way. In the artist's realm, characters and ideas seamlessly transcend into various mediums and publications, poems transform into paintings, ideas harmonise into musical compositions, and stories metamorphose into captivating videos. This seamless interplay of creativity is, to the artist, simply second nature.

heinzross.com

No art, and all will fall apart.

www.ingramcontent.com/pod-product-compliance
Lightning Source LLC
Chambersburg PA
CBHW051113300726
48981CB00001B/117